A KISS OF SAND AND SORROW

A KISS OF SAND AND SORROW

A GARRISON GAGE MYSTERY

SCOTT WILLIAM CARTER

FLYING RAVEN
PRESS

For R.C.

And the Elvis
Who Has Not
Yet Left the
Building

GARRISON GAGE MYSTERIES

1
———

The key worked, barely. It took a fair amount of finessing, a bit of a jiggle, and some rattling about with a few choice curse words thrown in for good measure, but Gage eventually got the deadbolt to turn. He was just opening the door, cringing at what might await him inside the supposedly empty office, when a woman spoke to him from the other end of the hall.

"Are you Garrison Gage?"

She sounded young, mid to late twenties, maybe, so he was surprised when he turned, leaning on his cane, and found a brunette with gray streaks in her hair and crow's feet around her eyes. She wore jeans, a purple-and-gold UW sweatshirt, and open-toed leather sandals, typical beachwear on the Oregon coast. He pegged her as early forties, squarely in the bucket of middle age, but that turned out to be wrong. She looked older, but she was actually closer to the age of her voice. If age was only counted in years.

"Yes," he said, cautiously.

"My name is Lacy Carson," she said. "I'd like to hire you."

"Wow, that was fast."

"Excuse me?"

"I haven't even rented this place, and I'm already getting clients. How did you find me?"

She blinked a few times, the way someone blinks when caught doing something embarrassing, and Gage immediately felt bad. He had no reason to feel bad. It was a perfectly reasonable question, but he would soon learn that this was the effect that Lacy Carson had on people. You felt for her. You wanted to protect her, to shield her from bad things. You didn't know why, but you did.

She was carrying a monster of a smartphone in a purple plastic case, and she glanced down at it as if looking for the answer there. It gave Gage a moment to appraise her more fully. Her hair, mahogany brown where it wasn't streaked with gray, fell to her shoulders in loose curls. He caught a whiff of saltwater taffy, but then she might just have carried the smell with her when she'd passed Thackleforth Candies downstairs. She was short enough that she could have stood under his chin with room to spare. She was also on the petite side, but then her jeans were at least a size too big, and there was a certain gauntness in her face, a hollowness, that made him think she'd lost weight recently … if it wasn't for the sweatshirt, which was at least a size too small.

Had she been a different woman, Gage might have concluded she'd worn the tight-fitting sweatshirt to show off her cleavage, but she didn't have a lot of cleavage to show off, and Gage didn't get the sense that she was the sort of person who ever tried to show off anything.

Genuine. That was the word that came to mind when he met Lacy Carson, and nothing that happened later dissuaded him otherwise. She might have been a little thing, but there was an authenticity, a realness to her that filled the hall. It was a dingy hall, narrow and poorly lit, with bland off-white walls and threadbare carpet that smelled slightly dank, and she brightened it with her presence, even if he could already tell it was a troubled presence. He liked her immediately. Maybe it was partly that she hadn't bothered to wipe the sand off her jeans and sandals. The sand was gritty and gray, damp from the morning rain, a fine coating from her knees down to her toes.

He'd think about that later, how she was only sandy from her knees down. It was the way sand stuck to pants after kneeling before the ocean. He knew this from personal experience. Kneeling in awe. Kneeling in prayer. Kneeling in surrender. Sometimes all three. Sometimes kneeling simply because the awesome power of the ocean demanded it.

"Um, well, maybe I've come to the wrong place," she said, then read off the address and suite number of the room Gage had been about to enter. She looked up, blinking again, her pale-green eyes coated with the kind of film that made him think of morning dew on parched grass. "That is the correct address, right?"

"Well," he said, "I've already told you I'm Garrison Gage, so whether this is the correct address or not, I think you've achieved your objective."

"Oh, right."

He'd thought he was being funny. She must have disagreed because she burst into tears.

"Oh no," Gage said.

"I'm—I'm sorry," she said.

"No need to apologize."

"It's just—it's been so hard."

"I understand."

Although he didn't. He didn't understand at all, but it was something to say, and he needed something to say because, as usual, he was rendered helpless when confronted with a crying woman. There was a lot of sniffling and blinking, and Gage finally opened the door, hoping to find something inside to offer her, a box of tissues, a folding chair, anything, even a distraction like "Hey, look at the cobwebs up there," which would get them out of that hall, at least. He was sorely disappointed when the room was empty.

Truly empty. As in, not only were there no tissue boxes or folding chairs, but there was no carpet either. There wasn't even carpet *padding;* it was just plywood with a few staples and tufts of yellow where the underlayment used to be. There were picture hooks on the plain white walls, but nothing else. When Gladys Thackleforth, who owned both the candy shop as well as the building, had told him the room had been cleaned up and stripped bare for the next tenant, she hadn't been joking.

It was maybe two hundred square feet, big enough not only for his desk but for a reception area too. He didn't think he'd ever need a receptionist—heck, he still wasn't sure he needed an office—but it was nice to know there was room for one. There was a tiny closet that might have once had a door but now only had hinges. He wondered why. When Gladys handed him the key a few minutes ago, she'd told him that the previous renter had been a massage therapist, tax filing consultant, and part-time psychic—an improbable combination for one person maybe, but such combinations were not all that rare in Barnacle Bluffs, Oregon, where year-round locals, the ones not rich when they moved to the coastal tourist town, often had to patch together various income sources to get through the leaner winter months.

He wondered which one of the three jobs required a closet with no door.

While he was pondering this deep question, Lacy walked to the single window, gazing out onto Highway 101 that passed directly in front of the building. The window was cracked open, probably to clear the haze of dust that still hung in the air, and he could hear the traffic but not the ocean—summer traffic, obnoxious and persistent. It certainly wasn't the leaner winter months now.

Her shoulders shook as if she were still crying, but he couldn't hear her. It was the middle of August, just after nine in the morning, and the sunlight, still coming from the east opposite the window, was gray and flat. The limp quality of the light did something to the roots of her hair, gave them a contrast in a way that bright sunlight wouldn't have. It was pretty in its own way, but Gage wisely decided not to say this to her. There was almost no way the words "gray" and "hair" could be arranged so they were a compliment.

"I went to the bookstore," she said.

"What's that?"

She wiped her eyes with the sleeve of her sweatshirt, then looked at him. She wasn't crying, but her cheeks were red and puffy. "You asked me how I found you. The guy working there, he told me you might be here. If I hurried."

"Ah."

That solved one mystery. Alex Cortez, the owner of Books and Oddities on the south end of Barnacle Bluffs, was just the sort of meddling do-gooder that would insert himself into other people's business. His only excuse was that he also happened to be Gage's best friend.

"I'm looking for my husband," she added.

"Ah." That solved another mystery. He really needed to stop saying *ah*. It could get annoying in a hurry.

"I have some money," she said.

"Mmm." That was not much better, but at least it wasn't *ah*.

"Can you help me?"

Gage hesitated. He wasn't actually looking for clients. After everything that had happened with Zoe the previous winter, he'd taken an extended hiatus from his work as a private investigator just to get his bearings. *Taken a hiatus* might have been the wrong way to put it. That implied that he'd chosen it. *Slipped into a hiatus by default* was probably more accurate since his mood had been so bleak since Zoe went back to school in Portland that he simply hadn't been able to summon the energy to take on even the most trivial work.

He was really only here as a favor to Alex, who'd informed him that Gladys, a friend of Alex's through the local chamber of commerce, was on the verge of declaring medical bankruptcy because of her husband's lung cancer. She'd probably lease the walk-up above her store to the right person for a song, Alex suggested, and Gage, in a moment of unrecoverable optimism, had previously mentioned that maybe, possibly, if the conditions were ideal, he might be thinking of renting a place of his own instead of working out of his house. Or Alex's bookstore. Or Alex and his wife Eve's B&B, the Turret House. In other words, Gage suspected that Alex had an ulterior motive in mind.

All this was going through Gage's mind when Lacy Carson asked for his help. He opened his mouth to tell her no, it wasn't the right time, he wasn't in the right headspace, there were a lot of reasons he wasn't the right person for the job, and he was therefore surprised when what came out of his mouth was entirely different. "Why don't we sit down?"

She blinked at the empty room, not because she was trying to hold back tears this time but out of surprise. "On the floor?"

"I'm okay with it if you are."

She glanced at his cane. He caught her looking, and she cringed when she saw that he saw. When most people worried about his bad right knee, it annoyed him, but not with Lacy Carson. He actually felt bad for giving her cause for concern.

"It's okay," he said. "My cane is purely decorative. I just

carry it around because I think it makes me look more sophisticated."

"Really?"

"No, not really."

"Oh."

"I joke a lot. Too much, people tell me. You can stop me if you find it annoying."

"No, it's okay," she said. "I usually laugh a lot more than this … Too much, people tell me."

She smiled, a furtive smile that was just as fleeting as the sun could be on the Oregon coast, and just as rewarding. It was a promise of not only more smiles but maybe laughter too. Gage hoped he got to hear her laugh.

———

THEY SAT NEAR THE WINDOW, cross-legged on the floorboards like two nervous kindergartners. The breeze flitting above their heads was cool and smelled of the ocean.

The Willamette Valley fifty miles to the west might have been suffering through a relentless heat wave, but in Barnacle Bluffs it hadn't topped sixty degrees this month. That partly explained the steady drone of traffic outside, heavy even for the summer. Everybody without air conditioning, and probably even half the people who did, had descended on the Oregon coast seeking relief. It also explained why he kept smelling popcorn, cotton candy, and saltwater taffy on the breeze. Below them, Gladys must be doing brisk business. He was glad.

Gage was dressed in a leather jacket over a white cotton cable knit sweater, a gift from Zoe last Christmas, and he still felt cold. He was cold way too much these days. Was it because he was getting old? He kept telling himself he was still a middle-aged man, but it was getting harder to believe it. There was a wall insert heater in the corner, the only kind usually required on the temperate Oregon coast, but he hadn't thought to turn it on before beginning his long journey to the floor. It had been an excruciating ordeal, Gage's knee screaming in agony the whole way down, but he'd refused to show even the slightest sign of discomfort.

He didn't know if he'd succeeded because Lacy was still looking at him with grave concern, but at least she didn't say anything about it. She didn't say anything when he set the cane on the floor behind him either. Instead she nodded toward the door, now closed.

"You don't think she'll mind?" she asked.

"Who?"

"The landlord. You said you hadn't rented this place yet. You don't think she'll mind that we're, you know, meeting in here? Doing actual business?"

Gage waved this concern away. "She told me to take all the time I needed. It's not like there's a great demand—none of the other offices up here are rented either. And what better way to see if it's going to work than giving it a test run?"

He could see by her dubious expression that she wasn't entirely convinced. That was fine. He wasn't entirely convinced either. He wasn't even sure what he was doing here. With her. On the floor. Any of it.

"Nice sweatshirt," he said, mostly just to be saying something. She obviously had a lot to tell him, but he wanted her to tell him in her own way, at her own pace. "University of Washington. Did you go there?"

"Oh," she said, glancing down. "I—I forgot I was even wearing this. It's actually Wade's. My husband. It's—it's his sweatshirt."

"Ah," he said. That explained why she was wearing a

sweatshirt too small for her. It also raised a lot of questions. "He went to UW, then?"

"Yes. Yes, he did. For their MFA program, actually. He's a very talented writer."

"Oh. Novels? Poetry?"

"Some. Short stories mostly."

"I see. Is there much money in short stories these days?"

For the first time, he saw something in her eyes akin to if not anger then at least irritation. "There is if you're *good*. Wade has actually had stories considered for publication by *The New Yorker*."

"Oh, wow, that's awesome," he said and raised his hands in apology even though he knew that being *considered for publication* could mean anything from a form rejection to an encouraging letter from the editor. "I didn't mean for my question to be condescending. I love a good short story—Hemingway, Jackson, King, doesn't matter the genre. Some of what I consider the best literary gems are at the shorter length."

"No, no, no, I'm sorry," Lacy said. "I'm just so ... on edge. And so protective of Wade, you know? I've always been."

He was afraid she was going to cry again. He could see it in her eyes, the way the misty veil descended over them. Weren't they green before? They looked more blue now. Or was it gray? It depended on the light. It depended on how she turned her head.

"So why don't you tell me—"

"I went to Boise State," she said.

"I see."

"For their nursing program."

"Oh."

"That's where we met. We're both from there—Boise, I mean. We didn't know each other as kids. I mean, we were kind of kids, we were only eighteen when we met during the freshman orientation, but … I'm sorry. I'm kind of babbling, aren't I? I just don't know what's important. I've—I've never done this before."

"Sat on the floor in an empty office with a complete stranger?"

"No, I mean hired a private investigator. I've never … Oh, you're joking, aren't you?"

"A little."

"Right."

"But to your point, it's hard to know what's relevant until I know a little more about *why* your husband is missing."

"Of course. Sure."

She blushed and looked down, and the blush made her look young, gave her some years back. He wondered if her husband was the one who'd robbed her of those years. But then why would she be looking for him? Why would she be wearing his sweatshirt?

"I'm sorry about the sand," she said.

"What's that?"

"On the floor. I'm getting sand on the floor."

He laughed. "I don't think it will hurt the carpet."

"What carpet? Oh, right. Silly me. You're making another joke."

"I can't help myself. I'm kind of a joke junkie. Addicted to sarcasm, you might say."

Her face clouded at this. At first, he didn't know what he'd said to set her off, figured it was just the enormity of her situation overwhelming her again, but then it came to him.

"He's an addict, isn't he?"

She nodded solemnly, her face remaining fixed on the floor, and when she spoke again, it was in a voice so soft that he had a hard time making her out over the semi truck that happened to be rumbling past at just that moment.

"Yes," she said. "A recovering one, but … yes. Once a drug addict, always a drug addict. That's what Wade always says anyway. That and …"

"What?"

"It doesn't matter." She sighed and shook her head. "He started doing meth our second year in Seattle—this was when it was still possible to buy it without it always being mixed with fentanyl, xylazine, or any of that cheap, even more dangerous synthetic stuff, thank God, or I don't think he'd be alive today. Flamed out of grad school, but he did make it through rehab. We moved to San Diego for a fresh start a couple years ago. I got a job at UCHealth. I really thought he was doing better. He was going to NA meetings. He was even writing again. Then his dad died, and all the wheels came off."

"When was this?"

"Oh, about a week ago, I guess. What is this, Thursday? I'm kind of losing track of the days. Yeah, his mom called late last Friday, very late. She was crying. She said Stan— that's Wade's dad—shot himself in his study. This is back in Boise. He is—I mean he *was* the owner of Carson Clocks. They make wristwatches, grandfather clocks, everything you can … Sorry. You probably don't need to know that."

"I've heard of Carson Clocks. Did Wade start doing drugs again?"

"I don't know. He insisted he was clean. But he was all amped up and agitated after that call. He talked about moving, getting another fresh start, maybe even Mexico."

"Mexico!"

"Yeah. I tried to get him to talk to me, figuring he was just, you know, trying to process his grief, but he wouldn't quit going on about how we needed to move. His mother was so distraught she needed help with the obituary and the funeral arrangements, but I could barely get Wade to focus on it. I got off early on Monday and walked in on him yelling at somebody on the phone. I heard him say *'I can't go through with this!'* before he clammed up."

"You didn't catch a name? "

"No."

"Man or woman?"

"I don't know. Sorry. I figured it was something about drugs, like maybe he was trying to back out of a deal. I begged him to come clean, telling him we could get through anything if he'd just be honest with me, but he burst into tears. He's ... he's kind of sensitive, you know."

"I see."

"He just kept saying I had to trust him to work things out. But when I came home on Tuesday after work, he was gone. And so was our old Ford Ranger. No note, nothing. He didn't take a suitcase. He didn't take any clothes that I could see, or any of his bathroom stuff, but it does look like he took the backpack we sometimes use for hiking."

"And you think he came all the way to Barnacle Bluffs? Why?"

She looked at her phone and tapped the dark screen. "This. He must have forgotten that we'd both turned on Google tracking so we could always find each other. Since he wasn't answering my calls or texts, I got in the Prius and followed him up here. He drove all night, stopping Wednesday morning at the Golden Eagle Casino. I was a couple hours behind him. But right before I got to town, about noon, his icon vanished from the map, and now when I call him, it goes to voicemail. The truck wasn't at the casino." She shook her head, and the tears that had been threatening to spill again finally did, just a few tiny, spherical diamonds rolling down her cheeks. "I've got to find him, Mr. Gage. I've got to find him before it's too late."

Gage hadn't known her long, and he wasn't one for a lot

of touchy-feely stuff anyway, but he still felt compelled to pat her knee. It was her power, again. He couldn't stand to see her in pain. "It's going to be all right, Lacy. Can I call you Lacy?"

She nodded.

"Good. And you call me Garrison. I'm going to help you find him, Lacy. You're not alone in this. You're afraid he's going to relapse, is that it?"

She took a steadying breath, then nodded. "That's part of it, yes. The new meth, it's so much scarier than the old stuff, and the original was plenty bad. I don't think he knows how dangerous it can be, how easy it is to die from an overdose. I mostly work in the ER, and I've seen firsthand what it can … Well, anyway, I *am* concerned about that, but that's not my biggest worry."

"It's not?"

"No. You see, I did notice one thing missing other than the hiking backpack. It was a gift from his father when Wade turned twenty-one. Stan, he said every man should have one, whether … whether they were the sort of person who ever saw fit to use one or not."

Gage didn't see where this was going. "What, a pocket watch?"

She swallowed. "No, a handgun. You see, Mr. Gage, I'm afraid my husband is going to take his own life just like his father did."

2

———

S *uicide*. The word hung in the air in that empty, second-floor office, as present as the motes of dust in the sunlight, even though Lacy hadn't said the actual word aloud. For the first time since they'd sat, the traffic outside had died down enough that Gage could actually make out the ocean, the steady, rhythmic crashing of the waves on the beach across the road and a few blocks down the hill.

The sky in the window above her was already overcast, but the sun must have retreated even more because the room darkened noticeably. The breeze ruffling his hair grew colder. Others might have seen the change as an ominous portent of what was to come, but Gage did not believe in such things. Maybe Wade Carson, with his highfalutin literary pedigree, would, but not someone like Gage, who'd spent so much of his life trudging through the sewers of human experience.

He knew as well as anyone that a man could put a bullet through his brain on sunny and cloudy days alike.

"Has he ever talked about ... that before?" he asked.

Gage may not have been superstitious, but he was still hesitant to say the word. This was partly because he didn't want to upset Lacy, but if he was honest, it was mostly because he'd always been deeply uncomfortable with the very idea. He told himself it was because he'd never regarded pain, misery, and suffering, no matter how bleak, as reasons enough to end things. Sometimes his pain and misery and suffering were the only things keeping him going. But there was something else too. The word was like a doorway to part of his heart that he preferred to keep tightly shut. "I mean, I know him taking the gun and saying things couldn't go on like this are bad signs, but are you sure he didn't just hit the road because he needed some space?"

"I'm not sure about anything, Mr. Gage. I'm not even sure I know who my husband is anymore. I just know I love him. And I'll never stop."

"Okay. Garrison, though, remember?"

"Right, sorry. Garrison."

Gage held up a finger in mock warning. "No more apologies, Lacy. I mean it now. I think you're up to five or six, and I haven't even known you an hour."

She smiled a little. Still not a laugh, but it was something. "I'll do my best. I'm kind of an over-apologizer."

"Well, I'm something of an over-offender, and I almost never apologize, so maybe that means we'll get along just fine. Or we'll drive each other crazy. One or the other. How do you know Wade's still in town? Maybe he's headed north again. Did you check with the casino, see if he booked a room there?"

She nodded. "I told them my husband might have checked in before me and asked if he'd left any messages for me. They said they didn't have anyone staying there under that name."

"How about his credit card activity? Do you have access to those accounts?"

She tapped her phone again. "Yeah, I checked those too.

I'm the one who pays the bills, and I've got all the apps right here, so it was easy. But there's been no activity. Nothing on our checking account either. Not even any cash withdrawals."

"Well, look at you," Gage said, "acting all private-eye-like. You probably don't need me at all."

"No, I really do need you, Mr. Gage—Garrison. I'm all alone in this. I—I don't even know what to do next."

"Hey, hey, it's okay. I just meant you're doing well, that's all. And I assume you probably drove to some of the other hotels looking for his truck?"

"Yeah. I haven't seen it anywhere."

"See, that's what makes me think he was just stopping for a breather. Even if he didn't check in, maybe he just wanted to take a quick nap. It's a big, busy parking lot, so it's easy enough to do without anybody bothering you. Or maybe he just wanted to play the slots for a bit, you know, blow off some steam that way, before hitting the road again."

She shook her head vehemently. "My husband hates gambling. That's one thing I'm absolutely sure he wouldn't do."

"Okay, but he *could* have hit the road again, right?"

She shrugged. "I just don't think he would have been parked at the casino so long unless he was planning on booking a room there. He just changed his mind when he noticed I'd followed him. I think he's staying somewhere else in town. There's just so many hotels, you know? And there's —there's just so many people everywhere. It's overwhelming."

Gage knew she was right about that. Even without including vacation houses and other Airbnb-type rentals— which Wade would have found it difficult to book on short notice without using his credit card—there were dozens of hotels, motels, inns, and B&Bs that would gladly take cash.

The official population of Barnacle Bluffs was around ten thousand, but those were the permanent residents, and the city often averaged fifty thousand in the summer months. And on a day like today? It might have even been double.

They weren't just looking for a needle in the proverbial haystack. They were looking for a needle in a whole field of haystacks—if Wade was here at all. At this point, Gage still thought it more than likely that her husband was long gone.

"There is a beach right next to the casino," he said. "Maybe he just stopped to look at the ocean for a bit?"

"Maybe. He does love the ocean. That's one of the reasons he chose UW. He'd sometimes ride the ferry to Bainbridge Island and back just to be out on the water. He said staring at the ocean helped him write. It also helped him forget …"

"Forget what?"

She shrugged. "Oh, just, you know, all his troubles. Looking at the ocean helped him clear his head. That's what he always told me."

As a man who'd used the ocean to forget plenty of his own troubles, Gage could certainly relate, but he sensed she was holding something back. "Anything specific?"

"What?"

"His troubles. Was there anything *specific* he wanted to forget?"

"No, no, just his troubles in general. I mean, his addiction too. That was a big part of it, you know. I think—I think looking at the ocean helped with that side of him too."

"Hmm."

She swallowed. "Do you?"

"What's that?"

"Um, like the ocean?"

He smiled, more at her tentativeness than the question. "I wouldn't be living here if I didn't," he said. Then, because that came off as flippant when he was trying to get her comfortable, he thought he should elaborate and surprised himself with what he chose to add. "Even when I was in New York, I loved it. My wife and I would often ride the subway out to Coney Island or Rockaway Beach, even in the winter."

"Does she like it here? Your wife, I mean?"

"Ah. Janet died, I'm afraid."

"Oh! I didn't know! I didn't mean to—"

"No, no, it's okay. It's been a long time. Nearly a decade. I still miss her, of course, but I ..." Gage shook his head. If he kept going, he'd eventually have to tell her how Janet had died because of a mafia hit gone wrong, a hit that was supposed to be for *him*, and how he'd originally moved to this far-flung little city to try to cope with his guilt, and that wasn't information Lacy needed right now. She didn't need any discussion of guilt because he was sure she was feeling plenty already, whether justified or not. "Anyway," he said, "let's get back to Wade. You don't buy that he left town, do you?"

Lacy sighed. "I just ... *sense* that he's here. I'm sorry, I know that's not much to go on."

"What did we say about apologies?"

"Right, right."

"Have you told anyone else? About your husband taking off? The police? In Oregon, there's no waiting period to file a missing person report."

"I called the Barnacle Bluffs police early this morning. I was hoping if I gave them the license number of the truck, they could look for it, but they said just because he left doesn't mean he technically qualifies as a missing person. They said if I thought he was in danger, that they'd file the report, but I just ... " She shrugged.

"You didn't tell them about the gun? Or that you're worried what he might do with it?"

She shook her head. "I thought about it, but I didn't want him to get into trouble. He would *hate* it if I did that. He was so embarrassed about everything that happened in Seattle. He'd never want that kind of attention."

"I think we're past worrying about that sort of thing, Lacy."

"I know, I know."

"Does he own the gun?"

"Yes. It's licensed to him."

"Then there's no trouble he needs to worry about. He's a risk to himself, and that should make him a priority to the police. What kind of gun is it?"

"Um, I think it's a … a Smith and …"

"Wesson?"

"Yeah, that's it. He called it a snubbie. I teased him about nicknaming his gun, but he said that's what it's actually called. I could get you the license number, probably."

"If it's a snub-nosed revolver, then your husband's right. The police can actually pull up all that information. I tell you what, I'll talk to them and see what I can do. The local law enforcement knows me quite well."

"Oh good."

"I said they know me well. I didn't say they liked me."

"Oh."

"But a few of them, particularly the new police chief, at least *respect* me. That might count for something. Anyway, let's hope we can find him quickly for you, one way or the other. Other than the cops, did you tell anyone else?"

She nodded. "I called Ellen right away on Tuesday night —Wade's mother. At first, I thought he might have been heading there. You know, to console his mother, getting there early for the funeral, that sort of thing. Maybe taking a long way so he could stay close to the ocean. Like I said, he's always liked the ocean. But she hadn't heard from him." She frowned.

"What is it?"

"What?"

"The look on your face. You looked like somebody who just found a bone in her halibut."

"Oh, it's nothing."

She shook her head, but he could see that it wasn't nothing. It was definitely something, and Gage had learned early on in his career as a private investigator that what people assumed was nothing that turned out to be something was often the very something that contained most of the clues he was looking for. This was also the second time he got the feeling she was holding back on him, and he couldn't let her keep doing it. "Lacy, come on. We haven't known each other long, but if I'm going to help you with this, you have to be honest with me."

"It doesn't have anything to do with Wade being missing."

"Why don't you let me be the judge of that, okay?"

She sighed. "Ellen doesn't like me. She never has. She even had the gall to …" She shook her head.

"What?"

"Well, she pretty much told me that if something happens to Wade, it's my fault."

"Ugh."

"She didn't *quite* say it out loud, but she almost did. She said that if Wade took off, there must be a very good reason for it, a reason he'd be so upset. I didn't tell her about the gun, about being afraid he might … She'd just blame me for that too. It's always innuendo with her, so she can, you know, deny later that's what she meant if Wade confronts her about it. Not that I tell him about stuff like that very much. I've learned it doesn't solve anything, getting him all upset, and it only makes her hate me more. I just try to be really kind to her. I always figure I'll win her over eventually."

"You're way too nice, Lacy."

"Oh, I don't know about that."

"I do. I can already tell. But I don't mean to suggest it's a character flaw. I mean you're too nice for this world, that's all. The world as it is doesn't deserve people like you, especially a world full of people so toxic they can't recognize a truly good person when they meet one."

"I don't know if she's toxic. She's just … Well, he's her only son. Nobody's good enough for him. I think she'd treat any woman married to her son this way."

"There you go with that nice thing again."

"Yeah. I guess I do try to see the best in people. Are you really going to help me?"

"I really am, and *especially* because you're so nice."

This time, her sigh was one of relief, her shoulders sagging so much that he thought she might slump right onto the floor. "Thank God. I'm so exhausted I can barely think straight. I haven't slept for two days. I tried last night, but my mind kept racing. I don't think I can do this on my own."

"And you don't have to," Gage assured her. "Hopefully, we'll find him very quickly, okay?"

"I hope so. So what do you charge?"

"For you, nothing."

"Huh?"

"I'm going to do this for free."

"No."

The firmness of her reply surprised him. "Excuse me?"

"The guy at the bookstore said you'd say that. He said not to let you get away with it."

"I have enough money. I don't need yours."

"He said you'd say that too. He said it isn't true."

"Well, he's a liar."

"He said you'd—"

Gage held up a hand. "I think we can both attest to the fact that Alex Cortez, the nosy, self-righteous bastard who owns Books and Oddities, *thinks* he knows what's best for me, but in this case, he's dead wrong."

"I really don't want charity."

"It's not charity. It's a gift."

"Look, Wade's family is very rich. She may not like me, but one thing I know is she'll pay anything to find him. She even told me that on the phone."

"It doesn't matter."

"But—"

"No buts. Seriously. Where are you staying?"

"The casino," she said. "I thought, you know, since he was probably going to stay there originally—"

"That he might come back," Gage finished. "Right. It wasn't a bad thought, but the opposite is probably true. Do you like it there?"

She shrugged.

"Me either," he said. "I used to play a lot of poker at casinos in my younger days, but I never liked staying in them. Too full of grouchy, petulant, self-centered jerks ... You know, like me." He smiled.

"That doesn't seem like you at all."

"Oh, give it time. Listen, here's what I want you to do. The best place to stay in town, bar none, is the Turret House Bed and Breakfast. It's actually more of a boutique hotel, and their breakfasts are to die for."

"Can I afford them?"

"Oh, they won't charge you either. Especially after I talk to them about you, though I doubt I'll even have to do that."

"You *don't* have to do that, Garrison."

"Of course I don't *have* to. That's what makes it so much fun. Anyway, the same guy who owns the bookstore co-owns the Turret House with his wife, Eve. You tell them I sent you, okay?"

Lacy frowned. "Didn't you just call him a bastard?"

"Oh, he's definitely that. But his wife is an angel, so that redeems him—a little anyway. She also happens to be our crazy town's current mayor, though how someone with her personality can stand the cesspool of local politics is beyond me. She's part of that too-nice-for-the-world club, like you."

"Thanks. I think."

"Listen," Gage said, "even being mentioned in the same breath as Eve Cortez is a compliment, trust me."

"I didn't mean—"

"No, no, don't you start apologizing on me again, Lacy. I want you to go get some rest right away—even a short nap will help a lot, I think. If we're going to find Wade quickly, I need you thinking clearly. I'll talk to the cops, do a little searching on my own, and if he hasn't turned up in the next few hours, I'll swing by to check on you and maybe get a little more information. Oh, do you have a picture of him?"

"I can email you one."

"I'd prefer a physical copy, if you have one."

"Oh. I don't know if … Wait, I think I *do* have one. It's in the Prius, the glove box. It's kind of silly, though."

"Silly in what way?"

"Well, we were dressed up as … pirates."

"Pirates!"

She blinked a few times, and for a moment, Gage thought she might cry again. "Yeah. It was our first day in San Diego. We went down to Seaport Village. It was a gorgeous day. One of the things we did was, um, visit the HMS *Surprise* at the maritime museum there. It's that eighteenth-century ship—I mean, a replica. It was even used in those *Pirates of the Caribbean* movies."

"Oh yeah?"

"Yeah. So afterward, we were walking along the, uh, the promenade on the bay, and we came upon one of those photo places. You know, with costumes and stuff. So for fun, we took some photos dressed as pirates. To kind of celebrate a fresh start. We looked so goofy and happy in them. We hadn't been happy like that in a long while. Wade, he, uh, he said we should keep a copy in the car. Just to pull out if we were ... if we were ever feeling down ..."

"Hey, hey, it's okay now."

She took a deep breath, steadying herself. "Wow, that—that hit me kind of hard. I just—I kind of forgot about it until now. We just ... we never needed to take it out, you know? I thought we were doing better. I really did."

"We'll find him," Gage said.

"I hope so."

"We *will.* Now, one last thing just to get me started. I'll need some info about your husband—birthdate, social security number, height, weight, the clothes he might have been wearing, if you know it. That sort of thing. The basic stuff that might help. Maybe you can jot down a few things for me." Gage cast his gaze around the empty room. "My office does seem to be short on supplies at the moment, though."

Lacy turned on her phone. "How about I just text it to you? Do you have a business card?"

"I don't have a card."

"Oh. Well, what's your number?"

"I don't have a phone either."

"You don't have a phone?"

"No. I heard cell phones cause cancer." Still no laugh. It was a weak-ass attempt anyway. He pressed onward. "I know what you're thinking. No card. No phone. No office. I'm not making much of a first impression, am I?"

"Well ..."

"It's all right. I deserve it. In fairness, though, I work cheap, so there's that."

"I really do want to—"

"Nope, nope, nope. Don't you dare bring up money again, Lacy. Now, I'm sure they have some paper in the candy shop we can use, so let's go hunt some down. Plus my ass is starting to kill me. It's not meant for sitting on hard floors. More of a plush recliner sort of ass, really."

They stood. For Lacy—for most people, really—this was a simple matter of rolling onto hands and knees, then rising onto one's two good feet. For Gage, it was a complicated and painful procedure that involved strategy, brute strength, and of course his cane, a process that took a lot longer than Lacy's effortless upward hop.

At least she didn't offer to help. That indignity might have been too much to bear, especially when the offer came from a wisp of a woman hardly more substantial than his cane. The traffic outside was a steady, noisy roar. Now that they were standing, the wan, overcast light from the window fell fully upon her face, and she looked older than her years again, her skin full of crevices and wrinkles and lines where before there had only been smoothness. The breeze rippled a strand of hair across her face, but she made no effort to push it away. He wondered about the kind of man who could ever leave such a woman behind, someone so devoted to him, someone so purely good, someone who'd given up so much of herself looking after somebody who probably didn't deserve it.

"How am I going to reach you?" she asked.

Gage had been so lost in his own thoughts that at first he assumed she'd read his mind somehow, that she was speaking metaphorically. "What's that?"

"If you don't have a phone, how am I—"

"Oh, right. You can leave a message with Alex, either at

the bookstore or the Turret House. He loves it when I use him as an answering service. It's like his favorite thing in the world."

"Ah."

Not even a chuckle. She really was a tough cookie. "You keep watching those accounts," he added. "Even if Wade takes out a cash withdrawal at Safeway or something, we'll know he's here. And his activity will give us something to go on."

"All right. You know, he did say something else about you. Your friend Alex."

"I'm almost afraid to ask. And let's not get ahead of ourselves. I never called him a friend."

"He said you're the best there is. He said that if anybody can find my husband, it's you. He said that once you take an assignment, you'll never quit."

Gage's face warmed at the heartfelt endorsement, and when he spoke, his voice betrayed him with its hoarseness. "See, I told you he was a bastard. Now let's go see if Gladys has some pen and paper."

He gestured to the door, awkwardly, a little too abrupt with it, but then Gage wasn't going to let himself turn into a quivering pile of emotional goo in front of her. Later, in the solitude and sanctity of his van, he could let himself fall to pieces maybe, but certainly not in front of Lacy Carson.

Fortunately, she spared him any more embarrassment by heading for the door. Gage started to follow, but then something caught his attention—a glint of metal, a quick flash, outside and below. Gage was standing at the window, but he hadn't looked outside yet. Now he did, leaning into a breeze that smelled of car exhaust and popcorn.

A Chevy Silverado towing an Airstream was chugging slowly past on Highway 101, and Gage thought the glint might have come from the trailer. The traffic was bumper to bumper, creeping along barely over walking speed. Gage saw a family of four, the boy and the girl eating ice cream cones, on the sidewalk below. He saw, over the top of the Airstream and the buildings on the other side of the highway, a long strip of ocean along the horizon roughly the same color as the barrel of his Beretta, safely at home under his bed.

Gage never brought the gun with him unless he had cause to do so, which made it odd that he would think of it now, but later he would wonder if his subconscious was already trying to tell him something. For when the Airstream inched out of the way, clearing the line of sight between Gage and the other side of the highway, he saw the source of the glint.

There was a black Ford Mustang parked in front of the sandwich shop across the street, a newer model, bulky and muscular but somehow sleek at the same time. The car made him think of a crouching black panther. The glint of metal did not come from the Mustang, however, but from the driver draping his left arm outside the window. The man was dressed in a black tracksuit jacket, his arm, like the car, both bulky and sleek, and he was holding a knife—a curved blade, like a tiny scythe. It flashed in and out of the sun as the man tapped the knife against the door.

Then Gage saw that it wasn't a knife at all. The man was actually holding a hook.

In fact, he wasn't *holding* anything. There was no hand at all, not unless the man was deliberately keeping his left arm tucked inside his sleeve, which would have been hard to pull off because the sleeve was so tight that Gage could see the man's ropey forearm muscles. The hook was a prosthetic. The angle, and the shadow from the resurgent sun, made it difficult to see much except a square face and dark sunglasses, but Gage had the queer feeling the man was looking right at him.

Ting, ting, ting.

That was the sound that the hook made when it tapped gently against the Mustang. Even over the hubbub of traffic, ocean, and wind, Gage was quite sure he could hear it.

Gage spoke without turning. "Lacy?"

"Yeah?"

"Do you know anybody who wears a prosthetic hook on his left hand?"

"A *what?*"

That answered that question. She joined him at the window.

"Recognize the car?" he asked.

"No," she said.

"Me either."

"Why?"

He was thinking how to answer this question when the Mustang pulled into traffic. Gage never got a good look at the driver. The Chevy Tahoe immediately behind was too wide for Gage to make out the license numbers of the Mustang, but he glimpsed enough to make out the dark red-and-blue style of the plate.

Idaho.

The state that both Lacy and Wade were from. That didn't mean anything particularly, not by itself. After Oregon plates, the three most common in Barnacle Bluffs were Washington, California, and Idaho, in that order, and he always had the feeling that the only reason Idaho ranked third in that list was because it was by far the least populated. Lots of people from the landlocked potato state who craved the ocean came to Oregon.

"It's probably nothing," he said.

But inwardly, he wasn't so sure. Gage didn't know any men with prosthetic hands, at least nobody that came to mind, but he really did get the feeling that the guy was looking right at him. Long after the Mustang disappeared into the throng of traffic winding its way south along Highway 101, Gage thought he could hear the man's hook tapping against the side of the car.

Ting, ting, ting.

3

———

Lacy Carson hadn't been lying about the photo. It *was* silly. It was also endearing.

The three-by-five print, in good condition except for some light foxing around the edges, pictured her and Wade in pirate outfits, him in a black tricorn hat, her wearing her hair tied up in a red bandanna. A treasure chest overflowed with gold coins between them. Behind them, climbing out of a backdrop image of a frigate with raggedy black sails and fraying rigging lines, was a huge octopus. At the bottom of the photo, in a sweeping yellow font reminiscent of the old adventure pulps, it read *The Kraken Strikes!*

That was the silly part. The endearing part was the look in their eyes. They weren't looking at the camera. They were looking at each other, their gazes so tender, so full of adoration and love, that when Gage looked at the photo the first time, he felt his initial irritation with Wade melting, if only a little. He still thought it more than likely that Lacy Carson had married an entitled man-child, one who probably talked about his "art" in a way that made earning money seem somehow beneath him, but Gage could see at least one

30

redeemable quality in Wade's eyes: the man knew what he had.

He knew how special Lacy was. It was as obvious as the brass buttons on Wade's pirate vest, that look in his eyes, and because he knew what he had, and probably knew how lucky he was to have it, he wasn't completely hopeless. Whether this was true or not, Gage was still going to find the guy, but it would make his job a lot easier if he didn't hate him while doing it.

"Cute couple," Jo said.

The police chief had swiveled her chair toward her office window to better make use of the daylight as she studied the photo in her hand, and Gage in turn used the opportunity to study *her.* Nobody in Barnacle Bluffs, past or present, had ever irritated him more, but he still didn't mind the view. A sturdy yet slender woman with slate-gray eyes and blonde hair as straight as broom bristles, she wore a crisp white shirt and sharply creased charcoal slacks, and there was little about her straight-laced appearance that carried even a whiff of sexuality … and yet the effect was just the opposite. For him, at least.

Oh, who was he joking? For *all* hot-blooded men, and plenty of women too. He'd already seen her rebuff propositions from both genders. No matter how many times he told himself that Josephine Roland was the devil incarnate, he still couldn't shake the feeling that she was also the most beautiful woman alive.

"Go ahead," Gage said.

Without turning the chair back, she shifted her attention to him and arched her left eyebrow. "Go ahead what?"

"Put your feet up on the desk. I know you want to."

"Oh God, not this again."

"Just once. It'll feel so good, trust me."

With an exasperated sigh, she swiveled back around and

tossed the photo on the desk. It was a huge, ugly desk with scuffed and dented metal sides and a thin vinyl top chipping along the edges. It had once belonged to her predecessor, Percy Quinn, and it seemed at once too large and too small for her: too large for her physical presence, which, as intimidating as it was, still landed on the petite side; but too small for the force of her personality, which strained the walls of the room.

"As I already told you," she said, "we'll keep a lookout for him, but there's not a lot we can do otherwise. Mr. Carson is a legal adult. He owns the vehicle. According to Lacy Carson, he left San Diego of his own volition. Just because he might be a little depressed doesn't mean—"

"Come on," Gage said, "just one foot. That's all I'm asking for. Even Quinn did it a few times."

"I don't have time for this. Do you have any idea how nuts it gets at the BBPD when the town gets this busy?"

"It's your office, you know. It really is okay."

She smirked at the photo. The way the print had come to rest, the cracked-open blinds over the window cast shadows over Lacy and Wade that made it appear as if they were in jail. Or maybe, Gage thought, *he* was the one behind bars, with Wade and Lacy looking in on him. He was here in prison with the great and beautiful Jo Roland, who, like Gage, was another broken soul serving a lifetime sentence for past mistakes that could never be undone.

Gage was well acquainted with his own past, but he knew only enough of hers to understand why she was haunted by it. Ten years ago, she'd been a detective on the rise in Seattle until she'd shot the Narcotics chief right between the eyes when she'd caught him among the containers at terminal five overseeing a drug deal himself. Apparently, there'd been some question whether the use of lethal force had been necessary and even a whiff of suspicion that she might have been in on the take.

This was partly because the Narcotics chief had also been her husband.

"Look," Jo said, "you're now the third person to call about Wade Carson, okay? I get it. You're all very concerned that—"

"Third?"

Jo leaned back, studying him as if she was reassessing the situation. Or maybe she was reassessing him. He didn't like it. He didn't like being judged by her, nor did he like being in the dark about who else might be calling about Wade. He could tell by the look in her eyes that she *enjoyed* that he was in the dark, as she seemed to enjoy anything that put him at a disadvantage.

She'd leaned back far enough that she was fully out of the striped bands of sunlight, leaving her hands, clasped on the desk, more fully illuminated. He caught the gold glint of her wedding ring. A simple band. No nonsense, just like her. It was an odd thing, that ring. She'd shot the man who'd given it to her, but she'd gone on wearing it. He'd never had the courage to ask why. He didn't know anyone who had.

Situated next to her computer was a photo of her and her mother. Each time he saw it, he couldn't help noting how much alike they looked. Her mother was older, of course, with more wrinkles and hair a similar silver color as the frame, but they both had the same severely straight hair, the same slate-gray eyes. A plain white coffee mug sat next to the picture, one with a tea bag hanging off the side, and the room smelled of the Earl Gray tea she must have been drinking. He didn't smell any perfume. He knew she sometimes used lavender soap, but he didn't smell that either. That made him sad. He liked those little hints of personality from her.

He heard commotion outside and down the hall, men yelling about something. Her office was a long way from both the bullpen and the front reception, but it was close to the jail cells, so he assumed the sound was coming from them. Jo saw him glance toward the door, and she nodded.

"See?" she said. "I told you it's crazy here. Too many drunk tourists. Too narrow a highway. Bad things are bound to happen."

"Who was the third person?"

"I'm not sure that's information you are required to know."

"Oh, come on. Really?" Then it occurred to Gage who the person must have been, the only person it probably *could* have been. "It was Wade's mother, right?"

She shrugged. "It doesn't really matter. The point is—"

"It was, wasn't it?"

"Garrison—"

"I do like the fact that you at least refer to me by first name now. That warms my heart. You may not be willing to put your feet on your desk, but there's hope for you yet, Jo Roland. Or can I call you JoRo? I've always thought it would be a neat nickname for you."

"Absolutely not," Jo said. "And listen, I know you're all very concerned about—"

"Surely I can't be the first, right? JoRo was just sitting right there, in plain sight."

"*Don't* call me JoRo. I'm serious … Wait, what are you doing?"

Gage smiled. "What does it look like I'm doing? I'm putting my feet on your desk."

"Stop that."

"Look, if you're not going to enjoy the fine privilege of having a desk, then I'm going to enjoy it for you."

"Put your feet down. *Now.*"

Gage snorted and dropped his feet back on the floor. "You're no fun. What did Wade's mother say? Did she tell you anything else about him?"

"You never quit, do you?"

"It's one of my more endearing qualities. Come, just tell me. Don't make me put my feet on your desk again."

"Fine," Jo said, "but there isn't anything to tell. She said it was of 'utmost importance' that we find her son. I told her what I told you: I'd do what I could, but her son was an adult, not truly a missing person, and our resources were stretched thin."

"And she was okay with that? I've heard she's a very … interesting woman."

"Well … if by okay you mean that she insisted that I call the National Guard to find her son."

"Wow," Gage said. "Did you?'"

Jo rolled her eyes. "I'd like to call them right now—to get rid of you."

"Ah! Good one. Listen, I know you're slammed, but I really, really need you to file a missing person report on him. Officially."

She shrugged. "Okay."

"Okay? Just like that?"

"Sure. If the three of you are that worried about him, we can at least do that. "

"But you'll put some actual resources toward finding him, right?"

She sighed. "Gage, I just told you—"

"Gage? What happened to Garrison?"

"Will you *listen* for once? I just told you how busy we are, so it's not like I have a lot of man hours to spare even if—"

"And we were making so much progress too," Gage said. "First names. My feet on the desk. I have to admit, you using the term *man hours* is surprising, you being a woman, but then

I've never been one to quibble too much about political correctness, JoRo."

"I told you not to call me—"

"*Person-hours* is a little clunky, isn't it? How about *staff hours*? That's at least a little better. Here's the thing. I know how busy you are. I get it. But I also know that you've got all hands on deck exactly *because* the city is so packed, which means you have a lot of cops crawling up and down Highway 101 at this very moment. There wasn't a single cop car parked out back. Can't you at least put out a BOLO on him?" He smiled. "As a personal favor to me?"

She blinked in surprise. Of all the things he'd said since walking into her office, of all his banter and hijinks, this was the thing that finally got her to bore into him with those gun barrel eyes. "As a personal favor to *you?*"

"That's right."

"The man who once said I was something less than a woman?"

Gage swallowed. "I apologized for that."

"It's kind of a hard thing to forget, even with an apology."

"I was angry. I was upset about what was happening with Zoe. I think I also added that I actually think you're a strikingly beautiful woman. Don't you remember that part?"

"Oh, I remember that part. Unfortunately, flattery tends to make apologies seem a little less sincere."

"It wasn't flattery," Gage said.

She didn't answer this, returning her attention to the photo. He thought he saw a hint of red gracing those sharp cheekbones. Was it from embarrassment or anger? "It doesn't change my answer," she said. "I'm not going to put out a BOLO for his car. I'm stretched thin as it is—one spot still unfilled, two out with COVID—and I can't have my officers looking for a runaway husband who's free to come and go in this country just like everyone else. I said we'd file the report, okay? Have Mrs. Carson call and give us all the necessary information."

"Which one? The wife or the mother?"

"Either!"

"And that's it?"

"That's it," Jo said. "Unless he's considered a danger to himself or to others, there's nothing more I can do. All my officers read the missing person reports. You keep me informed if anything changes and … What is it?"

"What?"

"That look. You want to say something."

Gage hesitated. The truth was, he *did* want to say something, but he was unsure. He knew Lacy was uncomfortable telling the police her real concerns about Wade, but he also believed that Lacy would trust him to divulge what he felt was necessary if it meant increasing the likelihood of bringing Wade safely home.

"What if I told you he has a gun with him?" he asked.

Jo leaned forward, her chair squeaking. "Okay, so now you've got my attention. Do you think he plans to do someone harm with this gun?

"To himself maybe."

"To himself."

"Yes."

"As in suicide?"

"Yes."

"What was that for?"

Gage frowned. "I'm sorry?"

"That look on your face," Jo said. "You winced."

"Did I? Must be the smell of Earl Gray. Never liked it much. Why aren't you using that lavender soap anymore?"

Jo gave him a look that could have cleared all the tourists

from town in five seconds flat. "Does Wade Carson have a license for this gun?"

"I believe so, yes."

"I see. And do you have actual evidence that suggests he might be considering suicide? Like a note maybe?"

"There's no note."

"No other evidence?"

"Well ..."

"Garrison."

"He told Lacy things couldn't go on like this."

"I see. And she had reason to believe he was referring to his own life?"

"She thinks so, yes."

"She *thinks* so."

"Right."

"Why didn't the mother tell me this?"

"Lacy didn't tell his mother."

"Why not?"

"I don't know. Something about breaking the cardinal rule about coming between a mother-in-law and her only son."

"Uh huh. And that's all you have?"

"Isn't that enough?"

Jo drummed her fingers on the desk, her gaze drifting to the coat rack where her black London Fog trench coat hung as well as her side holster. He wondered if she was looking at her government-issued Glock 42. He wondered if she was thinking about shooting him. Gage waited silently. Best not to tempt her. The hall outside her office was quiet. He hoped it remained that way. If it stayed quiet, then maybe she wasn't thinking about how slammed her department was. Or about shooting him.

Outside, in the parking lot behind her office, a seagull squawked. Then another joined it. The BBPD was located a half mile from the ocean in a shady grove of Douglas firs near Big Dipper Lake, an area more reminiscent of the Cascade Mountains than the Oregon coast, but the seagulls were a reminder that the beach was also close at hand. And everything that came with it.

She returned her attention to him, lifting a finger in such a way that he knew the answer was going to be *no*, that she really had done all she could do, when the phone on her desk rang—a black, multiline behemoth with lots of flashing lights and a plastic receiver bulky enough to use as a weapon. After staring at it for two rings, she snatched it up.

"Barb," she said, "I thought I told you I didn't want to be disturbed unless … Who? All right, put her through."

"Put *who* through?" Gage asked.

Jo glared at him and swiveled her chair far enough around that her back was to him, but she didn't ask him to leave. He took that as a positive sign. She spoke in a low voice, and he couldn't make out much of what she was saying, but he heard "yes, ma'am" a few times as well as "I think we can do that."

While he waited, Gage thought about why Jo had asked not to be disturbed. Because of him? That hardly seemed likely, but then he couldn't think of another explanation. Was an impromptu visit from Gage enough reason to ask not to be disturbed? When he'd arrived at the station and asked to speak to her, Barb had called back, and the two had spoken. She might have said it then. She also hadn't made him wait, having Barb send him right back. What did that mean? Did she secretly look forward to seeing him? Did she like him or hate him—which one was it?

The questions felt juvenile, worthy of a teenager more worried about bad acne than bad mortgages, but he was still thinking about them when Jo hung up the phone.

"All right," she said.

"All right what?"

"We're going to put some resources into finding Wade Carson."

"Really? Just like that?"

"We're still slammed," Jo said, "so I still can't guarantee much will come of it, but we'll—"

"*Who* was that?"

"None of your business."

Gage raised a finger in warning. "I'm going to put my feet on your desk again."

"God, you're impossible. It was our mayor, all right?

"*Eve* just called you?"

"Do you know of another mayor?"

"No need to get snarky."

"Snarky? You, of all people—"

"Did Lacy check in at the B&B? Is that why she called? What did Eve say? Tell me her exact words. I want to take notes, for the next time I need something from you."

"Nope," Jo said. "That's where I'm drawing the line. Besides, it really won't help you."

"You're not going to tell me?"

"No. Sometimes you don't always get your way, Gage."

He sighed. "Gage again. Oh well. So let me get this straight, JoRo. I ask for something, and you say no, but Eve Cortez calls and asks for essentially the same thing, but you say yes? That's the gist of it?"

"It *is* true that you're much easier to say no to."

"Golly gee. At least I'm good at something."

"However," Jo added, "in this case it had more to do with the fact that she received a special call from the governor."

"The governor!"

"Yes."

"Himself?"

Jo raised her hands. "That's all I know, and that's all

you're going to get. You'll have to talk to Eve if you want more. She said the governor called her to ask if we could do anything to find Wade Carson. She just told me to do what I could, to use my best judgment about where the priorities should be, and that she'd back me up with whatever I did. You see how easy that is, Gage? Trusting people to do their jobs? You should try that approach."

For once, Gage had no words. This had less to do with Jo's reprimand than it had to do with the mystery of why the governor of Oregon had called. He could think of only one plausible explanation: Ellen Carson had some serious juice. Had she called in a favor? Had one governor put in a call to another? Gage had figured that Carson Clocks was a fairly prominent company, especially in Idaho, but he wouldn't have thought the Carson family would have *that* kind of sway. Whether he found Wade quickly or not, he would have to find out more about them if for no other reason than to sate his own curiosity.

When Gage finally returned his attention to Jo, she was looking right at him, as if to say *Are we done?*, but then it changed. There was something behind the gray veil of her eyes, a flicker of vulnerability, and maybe that's why he said what he said next.

"Do you want to have dinner sometime?"

She blinked a few times. The question surprised him as much as it surprised her. It certainly wasn't premeditated. He didn't know where it came from, but now that it was out there, it was too late to take it back. He found, however, that he didn't *want* to take it back.

"Dinner?" she said.

"Yes."

"As in … a date?"

"Something like that. People have to eat, don't they?"

"Is this a joke?"

"So that's a no?"

She rolled her eyes and turned to her computer. "Get out of my office, Garrison."

"You called me Garrison again."

"Out. *Now.*"

4

"I don't know what I was thinking," Gage said. "I really hate that woman."

"No, you don't," Alex said. "And take your feet off my counter. You're scuffing it up."

Gage, sitting on the stool, dropped his feet off the glass-topped case and onto the thin carpet, not so much because Alex wanted him to but because Gage was too upset with himself to sit for long. He needed to pace. He was not generally a pacing sort of person, more of the sit-and-brood type, but he was also not the sort of person who asked out women he despised. It was not easy pacing in such a confined space, especially with a bad knee and even more especially without using his cane, which he'd leaned in the corner between the cash register and the dog-eared stack of Nora Roberts paperbacks.

The highway just beyond Horseshoe Mall's gravel parking lot may have been packed with cars, but inside Books and Oddities it was so still that Gage could make out the faint buzz of the lights that hung over the rows of packed bookshelves. It smelled of old books, pine, and the freshly baked donuts that sat in a box on the counter, all smells that Gage usually found comforting, but not today. Today he was too agitated to take comfort from such simple things.

"I must have lost my mind," Gage said. "Asking her out? I went temporarily insane, that has to be it. Or maybe I've been possessed by a demon. Do you have any books on how to perform a self-exorcism?"

Alex Cortez, seated at the computer desk, put down the thirty-year-old Volkswagen repair manual he'd been in the process of pricing, so he could list it on one of the online marketplaces, and swiveled around so he was facing Gage. He looked at Gage over the tops of his reading glasses. The look was a mixture of dismay and disappointment that Gage imagined Alex's two daughters, now grown and with children of their own, must have seen lots of times when they'd disappointed their father, though Gage doubted that the girls had seen the expression as often as he had.

Alex had a face ideally suited for that kind of look, a dark complexion with saggy jowls and deep bags under his eyes. The front pocket of his blue-striped shirt bulged with pens, pencils, a tiny spiral notebook, his phone, and, buried somewhere in there somewhere, the Holy Grail, for all Gage knew. His gray mustache was so thick that it hid his upper lip. For how full his mustache was, the top of his head was just as bald; only a ruffle of silver remained, thinner with each passing year.

Alex liked to joke that he didn't start losing his hair until his daughters became teenagers, but Gage knew that wasn't true. Alex started losing his hair long before that, when he was working as an instructor in Quantico and had the misfortune of meeting a bullheaded cadet who, despite his obvious talents, would get expelled because of his problems with authority.

"Just for a moment," Alex said, "I'd like you to consider

an alternate theory. Has it occurred to you that you asked out Jo Roland because, just maybe, you actually like her?"

"Impossible," Gage said.

"You've commented on her beauty quite a few times, I'd like to point out."

"Lucifer was also considered beautiful."

"I think you once told me that she was like a rare jewel that it would take the right man to appreciate."

"I never said that."

"You most certainly did. And whether it's with Jo or not, it would be good for you to go out on some dates. Maybe you wouldn't be so lonely."

"Lonely? I'm not lonely."

"Right. Is that why you've been hanging around here practically every day?"

"I like to read," Gage insisted. "Haven't I bought a ton of books from you?"

"Sure you have," Alex replied. "Dozens and dozens. Whether you've had time to read them, with all the time you spend here, is another matter."

"If my company isn't wanted," Gage said, "I can certainly take it elsewhere."

"Don't get grumpy. I'm just saying, ever since Zoe went back to PSU, you've been a little off your game, that's all. Plus didn't you finally get Percy Quinn's widow into a retirement home down in Newport?"

"So?"

"So, my point is that as long as you've had Zoe, Ginger, or other stuff to focus on, you haven't had to focus on the huge void in your life. A date with a strong-willed woman could be just what you need. And will you *stop?*"

"Stop what?"

"Pacing! You're going to scare the customers."

"What customers?"

"Don't be snide. Somebody's bound to show up any moment, and I don't want them to get the idea that some homeless tweaker just wandered in off the street."

That, finally, was the thing that got Gage to stop walking. "Homeless?"

"Sit down and have a donut."

"I don't look homeless. And I don't feel like having a donut."

"You're the one who brought them!"

"Those are for you—you know, for the use of your computer. I pay in carbs."

Alex sighed. "You know, for once I'd like to think you stop by just to see me, not because you're still stuck in the nineteenth century. And I've told you many times that I've cut way back on carbs. Plus I generally don't eat before noon."

"Since when?"

"A year, Garrison. That's how long I've been doing intermittent fasting, and don't pretend you don't—"

"You're still doing *that?* I thought that was just a fad."

"I lost twenty pounds, thanks for noticing, so I'm sticking with it. And you're trying to change the subject. Let's get back to your obsession with our police chief."

"I'm not obsessed," Gage said. "And it doesn't matter anyway. She said no."

"No, she didn't," Alex said.

"What? I was there. I heard it. She *definitely* said no."

"You told me she asked if you were joking."

"Right," Gage said, "exactly. A no."

"That wasn't a no, it was a question. And when she asked if you were joking, you said, 'Something like that. People have to eat, don't they?' Weren't those your words?"

"And your point?"

"That maybe she wasn't sure if you were serious. That

maybe you kind of ruined it, asking her out in a half-assed way."

"I didn't mean to do it at all!"

"And *maybe,*" Alex continued, "just maybe—hear me out here—she's in pretty vulnerable place when it comes to relationships, understandably, given what she's been through, so when a guy she's interested in asks her out in a kind of flippant way, she's not really willing to take a risk, right? So she evades the question without really saying no."

"She definitely said no."

"No, she didn't."

Gage groaned and started pacing again, using one hand for support, working his way along the case and the counter. A green Buick Regal pulled into the lot and parked on the other side, kicking up a cloud of gravel dust that plumed over Gage's '71 Volkswagen. Ordinarily, he wouldn't have cared about dirt getting on his old van, but yesterday had been one of the rare times he'd washed it, and the mustard yellow actually looked mustard yellow rather than the color of the dust settling on it.

That dust still hung in the air when a stoop-shouldered geezer in denim overalls and red suspenders clambered out and disappeared into the baseball card shop. Not for the first time, Gage wondered if he should take up a hobby like baseball cards. He didn't know the first thing about it, but it had to be a better way to pass the time than spying on cheating spouses or someone faking a back injury, which sadly always ended up making up the bulk of his caseload. If he took up baseball cards, he'd probably never have to talk to Jo Roland again.

"Don't worry," Gage said, "that guy's not here for you, so he won't be scared witless by my menacing pacing. And he looks more homeless than I do."

Alex stood and peered out the window. While Gage was

nearly a foot taller than his rumpled friend, Gage could never quite shake the feeling that Alex towered over him. The morning clouds blanketing the sky had long since dissipated, and as the dust settled, the sun was so bright that it looked like a pool of melted gold on the gravel. Alex smiled.

"That's Carl Gordon's Buick," he said. "He'll be in here next. Likes Louis L'Amour. I've never had the heart to tell him he's been buying the same books for years. Nice guy, though. You know, he told me that the first time he met his wife, it was love at first sight. The problem was, it took him a year to figure it out. It was the most miserable year of his life."

"What's that got to do with anything? And why are you holding your pants like that?"

"They've been married fifty years. He likes to tell the story just like he likes his Louis L'Amour. So who cares what anyone else thinks, huh? He's a man who's figured out what he likes. And I told you, I've lost a bunch of weight. I just haven't made time to buy new pants yet."

Gage thought it more likely that Alex worried, at least subconsciously, that he'd gain the weight back, but Gage decided to keep the snarky remark to himself. Some jokes hit too close to home. Gage knew that better than anyone. He also knew Alex's blood sugar levels had been pretty elevated, as well as his blood pressure, and Gage selfishly wanted as many years with his friend as possible.

"Speaking of wives," he said, "where's yours? I swung by the Turret House, but she wasn't there."

"I'm not her keeper, Garrison. And did you try city hall? That is where a mayor is often found, you know."

"I have a strong allergic reaction to bureaucracy, and that place reeks of it even more than the police station. Plus I don't want to bother her if she's in the middle of official business."

"That's never stopped you before. There is, of course, this little invention called the telephone."

Gage watched the steady stream of traffic on the highway, hoping he'd spot a red 2008 Ford Ranger with a white topper—the description Lacy had given him of Wade's truck—inching along with the rest of the fools. That would put an end to this thing in a hurry. He wondered if the best strategy might be to just plant himself in a lawn chair next to the highway down by Arrow Outlet Mall. The vast majority of Barnacle Bluffs existed in a narrow band a dozen miles along Highway 101, with few ways to get from point A to point B without using the highway, so odds were decent that Wade Carson would drive by at some point.

"Earth to Garrison," Alex said.

"What? Oh, yeah. I really need to talk to your wife. I need to find out what the governor said when he called."

"The governor! As in Jim Harmon? *Our* governor?"

"Right. Governor Harmon. That's what JoRo said. She said Eve got a call from the governor, asking her to do what she could."

"JoRo?"

"A little nickname I gave her. Trust me, she likes it."

"Uh huh. I'm sure. Okay, you've got my attention now. Sit down and start from the beginning. All Lacy told me when she stopped in here is her husband is missing."

Gage fished the pirate photo out of his leather jacket and handed it to Alex, then they both sat, switching places with Gage at the computer and Alex on the stool. After he was done telling Alex everything Lacy had told him, Gordon wandered in with a stack of Westerns in trade, followed soon by a mother and son who wanted to know where to find Captain Underpants books, so Alex's attention was required elsewhere.

Gage was relieved. It wasn't so much that Gage minded

Alex leaning over his shoulder while he used the computer. Not everyone had a decorated former FBI special agent in their back pocket, so his commentary, while sometimes annoying, often proved highly useful. No, Gage's relief had more to do with Alex's armchair psychoanalysis.

Was he lonely? Was that *really* why he'd acted like such an idiot? Jo Roland? He couldn't be *that* desperate, could he?

Putting aside that nonsense, he turned his attention to what he'd come to call The Great and Powerful Hive Mind. Using the logins and passwords to Wade's social media accounts that Lacy had jotted down for him—apparently Wade had voluntarily given them to his wife after rehab— Gage fleshed out his knowledge of the missing husband. The twenty-seven-year-old budding writer seemed pleasant enough online, his posts mostly of the bland, we-must-save-the-world-through-clicking-and-liking variety, but there was something about this petite, small-boned man with the wispy blond hair and slightly crooked smile that seemed too precious to be real. Like it was an act. Like he acted fragile so a strong woman like Lacy would swoop in and take care of him.

A harsh judgment? Maybe. The private messaging areas were mostly full of spam, though there were a few back and forths with his MFA classmates at UW. In these, he came off as intelligent yet somewhat pretentious, with a lot of half-baked analysis about symbolism and metaphor, but that was true for his fellow MFA students too. There wasn't much posting more recently, just a couple random pictures of Balboa Park, Coronado Island, and a few other places in San Diego as well as some "remember to vote" posts around the election.

His mother, Ellen Carson, liked or commented on everything that Wade posted, usually enthusiastically, though Wade seldom commented back. In her profile picture, she looked like Queen Elizabeth ... and then Gage realized it *was* Queen Elizabeth. Ellen must have been one of those people who didn't post her own photo. She was also one of those people who had her own account completely locked down. Interesting.

He also found it interesting that Wade's father didn't comment or like any of his son's posts, especially considering that Stan not only had accounts on all the major platforms but open ones too. They *were*, however, highly corporate, all about Carson Clocks. Stan looked like a beardless version of Santa Claus with his snowy white hair and round, ruddy face.

Stan had stopped posting last Thursday, but in recent days his friends and colleagues had been lighting up his accounts with condolences, personal anecdotes, and lengthy testaments to his character. The man came off as a regular George Bailey, the bedrock of the Boise community—Rotary, Elk's Club, Chamber of Commerce, even the Boy's and Girl's club, for God's sake. Gage could find no obituary yet, though an article in the *Idaho Statesman* titled "Prominent Local Businessman Dies," published last Sunday, partly functioned as one. No surprise, it contained a lengthy list of all the causes, events, and charities Stan had supported. It didn't mention Stan's cause of death except to say it was "sudden and unexpected." Did the newspaper purposely not mention it in deference to the family?

It was easier for Gage to believe that the Carson family's political sway extended all the way down to the local police, who might have kept a tight lid on the cause of death, than it was for him to believe that a big media outfit like the *Idaho Statesman* would sit on that juicy bit of information. Just how powerful was the Carson family anyway?

Gage was pondering this question when Alex finally

extricated himself from the chatty little old ladies long enough to join him at the computer.

"See," he said, a bit huffily, "I *told* you customers would show up eventually."

Gage placed his hand over his own heart. "I stand corrected, sir. You are the once and future bookseller."

"I don't even know what that means. What else did you find out about Wade?"

Gage told him. It didn't take long, though it was long enough for Alex to idly lift the lid of the donut box three times.

"So you think that's why the kid had a meltdown?" Alex asked. "His dad dies and he … what? Realizes he'll never be able to live up to his father's expectations now that the old man is gone?"

"It's one theory, I guess."

"And that makes him suicidal? Doesn't seem like enough."

Gage winced, an involuntary response that irritated him, not so much his unease with the word as his inability to control his reaction to it. "What's enough when somebody's in that state of mind?"

"Fair point. So what do you plan to do next?"

Gage's attention was caught by two squawking seagulls outside chasing a plastic bag bounding over the gravel. A diminutive dust devil swirled behind the birds and vanished, probably stirred up by the relentless highway traffic, which unfortunately only seemed to be getting worse, if that was even possible. At this rate, Gage would be better off walking around town. "You know that guy with the Thor hat that sometimes panhandles on the corner next to the outlet mall?" he asked.

"Yes."

"I was thinking of parking myself next to him and

watching traffic until the Ford Ranger shows up."

Alex frowned. "I think Lacy's paying you too much."

"I'm not charging her."

"She's still paying you too much."

"That's four times."

"Excuse me?"

Gage pointed at the donut box. "That's four times you've touched the donut box. Your subconscious is telling you something. Go ahead, have one."

Alex glanced at the donut box, saw that his fingers were brushing the cardboard, and jerked his hand back. "No, I wasn't."

"There's a chocolate donut with sprinkles on it."

"Stop. I'm going to stay strong."

Gage would have gone on teasing his friend, but another customer came in, a young guy in a North Face windbreaker who wanted to know where the hiking books were, and Alex was pulled away. Gage turned to the computer to do more research, but he hadn't gotten far when the phone rang. Gage answered it.

"Books and Oddities," he said, "at the intersection of Literature Lane and Fun Boulevard in the great little town of Barnacle Bluffs, Oregon. How can I help you?"

There was a pause. "Garrison?"

It was such a surprise hearing Jo Roland's voice that it took Gage a moment to reply. "Jo?"

"Why are you answering the phone?"

"Why are you calling here?"

"I asked first," she said.

"Alex is with a customer. I'm just helping out."

"Oh, right, of course. Well, I'm actually calling to talk to you."

"You called to talk to me, but you were surprised to find me here?"

"No, I wasn't surprised to find you there. Or at least, I knew calling Alex was the best way to get a message to you. I was just surprised that he'd let you answer the phone. That, you know, he'd think that was a good thing."

Gage sighed. Every conversation with this woman felt like walking naked through barbed wire. He was about to come back with an insult of his own when he heard someone sobbing in the background. "What's going on?"

"That's Ms. Carson, I'm afraid," Jo said. "Lacy Carson. She's in my office."

Gage tightened his grip on the phone. "What's happened?"

"We found Wade Carson's truck."

"Oh."

"It's parked at the public beach access on 32nd street—you know, the one next to the Starfish Motel."

"I know where it is. It's at the bottom of the hill across from my house." Gage swallowed. "And Wade?"

"No, it's just the vehicle. My officer already checked the Starfish and the beach, but there's no sign of him."

"How did you find the truck?"

"A neighbor complained. I guess the truck has been there all night, which isn't allowed in the public parking spaces. No overnight camping, you know. Ms. Carson came to the station to give us a little more information about her husband when the call came in. I thought you might want to join us—since she's your client, of course."

"Thank you, I appreciate the call." Then, more to Alex, who'd just returned from the back of the store, he added, "So much for parking myself on the side of the highway in a lawn chair."

"What?" Jo said.

"Never mind," he said. "Tell Lacy I'll meet you both there."

5

———

Thirty minutes later—three times longer than it would usually take—Gage escaped the caravan of madness and turned onto SE 32nd Street, easing down the steep hill until he'd reached the Ford Ranger.

It was parked in the first of three designated public beach access spots. The other two were taken by midsize SUVS. Wade's truck may have originally been maroon, but the years had faded it to puce and pale pink. The topper was white, at least where it wasn't rusted. The truck still had Washington plates.

Past the barricade, the ocean was as blue as it ever got in Barnacle Bluffs but full of white caps and churn. A boyish cop with a blond buzz cut waited next to Wade's truck, his BBPD Explorer parked behind the Ranger and partially in the drainage ditch at the bottom of the cliff face to the left. Wooden stairs led to the houses up there. Jo and Lacy were just getting out of a second police Explorer parked along the road.

As Gage parked behind Jo's cruiser, the wind was so strong that it felt like an elephant leaning against the van. It

55

was an unusually warm wind, though. He felt that as soon as he got out, a warm, dry wind that rippled his leather jacket and swirled between the cliff face, the Starfish Motel, and the houses on the other side of the road. He left his fedora but took his cane, hating when he had to use the damn thing in front of cops but not trusting himself without it in this wind.

It smelled fishier than usual. With no bay in Barnacle Bluffs, it was a smell they didn't have to endure often. Lacy Carson's face was pink and blotchy. Even from a distance he saw that the key she held in her hand was shaking. He joined them at the truck in time to hear Jo telling the cop to check with the other two motels farther down the road. With her black overcoat billowing around her legs and her blonde bangs sweeping across her face, she looked like she'd stepped off a fashion shoot. He wished she wasn't so damn beautiful.

"Mr. Gage," Jo said, even more stiffly than usual.

"Chief Roland," he said. He thought he'd try a more formal approach himself to see how that went. No jokes, no sarcasm. "Still no sign of Wade Carson, I take it?"

"Not yet," Jo said.

"Well, I guess I'll unlock it," Lacy said.

The way she said it, it was more like a question. She kept pushing her hair behind her ears in a futile attempt to keep it out of her eyes.

"Do you want me to do it?" he asked.

She nodded in obvious relief and handed him the key. It was attached to a San Diego Zoo keychain. Old style key, no fob. When he opened the passenger door, he was greeted by the smell of warm vinyl, stale sweat, and, faintly, pepperoni. The inside was worn but tidy. He found a receipt on the floor from Pizza Pat's, a popular joint down the road from the casino. A twelve-inch individual pizza to go and a large Dr Pepper, purchased Wednesday at 6:15 p.m.

He searched under the seats, behind the seats, and in the glove box, finding insurance cards, wrinkled maps, playing cards, travel tissues, plastic silverware, and lots of other stuff, the usual flotsam found in most people's cars. It wasn't long before Lacy, despite her initial reluctance, joined in, as did Jo, although not without first asking if she had Lacy's specific permission to do so.

They found nothing of significance. Lacy started to cry.

"Hey, hey, it's okay," Gage said. "This is a positive development. We'll find him."

"I just don't understand," Lacy said. "He loves this truck. He's had it since even before I met him. Why would he park here and then leave?"

Gage suggested they check the beach, just in case Lacy, more familiar with her husband's shape and mannerisms, might be able to pick out Wade from a distance. Jo retrieved binoculars from her cruiser. Before heading down, Gage caught a whiff of pepperoni from the garbage can. Inside he found the cardboard box from Pizza Pat's. He used his cane to lift the lid; only one piece was missing.

"Who buys an individual pizza," Jo said, "and only eats one piece?" She looked at Lacy. "Is that normal behavior for your husband?"

Lacy shook her head. "No, he loves pizza."

"Comes here to eat," Gage said, "but then he loses his appetite."

Lacy swallowed. "Because ... because he's thinking about ..."

Suicide. There was that word again, hanging in the air like a toxic cloud. "There's another way to look at it," Gage said. "He could have left the pizza in his truck, right? But he didn't want to. What does that tell you?"

Lacy just chewed on her bottom lip and stared, but Jo answered the question for her. "That he's planning on coming back to his truck, and he didn't want it to smell like pizza."

"Exactly," Gage said. "Let's go down to the beach. Maybe he's sitting there right now and this will all be over."

They followed the concrete steps, squinting into the gusts that grew even stronger once they'd dropped past the first berm. Lacy's brown hair billowed all over the place, as if she were caught in the middle of her own personal storm cloud, but there was something about Jo's rigid blonde hair that seemed immune to nuisances like the wind, just as her personality seemed immune to his jokes. They were quite the pair, these two women walking ahead of him, one short, one tall, one all goodness and feeling, the other all business and ice.

He'd walked in the rear to avoid the indignity of them seeing him use his cane, but the wind was too strong, and his knee aching too much today, for him to worry about his pride. The concrete steps were in good shape at the top but crumbling and broken farther down, where the steps not only had to contend with waves at very high tide but also the consistent, trickling runoff from the east. There was certainly no high tide now. The ocean was way out, as far out as it got on this beach, Gage well knew because he'd walked down here many times.

They passed tangled kelp, sun-bleached driftwood, and the ashy, blackened stones from last night's firepits. The runoff thinned and widened the closer it got to the ocean until it fanned into a glimmering sheen along the top of the darker, deeply packed sand. They did not walk all the way to the water. There was no need. The coastline did not bend much for miles in both directions, so they only needed to walk a dozen paces to be afforded an extended view.

Sand pebbled their faces. Only a few brave souls were trying to make a go of sunbathing, but plenty were walking barefoot, splashing in the surf, and fighting to keep hold of kites. The public access points were marked with black numbers on yellow signs, but there were plenty of other private steps Wade could have used. Using the binoculars, Lacy scanned both south and north for quite a while. Standing next to her, Gage could feel her desperation growing.

She finally handed the binoculars to Jo, who started searching to the right along the top of the bluff.

"Maybe he's tucked back in some little cave or something?" Lacy asked.

"Well, there's nothing quite like that close by," Gage said. "Trust me, I'm pretty familiar with this stretch. I walk it all the time."

"I know," Jo said.

Gage looked at her. She didn't actually blush, but she did swallow hard. She lowered the binoculars and looked at him.

"I see you sometimes," she explained. "Walking on the beach, I mean. I live just south of here, on Alva."

"You watch me?"

"I said I see you walking. I didn't say I watch you. It's not the same thing."

"Like a peeping Tom."

"I just said—"

"Do you use those binoculars?"

She rolled her eyes and headed for the stairs, her posture even more rigid than before. If the collar of her trench coat hadn't been turned up, he wondered if he would have seen red on her neck. Lacy gave him a funny look. He shrugged and they fell in step behind their suddenly-in-a-hurry police chief. Five minutes. He'd told himself he'd refrain from jokes and sarcasm, and he hadn't even been able to last five minutes. It was hopeless.

Alva. He kind of remembered seeing the street on a map

when he was first thinking of buying his house here. It was probably a two-minute drive south of his place, maybe fifteen minutes on foot via the beach, just one of the many dozens of side streets in the long but narrow strip of land between the ocean and the foothills of the coastal range that constituted Barnacle Bluffs. He wondered about Jo's house. If she could see him on the beach, that meant she had a view. View meant expensive. How much did she make as a police chief anyway?

Halfway back to the concrete stairs, Jo stopped. She raised her binoculars, looking up and to the right. She was still looking when Gage and Lacy caught up with her. He was going to make a crack about naked men in hot tubs, but he noticed that the binoculars were trembling slightly.

"Jo?" he said.

She kept looking. Following the direction of the binoculars, he saw the usual mixture of houses, decks, gazebos, and wooden steps to the beach, but with unaided sight, it was all mostly a jumble.

"Jo, what's wrong?"

She lowered the binoculars. Her face was whiter than the most bleached driftwood in front of them.

"Did you see Wade?" Lacy asked.

"No," Jo said. "I thought I saw ..."

She trailed off, then looked back at the bluff without the binoculars. There was nothing there, nothing obvious anyway.

"You saw what?" Gage said.

"Nothing," she said, but her voice sounded pinched. "I probably just imagined it."

"Jo, come on, let's be a team on this thing. If you saw something, just say so."

She gave him a look that could have started a campfire all on its own, but when she spoke, her voice had an odd quaver. "What I *thought* I saw has nothing to do with Wade Carson, Garrison. Look, I just remembered something I need to do. Would you give Ms. Carson a ride back to the station so she can retrieve her car? If you want to leave the truck here in case he comes back, I'll make sure it doesn't get towed for a few days."

He started to speak, but she was already gone. She held the binoculars in her left hand, but her right kept touching the part of her overcoat where he knew her side holster was. It might have been an unconscious gesture, but it still alarmed him.

"What got into her?" Lacy asked.

"I wish I knew," he said.

He looked at the bluff. For just a second, he thought he saw the glint of metal in a gap between two houses.

6

———

When they got to the van, Jo was long gone. The boyish cop, just climbing into his own cruiser, told them none of the other three motels on the street had a record of Wade Carson staying there, nor did they recognize his picture.

Gage and Lacy canvassed the neighborhood together, knocking on doors, talking to tourists and locals alike. Nobody had seen Wade. Nobody had seen anything suspicious. For those who'd even noticed his Ford Ranger, they said it had simply been there in the morning—quite early, according to a woman vacationing from Montana, who'd gone out for a run at 5:00 a.m.

The lack of observation was not all that surprising for a tourist town like Barnacle Bluffs. There were always people coming and going, so it was hard to know who deserved a second look. After a few hours of this, it was obvious that Lacy was about to fall over from exhaustion, and he insisted, over her objections, on taking her back to the Turret House to get some rest. He assured her that he or Alex would run her down to the police station to retrieve her Prius as soon as the traffic situation was better.

Starting up the van, his rumbling jalopy groaning and protesting as usual, Gage debated his next move. He still thought it more than likely that Wade could turn up without too much trouble, and Lacy looked so close to a nervous breakdown that he feared pushing her over the edge, but he still had the gnawing sense that she was holding something back. If Wade really was an immediate danger to himself, Gage needed any edge he could get.

With his hand on the gear shift, vibrating so much that he felt it all the way through his body, he turned and looked at her. In the shadowy interior of the van, made even duskier by the dirty windshield, she made him think of a lonely flower wilting away in a forgotten greenhouse. She even smelled like a flower, a floral scent mixed with the sweat of her exertions and her anxiety. He wondered if it was Wade's favorite perfume. If Gage didn't tread lightly, that flower might crumble to pieces before his eyes.

"Before we go," he said, "can we talk about something?"

"Okay."

"Wade's addiction. You said he got addicted to meth your second year in Seattle, right?"

She nodded, blinking rapidly.

"And he showed no signs of being addicted to anything before then?" he asked.

"Never. In fact, he was kind of a prude. Didn't drink. Didn't do drugs. Nothing. Not even weed. Maybe deep down he always knew he had the gene for addiction, I don't know."

"Okay. Is there anything that happened in Seattle that might have sent him down that path?"

"What do you mean?"

"Anything that triggered it? Him turning to drugs?"

"I think he just fell in with the wrong people. Some of his grad student friends were a little on the wild side."

"Okay."

"And he might have been a little depressed about his writing. He had writer's block a lot. He said being around so many talented people made him realize how stiff the competition was."

"I see. How about his parents? Either of them addicts?"

"Well, Ellen does drink a lot."

"An alcoholic?"

"Probably. She'd never admit it, though. If she is, she's a functional one, but then it's a lot easier to look functional when you've never had to have a real job."

Gage smiled. Even when Lacy said something cutting, she gave it a sympathetic ring. "And his father? Stan?"

"Maybe a glass of wine at dinner," she replied, "but that's it. Oh, he smokes a pipe a couple times a year, I guess. Does that count? Mostly he was straight as an arrow."

"What was their relationship like? Wade and his father?"

"Well, Wade worshipped the ground his father walked on."

"And Wade's father, Stan—he wasn't disappointed in his son for some reason?"

"For what? That he married me? No, not like Ellen. Stan adored me. He was such a sweet, gentle person."

"How about that Wade wanted to be a writer? Or that he didn't want to go into the family business?"

"No, Stan was super supportive of Wade. Paid his full MFA tuition. Told him to pursue his dreams."

"How about Ellen? Did she feel the same way?"

"Well, she didn't actively fight it, but she made it clear she would have been happier if Wade took over for Stan eventually. Or really, if he'd just never left the house, honestly. She would have been perfectly fine with that too. Anything to keep him close by. She never put any pressure on him. Wade was always her perfect little boy."

"And Stan and Ellen? They get along all right?"

"What do you mean? Their marriage?"

"Yes. Having an alcoholic in the house is not usually a recipe for marital bliss."

"Actually, they got along great. Ellen could never see a flaw in either her son or her husband. I mean, Stan never confronted her about the drinking. If she got really bad, at dinner or something, he'd just get up and leave. That was probably the worst thing he did to her, and I know it really bothered her. She didn't like being rejected by either of them.

"I see."

Lacy rubbed her temples. "I'm sorry, I'm really trying to be helpful. I just—I just don't see how this will help us find him."

"Sometimes people use drugs and alcohol to avoid confronting things," Gage said. To avoid feeling things. Because they feel guilty about something, or ashamed."

She shook her head, but he saw the hesitation there, the doubt. "We were fine. The two of us were *fine.*"

Gage found it interesting that she used *we* rather than *he.* "Forgive me for asking, Lacy, but did Wade ever … stray?"

"Cheat on me? No! I would know. Trust me, I would know."

"Okay. You just said some of his writer friends in Seattle were a little wild. I just thought—"

"He loves me, Garrison. I know how much he loves me. There's no question about *that.*" The quaver in her voice, the tears in her eyes, she was about to lose it big time. She turned away, looking at the Ford Ranger again, but there was nothing new to see there.

Gage put the van in gear. He knew she was close to

falling apart, but he also knew there was something there, *something* she was not saying, but he needed a different approach with her, a more gentle one. As he waited at the top of the hill for a break in traffic, he drummed his fingers on the steering wheel, thinking about possible conversational angles he could take.

A red Camaro finally waved him in, and Gage gunned the engine and veered hard to the right. He gave the Camaro a friendly wave, but he wasn't sure the driver could see it through the thick cloud of black smoke the van left in its wake.

Like most people unaccustomed to the van's high center of gravity, or its rattling, off-the-rails vibrations, Lacy held on as if she'd suddenly found herself on a roller coaster that should have been shut down years ago.

Gage laughed. "It's not exactly a Cadillac, is it?"

"Your van is … interesting."

"It's kind of like me—loud, boxy, and always on the verge of breaking down."

"Oh, I wouldn't say that."

"Of course you wouldn't. It's that nice thing again. But just because a truth is unpleasant doesn't mean it's not true."

He hadn't intended his comment to bear on Wade's situation, but the way Lacy swallowed and stared forlornly out the window, she probably took it that way. He hated hurting her. It was maybe why, when he spoke again, that he said something that surprised both of them. "My dad had one. A van, I mean."

Lacy looked at him. He immediately wanted to take it back. He didn't like talking about his childhood. He didn't like talking about his past at all, but he particularly didn't want to talk about his childhood. But he realized that this might be the more gentle approach he could use with Lacy. If he was willing to talk about uncomfortable things, then maybe she would do the same. It was not a bad theory, but the tightness in his throat and the heat in his face made it more difficult than he'd anticipated.

As they crawled along in the traffic, he cracked open the window. He hoped the ocean air would provide some relief, but it was choked with car exhaust.

"He got it when I was kid," he added. "I think I was eight. He had it for about five years. His was a '67 Volkswagen—got it when one of his bank clients had to sell it after a nasty divorce. He used to take Mom and me camping in it—or at least I camped in it. My parents camped in a tent outside. I guess I always … you know, felt safe in the van." His face was burning up. What the hell had gotten into him? "I guess that sounds a little silly, huh?"

"No, that sounds nice," Lacy said. "We used to camp a lot around Sawtooth. Tent camping at first, then Dad got a fifth wheel."

"Ah. How about Wade? Did he go camping as a kid?"

"No. His parents hated that sort of thing. Or at least his mom did. I think her idea of roughing it would be staying at a Super-8."

He laughed, hoping she'd do the same, but it was still too big a leap. He did see the corner of her mouth curl up, teasing a smile. It emboldened him.

"I had a complicated relationship with my father," he said. "I knew … I knew he was disappointed in me, for originally going into law enforcement. I put a lot of distance between us so I didn't have to face his disappointment—both real and figurative. The distance … well, it became a habit."

Each word felt like one more crank of the vise tightening around his throat. The gap between him and the Hyundai Elantra ahead of him increased, the chain of brake lights not lighting up quite so often. Traffic picked up a little as they curved around the bend where the Inn at Sapphire Head, the palace-like stucco resort that many considered the finest on the Oregon coast, perched on the highest bluff in town with a sweeping view of the Pacific. As hilly as Barnacle Bluffs was, there weren't many places where he could look *down* and spot seagulls soaring on the thermals.

The sun, gleaming on the tops of the orange metal roofs, imbued Lacy with a reddish halo.

"He said the FBI was a waste of my talent. He said I'd never stick it out anyway because … well, because I'm me. Because I don't like being told what to do. He said I was just going into law enforcement to spite him. Here's the kicker: my dad was right."

He let that last sentence hang there as he turned off Highway 101 onto the winding road that would take them to the Turret House. The homes near the highway, nestled among yellow-flowered Scotch broom and a few lonely fir trees, were smaller, cottages and bungalows, but the houses got increasingly more impressive as they descended the hill.

"He was right about *me*," Gage said. "Not about the FBI —not that it would be a waste of my talent … Well, it might have been. My own feelings about cops are complicated."

"I've kind of figured that out," Lacy said.

"Yeah, I make that obvious, don't I? But Dad was right about how the FBI was a bad fit. He was right that I wouldn't stick it out, because I didn't. I hated that he was right. I was embarrassed to admit it. That wasn't even the worst of it. The worst of it was that he was right about *why* I'd tried to join in the first place."

"To spite him?"

"Exactly."

"Why?"

As the Turret House came into view, Gage saw Carmine watering the begonias near the entrance. The B&B's diminutive assistant, dressed in the yellow, daisy-design apron she used for baking her famous scones, was already looking in his direction and smiling. He hadn't been planning on going inside, but it would be rude not to talk to Carmine, and he also realized that a change of setting might be a great help here.

"I'll do my best to answer that question," Gage said, "but let's go inside first. I want to show you the most special place at the Turret House, and it's a great place to talk."

"But don't you need to look for Wade?"

"This will only take a minute."

She nodded, but he could see by the way she pinched her lips that she wasn't pleased. But Gage still thought that there was something Lacy wasn't telling him, something important, and until he knew what it was, he would not be able to look for Wade without feeling like he was wasting his time.

7

It might have been going on four o'clock, but the sun rode so high in the blue canvass that stretched over the wood shake roof that it would be hours yet before sunset. The wind rippled the grass and the wildflowers atop the embankment at the end of the road, but the alcove where Carmine was watering the begonias was so sheltered that even the rainbow-colored whirligig above her barely moved.

The Turret House may not have been as famous as the Inn at Sapphire Head, but it was just as impressive in its own way. People often described it as a castle, though with its wood shake siding, shutter-flanked windows, and two wrap-around decks, there was little about the three-story structure that could technically be described that way. Even the turret on the southern corner, the very thing that had given the place its name, was more reminiscent of a fort than anything else.

And yet, there *was* something about the place that felt like a castle, perhaps because of the feeling of security and comfort it invoked in its guests.

Gage gave Carmine a friendly wave, who lifted her

watering can in return. When he and Lacy got out of the van, the breeze was cooler. They made small talk with Carmine, who insisted, at least three times, that they have one of the cranberry scones she'd just baked, then Gage asked her if it would be all right if he took Lacy to the turret.

"Did you ask Alex?" Carmine said.

"No."

"Good. Because then he would have said no. Go ahead. Just don't tell him I said so."

"Your secret's safe with me, Carmine. Besides, I might be able to live without Alex, but I'd never be able to live without your cranberry scones."

Carmine wrinkled her freckled nose. "Oh, you silly man. You know I'd go on baking for you after what you did for Tommy."

"Don't be ridiculous," Gage said. "You know you'd bake for me anyway even without that."

She laughed. "You're probably right."

Gage and Lacy took the flagstone path to the parlor. The air was fragrant with Eve's rose bushes. The ocean, on the other side of the building, was a soft but steady whisper.

"Who's Tommy?" Lacy asked.

"Oh, that's Carmine's cousin," Gage replied. "A couple months ago, he was getting roughed up by some bad dudes, and I made them back off."

"Wow."

"Don't be too impressed. Tommy is in sixth grade. I just gave his tormentors the impression that Tommy's father just *might* have been in the CIA and that people who messed with his family tended to disappear in the middle of the night."

Gage almost got a laugh out of her right there, but in the end it was just a playful snort. He would have liked to count it, but he had to be a stickler about this sort of thing.

They stepped into the parlor, with its sliding glass doors

that overlooked a paver patio, the backyard with its glistening grass and blackberry hedge and, beyond all this, the ocean, then passed into the connecting space. A cast iron staircase led to the turret. Up they went, Gage realizing he'd forgotten his cane as usual, but he endured the sharp stabs in his right knee with manly vigor. What he lacked in the manly department he always figured he could make up for with added vigor.

When he opened the door at the top, Lacy gasped in astonishment. It warmed his heart. That meant she was worthy. The study, the refuge, the Tower at the End of Time, Alex's Sanctuary for the Soul—there were many names that had been given to the turret over the years, some more grandiose than others, but none really did it justice. Like all such special places, it needed to be experienced to be appreciated, and even then not everybody did. As far as Gage was concerned, however, all *good* people did, and he was glad to count Lacy among them.

"Oh gosh," she said, "if I had a place like this, I don't know if I'd ever leave. It's like a little piece of heaven."

"Yet another word for it," Gage said.

"What's that?"

"Please, take a seat."

Eyes wide, she crept into the cozy, hexagonal room like a worshipper into a sacred place. For just a moment, it seemed she'd forgotten about all her troubles, which was what Gage had hoped would happen. The view, of course, was spectacular. There might have been a better one in Barnacle Bluffs, but if so, Gage had never found it—an expansive, one hundred and eighty degrees of the Pacific Ocean in all its glory, the tiny glimpse of the jagged, fir-lined cliffs to the south somehow making all that water even more impressive. Two seagulls soared past them. A trawler, so far away it blurred into the turquoise haze, crept north.

It smelled of leather, old books, and walnut shelving. The mechanical blackout blinds, programmed to come down at sunset, were open, revealing the leatherbound volumes on the western side between the windows to protect them from the sun. Two leather recliners were situated to best take advantage of the view, a beaded green glass lamp between them. The yellow glow of the lamp on all that dark chocolate leather practically begged people to sit. Gage and Lacy did so, and as always, to Gage it felt like coming home.

"Are you really sure it's all right to be in here?" she asked.

"The only thing Alex *might* be irritated about," Gage replied, "is that I got to take you up here before he did. Now let me tell you the rest of my story before I lose my nerve."

Gage leaned back, drawing both courage and comfort from the familiar way the leather, already warming from his body heat, molded to fit his back. "My dad was right about a lot of things," he said. "I *did* try to join the FBI partly to spite him. I couldn't see it at the time, but it was true. You see, my father was the son of a cop."

"In Montana?"

"No, this was back in New York, where he was from. Long Island. But my grandfather, he might have been a good cop, at least people said so, but he was bad at home. Heavy drinker. Abusive. And my dad, he was kind of a gentle kid, good with numbers and puzzles, but small, not physical. When he got older, he wanted to get as far from his father as he could. He graduated a year early and moved into an apartment with some friends, working at a bank and taking night classes in finance at NYU."

Gage, feeling his throat tighten, stared out at the ocean. "He was smart and he worked hard. I think he was planning on trying to land a job with one of the big Wall Street firms, but he met my mother when he came out to Montana the summer between his junior and senior year. He was there to do an internship at a bank in Missoula, his little stab at adventure. When he graduated, he came back and married her. He ... Hold on. Just a second."

"Are you okay?" Lacy asked.

"I'm fine. This is just ... Give me a second."

"We don't—"

"No, it's important I say this. I grew up in a little town in Montana called Red Castle, near Yellowstone. My dad was the president of a bank there. When I was in fourth grade, this kid moved in down the hill from us who saw it as his mission in life to make me miserable."

"I'm sorry," Lacy said. "I had a few bullies when I was growing up too."

"Well, if there's a class on how to be a bully, Dirk would have been a star pupil." Gage shook his head at the memory. "That was his name. *Dirk.* Has there ever been anyone nice named Dirk? It certainly wasn't his father, who was also named Dirk. Moved to town after his wife ran out on him in Spearfish, and got a job at the mill, but I think his real purpose in life was ensuring all the local watering holes had at least one steady customer. So it was Dirk Senior and Dirk Junior, real winners, both of them. Dirk Junior stuck my head in the school toilet. Put slugs in my lunchbox. The worst. I was a scrappy kid, but he was two grades ahead of me and outweighed me by thirty pounds, so it wasn't a fair fight. And remember, this is Montana. Their idea of Child Protective Services is making sure that kids aren't locked up in the basement in chains. Anything else is fair play."

"I'm not sure Idaho is that much better," Lacy said.

"I bet. I was a stoic kid, never wanted to complain, but I had scratches I couldn't explain—from when Dirk thought it'd be a hoot to carve a D on my neck with his pocket knife so kids would know I belonged to him. Dad forced me to come clean about what ... what was going on."

Gage had been on a roll, but his throat seized up again. His chest felt warm and tight. He took off his leather jacket, leaving it on the recliner as he walked to the window, hoping a change of scenery, even a small one, would help. It didn't. If anything, his vague reflection in the glass, the hard cut of his jaw, the silver glint in his sideburns, made speaking even more difficult. It was as if the ghost of his father floated in the air just outside.

He forced himself to continue. "So my father, he says, let's … let's go see if we can work this out. Let's go down there and talk about it. That was his way, you see. He always thought he could reason with people."

"He sounds like a good man," Lacy said, behind him.

It could have irritated him, because it sounded as if she was siding with his father, but instead it made him smile. He realized now why he liked her so much. She reminded him of his father. He was good at heart too. And yet, this realization made his face tighten with even more anguish at the memory.

"When we knocked on the door at Dirk's double-wide," Gage said, "his dad answered in a sleeveless undershirt some people call a wife beater, a can of Budweiser in his hand, a smoldering Camel cigarette hanging from the corner of his mouth. How cliched is that, right? Dirk Junior is there behind his dad, peering through a hole in the screen door, a sadistic grin on his face. The only thing that wasn't cliched was their dog. You would expect a pit bull or a Doberman or a rottweiler maybe, but they had this toy poodle—belonged to his runaway wife, I think. It looked like a rat with mange."

The memory elicited a rueful laugh from Gage, but that only made what he said next more painful in contrast. "So Dad, he points to my neck and says, your son did this to Garrison, and this sort of behavior needs to stop right now. Dirk Senior sips his beer. Dirk Junior actually snickers. That little rat dog is barking the whole time, this high-pitched yapping, and I feel myself getting real small. And Dirk Senior just shakes his head and says his boy wouldn't do that. My dad insisted that he did. Dirk Senior asked if my dad was calling him a liar."

Gage stopped to gather his thoughts. Below, on the strip of beach he could see, a boy came into view. The wind tousled his strawberry-blond hair and stuck his Superman T-shirt to his thin torso. He carried a blue bucket, and he barreled toward the water in obvious delight. From Gage's high vantage point, the footprints left by the boy's bare feet looked like cinnamon sprinkles on a sugar cookie.

The boy was alone. Where were the parents? He was only steps away from the ocean. Gage, heart in his throat, started toward the door, but then a big guy in a Hawaiian shirt charged into view. As he swept up the boy in his arms, the man's straw hat blew off his head. Trailing behind him, a woman dressed in a white coverall over a pink swimsuit stopped to pick it up.

"Something wrong?" Lacy said. "Do you see something out there? It's not—it's not Wade, is it?"

"No, no," Gage said, "it's just a … a family." His voice caught on that word, a funny thing. It conjured up feelings of longing and regret he was not prepared for even though he should have been, considering what he was talking about, and he had to swallow hard before continuing. "Anyway, you can see where this is going. My dad says he just wants to talk, but then Dirk Senior blows out of the house, yelling, pushing Dad, spitting profanity in his face, and Dad just takes it. He takes it. And it doesn't stop. Dirk hits Dad in the face, and Dad staggers back, his nose bleeding. Dirk hits him again. And again. And finally Dad drops to the ground. And here's the thing, Lacy. He never threw a punch. For God's sake, he didn't even lift his hands. It was like he *wanted* to get beat up.

And you know the really horrible part? I just stood there and watched it happen."

"You were just a kid," Lacy said.

Gage resisted the urge to look at her. If he looked at her, he'd never get out the rest. "Yeah, I was just a kid, but it doesn't matter. At least, it didn't matter to me *then*, and how you feel when things happen, no matter how old you are, well, that stuff sticks with you. It goes in deep. I felt scared. I felt weak. Most of all, I felt guilty for not helping him. Maybe it wouldn't have made a difference, but then at least I could have lived with myself, you see. I could have lived with at least trying."

"Did you guys talk about it?"

"Oh, I'm sure he talked plenty. Talking was Dad's way. I'm sure he said stuff about violence never being a great solution, how it really should be avoided at all costs. About how giving into anger just got you into trouble. About how the more people lashed out with their fists, the more scared they showed themselves to be deep inside. That was stuff he said all the time, but if he said it after that day, I don't remember. I wasn't listening anymore. I … I was ashamed of him."

"I'm sorry."

Gage laughed softly. "There you go apologizing again, Lacy."

"I guess I just don't know what else to say."

Gage looked at her. "You're wondering why I told you all this, aren't you?"

"Well …"

"It comes down to this," Gage said. "My dad wasn't totally wrong about violence rarely being the best solution. But he *was* wrong when he said it should be avoided *at all costs.* Because sometimes there is a cost to avoiding violence that is just too great. Sometimes, when all other options have been exhausted, it's the *only* way."

She shook her head. "But not everybody can fight with their fists. Maybe your dad-—"

"Everybody can fight, Lacy. That doesn't mean everybody can win. But everybody can *fight.*"

"I'm not a fighter."

"Oh, I think you might surprise yourself." When she started to protest, Gage raised his hand. "But that's not really what I'm getting at here. You see, being ashamed of my father, it ate at me. I let it get between us. We barely talked in his later years. It was only after he was gone that I realized how much I missed him. Whether he made a mistake not standing up for himself with Dirk, well, maybe that's up for debate, but I definitely made a mistake. And it cost me."

"What? That you couldn't see past his weaknesses?"

"It was more than that," he said. "I held him up to an impossible standard. I didn't have enough compassion for him. I didn't have an abusive, alcoholic father. He did."

Lacy nodded. "Maybe there was something inside he was scared of. Maybe he had his own anger. Maybe he was afraid that if he let it out, even a little, it would overwhelm him. Maybe he was afraid he'd become just like his father."

Gage, hoping she would make this connection, smiled. "You're a wise woman, Lacy Carson."

"Oh, I don't know about that."

"And to be honest, I've thought that before too—that he had some deep reservoir of rage that he felt he had to keep bottled up or he'd lose control."

"But you still can't forgive him?"

"It's not really about forgiveness. It's about acceptance. I just had a hard time accepting who he really was, and what made him that way, and by the time I figured it out, it was too late."

The sun, lower in the sky even as they talked, shifted the shadows in the room, drew them back, gave her face a paler, starker quality. Gage could see that she was fading by the moment. But her exhaustion might have also opened a window, lowering her inhibitions, her resistance to whatever *she* had bottled up inside of her. He didn't like taking advantage of her, but if he was going to make his move, he needed to do it now.

"We all have secrets, Lacy," he said. "We all have parts of ourselves that we hide away from others. A lot of these secrets have to do with our childhoods, scars that run deep."

She swallowed hard. "Are you saying Wade has secrets from me? That he might not be who I really think he is?"

"You tell me."

"That's why you told me all this?"

"No, I told you all this because I trust you. And I want you to trust me."

"You just met me. How can you trust me?"

"Whether you trust somebody isn't about how long you've known them. Trusting somebody is a choice. I'm *choosing* to trust you. I want you to make that same choice, with me."

"But if Wade has secrets, how would I even know?"

"Lacy," he said, "I'm going to do everything I can to find your husband as fast as possible—tonight, if I can. But if there's something else I should know about, now's the time to tell me. It could make a difference."

"There isn't."

"Remember when you told me that Wade said, 'Once an addict, always an addict?' Isn't that what he said?"

"Yes."

"And then you hinted there was something else he liked to say. What was it?"

"I don't know. I can't ... I can't remember what I was thinking."

"Earlier, when you said Wade liked to go to the ocean to forget things, I got the feeling there was something more."

"More?"

"More specific."

She shrugged. "Just his troubles. He had his demons."

"But *what* demons?"

"I don't know, okay! I don't know! And—and it kills me that I don't know. I should know! *I'm his wife!*"

This last bit was delivered with a rising crescendo, a shout that bounced off all the glass and wood and paper. It shocked them both. She glared at him for only a second, the best imitation of rage that someone like Lacy Carson could muster, but even this was too much for her. Her eyes misted up, and she stared at the floor. "I … I can't believe I just did that. I never yell."

"Well, I deserved it."

"No. No, you were right. There is … There is something. I just … I just don't think …"

She shook her head. He returned to his recliner, hoping that if he gave her time that she'd come out with it eventually. They became very still, the waves crashing on the rocks below filling the silence.

"I just don't think it's relevant," she said.

"Why don't you let me decide?"

"You have to promise never to tell him I told you. He made me promise."

"Okay."

"You promise?"

"I'll do my best, Lacy. But I can't promise before I know what it is. That's where the trust part comes in."

She stared at the ocean again, as if looking for permission out there, or guidance. "I don't know if it's a big deal. But it would kill him, me telling you this. I just don't want to do anything else that would—well, he's so fragile now, you know?"

Gage nodded, but he didn't say anything. He didn't want to do the slightest thing to get in the way. As it was, she was fidgeting constantly—with her seat, her hair, her UW sweatshirt. As she smoothed out the wrinkles in the sleeve, she stopped.

"I bought him this, you know," she said.

"Yeah?"

"We were visiting campus. He hadn't even applied yet. But he decided to apply while we were there. We were sitting on the library steps. Suzzallo Library. Beautiful place. And I said we should buy him a UW sweatshirt. Seattle can be a little on the chilly side, you know? He asked me what if he didn't get in? I told him he would, and he would do well."

"You believed in him."

"I love him."

"It's not quite the same thing, though, is it?"

"To me, it is. And so I insisted. We bought the sweatshirt, and he wore it all the time. And he *did* get in, and he did very well until … Well, you know. And later, in San Diego, he caught me trying to hide the sweatshirt away. He hadn't worn it in months."

"You thought he wouldn't want to be reminded of what happened there?"

She nodded. "But he took it from me and put it back in his closet. He said it reminded him not so much of the bad stuff that happened in Seattle but how much I believed in him. How much I … I loved him."

"And you thought, if you wore it …"

"He would remember how much I love him. He would know that I'm here for him. I'm *always* here."

"He's lucky to have you."

She shook her head. "A lot of people have told me that

over the years, but you have to understand something, Garrison. I think it's the opposite. He's my north star. I was never somebody who believed in soulmates, but then I met Wade. And I still don't know if I believe in that stuff. I just know that I'm not whole without him. I'd be lost."

Gage knew what she meant. While he'd loved quite a few women in his life, there was only one he would have described as his north star. Janet. It was also the love that was most inexplicable to him. They were opposites in so many ways. He was crass. She was refined. He saw all the bad where she saw all the good. He could never describe *why* he'd loved her so fiercely, not really, not to others, not even to himself. It just was.

He wondered if that was why there was part of himself he'd always held back from the women he'd been with since Janet. He wondered if these women, on some level, knew that. While Lacy stared at the ocean, as vast and unfathomable as the kind of love she was describing, Gage wondered about why people loved the people they did. He wondered how much choice they really had in the matter.

"The past doesn't have to define our present," Lacy said.

This brought Gage out of his reverie. "What?"

"When you asked me before, about the other thing Wade likes to say. That's it. He says, 'The past doesn't have to define our present.' It's his way of saying you have to let go of the past."

There they were. They'd finally arrived at whatever it was she was holding back. They were knocking on the door. Soft knocks. Gently, now. "And was there something Wade had to let go of?"

She pursed her lips. "I don't really know what it is exactly. It was just something he said once. It was when he was in rehab—a place called New Beginnings, down by the wharf. I went to visit him, as he was, you know, drying out. He was the lowest I'd ever seen him. He said his dad did some stuff he should be ashamed of."

"What?"

Lacy responded with a half-hearted shrug. "I tried to get him to tell me, but he just got angry, screaming that his father was a great man and how dare I question that. And he told me I should forget what he said and never, *ever* bring it up again."

"Was his dad in some kind of financial trouble?"

"Maybe. Stan was never great at business, you know. His father was the one who started it."

"But why would that make Wade … suicidal?"

Even after all this, Gage still had a hard time saying the word. If Lacy noticed his reticence, she showed no sign.

"I don't know," she said. "That's—that's why it's so frustrating. You see, Wade said some pretty awful things to me when he was in rehab. I just …I don't like thinking about who he was there. He wasn't himself."

"Okay."

"He apologized and I forgave him, but … this thing about Stan, whatever it is, it's what triggered it. And I'm afraid … I'm afraid …"

"That if it gets brought up again, he'll turn back into that person."

"I guess, yeah."

"Did he keep any journals?"

Lacy shook her head. "No, he said he liked to channel his emotions into his short stories. But even if he'd *had* a journal, I wouldn't have read it. I wouldn't do that."

"Can I ask you why he checked himself into rehab?"

"What do you mean, why?"

"Did you confront him? Stage an intervention? Give him an ultimatum?"

"I did confront him, but he ignored me. And no, I'd never give him an ultimatum. That's not who I am."

"I know. I was just—"

"It's okay. I'm getting defensive. I don't know why he went. He just called me from New Beginnings one morning and said he was getting clean. Why, is that important?"

"It's a little unusual, in my experience. Most addicts won't change course without an impetus of some kind. Can you think of anything that happened during that time? Something with his father maybe?"

"Not really."

Gage didn't sense any subterfuge on her part. "How about with any of his friends? With a teacher maybe?"

"No. But he wasn't really being honest with me, you know. He was … hiding a lot."

The way she winced, it was obvious that Wade's lying, even more than the addiction itself, was what caused her the most pain. "That night he called you from New Beginnings," he said, "do you remember anything else about it? Did he say where, exactly, he'd been before he checked himself in?"

She shrugged. "He just said he had to make a choice, and he made it. He said he loved me. He said he was sorry. He said if I stuck by him, he'd spend—he'd spend the rest of his life making it up to me. He … He …"

She wasn't quite hyperventilating, but she was getting there, her breathing coming in short, sharp gasps.

"It's okay, Lacy," he said. "You've told me everything you can."

"I wish I knew more."

"I know."

"If I think of something else—"

"I know. It's okay."

She let out a long, shuddering breath. Gage patted her arm, then stood.

"I'm going to go find your husband," he said. "You get some rest. Stay in here as long as you want."

She frowned. "What about my car?"

"I can take you to get it in the morning, or Alex can take you later tonight if you really want it before then. I'm going to stay after this, Lacy. I'm going to work all night."

"You don't have to—"

"Stop right there. No more protests."

She nodded, eyelids drooping, exhaustion robbing her of any last protests. At the door, he looked back at her. The light in the room was already changing, the shadows growing longer, the deeply stained walnut imbued with a golden glow. She was so still that she could have been a doll. He had his hand on the knob when she spoke to him.

"It turned out all right, didn't it?" she said.

"What's that?"

"With Dirk. He stopped bullying you?"

"He did, yes."

"Oh, that's good."

Her voice was fading, as if she were speaking to him from a dream. He almost left right then, and it probably would have been better if he had, but as usual, he could never leave a good thing alone.

"But only because I went to school the next day," he said, "and punched that fucker in the nose."

8

———

The drive north was a stop-and-go affair, with the emphasis on stop, the traffic even worse than before. As maddening as it was, this was no surprise to Gage. The brief improvement earlier, when he and Lacy had turned off Highway 101, had been a mirage, just the tourists *already* in town heading back to their hotels for the day. Now, at just before 5:00 p.m., they were contending with a whole new wave of people from the valley in search of a cooler climate, the tip of another weekend surge. That meant tomorrow, a Friday, would be even worse.

It was a good thing he'd left his Beretta at home. The Dennis the Menace lookalike in the back seat of the Honda CRV in front of him, who was currently giving Gage the finger, would have been too tempting a target.

The sun, lower on the left, blasted him in the face and heated up his van like a Crock-Pot. On the temperate Oregon coast, he seldom regretted the VW's lack of air conditioning, but he did today. Even rolling his windows down brought little relief. Not only was the air warm and choked with exhaust, he didn't even get the mild benefit of it moving through the van. Gage never would have been stupid enough to put himself in this mess if it weren't for the task at hand, but he didn't see how he had much choice.

He may have still been skeptical that Wade was really here to put a bullet in his head, but if the kid actually did it tonight while Gage was curled up in his easy chair, drinking bourbon and filling out crossword puzzles, he'd never forgive himself.

Not that he thought he'd have much luck tonight. He didn't find Wade trudging along the highway. He didn't find him hanging out on any side streets, at the cineplex, or the high school. He showed people Wade's picture and got nowhere. He didn't find him back in his truck or on the beach below. Even covering this small amount of ground took the better part of two hours in this herky-jerky auto circus, and Gage was thinking of saving the rest of the town for later when he spotted a familiar vehicle creeping toward him on the highway.

A black Ford Mustang with Idaho plates.

With the glare of the sun on the Mustang's windshield, the driver was hard to make out, but as the car crept closer, Gage clearly saw that it was the same guy who'd been parked across the street when he and Lacy were in the office above Thackleforth Candies—black tracksuit, broad shoulders, dark buzz cut. His square chin was like a mallet.

As they passed one another, Gage leaned out his window. "Hi, do we know each other?"

The guy stared at him, expressionless. In the mirrored sunglasses, Gage saw his own haggard face.

"How about Lacy Carson?" Gage said. "You know her?"

Still no response. The Mustang drove on. One good thing came out of it, though: Gage got the license number.

There was no real proof this guy was anything but

another weird tourist, but Gage's unease with the encounter was enough to change his mind about heading home.

He checked a few other side streets. He checked a few bars. He braved the parking lot at Arrow Outlet Mall. He fought his way all the way north to the casino, striking out everywhere, then doubled back, using some of the roads bordering the beach, a route well known to locals if not the tourists, to avoid much of the highway madness, not finding Wade anywhere, and finally emerging at the drab concrete building that contained both the library and city hall at eight o'clock on the dot.

The sun dangled over the ocean like a button on a string. Sunset was *still* a half hour away, but it was close enough that the light had begun to fade, the sky more lavender than blue. JayBee's Grocery was just across the parking lot. Gage, who hadn't eaten anything since breakfast, was thinking of picking up some chicken tenders from their deli when he spotted Eve's teal Toyota Sienna van parked in the employee lot between the two buildings.

Working late, as usual. He parked and went inside, not finding it surprising that the door was unlocked at such a late hour. Eve probably insisted on it. The interior was just as drab as the outside, with the scuffed stone flooring, wood doors with opaque glass windows, and a dank, musty odor that conjured up memories of Gage's fifties-era high school.

He found her hunched over a stack of manila folders, her reading glasses, the same powder blue as her blouse, perched low on her nose. If the building were a high school, then Eve was the perfect picture of the no-nonsense principal.

"You really should get some better security," he said from the open doorway. "They'll let just about anybody in here."

She didn't look up at him, but she smirked. Her office, at the back of a bullpen of sorts, was dark except for the banker's lamp. She was signing her name on a document. "I had some security," she said, "but they kept throwing out my husband because they thought he looked too suspicious."

"Well, they were right. It's all those pens he carries around in his front pocket. Who needs that many pens? Only people up to no good, that's who."

Eve set her own pen down and looked up at him, her rich, Mediterranean complexion growing darker the farther she got from the banker's lamp. Her chest was much flatter since her double mastectomy a few years back, since she'd opted not to have implants, but it had not diminished her beauty. He caught the scent of vanilla and wondered if it was her perfume. She was always trying different perfumes.

"And to what do I owe this unexpected pleasure?" she asked.

"What, a citizen of our lovely town can't just stop in to say hello to the mayor?"

"It certainly *can* happen, though I can't say it ever has. People usually stop by to complain or because they want something."

"Wow, Eve, if somebody else said that, I'd say they were pretty cynical."

"What does it sound like when *I* say it?"

Gage eased himself into one of the office chairs across from her. "Honest. But you have a way of making even honesty sound like a compliment. You know everybody out there has gone home, right?"

"Mmm. I think I know why you're really here. It's about Wade Carson, isn't it?"

"Alex told you his wife hired me?"

She nodded. "He called this afternoon. I imagine you want to know the same thing Alex wanted to know: why Governor Harmon asked for my help."

"It's been on my mind, yeah."

"Unfortunately, I don't have a lot to tell you other than

that Governor Harmon said that Governor Cramer—that's the governor of Idaho—called *him* to ask if anything could be done. Cramer said the boy's father committed suicide a few days ago and the boy was quite distraught. She said he'd last been seen in Barnacle Bluffs today."

"And Cramer called Stan Carson's death a suicide?"

"Why, do you have reason to think otherwise?"

"No, but the cause of death wasn't in the papers, so it's just interesting he was so forthcoming about it. I've been looking for him most of the evening with no luck."

"So has Chief Roland, apparently. I just got an update from her a few minutes ago. She hasn't had any luck either."

"I see. How did she sound?"

Eve arched her eyebrows. "How did she *sound?*"

"Did Jo sound worried? Distracted? She left in a hurry—when we were on the beach, checking out Wade's truck. Very abrupt, even for her. It was like something had suddenly occurred to her. Or she'd … I don't know, seen something."

"Well, she didn't mention anything to me."

"Ah."

Eve, eyeing him curiously, tapped her pen on a stack of binders.

"What is it?" Gage said.

"Hmm?"

"Mayor Cortez, I'm getting the distinct sense that you're not telling me something."

"Well, it's not really something I should disclose."

"Is it about why Jo acted so strangely earlier?"

"Garrison."

"Is it about Wade?"

"No. At least I have no reason to think so."

"What do you mean you have no reason to think so? If it's about my client—"

"It's not about your client."

"But you just said—"

"All right, all right." Eve sighed. "I know you won't stop badgering me until I tell you *something*, but she just told me she needed to take tomorrow off to deal with a personal matter, all right? That's all. Now will you stop? "

"Why couldn't it wait until Saturday? Is wherever she needs to go not open on the weekends?"

"Garrison—"

"She must be leaving town, right? Why else would she feel the need to tell you? Where is she going?"

"God, you're impossible."

"Salem? Portland?"

Eve, narrowing her eyes, continued to tap her pen on the stack of binders with increasing frequency. "Are you sure you're not asking all these questions about Jo Roland for another reason?"

"What's that supposed to mean?" Then Gage knew exactly what she meant. "Oh God. She told you, didn't she?"

"That you very clumsily tried to ask her out on a date?"

"She used the word clumsy?"

"Relax, she didn't make it sound like a bad thing. She just joked a little about it, that's all."

"Great. Now I'm a punchline."

"We did laugh, but not about you specifically. About men in general. About how difficult they can make things."

"I'm not sure that makes me feel much better."

"Look, I probably shouldn't tell you this, but I think she was just trying to get a sense of what kind of guy you are."

"She asked that?"

"No, but a woman knows, Garrison. And since I sensed that was what she was trying to figure out, I told her that I feel fortunate to have two of the finest men I know in my life."

That rendered Gage temporarily mute. From someone

else, such a compliment could have been laughed away with the usual sarcastic quip, but not coming from Eve. He finally managed to mumble a thank you.

"Oh," she said, with a smile, "did you think I was referring to you?"

"Ha ha."

"Just be careful with Jo, all right? That woman has been through a lot." And when Gage straightened in his seat, eager to probe this obvious opening, Eve held up her hand. "I don't know more than you, okay? Really, I don't. But I see things. I'm not blind. She may act tough, but ..."

"But what?"

"Just be careful. If you're really going to ask her out—"

"That was a mistake."

"Well, if you change your mind—"

"Not going to happen."

"Right, well, all I was going to say is that I get the sense she doesn't let many people inside her circle but can really be quite vulnerable with those she does. She let her guard down just a teensy bit with me, and I saw that vulnerability. She reminds me of someone else I know."

"I don't know what you're talking about," Gage said.

"She's also not that self-aware."

"Uh huh. I don't know what I'd do with myself if I didn't have you to pick apart my psyche, Eve."

"Oh, I think Zoe does a pretty good job just by herself. How is she, by the way?"

Gage, relieved to talk about something other than his own inadequacies, breathed out a sigh. "Good. I think."

"You think?"

"Well, I haven't talked to her in a couple weeks."

"Oh."

"Don't look at me like that."

"Like what?"

Gage looked down the length of his finger as if it were a rifle scope. "Like *that*. Whatever that is. Pity? Zoe's been busy. New job, working as an administrative assistant for that counseling center. Since summer quarter's over, I think she's helping one of her psychology professors with a research project. I've left a couple messages."

"But how would she reach you? You don't have a phone."

"Don't start on that again. We *have* exchanged emails."

"Which you use my husband's computer for, right?"

"Oh God, here we go. Zoe went through a lot last year. I just got the sense she needed some space—you know, to deal with what happened. To process it."

"She's not the only one."

"What?"

"I'm not trying to needle you, Garrison. I know your … aversion to having a phone is a philosophical choice. Unlike my husband, I'm more sympathetic about your various … idiosyncrasies. I actually find them a bit endearing."

"Why do I get the feeling you're talking about a pet dog?"

"But I'm worried about Zoe."

"Well—"

"And I'm worried about you too."

"Oh, I'm fine."

"Are you, though? Really?" Eve held up her hand before Gage could reassure her. "You *both* went through something terrible last year. It's not just Zoe."

"She had it a lot worse than me," Gage insisted. "She was arrested for murder!"

"And that's what I'm getting at. You must feel guilty about what happened, about how … powerless you felt. And so you're pushing her away."

"I'm not pushing her away."

"Are you sure?"

"I'd *never* do that. She's just been busy, that's all. I'm always here for her, if she needs me."

"I don't think that's ever been a question in Zoe's mind. What about when *you* need *her?*"

Gage felt a searing heat in his face, the sense that the walls in her office were closing in. He tried to speak, but all he could manage was to shake his head.

"When you really love someone," Eve added softly, "and you can't do anything to help them … It's one of the worst feelings in the world. Then you start suppressing your own needs because you tell yourself that what you're feeling is not … justified. That it doesn't compare."

"I can't burden her," Gage managed.

"Alex felt that way too."

"Alex?"

"Yes. When I was …" She motioned to her chest.

"Oh."

Eve swallowed. "He was going through hell, but he didn't want to be honest with me about it because he thought I had enough to deal with. He didn't want to … what was your word? *Burden* me."

"I should have been there for him," Gage said.

"That's my point. It wasn't up to you—or me. It was up to Alex to let us in. To ask for help. He didn't want to burden me, but it just made me feel more alone."

It strangely made Gage think about Lacy Carson, the parallel there. She probably felt powerless too, didn't she? Under other circumstances, Gage might have been irritated that Eve had managed to rip open a wound that he didn't even know he had, but instead he found himself in awe of the woman sitting across the desk from him. A no-nonsense principal? Hell, she was an angel on Earth.

"Where did you come from, Eve Cortez?" he asked.

"Excuse me?"

"You were always strong, but it was a quiet strength. You didn't like conflict. You didn't even like it when people said a cross word at dinner."

"I still don't like cross words at dinner," she said.

"And yet, there you sit in the mayor's chair, where you have to deal with cross words all day long. Why would you put yourself through that?"

Eve lowered her eyes. "What I went through, it changed me. It changed the direction of my life—what I wanted, what I needed. Not the big things. But I did decide I wanted to make a difference in a bigger way. Or at least try. I'm fortunate I'm surrounded by people who want to help. I just wish some of them would know that making a difference—for me, at least—starts with the people I care about most."

The message, to Gage, was abundantly clear, and he found all his usual arguments petty and hollow. "I'll get a phone. I promise."

"I'll hold you to that, but it's not about the phone."

"And I'll use it to call Zoe."

"It's not about whether you call her either."

"Okay, now you've lost me."

"It's about letting her know that you need her help," Eve said, "just like she needs yours. Phone, email, however you do it is not important. Although I think these things are usually best done *in person*."

"I see."

"Zoe is a lot like you, Garrison. Life has thrown her so many challenges that she's decided that in the end she can only rely on herself. She wants to be a knight in shining armor just like you. But even the most valiant knight has to take that armor off occasionally."

Gage nodded, but he was feeling pretty armor-less as it was. It exhausted him. Time to change the subject. "One other thing," he said. "Do you know of any man with a prosthetic hook on his left hand?"

"What an odd question," Eve said. "No, not that I'm aware. Why do you ask?"

"Caucasian, square jaw, Marine-looking sort of a guy?" When Eve shook her head no, Gage went on. "I've seen him around driving a black Ford Mustang with Idaho plates."

"And you think it has something to do with our missing Wade Carson?"

"Maybe." He grabbed a sticky note from her desk and jotted the license plate number on it, which he handed to her. "I was going to ask Jo if she'd look it up, but if she's going to be out of the office tomorrow …"

Eve tapped her pen on one of the binders. "And I imagine you don't know a lot of other people in the police department willing to do that for you?"

"I think the majority would like to shoot me on sight."

"Right. Well, I can put in a call."

"Whatever you find out, pass it on to Alex."

"No, I'll pass it on to *you*. Because you're going to buy a phone, remember?"

"Right."

They both laughed. Gage was about to thank her, but a man spoke from the doorway before he got the chance.

"I'll save you folks the trouble," the man said.

Just based on Eve's eyes, Gage knew who it was. After a startled glance upward, her gaze shifted down, to what was the man's most unique trait. For when Gage turned, the first thing he focused on wasn't the man's face but the prosthetic hook.

The point was as sharp as a dagger.

9

———

The man filling the doorway—and it somehow diminished him, reducing him to such a simple noun as *man*—was a tower of muscles, scars, and sharp angles. He still wore mirrored sunglasses and a black tracksuit, white pinstripes running down each leg. Like a mountain, his mere presence changed the airflow and the quality of the light. It was darker, more still.

Also like a mountain, his face had been ravaged by time and exposure, full of crevices, ravines, and patchwork discoloration. The scars were many but faint, like the geological signs of some distant, more violent age.

"Hello, sir, how can I help you?" Eve said, her voice unusually chirpy. She was ordinarily one cool customer, so it was noteworthy how much she'd been rattled. "I'm—I'm Mayor Cortez."

The man removed his sunglasses. His eyes were deep blue, all the more arresting because of the hashtag scarring around them. The nose looked like it had been set at least once. When he smiled, his teeth were so white and perfect that Gage guessed that almost all of them were crowns.

"Hello, ma'am, nice to meet you," he said, with a downhome friendliness that came off a bit too practiced. "I'm Tag Macklin. My birth certificate reads Garrick Macklin—that's the name my daddy gave me, but most everybody just calls me Tag. Some folks call me Big Mac, on account of my size, you understand, not because I'm a fan of McDonalds, so you can go with that one too if it suits you."

"Oh," Eve said. "What can I do for you, Mr. Macklin? This is my dear friend, Garrison Gage, by the way."

"Oh yeah?" Macklin said. "Well, it's good to have friends in high places."

He had a southern accent, but the edge of it was worn off, and it was like he was trying to compensate for the loss with his folksiness. The man's name sounded vaguely familiar to Gage, but he didn't know why. They shook hands. Or Macklin did. It was more like Gage's hand was engulfed in a catcher's mitt.

"I heard you talking," Macklin said to Eve. "Sorry, my momma always said it's impolite to eavesdrop, but it just sort of happened. I wanted to see you anyway, so I guess it's good timing. I can clear up any confusion. See, I'm a private investigator. I'm here looking for a young man named Wade Carson."

Now *that* was not something Gage expected. "Did his mother hire you?"

"That's right. How'd you know that?"

"Garrison is also a private investigator," Eve said. "He's been hired by Wade's wife."

"Oh! Well now, isn't that interesting. I didn't know I was going to have competition." He chuckled. "I guess two heads are better than one and all that, right?"

Gage couldn't get over the man's congenial manner or the sweet home Alabama voice. It didn't seem to fit the hulking, battle-worn figure. It was like a ventriloquist was using the guy's body. "Were you following me?" he asked.

"What's that?"

Gage may not have been able to beat the man in a hand-shaking contest, but he could throw him off balance in other ways. "When I saw you on Highway 101, you were going the other way."

"Huh. If I passed you, I don't rightly recall, but then I'd never met you before. I'm staying at the Sea Witch just down the road a spell. I saw the city hall sign and took a chance."

"And this morning?"

"How's that?"

"I was talking to Lacy Carson in the empty office above Thackleforth Candies. I saw you parked across the street."

"Oh. Well, I did see Lacy Carson go inside that building. Didn't know she was there to meet you."

"Why were you following Lacy Carson? I thought you were looking for Wade."

"I most assuredly am, sir. I'm not at liberty to discuss my client's instructions, but since you're in the business too, you can probably guess that Ellen Carson might have different concerns and considerations regarding her son's whereabouts than the man's wife."

"What, Ellen thinks Lacy is lying? Is that it?"

"As I said, I'm not at liberty to—"

"It's kind of late, isn't it?"

"Excuse me?"

Gage nodded toward the gold nautical clock that had been a gift from Alex. "It's a quarter to nine. Kind of late to be just stopping in on the mayor, isn't it?"

"Like I said, just thought I'd take a chance. I stopped by the police station a little while ago, and they told me about Wade's truck. I just got back from there. I just thought, if anybody can grease the wheels and get things moving, it might be the mayor." He tipped his head at Eve as if he were wearing a hat. "Ma'am."

"We'll do everything we can, of course," Eve said. "Do you have a number where I can—"

"Were you up on the bluff earlier?" Gage cut in. "I could have sworn I saw a glint of metal."

"I've been driving all over town," Macklin said, "but I don't think I was there. I'm sure I would have seen Wade's truck, if I had been." His omnipresent smile didn't fade, but his blue eyes took on an icy sheen. "What was the name again?"

"Garrison Gage."

"Right. Garrison." He chuckled. "Kind of close, isn't it?"

"What's that?"

"Garrick. Garrison. Maybe we're long-lost private eye twins?" He laughed again.

"Right," Gage said. "Separated at birth."

He bumped Gage playfully on the arm with his hook. It might have been a playful tap, but it felt like getting hit by one of those cranes used to erect buildings. "Now you're getting the swing of it," Macklin said. "So what do you go by, then? Gary?"

"Never."

"Ha! I guess you like your full name as is, huh? That's swell. I probably would have gone by Gary myself if Tag hadn't stuck. I always hated Garrick. Don't know what my daddy was thinking, honestly."

"Maybe he named you after the actor," Gage said.

"Excuse me?"

"David Garrick. He was an English actor in the eighteenth century, pretty famous for the time. He did a lot to revive the name of Shakespeare. There's even streets and buildings named after him in London's theater district."

"Huh. Who would have thunk it? But my old man, I

don't know if he could even read the instructions on a can of soup, that's how dumb he was, so it was more likely Garrick was just some old drinking buddy of his." He laughed, a big, hearty chortle that shook the room. "Anyways, now you know who I am and why I'm here. If I pass you again on the road, I'll make sure to wave hello if it makes you feel any better."

"I'll feel better when Wade turns up safe and sound."

"Well me too, partner, me too."

"I hope that's true."

"Come again?"

"We'll do everything we can to find him," Eve jumped in, before Gage could answer. "Do you have a number where you can be reached?"

"I'll surely do, ma'am, but I'll do you one better."

He reached into his back pocket with his right hand and retrieved his wallet, then fished out a couple of business cards with his prosthetic hook. A hole had been punched in the top of each card, obviously for this purpose, and he dangled one in front of Eve like a fisherman with a lure. She took it with a polite smile. Then Macklin held the remaining one out to Gage.

"One for you, too, partner," he said. "I sense you wouldn't be too keen on working together, and that's fine, that's mighty fine, but it wouldn't hurt for us to keep each other in the loop, right?"

Gage took it. It was heavy card stock and read *Tag Macklin, Investigations*, with a phone number, a Boise, Idaho, PO address, and an embossed graphic of a metal hook, much like the one on the end of Tag's arm, that circled the hole. The tagline beneath the contact information read *I'm on the hook for you!*

"I have to hand it to you," Gage said. "It's memorable."

Tag laughed. "I see what you did there. *Hand* it to you.

It's a good thing I'm not a bad sport about those kinds of jokes. I kind of figured, hey, this thing happened, but I might as well lean into it, you know? I still got two legs for leaning, right?" He chuckled. "Hey, you got a card yourself?"

"No. But since we're on the subject of your hand, you mind saying how you lost it?"

"Wow, you really are forward, aren't you?"

Eve frowned at Gage. "You'll have to forgive my friend. He can be a little blunt."

"Naw, it's okay," Macklin said. "If I don't tell you, you'll find it out as soon as you look me up anyway. I lost it in the line of duty, okay?"

"Police?" Gage said.

"Yessiree. So you got a number where I can reach you, at least?"

"Alas, I'm between phones right now, but I'll have one soon enough."

"In the meantime," Eve said, "just call me if you need to talk to Garrison, and I'll pass it on."

"All right, that's just peachy," Tag said. "Again, I'm sorry for barging in on you. I was just hoping we might work as a team on this thing. Is there anything else either of you can tell me that would help?"

"I can tell you that Lacy Carson has nothing to do with her husband's disappearance," Gage said.

"You're that sure, huh? Well, I hope that's true."

"You don't have to hope. It *is* true."

"Okay, pal. You don't have to put on the hard sell. I haven't met Lacy, but I'm sure I'd think the same if I had. I'm just following my client's instructions, okay? She's just real worried and doesn't want to leave any stone unturned. Don't shoot the messenger. In the end, we both want the same thing, right?"

"That's right," Eve said, "and I'm sure he'll turn up very

soon. I can understand where Wade's mother is coming from. If one of my daughters was missing, I'd be out of my mind with worry. Isn't that right, Garrison? If Zoe was missing, you probably wouldn't be thinking so clearly."

It was a not-so-subtle reminder of how Gage *had* acted when Zoe was in trouble, but Gage was too bothered by this guy to play nice at this point. "So how, exactly, did you lose your hand again?" he asked.

"Garrison," Eve said.

"Wow," Tag said, "you won't quit on that, will you?"

"It's okay if it's a touchy subject."

Tag's smile hadn't faded one bit, but his eyes were like painted rocks. "Is that another joke?"

"You said you didn't mind."

"I don't, as long as it's in good fun. Why do you have that cane?"

"It's not a cane. It's a magic wand, and I'm a wizard."

"Something happen to your legs? If you don't mind my asking, that is."

"Are you asking why my legs are so handsome? You should see me in shorts. Why did Ellen Carson hire you?"

"Excuse me?"

"Did she just Google you?"

"No, I done some jobs for her husband in the past. She must have remembered."

"What kind of jobs? From one private investigator to another, you know."

Tag shrugged. "Mostly fraud, disability claims, equipment theft—you know, the usual. As a private investigator yourself, you know I can't get into the details.'"

"Why not, the man's dead, isn't he?"

"Garrison, *please*," Eve said.

"It's okay, ma'am. I know he's just trying to rattle me, because he doesn't trust me. And that's okay. I probably wouldn't trust me either, if I was in his shoes. Look, man, I'll tell you this much. The first time Stan Carson hired me was *also* to look for his son."

"When was this?"

"About two years ago, when the kid was about to go down the tubes with meth. Everybody was frantic to find him. Stan started calling all the local PIs in Seattle who came up on a Google search, and I guess I was the first one who called him back. I found the kid and convinced him to check himself into rehab. What, Lacy didn't tell you any of this? That's interesting."

"Why is that interesting?"

"Just that you're so sure about her, and here she didn't tell you that."

It was a dig, and not a very subtle one. "Maybe Wade didn't tell her. Maybe he wanted to look more like a hero in her eyes, that he did it himself. Maybe that's all it is. So you're originally from Seattle, huh?"

"That right—well, Alabama back in the day, but that was before Momma wised up about Daddy and moved me across the country to Spokane when I was twelve. I'm glad those other PIs were busy because that turned out to be my lucky day. Stan was so grateful he offered me a job as head of security of Carson Clocks. I turned that down, because I didn't want a regular eight-to-five thing again, but he said if I relocated to Boise, he could pretty much guarantee he could keep jobs coming my way. So I thought, what the hell, and moved my ass to Idaho."

"Just like that," Gage said.

"Just like that. So you see why I feel real grateful to the whole Carson family. I'm going to find Ellen's son for her, and I'm not going to stop until I do. That woman has been through so much as it is."

"I get it."

"Good, fantastic. All right then, I'll be seeing you both."

He gave the doorframe a friendly tap with his good hand and turned to go. Gage was still thinking about Seattle. He didn't like coincidences.

"So did you know Jo Roland?" he asked. "When you were in Seattle?"

Tag stopped, still smiling, but there was a bit more hesitation in his eyes. "Your chief of police? Yeah, man, I actually served with her. We were both in Narcotics."

"Really. That's a hell of a coincidence."

"Tell me about it. In fact, I met her husband, Dell, at the police academy, so I knew him even longer. I was a little older because I did a seven-year stretch in the army first, and he just worked for a year at a lumber yard before deciding he wanted to be a cop, but we were both small town kids from eastern Washington, so we kind of bonded over that. Plus we both loved to read. I almost fell over when I walked into the police station here and saw Jo's picture hanging on the wall. I mean, I'm not surprised she's chief, she could do anything. It's just too bad, how things went down with Dell. You know all about that?"

"I do. So you really didn't know she was here?"

"Nope. But she pretty much cut ties with anybody who was part of her life in Seattle. Don't really blame her, the way things went down. She's not on social media. She changed her numbers and emails. I know because I emailed her a couple times early on, and they bounced. I figured she might reach out at some point on her own, but, well, you never know with Jo." He chuckled.

Gage thought about the strange way Jo had acted on the beach earlier. Now he was nearly certain Tag Macklin had been there, up on the bluff. "And you talked to her? At the station?"

"I did indeed, sir."

"And that was the first time you saw her in town?"

"Yep."

"Not when she was down by Wade's truck? Or walking on the beach below?"

Tag didn't stop smiling, but all the muscles in his face hardened. "Dude, I already told you I wasn't there. Why would I lie? I have no reason to lie about that."

"No reason," Gage said, nodding. "So when you were in Narcotics in Seattle, what was your relationship with her husband?"

"What are you getting at?" Tag said. "Are you wondering if I was in on the take too?"

"Well, were you?"

"Jesus."

"Garrison," Eve said.

Tag raised his hook in a gesture that was probably meant to look placating but still, because it was a hook, came off as slightly menacing. "It's okay, ma'am. Really. Again, if I was in his shoes, I'd probably wonder the same thing. But it's obvious Garrison here doesn't really know what went down that night at Terminal Five. If he did, his perspective might be a little different."

"Oh yeah?" Gage said. "And why's that?"

"Because I saved Jo's life," Tag said. "If it wasn't for me, her husband would have shot her dead instead of shooting me in the hand."

10

Tag Macklin told them they didn't have to take his word for it. They could read all about what went down ten years ago at Terminal Five in the *Seattle Times.* This was what Gage and Eve did as soon as Macklin left, Gage leaning over Eve's shoulder in her dimly lit office while she used her computer to scour the newspaper's archives.

The articles, and there were dozens, verified Macklin's account. The drug bust in the shadow of Mt. Rainier, the shooting amid all the stacked containers, the added drama of husband and wife officers being mixed up in all of it—it was a story for the ages in Seattle. Officer Garrick Macklin had been grievously injured while trying to protect Lieutenant Jo Baldwin and received special commendation for his service in the line of duty. (Roland was apparently Jo's maiden's name, which a bit more research revealed she'd gone back to shortly after leaving Seattle.) Disgraced Narcotics Chief Dell Baldwin had died at the scene, as did three known associates of the Tunez cartel.

Macklin was pictured in the hospital with both the mayor and the chief of police at his bedside, his left arm bandaged to the elbow. Macklin had the same larger-than-life smile to go with his larger-than-life body, though his face wasn't nearly so scarred.

"I wouldn't be alive today if it weren't for Officer Macklin," Jo was quoted as saying. "When I told him I thought my husband might be mixed up in something illegal down at Terminal Five, he insisted on coming along as backup."

Now Gage knew why Macklin's name had sounded familiar. Gage had skimmed these accounts last year, when he was frustrated with Jo's handling of Zoe's situation, and he was looking for something he could exploit to his advantage.

Too irritated with Gage's rude behavior to let him continue reading over her shoulder for long, Eve shoved Gage out of his office with a reminder that the Verizon store was open until ten. With a decent smartphone, he could do his own research. Spending even five minutes at the outlet mall, let alone a cell phone store *in* an outlet mall, sounded like torture on par with waterboarding and school board meetings, but Gage took her advice. A promise was a promise.

The experience in the store was even worse than he'd imagined, but somehow he survived with his sanity mostly intact and a few insufferable hours later was slouched at his dining room table with the brick-sized phone aglow in his hand.

The first call. He knew who it should be, but he hesitated. It was late. Maybe he should wait until tomorrow. His big, A-frame window was dark, no remnants of the sunset, the traffic down the hill finally dying off enough that he could hear the ocean. The packaging was strewn out on the table, his shadow long on the dark walnut surface, the only light coming from the tiny bulb above the sink behind him.

Other than the backs of the recliners, the rest of his living room was lost in a sea of darkness.

Two chairs. Matching green wingbacks with thin gold striping. When had he bought the second? Was it the first year she'd come to live with him or the second?

He dialed her number. He didn't expect her to answer since it would be coming from an unknown number, but he still hoped she would. The call went to voicemail.

"Hey, kiddo, it's me," Gage said. "I got myself a new phone. This is the number. I guess that's obvious, huh? Anyway, call me back. Or text or something. Love to chat … When you have a chance. Hey, I, um, I'd love to talk. I know I said that. Okay. Bye now."

He dropped the phone on the table with a clatter, disgusted with his babbling. It took him a moment to realize he hadn't hung up, and when he groped for the phone he managed to send it skittering onto the floor. Somehow the phone survived the experience, and he finally ended the call, though not without tossing in a few curse words. Zoe would certainly find his message entertaining.

She didn't call right back. That was okay. He typed in her contact information, even figuring out how to use the camera so he could add her picture—a picture of a picture, as it were. He used the photo on his dresser, the one Alex had taken at Eve's election night party two years ago, patriotic balloons and streamers in the background, a sea of red, white, and blue. Zoe had looked so radiant that he'd asked Alex if he could have a print at some point. Alex surprised him that Christmas with the photo in a sandalwood frame. Gage liked the picture even more now, though there was something about it that wasn't quite Zoe anymore. Even with the rocky childhood she'd had before entering his life, there'd still been a hopeful optimism in her eyes—a *fierce* optimism, yes, but still hopeful—and he seldom saw that anymore.

A picture frozen in time. It took him twenty minutes to figure out how to crop himself out of it, but in the end he liked it better with the two of them in it, so he left it the way it was.

Contact No. 1 saved.

———

SINCE IT WAS LATE, he texted the others about his new number—Carl, Alex, Eve, and finally Lacy. Carl was a garbage collector from Iowa whom Gage texted by mistake when he tried to text Lacy and got Carl instead, who immediately rang up Gage and launched into a screed of profanity. In the midst of all the insults, Carl added that he had to get up godawful early in Des Moines to collect people's garbage, so he didn't appreciate being disturbed. When Gage politely asked why Carl didn't use the phone's mute button, the man said something unsavory about Gage's mother and hung up.

Welcome to the twenty-first century, Gage.

That was word-for-word what Alex texted him after getting Gage's first message, and Gage started to type something unsavory about *Alex's* mother, but autocorrect and clumsy fingers turned it into a mishmash of nonsense mixed with a bunch of monkey emojis. *LOL* was Alex's reply. Gage managed to type the number Lacy had given him correctly the second time, telling her there was no sign of Wade yet but there was some stuff they could talk about in the morning, specifically adding that she didn't need to call tonight. So what did she do? She called him one minute later.

"You got a phone," she said.

"I know. Call the Vatican."

"Huh?"

"You know, because it's a miracle. They'll need to verify it."

"Oh, right." There was a pause, and he heard the unmistakable *thunk* of a car door slamming, then the waves crashing on the beach, loud and close. "No sign of Wade, though, huh?"

"Where are you?" Gage said.

She hesitated. "I'm … I'm down by Wade's truck. I just thought, you know—"

"Lacy, what the hell. It's almost midnight. I thought you were going to get some sleep."

"I know, I know. It's just—"

"How did you get there? I told you I'd take you to get your car in the morning."

"No, the Prius is still at the station. I walked."

"You *walked?*"

"Yes. I did sleep for a little while. Then I … I dreamed Wade was in his truck but he was drowning. I just had to come down."

Hearing this, Gage felt a stab of regret. She'd had a nightmare, and here he was yelling at her. "That's a long walk," he said. "I've done that myself a few times. Do you want a ride back? I'm one minute away."

"No, no."

"I'm going to drive the van down and get you."

"You don't have to do that."

"Just stay there, okay?"

"I'd really rather walk."

"Lacy—"

"But tell me, what's the stuff you wanted to talk to me about?"

"What?"

"You said there was some stuff to talk about in the morning. What is it? Just tell me. I'll wonder all night if you don't."

Gage sighed into the receiver. This wasn't the way he wanted to bring up Garrick Macklin, but he couldn't very well refuse her request. "There's another private investigator in town," he said. "He was hired by Ellen to find Wade. His name is Garrick Macklin. Goes by Tag Macklin. Have you heard of him?"

"No. Why? I mean, that's good, though, right? I wish Ellen would have told me she was going to do that, but the more people looking for Wade, the better."

Gage didn't hear the slightest hesitation in her answer. "Macklin told me he found Wade when he went missing a couple years ago, that Stan hired him. Macklin said he even helped Wade get checked into rehab."

"Oh. That's … okay. Wow."

"Wade never mentioned him?"

"No. This man—what was his name?"

"Tag Macklin."

"He's sure about this?"

"He sounded pretty sure."

Lacy didn't speak for a while, the ocean waves crashing into the silence. He heard her footsteps on the pavement, then the sound changed, softening as her shoes touched sand.

"You still there?" Gage said.

"Yes," she said. "I'm heading back to the Turret House now. I just … Wade told me he checked himself into New Beginnings. I'm just trying to understand why he would tell me that if it wasn't true."

"Maybe he just wanted to seem stronger than he really was. For you. He wanted you to think he was strong enough to do it on his own."

"Yeah, I guess. I don't know. I don't know what to believe."

"It's okay," Gage said.

"I don't want to be angry with him. That's—that's just wasted energy. I just want him home."

"I understand."

"I just miss him so much."

"I know."

She started to say something else, but the words came out too garbled to understand with all of her crying, especially with the growing roar of the ocean.

"Turn around and go back to Wade's truck," Gage said. "I'll come get you."

"N-n-no," Lacy said, struggling to even get that word out amid all the ragged breathing. "No, you … you don't have to do that. I really need to walk this off. It's good that I'm walking. It's helping."

"I'd feel better if I took you home. It's a long way to walk in the dark."

She took a few deep breaths. "Please, Garrison. I really don't mind walking. It's nice. The moon is out. I can see fine."

"I know. But you're literally just down the road from my house, and I was planning on doing a little more searching for Wade myself tonight anyway."

"You don't have to do that. You need sleep too."

"I'll be fine. You can even come with me for a bit, how's that? Then I'll drop you off at the Turret House. Just come back to the truck, okay?"

There was a pause, one long enough that Gage was going to speak again, when she cried out.

"Oh my God!"

"Lacy?"

"I think I see him!"

"Wade?"

"Yes, yes! He's way, way down there, but I think it's him.

I'd know his shape anywhere. I think that's the green sweatshirt I bought him. He's got his backpack on."

"Are you sure?"

"I'll—I'll call you back in a minute!"

"Lacy, wait. Leave the line—"

Open he was going to say, but she'd already clicked off. He was in his van and halfway down the driveway when he realized he'd forgotten his cane. Too late now. The moon was only a sliver, but she'd been right about how bright it was. It was bright enough that he didn't realize until he'd reached Wade's truck that his headlights were off. The Ford Ranger was the only vehicle parked in front of the barricade.

His cane wasn't the only thing he'd left behind. He'd also forgotten his leather jacket, and when he got out of the van, the air was still but much cooler than before. His polo stuck to his back. A man hefted a cooler across the parking lot in front of the Starfish Motel, his flip-flop sandals clacking against asphalt, but otherwise Gage saw no one. The garbage can smelled like someone's chicken dinner.

He made his way down to the beach in the moonlight, the ocean rising to greet his ears, but the wind, even there, barely noticeable. It was almost never this still. The yellow windows of the motels and houses loomed over him like the eyes of crouching wolves. He didn't see Lacy—left, right, anywhere. He heard the drone of a television. He heard a dog bark. He heard a man up on a balcony at the Starfish laugh, and then a woman joined him. The smell of pot, that distinctive burned grass stench, wafted over him.

As he trudged closer to the surf, a ribbon of white amid all that black, it was easier to walk because of the smoother sand and also easier to see without the ambient light behind him. The glittering houses stretched in both directions like the bejeweled back of a snake. Gage didn't even know which way to walk, so he chose south.

It was a good gamble. In the end, he very nearly jogged right past her. Winded, collar drenched with sweat, and his right knee throbbing, he'd just passed a small log when he realized that it wasn't a log. Logs don't cry.

It was quite a bit darker in this stretch, about halfway between the Starfish and the Inn at Sapphire Head, where there were fewer motels and houses casting their diffuse light on the sand. Gage found Lacy on her hands and knees not far from another public access point. He could clearly see the yellow sign next to wooden stairs.

"Lacy?" he said.

She was hugging her knees and rocking back and forth, making a keening sound so quiet he could barely hear it over the surf, even as still as it was. Gage crouched next to her. It wasn't like he had a choice. If he didn't crouch, he would have fallen over anyway.

"He—he ran away," Lacy said. "Why would he run away?"

"Just take a breath. It's okay."

"He was standing in that square of light over there. Right there! I think he r-r-ran up those steps. But. But I'm not sure. Should I go up there? I don't know. I don't—I don't know which way to go. He might … he might have kept running. I —I don't—"

"Lacy, breathe. Just breathe."

"He had his gun."

"What?"

"I saw the shape. It was in his back pocket."

"Breathe. Lacy, please, just breathe."

Gage put his hand on her back. Even through the sweat-shirt, her back felt as warm as a stovetop. The breathing slowed, became more rhythmic. When Lacy looked at him, her eyes gleamed with the light from the houses on the bluff.

"Why would he run from me?" she asked.

"I don't know," he said.

"He's going to do it. He's really going to do it."

"But he didn't, Lacy. That's good, right? Seeing you stopped him. And we'll find him. He's close by. I'll—"

"I just—I can't—"

"Lacy—"

"I can't live without him."

She collapsed against his chest, sobbing openly. She was not a big woman, but if he hadn't braced himself, he would have toppled onto his back. His fingers burrowed beyond the upper layer of warm sand into the gritty coolness beneath. He held her as she cried, straining to keep himself upright, and it was because of this extreme angle that he was looking over the top of Lacy's head at the houses on the bluff.

Jo Roland stood in one of the windows.

It was actually a glass slider. The door was closed, but the curtains were open, the light spilling onto the deck. She wore jeans and a black V-neck shirt, and she had her arms crossed underneath her chest. He thought she might have been looking at them, but it was too dark outside. Had she heard Lacy cry out? Not likely. The bluff was way up there, the equivalent of four stories, and the ocean was loud.

Jo's lips were moving. Who was she talking to? He was about to mention it to Lacy when a man walked into view behind Jo.

Tag Macklin.

11

The big private investigator towered over Jo Roland, who was not exactly short. Even from the beach, Gage could make out his toothy smile. Macklin no longer wore his tracksuit jacket, his biceps bulging in a long-sleeved white V-neck shirt that covered whatever bulky contraption—lots of wires and wraps, judging by the bulges and wrinkles in the cotton—that kept his prosthetic hook in place. If Gage was surprised to find Macklin in Jo's house, he was even more surprised at what happened next.

Macklin put his hand on Jo's shoulder.

It was not the gesture of a former colleague. It was too familiar. Jo patted Macklin's hand, then turned and disappeared. Macklin watched her go, still smiling, before disappearing into the house himself.

In the darkness, Lacy was still huddled against Gage's chest, not looking at the window, not seeing what was up there. The sand felt cold and hard. She sat up, wiping at her eyes. Gage kept his peripheral vision trained on Jo's living room window, but there was nobody up there now. Should he say something to Lacy? No, not until he knew more.

"I shouldn't have done that," Lacy said.

"It's really okay."

"I'm sorry."

"I'm docking you ten points," Gage said.

"What?"

"No apologies, remember?"

"Oh. Right." Her face was awash in shadows, but her eyes, catching the moonlight, revealed her anguish. "I better stay here. I better stay here unless he comes back."

"Lacy, come on. You can't stay out here all night."

"Yes, I can. If that's what it takes."

"He was heading this way. Isn't it a good bet he was going to his truck?"

"I guess so. But the gun—?"

"It was in his pocket, right?"

"Yes."

"It wasn't in his hand?"

"No … No, it was just in his pocket."

"If he doesn't want to face you yet, he might be heading through the neighborhoods to get back to his truck. He could use the steps on 32nd."

It was enough to get her moving. He looked back once, at Jo's house, and saw that the living room light was off. He felt like he'd swallowed a burning ember. When they got back to 32nd, the truck was still there, but there was no Wade. They waited in the van for an hour to no avail, the temperature dropping enough that Lacy started to shiver. They drove up to the streets on the bluff and back, not seeing him anywhere.

"He's probably hunkered down in an empty vacation house now," Gage said.

"I hate to leave," she said, but her drooping eyelids said otherwise. "What if he comes back and then drives somewhere else? Another town?"

"Well, we could take the air out of his tires."

"Oh, no, we shouldn't do that. I don't—I don't want him any more upset than he already is."

"Why don't you leave him a note?" Gage said. "Tell him you're staying at the Turret House. Tell him the room number. Tell him he can come there at any time. Tell him how much you love him."

"You think that will help?"

"Anything that reminds him how much you care can't hurt."

She did as he asked, finally relenting on going back to the Turret House.

———

After dropping Lacy off at her room, the clock on Gage's new cell phone read 1:37 a.m.—technically Friday, but it felt like the continuation of one long day. As he headed south again, a few lonely headlights swept past him on Highway 101. He was at Jo's place in five minutes.

It wasn't hard to find. Alva Street was in the hilly neighborhood just north of the Inn at Sapphire Head. The little white cottage, at a bend in the road, might have been modest compared to its neighbors, but it was in good shape, with a white picket fence, a well-tended yard of evergreen plants, and a bright red front door. Her '69 Chevy Malibu was parked in the attached carport. He didn't see Tag Macklin's Mustang.

A moment after he rang her doorbell, light illuminated the opaque panel to the right of the door. Heavy footsteps. The briefest pause. Then the snap of a deadbolt and there she was.

"Is he gone?" Gage said.

"What the hell, Gage! Do you know what time—"

"Don't play fucking games with me, Jo. Macklin was here just a little while ago, and I want some answers."

As she fumbled for a response, Gage edged his way through the opening. A carpeted stairway led upstairs. A few more steps inside, he came to a galley kitchen with a white marble countertop, kept going past a built-in bookcase decorated with blown glass, and ended up in the living room with its expansive windows. A peach couch and loveseat were positioned in front of a white brick fireplace. A goblet of red wine sat on the glass coffee table. Just one.

The decor, with pastel pillows, blue glass vases, and a water color of an ocean sunset was a lot more Martha Stewart than he expected.

"Gage, what the *fuck,*" Jo said. "You can't just march into my house. Tag is an old colleague. I don't know what your problem is."

In his flurry into the house, he'd really only noted her face—mostly the shock in her eyes—and didn't take in any other details. Now that he was really looking at her, two things stood out. The first was that she was dressed in skimpy silk pajamas a similar color as her peach couches. The second was that she was holding a gun.

A Glock 42 with a dull black metal finish. Her police issue handgun. She gripped the handle with such ferociousness that it looked like her bones might pop out of her flesh.

"Are you going to shoot me, Jo?" he asked.

She glanced at the Glock. A glow from the bookcase caught his eye. A cell phone in a black case rested on the top shelf next to a large teak box. She saw him looking and grabbed the phone, turning it off, but not before he was able to get a glimpse of what was on the screen. He read the headline *Secret Beach* above a photo of an ocean cove. There was a towering rocky island not far out in the ocean, an island topped with fir trees. It looked familiar.

"Where's Secret Beach?" he asked.

Her jaw was just as rigid as the barrel of her gun. "You need to leave."

"Why was Macklin here?"

"I'm not talking about this."

"Eve told me you were taking Friday off. Why?"

"Get out. *Now.*"

"Not until I get some answers. Why was Tag Macklin here?"

"I told you it's none of your damn business!"

Gage flinched. On the Richter scale of emotional outburst, her shout hardly registered, but by Jo Roland standards, it was as big as they got. "It's my business if it has something to do with Wade Carson," he said.

"What?"

"I don't like coincidences, Jo. Especially when I'm working on a case."

"Are you *insane?*"

"Then where are you going tomorrow?"

She stepped closer, alarmingly close, the Glock still at her side. He smelled wine on her breath. "You have some nerve, Garrison. Accusing me, the chief of police—"

"I'm not accusing you of anything."

"You're implying, though, aren't you? You're implying I'm up to something."

"Well? Are you?"

"Jesus Christ! A few hours ago, you were asking me out on a date, and now you're—"

"Just tell me what you're doing tomorrow."

"I told you, it has nothing to do with—"

"How did you afford this house anyway?"

"Are you kidding me?"

"What are you hiding?"

"Fuck you, asshole!"

He didn't think it was possible that they could move any closer, but they must have, because their noses bumped. The touch was an electric whip along his spine. He hated her. He wondered what she looked like naked. He hated her more than he'd ever hated a woman before. He wondered how it would feel to touch her. He wished she'd never moved here. She leaned closer, the heat of their bodies rising like an inferno between them. A fire could keep you warm. A fire could burn you up.

She moved away.

She didn't go far, a half a step to the right, turning so she was looking more at the windows than at him. "How—how did you know he was here?"

Gage swallowed. "I saw him. When I was down on the beach. A while ago."

They stood more side by side than face to face, leather brushing against silk.

"Oh really?" she said. "You were watching me from the beach. So who's the peeping Tom now?"

"It wasn't like that."

She chuckled softly, but even this had an edge. "Oh yeah? What was it like then?"

"I was down there with Lacy. I just happened to look up."

"What?"

He walked to the window. It was either that or tear her clothes off. Staring at his own reflection, he told her what had happened. The news appeared to deflate whatever remained of her fury. When he turned back to her, she just looked sad. She opened the teak box on the shelf, put her Glock inside, then closed the lid. There was a numerical combination pad, camouflaged so well he didn't notice it until now, which she spun a few times.

Jo Roland remained an enigma to him. It was like she wanted the Glock close at hand but not in a way that upset her calming coastal ambiance. He thought it was interesting that she kept it in the living room and not her bedroom. Some cops, he'd been told, didn't like having a gun too close at hand late at night, in those all-too-frequent desperate hours, when hope was harder to come by than bullets.

Staring at her hands, he realized she wasn't wearing her wedding ring, that simple gold band. He wondered what that meant. He wondered if it was gone for good, and if its absence had anything to do with Macklin's arrival, or if she simply removed her jewelry as part of her nightly routine.

"I'm sorry to hear that Wade ran off again," Jo said, fastening the top button of her nightshirt before turning to him again. "I'm not sure what I can do if he just doesn't want to talk to his wife."

"He still has that gun," Gage said.

"That's not a crime. Look, it's late. I've got to get up early to …" She trailed off.

"To what?"

"Never mind. I'm very tired. I really need you to—"

"Did you sleep with Tag Macklin tonight?"

"Jesus, Gage." Her eyes burned hot, like someone blowing on dying embers, but then it was gone. Her shoulders sagged. "There's just no line you won't cross, is there?"

"Did you have an affair with him back in Seattle? When you were married?"

"You're unbelievable."

"Or was it after? Maybe your husband's death drew you together?"

"You're jealous, is that it?" she said. "Is that what this is about?"

"Don't be ridiculous," he said. "I told you, I don't like coincidences. What happened at Terminal Five? I know Macklin was trying to protect you, but how did that go down?"

"You don't know anything."

"Then tell me. Let me help you."

"Help me? *You?* You've got to be kidding. I don't need your help. I don't need *anyone's* help."

"If you're mixed up in something—"

"Just leave. Please."

This last she said softly, but there was so much anguish in it that it stopped him cold. She bowed her head, exposed and vulnerable in her flimsy silk outfit. He felt something unexpected then, the desire to comfort her, but he steeled himself against the feeling and walked to the front door.

As he opened it, she was still standing by the bookshelf. She lifted her head, but not to look at him. She looked at the teak box with her Glock in it. There was no anger now. What he saw in her eyes, as he closed the door behind him, was far more disturbing.

It almost looked like *longing*.

12

"I need a favor," Gage said.

There was some rustling on the other end of the line, a groan, and a muffled voice. As usual, Gage had forgotten to say hello. He could have blamed it on fatigue, but despite not having slept at all last night, he still didn't feel tired. Fog rimmed the windshield from the inside. Outside, for the first time in over an hour, Highway 101 was completely still.

"Garrison," Alex said finally, "do you know what time it is?"

"I need to borrow your van."

"*That's* what's so important?"

"There's more."

"I should hope so since you're calling me at … 4:04 a.m. Jesus."

"I need you to close the bookstore tomorrow."

"Okay. Why?"

"Because you're going to be busy looking for Wade Carson. Think of it as a way to dust off those old FBI skills of yours."

"I'm confused. Isn't that what *you're* supposed to be doing?"

"Yes, but I'm following a hunch, and I'm going to be gone all day. I really want someone to be looking for Wade while I drive to Gold Beach."

"Gold Beach! That's four hours away. Why on Earth do you ... Hold on, let me grab my robe. Eve has an early meeting. Where are you? You sound like you're in your van already?"

"I am. Well, not my van. I'm in *your* van. I'm parked at the scenic viewpoint just south of Barnacle Bluffs. My van is parked in front of your place."

Alex sighed. "Of course it is. So you basically just broke into the Turret House and stole my van?"

"I had a spare key to the Turret House, remember? So I didn't break in. I snuck in. There's a difference. And the keys to your Kia were right there hanging on the rack in the kitchen. I was barely inside. I'll have it back tonight."

"But if you took my van anyway, why did you even call me?"

"I didn't want you to be surprised in the morning."

"You didn't think, just maybe, you could have called in the actual morning too?"

"It's technically morning."

"It's dark outside. That means it's not morning. And why on Earth would you ... Just a second, I'm heading up to the turret. I don't want to disturb the guests."

"Look, I can call you from the road in a bit. I really should go."

"Oh no, you've got me wide awake now, so you're going to tell me everything, including what this has to do with Jo Roland."

"Why do you think it has anything to do with Jo Roland?"

Gage heard the creak of another door, slippers slapping against tile, then the heavier thudding of footsteps on the spiral staircase.

"Because Gold Beach is not far from Port Orford," Alex said, "where she used to live. Because you're waiting just outside Barnacle Bluffs to see if she passes on the highway going south. I know that viewpoint. There's a place to park where all the junipers would block the view from anyone coming from the south. And you wanted to be in my Kia Carnival because it's pretty nondescript compared to that banana on wheels you drive."

"Hmm. Maybe your FBI skills aren't so rusty."

"Well, it doesn't take FBI skills to recognize how obsessed you are with Chief Roland."

"I'm not obsessed with her."

"Infatuated? Is that a better word?"

"You're being ridiculous."

"As ridiculous as stealing your best friend's van at four in the morning? All right, I'm settled in my chair. Tell me everything that's happened since I last saw you, then I'll judge for myself whether I need to stage an intervention."

Gage did, if only because he wanted to prove Alex wrong. He finished by telling Alex how he'd learned, when he'd finally sat down in his recliner at a quarter to three in the morning and used his phone's internet browser with all the speed and efficiency of a toddler using a crayon, that Secret Beach was located on the southern Oregon coast in the Cape Sebastian Scenic Corridor, just south of Gold Beach and just north of Brookings and the California border.

Or about a forty minute drive from Port Orford, where Josephine "Jo" Roland had worked in the tiny, four-person police department for almost ten years after leaving Seattle.

The picture he'd seen on Jo's phone had looked familiar

because he and Zoe had stopped at nearby Thunder Cove a few years back on a trip down to the California Redwoods. Despite its name, Secret Beach wasn't all that secret, deriving its name from the fact that most of the beach, sandwiched among giant rocky formations topped with stunted and windblown firs, disappeared at high tide. He and Zoe hadn't hiked it because they were only stopping briefly, but he remembered her showing him that same photo and remarking how they'd have to come back someday.

Now it looked like he might get his chance.

Outside, approaching headlights illuminated the wall of junipers, but when the car passed it wasn't Jo. He watched through the Kia's rearview mirror, the van parked so it overlooked the dark ocean. The waves were visible only as thin gray ribbons, and though he couldn't see them crashing against the rocks below from his vantage point, he could hear them. The hundred-foot cliff face behind him, on the other side of the highway to the east, smothered the moonlight and made the empty parking lot look like a pool of oil. The windows may have been all shut tight, but he could still smell both the junipers and the salty air.

"So," Alex said, "you admit that this isn't primarily about Wade Carson then?"

"I concede that our little town's police chief might be ethically compromised."

"Uh huh. What exactly do you think you're going to find down there?"

Gage glanced at the backpack on the passenger seat. Included in the bag, along with various snacks and supplies, was his Beretta model 92, along with an extra cartridge of 9mm rounds. "I don't know, but I want to be ready for anything. I'll admit this much: I'm hoping she *isn't* mixed up in something, okay? If she's in trouble, maybe I can be there for her."

"I thought you hated her guts."

"Things change."

"Aha!"

"What do you mean, 'aha?' There's no 'aha'. She's a person. I'm a person. It's okay to care about another person, you know, just as one human being to another."

"Mmm. How do you know she hasn't already left?"

"I drove by her house, and her Malibu was still parked in the carport."

"Wow, see, obsessed. And what if she doesn't go at all?"

"She'll go."

"You could end up just sitting there for hours."

"I don't think so."

"What if she recognizes my van?"

"Then she does. But since I have a pretty good idea where she's probably going, I'll hang back as far as I can."

"It's a strange way of asking her out on a date, that's for sure. Most women don't find stalking all that attractive, you know."

Gage was going to fire back a retort when he heard another car approaching from the north, this time a familiar rumble. Headlights swept over the junipers, then lanced across the highway. The topper was up. He caught a glimpse of the driver's silhouette, then the red glow of the taillights receded from view.

"Told you she'd show," Gage said, starting the Kia. "I'd know those distinctive Malibu taillights anywhere. Listen, Alex, hit the campgrounds, talk to some more neighbors, and tell Lacy I'll be back in Barnacle Bluffs this evening. Hopefully, he turns up on his own anyway. I really appreciate your help."

"I bill by the hour, you know," Alex said.

"I can afford all the donuts you can eat," Gage said and clicked off.

13

—————

Until sunrise, Gage didn't worry much about whether Jo saw him, figuring he'd just be a pair of generic headlights in her rearview mirror. As the sky in the east brightened, first with splashes of gray, then with crimson streaks over the Douglas firs that hugged Highway 101, he eased back and tried to keep two or three cars between them.

Traffic was blissfully light. She stopped only once, fueling up at an Exxon in Florence. When Gage passed the station, she was outside fueling the Malibu and fortunately had her back turned. Gage waited for her just after the Siuslaw Bridge. He didn't think she'd seen him, but he couldn't be sure.

Other than that, she drove straight there, past the many lakes south of Florence, whipping through rustic Reedsport and sleepy Winchester Bay, and over the majestic Conde B. McCullough Memorial Bridge into Coos Bay, the biggest city on the Oregon coast, the traffic picking up around touristy Bandon before easing up again shortly thereafter. The sun, in all its fiery orange beauty, sprang over the coastal range. The Kia drove easy, he had to give it that much, but to Gage it felt too easy; it was like trying to make conversation with one of those poor souls completely devoid of personality.

A quarter after seven, according to the bland-looking dashboard clock, Gage received a text. He'd gotten so accustomed to the company of the road noise and his own thoughts that the buzz made him jump. It was from Zoe:

Hey, welcome to the 21st century, bozo!! Srry didn't get back to you yet—cra-cra busy! Gotta be at work at 8, but let's chat soon, k?

There was even a smiley face emoji. Look at that. Here he was texting just like a regular person. Gage hated the whole idea of emojis, but even so, getting a yellow happy face from Zoe was strangely thrilling.

Mindful of her warning that she was off to work, Gage's first instinct was to just hit the thumbs-up emoji—that alone would probably make her fall out of her chair—but then he thought about what Eve had said. Was he just practicing more avoidance because he didn't want Zoe to think of Gage as a burden? Before he chickened out, he called her.

"Hey!" she said.

"Hey there, yourself. You got a few minutes before work?"

"Are you driving?" she asked. "I thought I heard a car."

"Yeah."

"You shouldn't be on the phone and driving. It's against the law in Oregon. You might get pulled over. Maybe you should call back when you get home?"

"That's going to be a while," Gage said. "I'll risk it."

"Well, at least put it on speaker phone. I don't have long, you know."

It took Gage a second, but he figured out the speaker button. Meanwhile, he heard nothing on her end except a strange hollow silence, like she was inside a phone booth. "There," he said, "did that work?"

"Yes. You don't need to shout, though."

"Great. I'll put it down on the seat here."

"Sure, but like I said, I only have a couple minutes."

"I know, I know. I just … I'm on a long drive south on 101, and … Well, I just thought it would be nice to chat for a few minutes. If you don't mind."

"Sure, okay."

Neither of them said anything. The pause might not have been more than a second, but the silence, as the highway hummed underneath him, felt interminable.

"So you got a phone," Zoe said.

"I did indeed," Gage said.

"A real phone. Not some crappy, pay-as-you-go thing. A real phone."

"That's right."

"Did you fall down and hit your head?"

"Ha ha, very funny." This was better. This was starting to feel more normal. "It's good to hear your voice, kiddo. Really."

"Hmm. I'm still not sure it's really you. Is this actually an elaborate phishing scheme? Are you really calling from some Eastern bloc nation, using a deep fake computer program to mimic my dad's voice? Prove that it's really you. What did I get you for Christmas last year?"

It took Gage a moment to hear her question because his mind paused when she said the word *Dad*. He liked it when she called him *Dad*. It had taken her quite a few years before she'd done it the first time, and now she said it all the time. Not that he'd asked her to. Zoe had come into his life at sixteen, a troubled teenager who'd already lost her parents to meth and then lost her grandmother to cancer on top of it, a saintly woman who'd asked Gage to adopt Zoe. Which he had—reluctantly, grudgingly, and not without plenty of misgivings. Now here he was feeling warm and fuzzy just because she'd called him Dad. Such a strange thing.

"Hello?" Zoe said. "Earth calling?"

"I'm here," he said. "You gave me a coffee mug. I think you bought it at Goodwill."

"I got it from eBay, and I paid top dollar for it, thank you very much. What kind of—" The rest was garbled.

"Zoe?"

"What's that?"

"I didn't hear what you said."

"Oh, your cell signal must be weak. I can hear it on my end too. How many bars do you have?"

"Bars?"

"The little lines in the upper right corner, Dad."

"Oh, right. Just one, I guess."

"There you go. Anyway, I was asking you what kind of mug it was?"

"Um … I forget."

"Liar. Nobody could forget this mug. Who are you? Are you calling from a bunker in Moldova?"

"It was a Smurf mug."

Zoe made a buzzer sound. "Close, but no cigar. It was actually a Gargamel mug. But I'll give you a final chance. What did I say to you when I gave you the mug?"

"Can I have a different question?"

"Five … four … three …"

"You said Gargamel was obviously my long-lost brother, which was why you wanted me to have it."

"Ha! So it is you! So, how *is* Garagmel's long-lost brother doing anyway? *Something* must be up, or you wouldn't have a phone, that's for sure."

"I got it because of a client."

"Ah."

It was a lie. Sure, the phone would come in handy with the search for Wade Carson, but he'd gotten it because Eve had badgered him about reaching out to Zoe. Why couldn't he just say that? Why was it so hard? He swallowed away the lump in his throat. A boxy motorhome rumbled past trailed by three cars in its wake eager to pass.

"Actually—"

"Well—" Zoe said at the same time. "Oh, sorry. Go ahead."

"No, no, it's fine. You first."

"Oh. Well, I was just going to say … You know, I'm glad you got it. For whatever reason. It's good to hear your voice."

"Yours too."

"Listen, I really do have to go—"

"How's that big research project you're working on?"

"Research project?"

"You know, with that professor."

"Oh. Professor Hane. Right. Actually, he actually came down with Covid, so everything's on hold. And I'm not sure his grant money was going to come through anyway. I thought I told you that?"

"No, I don't think so."

"Oh. Well, I actually got so busy with my second job at Senator Demming's office that I'm kind of glad that hasn't come together. I told you about that at least, right?"

"Sure, sure," Gage said, deciding to lie rather than admit that she hadn't. He knew Demming wasn't one of the two senators that Oregon sent to Washington, which meant it must have been a state senator. He vaguely remembered her talking about volunteering for a local politician. "Going to keep that job once fall classes gear back up?"

"Not sure. It's a big opportunity, actually becoming part of the paid staff. It pays better than the student job here in the psych office, which isn't saying much, but the student job is more stable. Really do want to help with the fall elections at least. I do see a future career in politics. I just don't know when."

"I know."

"So what's this case you're working on? *Reader's Digest* condensed version, I mean?"

Before he could answer, he heard someone say something in the background. A man.

"Who's that?" he asked.

There was a moment's hesitation. "Oh, that's Steve."

"Oh. A friend of yours?"

"Mmm hmm. So what about this case?"

The last time they'd talked, Zoe had said she was swearing off men until she was out of graduate school, so he found her about-face on this issue even more surprising than the news about her job situation. That warm feeling he'd gotten from her emoji seemed like a long time ago.

"Well," he said, "it's a missing person case. A young man from San Diego."

She didn't answer.

"Zoe?" he said.

"Yeah, still here. You're breaking up on my end."

"Oh. I said it's a missing person case—a guy from San Diego."

"Ah," Zoe said, "and that's where you're going? To California?"

"No, I'm … I'm actually, well, it's complicated. I can tell you more later."

"Okay, sure."

Silence again. He'd called to close the gap between them, and if anything, it seemed to be widening.

"I should go," she said. "I really got to get ready for work—Demming's office. I like her, but she doesn't tolerate tardiness. Kind of anal about it, actually."

The window was rapidly closing. "I understand," Gage said. "Talk again soon?"

A Safeway truck roared past. Whatever Zoe said was

drowned out by the roar of wind and the rattle of axles, so he asked her to repeat it. She didn't answer. When he glanced at the phone, he saw that she'd already clicked off.

———

SHORTLY THEREAFTER, Gage lost sight of Jo. He didn't see her in tiny Port Orford or as he descended into Gold Beach. He decided not to stop at either, pressing onward, and was relieved when he rounded the final, fir-lined bend in the Samuel H. Boardman Scenic Corridor and spotted her white Malibu parked along the shoulder exactly where he expected it to be.

At the trailhead to Secret Beach.

Hers was the only car in the dirt turnout. Not a huge surprise at half past 8:00 a.m. with fog so thick the ocean would be invisible. He drove past, keeping his head low, but he didn't see her. He parked at the Natural Bridges viewpoint just up ahead, a five-minute walk back to the trailhead to Secret Beach. A few cars were parked there, including a bulky Suburban he used to shield the Kia from view, just in case Jo was still lingering nearby. A man in an Oakland A's baseball cap was helping an older woman down the concrete path, where the viewpoint itself was hidden by fir trees and fog as thick as soup.

When he opened the door, the air dampened his face. He slipped on his black vinyl jacket and his backpack, then grabbed the walking sticks out of the back. They'd been a gift from Rita, the woman he once thought he was going to marry. He'd even proposed. And what had that whole ordeal gotten him? Better to hate the woman he was attracted to, perhaps. The hate could keep him warm, and nobody had to get hurt.

He had a canteen, a few power bars, a wool hat, and

some leather gloves. He didn't have much else, but the back-pack still felt heavy because of the Beretta. Guns made everything heavy. As he made his way north along the shoulder, a few lonely cars whipped past. The tops of the fir trees disappeared into white mist. The sky was nearly the same muted gray as the highway, the asphalt slick and gleaming under the fog.

Jo's Malibu was empty. Once onto the root-strewn trail shadowed by spruces, firs, and oaks, Gage felt the temperature drop another ten degrees. He put on his hat and gloves, but he'd barely made it past the second switchback and, sweaty and breathing hard, he was already taking them off. Ten minutes later and he was stuffing his jacket into his backpack too.

Inside the forest, the morning light was weak and gray. The trail descended at an alarming rate, sword ferns whipping at his legs and leaving watermarks on his jeans. Every exposed root, and there were hundreds, threatened to trip him. For a while, he could hear the occasional passing car on the highway, but soon this was gone and he was left with the droplets splattering on the ferns and his own ragged breathing.

He approached each bend with caution, but he didn't see Jo. Or anyone.

It grew darker, as if dusk had come rather than the dawn. It smelled of fir and damp earth. He stopped once to rest and gulp cold water from his canteen. Every now and then, a gust that smelled of the sea whipped up the path. It didn't take long, maybe half an hour, before he reached the bottom. First he began to hear the surf, whispering through the trees. A few minutes after that, he came around the last bend onto a rocky outcropping.

The view was remarkable and yet somehow alien, made even more so by the wall of fog that sealed off the cove from the rest of the ocean. Rocks as big as ten-story buildings loomed in the water, some topped with firs and bushes, others bare. The breeze rippled his sweat-drenched shirt, providing welcome relief even as the moisture collected on his eyelids with each blink.

The beach was empty. There were many footprints below, but none in the smoother, darker sand near the surf. He knew from what he'd read online that there was another beach beyond the glistening black rocks on the southern end, accessible without wading through the water only at low tide. It apparently wasn't low enough now. Someone would have to wade through the crashing waves to reach it. Was Jo over there?

Getting off the rock proved tricky, but he managed, scooting down the last bit on the seat of his jeans. Two seagulls pecked at the glistening pebbles and broken shells gathered along the surf's edge. A turkey vulture circled overhead. Near the cliff face, there were a few alcoves. He trudged closer to make sure she wasn't inside. She wasn't.

The rocks were slick with algae and smelled of fish. He caught the scent of something rotten a moment before he came upon a seal carcass, buried in the sand except for part of its head, one empty eye socket turned in Gage's direction.

"Have you seen Jo?" Gage asked.

As if in answer, there was a crackle from high above, on the trail where he'd just been.

It set his heart pounding. He looked up and saw Jo's scowling face emerge from the tall grass and ferns. She was gazing at the ocean, not down at him, her blonde bangs stuck to her forehead like wet tissue. He saw gray hiking pants. He saw a blue windbreaker, shiny with moisture. He saw black shoulder straps and a glimpse of a bulging backpack.

Before she could notice him, he ducked into the alcove. It

was deep and wide enough that he could hide from her if he wanted, which he did when she clambered down the rock, much faster than he'd accomplished the same feat. When she trudged in front of him, he saw the unmistakable box-like bulge at the rear of her backpack, about the size of a man's shoebox, maybe a bit bigger.

He held his breath, waiting for her to look his way, but she didn't. She walked with grim purpose, passing out of sight. He waited a minute, then two, unsure of himself, debating what to do next. He hadn't planned that far ahead. Finally he dared to lean out, and she was gone.

The next beach? It was either that or she'd been swallowed by the ocean.

With a growing dread, he made for the rock, picking up his pace, holding his walking sticks rather than using them. He splashed into the shallow surf, his jeans soaked to the knees, a salty spray wetting his lips. The water was ice cold. A wave, low but powerful, pressed against the rock as he struggled past it.

He saw Jo at once, alone on the smaller beach.

She didn't see him. She knelt on the sand, facing the ocean. Kneeling in prayer. Kneeling in surrender. Gage knew that pose well, and his throat seized up at the sight of it. What private anguish possessed her? Her bag rested nearby, as did a rusty steel box caked with mud and sand, its lid swiveled open, several large plastic zip bags next to it. A bunch of other things were strewn around her, most too small to determine from a distance, but one caught his eye.

It was bulky and dull black with a beveled grip. He recognized it for what it was just as she reached for it.

A gun.

14

The wind whipped around the outcropping where Gage, calf-deep in the cold surf, leaned against the rock for support. The salty mist stung his eyes, made it difficult to see, but Jo was definitely reaching for the gun.

It was happening too fast, the smaller, more compact beach, with its freighter-sized rocks in the shallows, towering cliff faces surrounding them like the walls of a coliseum, and even the oppressive gray fog, amplifying the ocean's roar, cranking it up until he could barely hear his own thoughts. It was like watching a silent film on fast-forward accompanied by an obnoxious orchestra where every musician was belting out a different tune.

There was only one reason, as far as he could tell, that a person kneeling before the ocean would reach for a gun.

"Hey!"

Gage put all his energy into the shout, hoping that somehow his voice would rise above the cacophony and snap her out of her reverie. It worked—too well, in fact. She didn't stop reaching for the handgun, instead snapping it up and whirling in his direction.

He blinked his eyes clear and watched the panoply of reactions play out on her face, clear enough even a hundred feet away: first shock, then disbelief, then hot, blazing rage. He returned this with a smile and a feeble lift of his walking sticks in a sort of wave, hoping to get a smile in return. She didn't even lower the gun.

Her face and hands were the whitest things on the beach; everything else was gray and muted in comparison. Was she going to shoot him? His Beretta was only inches away, but tucked into his backpack it might as well have been back in Barnacle Bluffs. He couldn't even let go of the walking sticks without fearing he'd fall into the water.

And what would he do with his gun anyway? Challenge her to a duel?

Fortunately, he never had to really grapple with this question because she *did* lower her gun—a little, at least, the barrel pointed more at the sand than at him. Her outraged expression didn't change, her eyes so wide, and her pupils so dark, that he could feel the heat of her anger even from here. With the way her legs were partially hidden beneath her, her crinkled black windbreaker glistening in the heavy morning air like fish scales, she made him think of a grieving mermaid who'd emerged from the depths in search of vengeance.

He splashed around the rock, toes already numb and aching, and sloshed across the sand toward her. His tennis shoes squished with each step. His soaked pant legs felt like lead. He must have cut a ridiculous figure. Garrison Gage, always the picture of the dashing hero.

She still didn't put down the gun. It was a Beretta 92FS, a similar model to the one he owned. They used to be common in police departments until the Glock rose in popularity. He'd never seen her with it before.

"I heard this is a nice beach," he said. "I thought I'd see for myself."

She still hadn't gotten up. Out of the surf and away from the amplifying effects of the rocks, the ocean did not seem so loud, so he didn't doubt that she'd heard him.

Her face gleamed like wet chrome. Her blonde hair looked like it had been painted on her scalp. He could see that there were lots of other things spread in a semicircle around her—a worn leather wallet, a phone in a green case, a buffalo belt buckle, a Swiss army knife, a faded and badly foxed photo in a silver frame, and lots of little things he couldn't identify at first glance, everything dusted with sand. While he could see that the aluminum box was empty except for the plastic bags, her backpack, behind her, was still quite bulky. He wondered what else might be stowed inside.

The way the light reflected off the glass-covered photo, he had to shift to the left before he could see that it pictured a man in an army uniform.

"What are you doing here, Jo?" he asked.

Until this point, her gaze had been unrelenting but unchanging, a single frame out of her silent movie, but now she blinked. "I don't believe this," she said.

"What do you plan to do with that gun?"

"What is *wrong* with you? You actually followed me?"

"Just tell me what you're doing with that gun."

She gazed at the ocean, or what little was visible with the fog. When she answered, her voice warbled with barely contained anguish. "Please just go. This has nothing to do with you. Or Wade Carson. You're just making this more difficult. You're just ..." She looked at him sharply, then down at the Beretta, still gripped in her bone-white fingers. "Wait a second. You think ... You actually think ..."

"I don't know what to think."

She dropped the gun as if it were scalding hot. "I wouldn't do that! I'd *never* do that."

"Then what *are* you doing?"

"Go! Leave!"

"You dug up that box, didn't you? You had it buried up there somewhere, and you dug it up?"

"It's none of your business!"

"I'll take that as a yes. What else was inside?"

"What?"

"Drug money maybe? Do you have wads of cash stowed in your backpack? Is that how you paid for that house of yours? What did you get yourself mixed up in, Jo?"

"Are you fucking serious?"

"Just tell me what's really going on. I can't help you if you don't talk to me."

She buried her face in her hands. "Oh my God. This nightmare just keeps getting worse."

"What nightmare, Jo? What's going on? Talk to me."

She moaned softly and rocked back and forth. He was taken aback by how different she appeared. The crumpled, waifish creature on the sand before him was like an entirely different species than the self-assured police chief he'd come to know. This was no vengeful mermaid. A strong wave could wash her away.

The pause gave him time to survey the other things strewn about her. He saw a gold watch, a Mariner's baseball cap, and a dog-eared John D. MacDonald paperback, *The Dreadful Lemon Sky*. He saw fishing lures, a walnut pipe, and one mud-caked men's hiking boot. A Han Solo action figure. A fishing lure. A baseball card with foxed edges. It was only then that Gage finally realized what all this was, what would have been obvious if he hadn't been so fixated on the gun.

It was a shrine.

The sand, stirred by the breeze, swirled around her jacket

in gentle eddies. Two seagulls, swooping behind the towering rocks, were the only other parishioners in this particular cathedral by the sea. Against all reason, all his anger and suspicion drained out of him, and he felt something for Jo Roland he had never felt before.

Compassion.

Gage knew what it was like to be unable to let go. He knew what it was like to carry a guilt that had cut so deeply it would never heal. He did not know if Jo's situation was similar, but he could see that there was regret, whatever had happened, and he could see that there was remorse, whether she was truly to blame or not, and he felt compassion for her that overrode all other concerns. He knew what it was like to be in pain. There was something else too, a feeling he could not yet name, brushing against his heart like the feathers of a bird swooping past him in the dark.

"I want to help you," he said.

She snorted, then spoke through her fingers. "I'd settle for you just leaving me alone."

"I won't do that."

"Gage—"

"I can't help you if you don't tell me what's going on."

With a low growl, she leaped to her feet. She stood so close he could see the sand freckling her nose, the icy blue shards in her eyes, and the wet gloss on her eyebrows. She had sand in her hair. She had sand on her forehead. She had sand even on her lips.

"Why should I?" she said. It came off as a yell, but in reality it was barely a whisper, and as she leaned in even closer, he felt the warmth of her breath on his chin. "You think I'm a criminal. That's what you just said."

"No," he said.

"No *what?* No, you don't think that? Why did you really come down here then?"

"I don't know."

"It's not just about Wade Carson. Don't even tell me that! Tell me the real reason you're here."

"I—I don't—"

"I'm not a bad person," she insisted.

"I never said you were."

She was crying now. He'd never seen her cry. The tear tracks gleamed in the thick air like hairline fractures in a vase, like the porcelain, painted to make look like metal but not nearly so strong, buckling under the strain of what was contained within. "I did—I did something terrible," she said.

"It wasn't your fault," Gage said.

"Yes, it was. You don't know. You don't know anything."

"Then tell me."

"Why? Why should I?"

"Whatever it is, I won't turn you in. I promise." And he knew, when he said it, that it was true. It was inexplicable, but it was true. He would not betray her trust, regardless of the consequences. "Please, Jo. Just trust me."

"But why, Garrison? Why on Earth should I trust *you?*"

Then Gage, in a halting fashion, said something that surprised both of them: "Because … I'm pretty sure … I'm falling in love with you."

"What?"

She stared. There it was, the brush of wing feathers in the dark, the feeling he had been unable to name. That didn't make the words any less true. Gage knew they were true even if he didn't want them to be, and he really didn't know what he wanted, not anymore. He just knew he'd finally said what needed to be said, what had to be said, and so he said it again. With more conviction this time.

"I'm falling in love with you."

She shook her head.

"I think you feel the same," he said.

"No, I don't. How could I …? No. I *hate* you."

Gage laughed. He was terrified, but no matter what happened going forward, at least he wasn't living in denial. That was something. "I don't think love and hate are mutually exclusive," he said.

"You think this is a joke?"

"I don't know what it is, but it's happening."

"It's not. It's not happening."

"Then why are you leaning forward?"

"What?"

"You're still leaning forward," Gage said. "If you hate me so much, why don't you walk away?"

"Don't tell me what to do."

"Just admit it, Jo. Admit you have feelings for me."

"If you're not going to leave," she said, "then I will. I'm leaving right now."

"Okay," he said.

"Right now."

"Fine."

"I hate you."

"I know."

Then she kissed him. He felt and tasted the sand, a touch of coarseness on lips that were surprisingly soft for a woman with so many hard angles. She pressed her body against his, not at all like the live grenade he'd come to know but desperate and yielding, filled with a particular brand of fragile tenderness borne from the deepest loss. Gage knew the feeling well. Her cheeks were still wet with her tears, and he felt the moisture against his nose. It was a kiss of sand and sorrow, and when it ended, when they stood with their breaths warm on each other's faces and the roar of the ocean joining the thumping of their hearts, neither of them said a word.

Then his cell phone rang.

The phone was in his backpack, still slung over his shoulder. He could barely hear the ring over the waves, but the sound was so jarring that it made both of them jump. In that moment, his hatred for cell phones was apoplectic, but he couldn't very well ignore it given the few people who had the number and the even fewer reasons they might call.

While Gage ripped off his bag, yanked out the phone, and finally answered the damn thing, Jo took a step back.

"Garrison?"

It was Alex. There was something wrong. Gage could hear it in his friend's voice right away.

"Yeah, it's me," Gage said. "What is it? What's happened?"

"It's Lacy Carson," Alex said. "She's missing."

15

———

The words *she's missing* seeped into Gage's mind as surely as the ocean water had seeped into his shoes, with a cold shock that brought him fully into the present. Jo, watching him, wiped the tears from her face and backed up a step, like a person moving away from a precipice. He heard voices and laughter from the other beach, another reminder, as if he needed one, that the wider world had not stood pat while he and Jo had shared their private moment.

"What do you mean, she's missing?" Gage said.

"It means what you think it means," Alex said. "I can't find her anywhere."

"Does she have her car?"

"No, not yet. It's still parked at the station. That's the first thing I did, was call down there and—"

"Maybe she went for a walk."

"Garrison, come on. I wouldn't call you if I thought there was an innocent explanation."

"I know, but—"

"I texted her a little after eight this morning, to let her know you were gone and that I would be helping her in the meantime, but she didn't write back. I figured she was exhausted. But when I didn't hear anything by nine, I knocked on her door. She didn't answer."

Jo mouthed the word *Lacy?* and Gage nodded. She dropped onto her haunches and started to gather up her things. He put the phone on speaker so she could hear. The phone's clock showed that it was half past nine.

"And so you went in?" Gage asked Alex. "I'm here with Jo, by the way. She's listening."

"Okay. Good. That's right. All of her things were there, but her bed hadn't been slept in."

"Well, she could still be—"

"There's something else, Garrison. Somebody found Lacy's phone on the beach a few minutes ago."

"What?"

"I texted and called again. I kept calling. I was about to give up and call you when somebody answered it. It was a guy going for a run on the beach, and he heard it ringing. It's just below the Turret House, a little to the north. It was just laying in the sand."

The aching cold in Gage's toes spread to the rest of his body. "Is Wade's truck still parked on 32nd?"

"Yes. That's the first thing I thought of too. Traffic is already horrible this morning, so it would take a while for me to get over there in person, but I called the desk at the Starfish Motel and asked if they could poke their heads outside and see if it's still there for me. It is."

"Do you have her phone back yet?"

"Not yet, but the guy's being kind enough to jog up here and give it to me. Should be here any second."

"Okay, see if you can get into her phone when he does. I want to know if anybody else contacted her."

"Got it. The phone might be locked, though. Do you think someone …"

"I don't know what to think yet. But since her room wasn't disturbed, it leads me to believe she went out again willingly. She might have gone back to search, or she might have been meeting someone. If she was meeting someone so late on the beach, it would have to be someone she trusted."

"Wade?"

Gage was going to answer, but Jo, wearing her over-stuffed backpack and standing in front of him, held up her right hand. With her left, she now held her own cell phone. The shock of pink around her eyes was the only sign of the broken woman from a moment ago, and when she spoke, it was again with the cool detachment of the consummate professional.

"Call it in, Alex," she said. "Tell the dispatcher you think she's been abducted. When the jogger shows up, ask him to wait until my officers get on the scene, and then have him take you all down and show you where the phone was found. I'll get one of my detectives down there too. We'll see if we can find any clues. I'm heading back now."

She started to walk past Gage, not looking him in the eyes. He covered the mouthpiece.

"Please wait," he said. "We can walk up together."

"I'd rather not," she said. "This never happened, Garrison."

"Jo."

But she kept going—head bent low, walking stiffly, heading for the other beach.

———

By the time Gage finally gasped and winced his way back to Highway 101, Jo's Mustang was gone. So was most of the fog; only thin tendrils clung to the tops of the Douglas firs. The sunlight lanced through the treetops like golden spears.

With the sweat cooling on his body, Gage tossed the backpack and walking sticks into the back of the Kia, then slumped into the driver's seat. He should have felt lighter, but he was weighed down with all the guilt he was carrying.

He was fishing out the cell phone when Alex called. It was a quarter after ten, according to the cell phone.

"I've been trying to reach you," he said.

"Reception is crappy in the forest," Gage said. "I take it Lacy hasn't shown up yet?"

"No, but the cops were here. And Detective Trenton. Not much they can do at this point but file a missing person report. We did go down to the beach, but we didn't find anything where her phone was found. No signs of a struggle —not that it would be all that obvious on the sand."

"Did you get into her phone?"

"No, it's locked. Facial recognition. It does have a pattern override."

"Pattern override?"

"Yeah, you know, nine dots on the screen and you connect them in a particular way with your fingers."

"But the cops didn't think it would be useful to take her phone? Maybe find a tech in Newport or somewhere else that could get into it?"

"They said at this point they couldn't without a warrant. I've tried lots of patterns, but nothing seems to work. I'm afraid to keep going or I might lock it permanently."

Gage thought about this. "Try a W. The shape, I mean."

"A W? Oh right, for Wade. Okay." There was a pause. "Yep, that worked. Good thinking."

"Check the calls and texts," Gage said.

"Hold on, hold on. I can only go so fast. Um, the last calls were from me and you. There is a text, though. Oh no."

"What?"

"It's not good."

"Just read it to me, damn it."

Alex cleared his throat. "It's from Wade. It says, 'I'm sorry I ran. Meet me at the truck. Don't tell anyone. I want to see you one last time but I won't show if I see anyone else. I'm turning off my phone again so just come.' It looks like it came in around 2:00 a.m."

"That was about a half hour after I dropped her off at the Turret House. Did she answer?"

"Yeah, she wrote, 'I'm walking there now on the beach. I love you. Please, please don't do anything until we talk.' About one minute after Wade's came in."

"And nothing else?"

"Nope. I'll check her email and other things on her phone to see if we can learn anything."

"Good idea," Gage said. "And since my cell reception is spotty, could you relay that information to the police?"

"Of course. Maybe that 'one last time' will get them to put more resources into finding him. Maybe they can even track his cell phone signal, at least find out where he was when he texted her."

"I hope so, but that will take time even if they—Oh! That reminds me. Lacy told me they could check each other's locations. Can you see if he turned that back on? Do you know how to do that?"

"Oh, sure," Alex said, "Eve and I do that as well. It's on the maps tool. Hold on … Hmm. No, it looks like the last time he showed up in Barnacle Bluffs was Thursday morning at Golden Eagle Casino. Was that the last time he had Google tracking turned on?"

"Yeah. It was worth a shot, though."

Alex was silent a moment. "What is going on with Jo anyway?"

"Nothing."

"Your voice doesn't make it sound like nothing."

"It doesn't have anything to do with Wade or Lacy, okay? At least I don't think so, and I'll explain more later. Will you just call the police and give them an update about the phone?"

"Of course. Anything else I can do?"

"Just keep looking for them," Gage said. "If you find anything else on the phone that might help, call or text me. With luck, I'll be back in town by three."

———

Luck apparently wasn't on Gage's side, because he wasn't back in town by three. He wasn't even back in town by six. The refugees pouring in from the heat-scorched Willamette Valley had not only overwhelmed Barnacle Bluffs but apparently the rest of the Oregon coast too, made even worse because it was a Friday. If that wasn't bad enough, all those drivers must have been half-crazed from heatstroke because his progress was slowed to a near standstill on three separate occasions from serious traffic accidents.

It was approaching sunset by the time Gage reached the outskirts of Barnacle Bluffs, where traffic wasn't just at a near standstill. It was at an *actual* standstill. For the safety of the other motorists more than anything else—it was not exactly a good thing that Gage had his Beretta close at hand—Gage parked on the side of the highway and, using his walking sticks, trudged on foot the rest of the way into town.

He didn't pass Jo's Malibu. He didn't see Wade or Lacy. A half hour later, he reached the Turret House, where he'd left his Volkswagen, and found Alex and Eve sitting glum-faced at their kitchen table sipping lemon tea. In the paned window over their sink, the sky showed the first blush of sunset.

"Where's my van?" Alex said.

"Parked alongside the highway. I'll get it later. Anything new on Lacy or Wade?"

"You abandoned my van?"

"I told you, I'll take care of it. No word from Lacy?"

"I can't believe you abandoned my van."

"Alex, focus."

His friend shook his head, then removed his glasses and rubbed the bridge of his nose. "Didn't you hear my voicemail? I told you the police can't do anything with the phone until we have probable cause there's been foul play. And I found nothing helpful on her phone."

"I heard it," Gage said. "I was just hoping something had changed in the last hour."

"No. I spent all day fighting through traffic, looking for them both, but I haven't found them. I just got back a few minutes ago." Alex, who'd set his glasses on the table, started to put them on but then stopped. "I really am sorry."

"It's not your fault," Gage said. "We had no reason to think you should watch her so closely."

"Well, then it's not your fault either."

Gage didn't answer this. Eve set a mug on the table, one already steaming and with a tea tag hanging off the side. Gage hadn't even seen her get up. Her hospitality was like that, some sort of magic. He had no interest in drinking tea or even sitting, but he found himself doing both in short order, his backpack and walking sticks deftly taken from him and placed in the corner. The strong lemon scent wafting up through the steam had a calming effect, taking the edge off his anger if not his regret.

"I shouldn't have left," he said. "It was stupid, taking off the way I did."

"We should focus on what we can do now," Eve said. "Unless you want to talk about what happened with Jo?"

"I don't. I've got to focus on finding Lacy. That's the only thing that matters. Can I see her room?"

"Of course," Eve said.

Mugs in hand, the three of them spent twenty minutes searching her room for any other clues of where she might be, but they didn't find anything. The brass frame bed was still made. Her suitcase, a pea-green hardshell one, was still there. When they opened it, they found her toiletry bag and her clothes tightly packed inside. Gage doubted she'd opened the suitcase since leaving San Diego.

It was hard to believe a day had passed since he'd met her. One day. That was all it took for him to fail her completely. They found no purse or keys. While Gage looked through her suitcase, finding nothing that might aid them, Alex fetched her phone. Sitting next to each other on the bed, they spent a few minutes going through her messages, her emails, and her recent call history, but Alex was right: There wasn't anything that could help them or that would get the police more involved.

After Wade took off on Wednesday, she'd sent him dozens of text messages pleading with him to call her that went unanswered—until the one last night.

"I'm going to walk down to the beach," Gage said.

"In the dark?" Eve said. "It will be hard to see anything."

"We'll come with you," Alex said.

"No, it's better that you stay here in case she comes back. I'm going to walk all the way home. No sense trying to drive my van now. I'll check the beach, his truck, and maybe the neighborhood around 32nd just to see what I find."

They were disappointed, but they agreed. Gage headed outside, finding that the air had cooled as darkness had settled. A light breeze ruffled the patchy grass on the hills of sand and dirt around the house, and the unobstructed moon painted everything with a milky white glow. He felt a bit ridiculous with his walking sticks, like someone trying to cross-country ski without snow, but every joint in his body, not just his right knee, throbbed with intense pain, so the walking sticks weren't really optional at this point.

After a few fruitless minutes searching around the Turret House with his cell phone flashlight, he took the stairs to the beach. Except for the driftwood, he was alone. He saw a distant campfire far to the south. They'd been banned because of the high fire danger, but there were always people who thought the rules didn't apply to them. He started north. Now and then, he thought he saw a body lying in the sand, but the flashlight always proved it to be a peculiar-shaped log.

There was a briny scent on the breeze. Farther out, the water was like black velvet, and the surf, where it was visible in the moonlight, was like braided white rope. The breeze may have been cool, but his face was warm, and his wind-breaker and his jeans felt glued to his body with sweat. Everything hurt. He felt old. Old, broken down, and all-around decrepit. How had he let that happen? This was no way to be a private investigator. This was no way to live either.

He didn't find anything of interest on the beach. At the stairs up to 32nd street, the Starfish Motel's windows were lit up like the candles on a birthday cake. He heard a man and a woman laughing on one of the balconies. He caught a whiff of popcorn. Everybody was having a good time. Except Wade and Lacy Carson, of course. Where on Earth had they gone?

As he reached the street, Gage was in for another surprise. A flatbed tow truck, its exhaust pluming in the red glow of its taillights, was backed up to Wade's Ford Ranger. The tow truck's bed was tilted at an angle. He heard the clank of chains over the rumbling engine, and the truck driver, a burly guy in denim overalls that barely contained his belly, rose up from behind the Ranger's bumper. He was looking down, his attention focused on his work.

"Who ordered this?" Gage asked.

The driver jerked back in surprise. "This yours, man?"

"Was it the police department?"

"Look, man, I'm just doing my job. If you have a beef with this, take it up with the lady over there."

"Lady?"

The guy tilted his head toward a black Lexus SUV idling at the back of the Starfish Motel parking lot, headlights off, parking lights aglow. Gage had barely looked in that direction and an Asian man in a white cotton turtleneck hopped out of the driver side and opened the back door. The first thing Gage saw was a pair of slender legs in dark tights, then two stiletto heels clicked onto the asphalt.

In the gauzy glow from the overhead streetlamp, a tall, slender woman emerged from the SUV, her form-fitting gray overcoat only extending to her knees, showing off her legs to great effect. She strutted toward him like a model on a catwalk, heels clicking one in front of the other, her dark cloud of hair staying firmly in place despite the breeze.

The man in the turtleneck made as if to follow her, but she gestured for him to stay in place—which he did but somewhat reluctantly, judging by the way he crossed his arms and glared. He was short and slight of build, but he'd made sure to wear a turtleneck so tight it showed off his well-chiseled physique. He may have been small, but he wanted to make sure people knew he went to the gym.

Then the woman was standing before him, collar upturned, the tow truck's tail lights bathing her porcelain skin in a red glow even as she was mostly lost in hazy darkness. Her eyes were completely shadowed. Despite her regal demeanor, Gage was struck with the feeling that he was peering into a long-abandoned mansion.

"Mr. Gage, I assume?" she said.

The voice was rougher than he'd expected, imbued with the authoritative tone of a woman used to getting her way.

"Yes?" Gage said.

When the woman took a step closer, Gage saw that the porcelain skin was something of an illusion, layers of makeup striving to hide tiny fissures around her eyes and mouth. Her cheekbones were as sharp as switchblades.

"I'm Ellen Carson," she said. "I'm here to find my son, and I'm not leaving until I do."

16

She was a beautiful woman, to be sure. There was a timeless quality to her beauty, in that same way that Jackie Onassis, John F. Kennedy's strikingly beautiful wife, possessed—both stately and swan-like, chin held *just so,* as if she had an invisible crown perched in that frozen cloud of hair. But the longer Gage looked at the woman standing before him, lit up by the harsh, reddish hue of the tow truck's brake lights and the more distant, gauzy glow of the street-lamp, the more apparent it became that Ellen Carson had crossed the threshold from luminous to ludicrous a long time ago.

All those layers of makeup may have hidden most of her wrinkles, but they also gave her skin an inhuman sheen, shiny and chrome-like, as if she wore a flesh-colored suit of armor. Brittle but ready for battle. That was what Gage thought in those first few seconds, standing there in the dark next to the rumbling tow truck and breathing in air thick with diesel exhaust and mixed with a floral scent only slightly less strong. She must have put on her perfume by the bottle.

Then he remembered the tragedy that she had endured

only a week ago, and he immediately regretted judging her so harshly.

"I'm sorry about your husband," he said.

There was a moment when Gage thought all those tiny fissures around Ellen's eyes were going to rupture, offering a glimpse of the real woman underneath all that makeup, but then the tow truck's gas-powered winch clanked and groaned and roared, making her jump. A hand fluttered to her chest, an enormous diamond ring glittering blood red in the tow truck's taillights, and when she lowered her hand and fixed her gaze on him again, she was safely back in her suit of armor.

"Yes, thank you," she said. "It was a terribly unfortunate thing, my husband's untimely passing, but the family is bearing up as best we can."

At this, Gage wondered if it was the suicide, more than the death, that most troubled her. *My husband's untimely passing.* What an odd way to put it. "It was indeed a terrible thing," he said. "Can I ask why you're having the truck towed?"

"It seemed the reasonable thing to do," she said. "I'm staying at the Inn at Sapphire Head, and they said I could park it in the east lot until I checked out. I didn't want it to get towed."

"Chief Roland assured us it wouldn't."

"Yes, well, I learned long ago that it's never a good idea to put your faith in government if there's something one can do."

"But don't you think Wade might come back for it? That's why we left it here."

She brushed a finger over her right ear, as if tucking away a strand of hair, but there was no strand to tuck. Gage was mystified how that dark cloud of hair, a lustrous bluish black, remained so fixed in place. Evidently she didn't just put her perfume on by the bottle; she did the same with hairspray. "Mr. Gage," she said, "do you take me for an idiot?"

"Excuse me?"

"Do I strike you as a dumb woman?"

"Ma'am, I think you've got the wrong—"

"If I was a dumb woman, would I have driven up in that Lexus? Would I have my own driver and bodyguard? Would I be dressed like this?"

Gage was taken aback by the tense turn the conversation had taken. Her tone hadn't changed. She still managed to speak with cool detachment, as if making small talk with other high society types at the opera, but there was something in her eyes, those big dark eyes, that pulsed with barely contained rage. This was not the woman Gage had imagined when Lacy Carson described her. He'd imagined a rummy-eyed drunk, heavy and saggy in the way that rich drunks get when they have too much money, too much time, and not enough places to put either. He hadn't expected such a formidable presence, and it made him wonder who the real center of power had been in her marriage.

"Mrs. Carson," Gage said, "our thinking was that if Wade came to his senses and wanted to go home, that we would make it easy for him. That was the only reason. I didn't mean to offend you."

She sighed. "I assure you, Mr. Gage, it would take a lot more than a two-bit private investigator in a squalid, half-rate town at the ends of the Earth to offend *me*."

"Ouch."

"I'm sorry, I didn't mean to offend you."

"Oh, I think you clearly did. But you're also clearly hurting, so it's understandable."

"I don't need your pity."

"Good," Gage said, "because I wasn't offering any. I was just saying I understand where your behavior is coming from.

Besides, I assure you it would take a lot more than a pretentious and entitled former beauty queen with more money than sense to offend *me* ... Mrs. Carson."

There was a moment when Gage thought the porcelain veneer might shatter, but then she smiled. "I like you, Mr. Gage," she said.

"Well, that's not what I expected you to say."

"Good. In my opinion, there's hardly a worse character trait than predictability. And whatever would give you the idea that I am a former beauty queen?"

"Well, are you?"

"I'm not going to answer that because it would contradict what I said about predictability."

Despite the tension in his jaw and the warmth in his face, Gage had to laugh. He wasn't quite ready to say he liked Ellen Carson, but he did like her sense of humor. He was about to say this, as a way to maybe reset things, but then the truck driver threw a switch and the wench system screeched and groaned even louder than before, dragging the Ford Ranger up the ramp. She winced and walked past Gage, gesturing for him to follow, and they reconvened at the barricade. The ocean breeze flitted up the path, clearing the smell of diesel if not the overpowering scent of her perfume. Gage saw no one down on the beach. Ellen saw him looking and shook her head.

"I did wait here for an hour before calling the tow truck," she said.

"I really wish you'd tell him to stop," Gage said.

"And leave Wade's truck here for any drugged up homeless lowlife to inhabit? I think not. I never approved of Wade keeping this ... monstrosity, but he wouldn't listen to reason, you see, even when I offered to buy him a brand-new one. I actually detest trucks, they're so low class, but he was determined to have this one no matter what I said. And if it's important to him, well, then it's important to his mother too."

Watching the Ford Ranger inch up the bed, Gage realized that all the wheels were turning without resistance. "The truck driver must have put the Ranger in neutral."

"What's that?"

"You must have had a key. For him to do that. Did Wade give you one?"

"Ah. Well, yes. I had one made. Just in case."

"In case of what?"

"Oh, you know. If a need should arise. And here we are, you see. So obviously my precaution was necessary."

"You mean to say you had it made without his knowledge?"

Ellen dismissed this with a playful slap at the air. "Oh, I wouldn't put it quite so dramatically. Heavens, that makes me sound like a common thief. This is my son we're talking about here. Isn't a mother allowed to be worried about her son?"

"Was there a reason you should be worried?"

"He asked me to stop badgering him about his truck. He said he bought it with his own money and he was proud of it and that nothing I said could make him get rid of it. So when he was visiting for Christmas a few years back, I had one made. Yes, I didn't tell him, but having the key in my possession allowed me to both respect his wishes and to sleep a bit easier. What if, I don't know, he was trapped inside after an accident and I was unable to get him out? I'd never be able to live with myself."

"And if he comes back tonight and the truck isn't here, what is he supposed to do?"

"Well, then he'll call me, of course. What else *could* he do?"

"Ah. Now I'm beginning to understand."

"Oh? How so?"

Gage knew she might take offense to what he was about to say, but he thought it worth saying anyway. "You're cutting away his options, trying to force him to come to you instead of … well, somebody else. Or leave town on his own. It's just another way of controlling him, which I imagine you've been doing since he was born."

She regarded him silently, like the bust of some sculptor's vision of the ideal woman. The intensity of her stare unnerved him. Then she turned her attention back to the truck driver, who was out of the cab and fastening locks to the Ranger's wheels.

"I'd like to hire you," she said.

Gage thought she might be joking, so he laughed, but Ellen Carson didn't smile. She didn't even so much as glance at him, acting as if it was already a settled matter, which irritated him.

"Lacy Carson has done that already," he said.

"Yes, but Lacy Carson is missing, isn't she? That's what I learned, when I checked in with Chief Roland when I got to town. I'm not surprised, you know. I always knew she'd abandon my son when he needed her most. She's probably on her way back to San Diego."

"Without her car?"

"Who knows. She's probably hitchhiking back, trading sexual favors for gas money."

"You can't be serious."

"You just watch, she'll turn up, I assure you. We should be focusing our efforts on finding Wade. Now, how much do you charge? Whatever it is, I'll at least double it."

Gage sighed. "Didn't you already hire Tag Macklin?"

"Yes, of course. But I don't see why I can't have two private investigators under my employ—or even more. What do you say?"

"I'd say I only work for one person at a time."

This, finally, got what appeared to be genuine surprise from her, though it still amounted to little more than a few rapid blinks and a half step backward. "You don't even want to know what I'd pay? Surely Lacy couldn't even come close. I know they were barely scraping by, despite how often I've offered to help them financially."

"It's not about how much you could pay. It's about keeping my word. When I tell someone I'm working for them, I *only* work for them. Among other things, it cuts down on any possible conflicts of interest."

"I'll pay you a thousand dollars an hour."

"The answer is still no."

"You don't even have to think about it?"

"No."

"I see. Despite your rather rumpled appearance, are you some kind of secret millionaire?"

"Rumpled?"

"I guess I have to admire your loyalty even if, in this instance, it's quite misplaced."

"I don't think I'm rumpled. Why do you think I'm rumpled? Casually dressed, sure, but rumpled?"

This elicited a faint chuckle, the first time Gage had heard anything akin to a laugh. It was not a pleasing sound. "I like you," she said.

"You said that already."

"It bears repeating. All right. Even if you're working directly for Lacy, I don't suppose you'd at least consider reporting to me what you report to her? I'll even pay you the same—a thousand dollars an hour. That's the easiest money you'll ever make."

"Ma'am, you could make it *ten thousand* dollars an hour, and my answer would still be the same. No."

"But what does it hurt?"

"Look, I'll say this much. When I find Lacy, I'll ask her if it's okay if I pass on what I report to you. If she says yes, I'll do it, and I won't charge you a dime, okay?"

"And if she says no?"

"I think you already know the answer to that one."

She wrinkled her nose. It was like watching tinfoil crinkle. "I don't like playing second fiddle to anyone, but I especially don't like playing second fiddle to that little tart."

Gage shook his head. He reminded himself that this woman had just suffered the loss of her husband, but he still couldn't stop himself. "What exactly is your problem with Lacy anyway? Is it just that she stole your precious son away from you, or is it more than that?"

With the pink glow of the tow truck's taillights on her face, it was hard to say for certain, but Gage thought she might have blushed. Whether she would have answered this question or not, Gage would never know, because they were interrupted by a familiar black Ford Mustang roaring down the hill and screeching to a stop behind the Lexus. When it had turned off Highway 101, Gage noted that the Mustang had come from the south. Not north, where Macklin was staying in the Sea Witch.

The truck driver was climbing back into the cab. Before he'd even managed to close the door, the one-handed behemoth in the black tracksuit had bolted out of the Mustang and crossed the distance between them. His mirrored sunglasses, perched on top of his Cro-Magnon head, caught the red glare from the taillights, making it seem like a pair of demonic eyes.

"Mrs. Carson?" he said. "What are you *doing* here?"

Ellen sighed. "I think that would be rather obvious, Mr. Macklin."

"You're towing Wade's truck? Why?"

"Do you only ask obvious questions? I don't feel like

explaining myself again. You can talk to Mr. Gage about my reasoning, if you like."

In the darkness, it was hard to read Macklin's expression, but there was no mistaking the rage in his voice. "I *told* you, ma'am, I got this."

"If you *had* this," she said, "then my son would already be found. But he isn't, is he?"

The tow truck clanked into gear and groaned up the hill. They watched it go. Macklin, finally, turned to Gage.

"I suppose she tried to hire you too?" he asked.

"He turned me down," Ellen said before Gage had a chance to reply. "It's such a rare occurrence that it still surprises me when some men can't be bought."

Without another word, she strutted back to her Lexus. The clicking of her heels on the pavement sounded like rifle shots up in the hills.

17

As the Lexus disappeared up the hill, neither Gage nor Tag Macklin said a word, but Gage could still feel the disturbance that Ellen Carson had caused rippling between them, like the wake of a shark's passing.

The night was still warm. The ocean, always a palpable presence even when it was forgotten, reasserted itself, the sound of the waves flowing into the silence between them. Standing next to this giant, Gage felt small. He seldom felt small, even next to the biggest brutes that the human race had on offer, but he certainly felt small next to Macklin. He wondered why. The walking sticks might have had something to do with it, but he couldn't very well get rid of them. Not unless he wanted to crawl home.

"She's a piece of work, isn't she?" Macklin said, smiling in that infuriating aw-shucks way again. "Some folks in Boise call her the Queen of Idaho. You can see why. Always thinks she can wave her magic wand around and everybody will just bow down and do as she wants."

"Scepter," Gage said.

"What?"

"You're mixing metaphors. Is she a queen or a witch? Come to think of it, witches don't usually have wands. Those are wizards. She could be a female wizard, I guess, but that'd be a little unusual too. I guess it'd be fitting for the age we live in, right? Maybe gender doesn't matter so much. If a woman wants to be a wizard and have a magic wand, why not?"

Macklin's smile petrified. "You're a real funny guy, aren't you? The jokes just never stop."

"How did you know she was in town?"

"What's that?"

"Ellen Carson. How did you even know she was here? You were surprised, so she obviously didn't give you a heads-up."

The smoldering stare remained for a second, then Macklin shrugged. "I didn't. I just thought I'd check Wade's truck again, maybe search the beach, see if either he or Lacy turn up. Kind of like you, right? Jesus. That woman thinks she's actually helping, being here, but she's more likely to …" He shook his head.

"What?" Gage said.

"I mean, if her kid's really thinking of offing himself, then having that woman close by probably won't make him change his mind. Sorry to put it so crude-like, but the kid, he's got mommy issues, and mommy's got all kinds of issues, know what I'm saying? Put the two together in a room and you'd need a dozen shrinks just to unpack all the things wrong with their relationship."

"How did you know Lacy was missing?"

"Word gets around."

"Jo told you?"

"So what if she did?"

"You were at Jo's place, weren't you? Just before coming here? And you overheard her talking to Ellen Carson. Jo's place is just south of here, which explains why I saw your Mustang coming from the south on the highway."

There was a beat, then Macklin chuckled. "So what if I was, man? What does it matter?"

"Why didn't you just say so then?"

"Maybe because it's none of your business?"

"What were you doing there?"

"Dude, what did I just say? It's none of your business."

"It is if it involves a certain missing couple."

"What? Are you saying I have something to do with that?"

"Well?" Gage said. "Do you?"

"I don't believe this. You're just spoiling for a fight with me, aren't you?"

Something had happened to the space between them. There was no wind, but the air was filled with an electricity that rippled around them. Macklin's hook, gleaming in the moonlight, looked large enough to lift a car. For one tense moment, Gage thought Macklin might take a swing at him with it, but then Macklin snorted.

"I'm not letting you bait me, Gage. What's going on with me and Jo, it has nothing to do with Wade or Lacy, man—or any of the Carsons, okay? It's just two colleagues catching up. I'm sure you know by now, we went through a lot together back in Seattle."

"If that's all it is, then why all the secrecy?"

"You're a peach, Gage," Macklin said, then started toward his Mustang. "We both have a job to do, so we should probably get back to it. Unless you want to work partners on this thing?"

"No, but you can give me a call if you need a hand with anything."

"Zing, zing. Just can't help yourself, can you?"

"I have to hand it to you, you've got me all figured out."

"Right. Like I said, a peach. I'm starting to see it."

"See what? That I'm obviously the better private investigator?"

Macklin chuckled. He reached his car and opened the door. "I can see why she's into you."

"Who?"

"Come on."

"Jo?"

"She has a thing for difficult men. But if I were you, I'd steer clear. That woman has a dark side like you wouldn't believe. She'll drag you down, man. She'll drag you down."

With that, he got into the Mustang and drove away. This time, he turned north.

———

THE MURMUR of the ocean followed Gage up the hill, amplified by both the angle of the road and all that smooth asphalt, the way even an actor's whisper carries to the farthest reaches of a theater. The night may have cooled, but he was sweating inside his leather jacket. Traffic on Highway 101 had finally died off, but he still had to wait for a jacked-up Camaro to roar past, men laughing inside. It was hard not to feel like they were laughing at him.

Why wouldn't they? He was a failure and a fool, and it must have been obvious to anyone who saw him. He was a failure for not finding Wade and for not protecting Lacy. He was a fool for admitting his feelings to Jo Roland, who would only use the confession against him.

That woman has a dark side like you wouldn't believe.

What the hell was that supposed to mean? It didn't matter. Jo was right. That kiss, that moment they'd shared on Secret Beach, it had been a mistake. He wasn't going to compound that mistake by obsessing about her psychology.

So what if she was into difficult men? Even assuming Macklin wasn't just trying to mess with him, Jo was so wrapped up in the wreckage of her past that it would take the jaws of life to open up her heart. Gage was not the man to do it.

He trudged toward his house, into the deeper darkness beyond the reach of the gas station lights at the bottom of the hill, where the road was shrouded by a pair of Douglas firs. As if feeling like a fool and a failure wasn't enough, he also felt an intolerable pang of loneliness. Alone in the darkness, with so many dark days ahead. Yes, they could be dark indeed, when even the briefest laugh or the most fleeting smile required an act of supreme will, and even then, even when he was really trying, he knew people could tell he was just faking it. They could tell he was just putting on a dog and pony show, every witty comeback and sarcastic jibe just a way of deflecting people from noticing the black hole of pain that was always there, *always*, right in the middle of his chest.

Wasn't that why the word *suicide* bothered him so much? Wasn't that why the very idea of it, the act of taking one's own life, clawed at his deepest, darkest fears? It was one sure way out of all that pain. While Gage believed he was strong, that he would never do such a thing, he was still afraid of looking too deeply into the darkness inside himself.

How many nights had he lain awake in that flat in New York in those first fitful weeks after Janet's murder thinking about the Beretta he'd locked in the gun safe in the closet?

She'll drag you down, man. She'll drag you down.

Love and loss. Two sides of the same coin. You flip it once, and life is roses. You flip it again and find a bullet hole where the coin used to be. The real secret, the one he always came back to, was not to pick up the coin in the first place.

The road gave way to his driveway, his walking sticks crunching on gravel. Draped in moonlight, the white oaks in the undeveloped land beyond his house rose above the wall of arbor vitae that lined the back of his property. He bought the place partly because it gave him some sense of solitude even surrounded by other houses, but now that solitude felt more isolating than comforting.

He shut the door behind him and flipped on the kitchen light. The junk mail on the tiled counter, the *New York Times* on the dining room table, the leather recliner with Hemmingway's *The Sun Also Rises* perched precariously on the arm—everything was exactly as he'd left it. It still smelled like the bacon he'd cooked for breakfast Thursday morning, which astonished him until he realized that it was still only Friday.

Not for much longer. The oven clock read 11:42 p.m. What now? He needed to get back out there and look for Wade and Lacy, but he didn't have his van. His decision to avoid the traffic and walk here now seemed foolish. More failure on his part. He needed sleep too, and rest for his weary bones, but that was not a luxury he could allow himself after all the mistakes he'd made. Yet what was the point in just wandering randomly around town when Wade or Lacy could be anywhere?

He needed some sort of plan of action, but he couldn't do that without more information. There were too many unknowns. There were too many unanswered questions. The urge to get out there right now and look for Lacy was over-whelming, but there were times, and this was one of them, when he knew had to resist the impulse to *do something* and just think. Action without intention, especially intention grounded in intelligence, was often worse than no action at all.

He turned on all the lights, in the vain hope that it would drive away some of his own darkness. He could have used a decent meal, but he settled for a peanut butter sandwich and an apple, which he munched on while he brainstormed ideas with a yellow legal pad, using his smart phone for research. He had to admit, the phone did come in handy. *Where is Lacy Carson? Where is Wade Carson?* He started with these two questions at the top of the page, then spent the next half hour reviewing what he knew about them, Stan Carson's death, Carson Clocks, and anything else that might help provide answers, scouring the internet for any new clues.

He didn't find anything useful, but he wasn't sure what to look for either. There were no damaging news articles about the Carsons or their company. There were no arrests, no rumors, nothing negative he could find with his admittedly mediocre online skills. Stan Carson really was the perfect picture of a model citizen, a pillar of his community, his résumé so sterling that he probably could have ran for mayor of Boise and won in a landslide. So why did he kill himself then? The cynic in Gage was always skeptical of the over-the-top do-gooders of the world since experience had taught him they were usually hiding something or, at the bare minimum, trying to assuage the guilt they felt over some past transgression. The inexplicable nature of Stan Carson's suicide made him even more skeptical.

As did Wade Carson's ominous words to Lacy: He'd said his father had done things he should be ashamed of. What? What crimes had he committed that were so egregious that his guilty conscience eventually drove him to take his own life?

Unless he *didn't* take his own life. Unless it was murder, made to look like a suicide. But that just raised other baffling questions. Who would do such a thing, and why?

In Gage's mind, the obvious suspect was Tag Macklin, if only because he instinctively distrusted the guy, but why would Macklin kill his golden goose? Unless Macklin was lying, and Gage could see no reason for him to lie, at least in this case. Stan Carson had given him a steady diet of work. Gage did some more online research on Tag Macklin, but other than the big news stories about what went down at Terminal Five in Seattle, there wasn't much there. Macklin's name popped up in a few unrelated court cases in which he'd worked as a private investigator, but not much else. He had no internet presence of his own to speak of—no social media, no web page, nothing like that.

To someone else, that might have been usual, but not to Gage. He had no internet presence to speak of either.

There was also what Ellen Carson had said just a little while ago as she'd walked away from Gage and Macklin: *It's such a rare occurrence that it still surprises me when some men can't be bought.* Was that just a general comment, or was it a dig at Macklin specifically? And did it have anything to do with whatever it was that Wade Carson felt his father should be ashamed of? The more time Gage spent thinking about all this, the more it led back to Tag Macklin.

And Jo.

Despite his reluctance to put his mind there, he wrote another question on the notepad: *What is going on between Jo Roland and Garrick Macklin?*

As he scribbled that question underneath the others, Gage found it interesting that he wrote Garrick rather than Tag. Was his subconscious trying to tell him that he should think of Tag Macklin and Garrick Macklin as different people? There was Garrick Macklin, the distinguished police officer in Seattle who'd raised his hand to stop a bullet, and there was Tag Macklin, the one-handed private eye who was mixed up in some mess with the Carsons.

Maybe those two versions of Macklin really should be treated as separate people, and the fact that Macklin ended up in the same town where Jo was police chief was nothing more than mere coincidence. Maybe Gage just kept insisting there was something more to it because he wanted a reason to be near her, and the sooner he got over his inexplicable obsession with her, the sooner he'd be able to see this case with more clarity. Gage hated coincidences, especially when it came to his work, but Macklin ending up in Barnacle Bluffs may have just been one of those random quirks of fate.

But maybe not.

And if it wasn't a coincidence that Macklin was in Barnacle Bluffs, then it wasn't a coincidence that Wade was here either. After all, he could have stopped at any number of places. Why here? That was a long way to drive just to end his own life. And if Gage allowed for the possibility that Wade had *chosen* to come to Barnacle Bluffs, then he had to also allow for the possibility that whatever that motivation was, it had something to do with Macklin. Which brought him right back to the last question he'd written on the yellow pad:

What is going on between Jo Roland and Garrick Macklin?

Jo may have insisted that whatever she was up to had nothing to do with the Carsons, and Gage didn't think she was lying, but he also wasn't sure she was in a position to know. After all, the Carsons had come into Macklin's life long after Jo had fled for Oregon.

She has a thing for difficult men.

Gage was surprised to find himself writing that sentence on the page. He almost scratched it out, not wanting to engage in a bunch of self-indulgent fantasizing that he'd already vowed would lead nowhere, but then he stopped. There was something here too, wasn't there? She'd gone to a lot of trouble to build that shrine on the beach, if that was indeed what it was. Was she really going to take her own life? Or had she been picking up the gun for another reason, as a sort of reenactment to try to make peace with the terrible thing she'd done with it?

And had there been something else in that rusty steel box? Drug money maybe? He couldn't rule it out. Maybe Macklin was no longer the hero the world thought him to be. Maybe, as the glory of his heroic act in Seattle faded and the reality of his one-handed existence laid bare how difficult his life would be now, he'd decided he was owed whatever drug money Jo had squirreled away in that box of hers. Maybe he had some kind of leverage over Jo that would make her give it to him. Gage couldn't quite parse the logic of all that, but his gut told him there was something there.

She has a thing for difficult men.

It wasn't so much what Macklin said as the question it raised. *Why* would Jo have a thing for difficult men? Whatever it was that made her that way, it probably didn't start with Dell Baldwin. Gage returned his thinking to that shrine she'd made on the beach. There was something about it that bothered him, and it wasn't just the money he assumed was still in the box. It was the picture of the young man who'd been decked out in an army uniform.

Gage remembered now that Macklin had said that he and Dell had gone straight from high school into the police academy. That meant it was highly unlikely that Dell had ever served in the army. There was also something about the photo, its faded and foxed quality, that led Gage to believe it wasn't a picture of Jo's husband. Gage hadn't gotten a great look at the photo, but now that he thought about it, from what he remembered of the cut and style of the uniform, it looked like one from the Vietnam era.

Then it came to him. It was the photo in Jo's office at the BBPD, the silver-framed one next to her computer that pictured her and her mother. The same kind of silver frame.

It wasn't about who was in the picture, though. It wasn't about what he'd seen at all.

It was about what he *hadn't.*

There were no photos of her father.

What did Gage know of the man, except that he and his wife had both been academics at the University of Oregon and that they'd both passed on to their daughter a love of Shakespeare? Gage swallowed hard and brought up a search box on his phone. He didn't know their names, but if they were tenured professors at U of O, it shouldn't be too hard to find that out. As he typed "Jo Roland, Eugene, University of Oregon, parents," his fingers left sweat stains on the screen. Why were his hands so clammy? This was ridiculous.

Gage was right. It wasn't too hard to find out their names. It wasn't too hard to find out everything else too.

"Oh, Jesus," Gage said.

———

GAGE WAS STILL HUNCHED over his phone at the dining table when he heard a familiar sound outside—the obnoxious grumble of a 1600 cc engine that more than a few people had compared to the death rattle of a lifelong smoker in the final stages of lung cancer.

As he stepped into the chill air, his boxy, mustard-yellow old friend, better known to the world as a '71 Volkswagen, skidded to a stop on the gravel. The smell of burned oil wafted over him. Alex rolled down his window and leaned outside. His gray mustache was the same color as his felt riding cap.

"I knew you'd still be up," he said.

"I'm not paying for delivery, if that's what you're after," Gage said. "I could have gotten the van myself in the morning."

"I was afraid you might report it stolen before then," Alex said. "Come on, let's go."

"Go? Go where? It's two in the morning!"

"Everywhere, my friend. Until we find her. Until we find both of them. Just like me, you know you're not going to sleep, so we might as well be doing something useful. Now, are you going to get in, or am I going to drive off without you?"

There was a lot of muttering and grumbling, and a few minute's delay while Gage popped back inside to use the bathroom and fetch his coat and walking sticks, but Gage eventually climbed into the passenger seat. Alex put the van in gear, and they rattled down the hill.

"What is it?" Alex asked.

"What?"

"You look like you were just punched in the gut. And you didn't insist on driving. For your own van, that's almost unheard of. Spill the beans."

Gage looked at him. They were at the bottom of the hill. The harsh light from the gas station deepened the dark bags under Alex's eyes. A sedan swept past, its headlights casting their shadows along the ceiling of the van.

"I just learned something about Jo," Gage said. "Or about her father, really. He committed suicide at Secret Beach when she was nineteen years old."

18

─────────

The particular way Richard "Richie" Roland had died was not in his official obituary published in the *Register Guard*, nor was it in the glowing write-up Gage found on the University of Oregon website under the Emeritus Professors and Distinguished Alumni page of the English Department.

Those both omitted the cause of death, which was something of a clue in itself, because the man had only been fifty-seven years old. If he'd been even ten years older, such an omission might have been overlooked, the cause of death assumed to be old age, even if that would still be on the young side by modern standards. But when a fifty-seven-year-old man died, it raised questions.

The first page of search results was mostly full of the man's poetry publications. Halfway down the second page, however, Gage found the answer he was looking for: a headline for the *Curry County Reporter* that read "Distinguished UO Professor Dies at Secret Beach." He steeled himself when he clicked the link, knowing full well what he was likely to find. If the cause of death had been a violent crime, he didn't think it would be on the second page of results, even after twelve years.

But a suicide?

Especially one carried out in a fairly straightforward fashion, with no kinky characteristics that would make the tragedy more newsworthy?

Yes, Gage could easily see *that* failing to rank highly in whatever mystical algorithm these tech companies used. And a fairly straightforward suicide it was, if overdosing on a cocktail of painkillers while sitting on a beach in southern Oregon at midnight on a balmy September day could be called straightforward. The most sensational aspect of the story was the desperate 9-1-1 call received by the Gold Beach Police Department a few hours earlier, when a frantic sophomore at the University of Washington claimed that her father had left a her strange voicemail a few hours earlier that led her to believe he might be thinking of doing harm to himself somewhere in the Cape Sebastian area. When pressed for reasons, she said he'd told her he was visiting one of their favorite places, that she shouldn't worry about him because he was at peace now, and that he loved her.

This was all in the article, even the bit about Richie Roland telling her daughter he loved her. The reporter noted that it was in the transcript of the 9-1-1 call. He tried imagining Jo telling the dispatcher the part about her father loving her. He wondered if it was something she just blurted out or if she'd said it quite intentionally, as if she didn't think the local police would act unless she told them this.

"Wow," Alex said, when Gage finished relaying all this to him. "I had no idea. Do you think that's why she eventually relocated to Port Orford? Because she was … I don't know, trying to get closer to him in some way?"

"Or it was an act of penance," Gage said, "because she blamed herself for his death. She was probably also pretty angry at the police for not acting swiftly enough. There was some minor controversy because the Gold Beach police didn't send an officer down to the beach until the next morning—and only because a hiker found Jo's father, already dead."

They were cruising north along an empty Highway 101, nearly to the Golden Eagle Casino. The moonlight, piercing the clouds, laid bars on the road ahead of them that looked like piano keys, but the drainage ditch on Gage's right was so dark it could have been a mile deep. Gage still couldn't get used to riding in the passenger seat. He had to resist the impulse to grab the wheel and jerk it to the left, so sure was he that the van was about to slip into the ditch.

There was no sign of Wade, Lacy, or anything else suspicious in nature. The hotel rooms may have all been full, but apparently everybody was asleep in their beds.

"Eve and I stayed in Port Orford once," Alex said. "It's a tiny place, very remote. Gold Beach and Brookings aren't exactly huge, but Port Orford is minuscule by comparison."

"I know," Gage said. "I just drove by there this—" He was going to say *morning*, but the clock on the US Bank sign read 2:35 a.m., so it was technically Saturday morning now. "Yesterday. God, it feels like one long day since Lacy walked into my office."

"You have an office?"

"I mean, the office I was looking at. The walk-up above Thackleforth—"

"Right, right. Thought maybe while all this was going on you actually rented it. Got me excited there. I figured I'd have my bookstore computer all to myself again. Of course, knowing you, just because you'd rent office space doesn't mean you'd actually put anything in it. Least of all a computer."

Gage ignored this. "What I'm trying to figure out is why

sui—suicide keeps coming up. Wade's father. Wade threatening it. Jo's father."

Alex fell quiet as he turned into the parking lot of the Golden Eagle Casino, one of the places, maybe the *only* place, in town still open at such an hour. "You really don't like that word, do you?"

"What's that?"

"Suicide."

"Oh."

"Care to elaborate why?"

"Do I need to elaborate?"

"I'm just saying, if you want to talk about—"

"I don't."

"Okay."

"You don't have to worry about me, Alex. I'm not going to eat a bullet anytime soon."

Alex said nothing for a moment, the van rumbling through the rows of RVs, both of them looking for anything worth looking at and coming up empty. "I don't like that you added *anytime soon*," Alex said.

"Will you quit? I didn't mean it that way. I just meant I'm fine."

"Are you?"

"Jesus Christ."

The parking lot was a well-lit place, with dozens of street lamps on tall poles standing vigil over all the chrome and steel, and so when Gage glanced at Alex, his friend's face was fully illuminated, every crag and crevice, every wrinkle and line, thrown into sharp relief. It made him look old. It also made it obvious that there was moisture in Alex's eyes. It shocked Gage into softening his tone.

"Look," he said, "I know you worry about me. I appreciate it. But I am fine."

"Well, you make it damn difficult, that's for sure."

"I'm sorry about that."

"Good. I'm glad we got that fucking settled. Do you want to look inside the casino or head somewhere else?"

It was the profanity, more than the quake in Alex's voice, that surprised Gage the most. Alex almost never swore. Finding his own face warm, Gage looked out the window and mumbled something about heading north again. They headed back to the highway in silence, the tires, humming beneath them, barely audible over the growling engine.

As they canvassed the town for the next two hours—cruising past Big Dipper Lake, Arrow Outlet Mall, and most of the larger hotels—neither of them hardly said a word. They didn't see Wade or Lacy either. A little after four in the morning, weighed down by dejection and disappointment, Alex pulled into the empty JayBee Grocery parking lot. The store's interior lights were all off except for the coolers along the back wall. The traffic light glowed a steady, forlorn green, no cars coming from either direction on Highway 101.

"I'm out of ideas," Alex said.

"They've got to be somewhere," Gage said.

"My brain's too fuzzy to even remember who it is we're looking for."

"Lacy and Wade Carson."

"I was joking."

It was dark inside the van, but Gage caught Alex's smile. It was a good thing. It meant the pall hanging over them was lifting.

"It's like I'm looking at this case all wrong," Gage said. "I'm missing something."

Alex yawned. "Sleep would be the obvious answer. Aren't you getting tired?"

"Let's pretend that Wade isn't here to do what everybody thinks he's here to do. Let's pretend he's in Barnacle Bluffs for another reason. What would that be?"

"Heck if I know."

"Yeah, I'm drawing a blank too," Gage said.

"Robbing a bank?"

"What?"

"You said you think Wade is robbing a bank?"

"No," Gage said, "I said I'm drawing a—never mind. I just don't think I have the full story. People are holding out on me. There's some big piece of information I'm missing."

"What?"

"Well, if I knew what it was, then it wouldn't be missing, would it?"

"See," Alex said, "you are tired. That's why you're getting snippy."

"And even if Wade *is* here to end his own life, what about his father's death would drive him to that? No, it just doesn't make sense. There's something else. That's why I keep coming back to the connection between Tag Macklin and Jo Roland."

"Right. That was ten years ago, though. I mean, how much of a connection is it, really?"

"You see why I find it so unlikely, though?" Gage said. "That Wade would just happen to come to the same city that … that …"

"That what?"

"Well, I don't know what! That's the problem."

"Lack of sleep is probably the bigger problem. Back when I was in the FBI—"

"You were in the FBI?" Gage said.

"Ha ha. Back when I was in the FBI, when you were still in diapers—"

"I think I was at least potty trained by that point."

"—I could pull all-nighters without any problem," Alex continued, "but it's a little more difficult when you're at the age when you're getting Social Security checks. "

"They still send *checks?*"

"Couldn't we table this discussion for a few hours? You're not exactly a spring chicken. I really do think some shut-eye would help you too. At this point, you've got to be running on fumes."

Gage scratched his stubbled chin. It felt like running his fingers over a cheese grater. "It's like a jigsaw puzzle, right? I may not have all the pieces, but I feel like I should at least be able to know what the puzzle's supposed to be at this point, but I don't even know that. "

"Maybe a fresh night of sleep would give you the appropriate puzzle clarity."

"What's blocking me? That's what I can't figure out."

"Fatigue. Fatigue is blocking you."

"There has to be something."

A silver Cadillac cruised past, the stoplight glowing a steady green on the hood of the car. It was the first car they'd seen on the highway since they'd parked. It wouldn't be like that for long. In a few hours, the town would be a crazy ant hill of activity, and it would be impossible again to get around. Gage felt a creeping sense of helplessness.

"That guy in the Cadillac is probably going home to get some sleep," Alex said wistfully.

"You know," Gage said, "this *was* your idea."

"I know. But it's one thing to actually be getting Social Security checks. It's another thing to *feel* like the kind of person who should be getting Social Security checks."

"You're really hung up on the whole Social Security thing, aren't you?"

"I'm old, Garrison. I'm hung up on a lot of things."

"I don't know what to do next. I just don't usually feel this way."

"I'd offer a suggestion if I could think of anything. I mean, you said it's like a jigsaw puzzle. Maybe instead of trying to make sense of the pieces you have, you should, you know, get a few more pieces?"

Gage nodded. It wasn't a bad idea. In fact, it was probably the best idea either of them had come up with that night, which said something itself about their state of mind. He sighed and opened the passenger door.

"Let's trade places," he said. "I'm taking you home."

19

———

Gage woke to the call of a rooster and the feel of cool, hard glass pressing against his temple. When he opened his bleary eyes, he saw tall, dew-glistening grass and a grove of Douglas firs, the trees casting their long shadows on a pole barn. The light was gauzy and gray. As if the godawful rooster wasn't bad enough, his head hurt like hell. It even sounded like someone tapping on his brain.

Only the sound wasn't in his brain. Craning his head to the right, he saw the source of this particular annoyance was a woman in a pink bathrobe, her hair like a tangled ball of orange yarn. She was clacking her fingernails on the passenger side window. They were the same orange color as her hair. Behind her, a manufactured home was tucked behind a grove of apple trees.

"You can't camp here, honey," the lady said.

Gage leaned back and wiped the slobber off his face with the sleeve of his leather jacket. It started to come back to him. After dropping off Alex, he'd driven into the hills bordering Barnacle Bluffs to do some more searching. Then his eyes had started to close against his will. Feeling it was better to take a quick nap rather than risk driving home, he'd pulled over before he ran down someone's mailbox. The nap apparently wasn't so quick.

"Don't worry," he said, "I'm leaving now."

"I called the cops, you know."

"Look, I said I'm leaving, okay?"

"You know who called me back?"

"The tooth fairy?"

"The chief of police."

"Oh. Jo Roland?"

"Yeah, that's the one. And you know what she told me?"

"To shoot me on sight?"

"She said you were mostly harmless. She said you'd probably be gone in the morning. She said if you *weren't* gone in the morning, then I should come out and tell you what she told me to tell you. "

Gage rubbed his temples. He was so groggy that trying to understand this woman was like trying to parse Algebra. "Uh huh. And that is?"

"That she'd send out a garbage truck to haul you and your ugly van to the dump if you didn't stop scaring the fine citizens of Barnacle Bluffs."

"I see. How very kind of her."

"You married to her or something?"

"What? What would make you say that?"

The woman chuckled, her curlers bobbing in her orange hair as she walked away. "The only person I talk about that way is my husband," she said.

———

WISPY FOG, as diaphanous as spiderwebs, hung over the ocean. Even at a little before nine on Saturday morning, Highway 101 was full of idiots in metal boxes. Another hour and it would be impossible to get around again. Barnacle Bluffs would have been a decent place to live if not for all the tourists. Of course, without the tourists, there would have been no jobs since Barnacle Bluffs, unlike Newport or even, a little farther south, the sleepy village of Waldport, didn't have any kind of marina.

Still, navigating the slow death of honking horns and fuming exhaust pipes, Gage would have gladly made the trade. It was either that or engage in mass murder. Was there a word for that sort of thing? *Touristcide?*

It was a joke in poor taste, even to think silently, but Gage was in a foul mood. He was furious with himself for falling asleep. He was even more furious after he called Jo for an update and she didn't take his call. He got Barb at the front desk instead, who told him, after leaving him on hold for five minutes, that Chief Roland was busy. Barb did tell him that there was nothing new to report on Wade or Lacy Carson, so the phone call wasn't a total loss even if the information only served to send him spiraling into a deeper funk.

It didn't help that when he finally rounded the corner onto his gravel driveway, the first thing he saw was the tail end of a black Ford Mustang.

Tag Macklin was standing on his front porch.

The massive, one-handed behemoth in the black track suit and mirrored sunglasses was holding his hook before the door, as if he were about to knock, and he turned and grinned at the Volkswagen's approach. It was the grin, even more than the unannounced visit, that really set Gage's heart pounding.

"What the hell are you doing here?" He said this as he got out of the van, stumbling because his joints were all fused together. Perfect. Macklin's grin didn't fade, but he did adjust his posture, leaning against the side of the house and resting his hook against his stomach. It glinted in the cool morning air.

"Hey, now," Macklin said, "what's with all the attitude? Your doorbell's broken, by the way."

"It's not broken. I unplugged it. I don't want people to get the idea that I want visitors."

Tag chuckled. "Figures. You *would* do something like that. You look like shit, man."

"Thanks. I appreciate that. Now, is there anything else, or is this just a welfare check?"

"No, seriously, man, you look ill."

"I'm fine. Now what the fuck do you want?"

Macklin didn't move. In the reflection of his sunglasses, Gage saw his own haggard, unshaven face, and he had to admit he *did* look ill—gaunt, skin waxy and yellow, with caverns where his eyes should have been. Macklin may have been leaning against the side of the house, but he was such a huge, hulking presence that Gage wouldn't have been able to squeeze past him without knocking over the pot of geraniums. Dead geraniums, Gage saw now, withered and brown. Something else in his life that he'd managed to fail.

"It's like this," Macklin said. "I thought it over again after we talked last night, and I really think we ought to put aside our differences and work as a team on this."

"You're joking," Gage said. "Did Ellen Carson send you?"

"No, no, I'm here on my own. Look, it doesn't help either of us if we're covering the same ground. You don't like me. I don't know why, but hey, you got a right to your opinion. But finding Wade and Lacy is more important than us being pals, right?"

"It's not that I don't like you, Tag. I mean, that's true, but I don't like most people. The problem is, I don't trust you."

"Look, man, it's simple. I'm a private investigator hired

by Ellen Carson to find her son. I don't know why you have to make more of it than—"

"Why did she say some men can't be bought?"

"What?"

"You heard me. It was like she was implying something about you. What would that be?"

"Christ, man, don't read too much into what that woman—"

"What really happened in Terminal Five?"

"Excuse me?"

"What's the real story?"

"I don't know what you're talking about. You read what was in the papers. That's the real story. Anything else is in your imagination."

"Why did Jo go down to Secret Beach yesterday?"

"Okay, now you've totally lost me. She went where?"

"Don't play me for a fool, Tag. You want something from her. What is it?"

"I'm telling you, there's nothing there. You're barking up the wrong tree. As my daddy used to say—"

"Oh, fuck your daddy."

"Whoa. Come on. That ain't a nice thing to—"

"Do you wear those sunglasses all the time because otherwise you're afraid people will be able to tell you're lying?"

"Wow."

"Were you in on the take with Jo's husband?"

Macklin sighed. He removed his sunglasses and leaned away from the house, back to his full height. It shouldn't have made him that much taller, but it did. He towered over Gage. The grin was gone. The eyes were hard. In the flat, gray light, all the many scars around Macklin's eyes looked like cracks in concrete.

"Dude," he said, "you can look right into my eyes if it makes you feel better, but the truth is the truth. I *saved* her life. I lost my fucking hand because of it. Why would I have saved her if I was in on the action with Dell? You see how that makes no sense? I was friends with Dell, sure, but he was my supervisor, so we weren't really that close. I really did come here hoping we'd work together on this thing."

"The fact that you won't give me a straight answer," Gage said, "leads me to believe that I'm onto something."

"You just won't quit, will you?"

"It's one of my more endearing qualities, Big Mac."

"Big Mac. That's cute. You think you can take me, old man? Is that it?"

"Old man," Gage said. "That's even cuter. Am I really that old? You're the one wearing a tracksuit like one of those wrinkled geezers at a Florida senior center."

Macklin chuckled, but there was no mirth in it, only more menace. "You're trying to get me to take a swing at you, is that it? Trying to provoke me? I don't get it. I'd gut you like fish, and you know it."

"Go ahead and try," Gage said. "People are always underestimating me. Why don't you just tell me what really happened at Terminal Five? Tell me what was left out of the papers."

"There was *nothing* left out of the papers, at least nothing that will make one damn bit of difference."

"Bullshit. There's still something you're not telling me. Did you two have an affair? Was that it?"

"What?"

"I saw the way you put your hand on Jo's shoulder at her place Thursday night."

"You were spying on us?"

"I was walking by. It's not the same thing."

"You've got it all wrong, man. You've got everything wrong."

"There was some kind of love triangle, right? That's why

you saved her. You had to choose between the drug money and her, and you chose her. But after it was all done, she pushed you away."

Macklin's resolve wilted. It was in the eyes. There was a fading, like a bulb going out. "You really have no clue," he said. "You're so far off course, it's like you're heading for a different country."

"So you admit there's something you're not telling me?"

"You're really not going to work with me, huh?"

"Tell me what happened at Terminal Five. For real. The whole story."

They locked eyes for a long moment, then Macklin laughed and pushed past Gage. "Okay, so this was a waste of time. Good luck finding her. If something happens to either of them because you were too stubborn to work together, it's on you."

Macklin walked to his Mustang. Gage, feeling helpless, watched him go. He knew there was something there, it wasn't in his imagination, but he didn't know how to get at it. This man was guilty of something. He had to be.

Then, after Macklin opened the door with his good hand, he swung back around. With his sunglasses on, and his grin just as wide as before, he was back to his old self.

"Look," he said, "it's fine that we're not working together, but I want to give you something to think about."

"Oh goodie."

"Did it ever occur to you that maybe Jo was the one who was in too deep with her husband? That the only way she didn't go down with him was because I didn't rat her out?"

When Gage didn't say anything, Macklin laughed. "No witty comeback this time?"

"You're still lying," Gage said. "There's still stuff you're not saying."

"Everybody's got stuff they don't say, man. Doesn't mean

it's illegal. Don't even mean it's a lie. It's just stuff people don't want to talk about, right? You know about Jo's dad? Yeah, you do. I can see you do now. This Secret Beach, is it down in the Gold Beach area?"

"You already know it is."

"No, I don't, man. But if that's the case, then you already know the real reason she went down there."

"There's got to be more than that."

"Ask her. Ask her about what I said. Ask her if she was in too deep with her husband, and ask her if her old buddy Tag gave her a way out. Watch her eyes. No matter what she says, watch her eyes. She's not a bad liar, Jo—except when the truth is staring her right in the face. Then you'll be able to see it. Judge for yourself, man."

"What truth?" This Gage croaked out in a whisper, but Macklin was already climbing into his Mustang. He started the car, flashed Gage one last smile as if he'd been there for nothing more than a social call, then peeled out of the driveway.

———

INSIDE HIS HOUSE, Gage felt as if he'd been gone for a year, even if it had barely been over a day. Everything appeared both comfortingly familiar and strangely foreign in the way a home often felt after a long absence.

The permanent scuff mark on his glass top oven. The lemon scent from the dishwasher soap. The way the dust motes floated in the shaft of light streaming down from the high, A-frame window. These were things he knew but seldom noticed. His absence, however brief, raised them back into his awareness.

His absence also made him even more acutely aware of

how alone he was. How lonely. This wasn't just a bachelor pad. This was a crypt.

Gage's failure to make any headway at all in finding Wade or Lacy Carson only deepened his loneliness. He needed a shower, a shave, maybe something decent to eat—all the petty details of life and living that needed to be dealt with even when those details only got in the way of doing what needed to be done. But *what* needed to be done? That was the question.

The Carson family had become a bedrock of the Boise community by making clocks. Gage felt there was a clock ticking right now—a timer for a bomb, set to detonate at a certain time, but he didn't know where it was or when it would go off. He didn't even know *why* it was. He could just feel it, that something bad was going to happen unless he acted, and time was running out.

Last night, Alex had told him he needed more puzzle pieces. It was good advice. Too many people were holding out on him. Gage couldn't quite bring himself to confront Jo, and Tag Macklin had proved to be a frustrating enigma, but there was another person in town who might be easier to crack.

If there really was a clock ticking, Gage didn't have time to play nice.

He headed back to his van.

20

In the short time Gage had been off Highway 101, the wispy fog had burned away, leaving an ocean so blue and a sun so yellow they looked childishly phony, like a mural on a kindergarten wall. The Volkswagen barely made it a quarter mile south in the tightly packed procession of metal and rubber before Gage gave up in favor of an old gravel logging road, unremarkable to the uninitiated but a lifeline to locals in the know.

The road led to other roads, winding its way east of the highway through forest so dense it felt like dusk, eventually connecting to another road, then another, lots of potholes and washboard ruts, a few lonely mobile homes glimpsed in the hills but mostly Douglas firs, ferns, and live oaks until eventually the van emerged next to the Inn at Sapphire Head —or rather, the adjoining golf course on the east side of the highway.

It had been a long and tortuous drive, but Gage would take long and tortuous *in motion* over long and tortuous *standing still* if he had any choice in the matter.

He parked in the main lot across the highway, then used

the pedestrian tunnel to cross under the road, navigating the uneven asphalt with his cane and standing aside as a golf cart with two potbellied men rattled past. Five minutes later he stepped off the elevator onto the top floor. There were only three doors. The first two were open and being cleaned by housekeepers, revealing a glimpse of the palatial suites and their sweeping views of the Pacific Ocean. He knocked on the last one.

"I wasn't expecting you," Ellen Carson said when she opened the door and found him standing in the hall. "It's not —it's not bad news, is it?"

Her black silk outfit might have been a dress, or it might have been a nightgown; it was hard to tell. Either way, the outfit was very prim and proper, no cleavage revealed, and the hem so long he couldn't see her feet. She held a tumbler, a tiny bit of amber liquid sloshing at the bottom of the ice cubes.

"It's nothing like that," Gage said. "They're both still missing, I'm afraid. I was just hoping we could chat. I have a few questions I was hoping you could help me with."

"They told you, at the front desk, what room I'm in?"

Her speech was slurred. It wasn't even noon. Her makeup, as thick as ever, was so shiny that it reflected the light coming from the ocean-view windows, giving her cheeks a bluish tint. He wondered if she'd slept in it. He wondered if she ever took it off. She made him think of a dilapidated Victorian house, one somebody had slapped several coats of paint on but had done nothing to repair any of the house's true problems.

"I just figured you'd be in one of the best rooms," he said. "Can I come in?"

"Yes, yes, of course. Please. You don't look well, you know. Have you shaved lately?"

When he passed her, he caught a whiff of bourbon, the

sweet and woodsy scent he knew so well. The room was big enough to hold fifty people and felt bigger still for how lightly furnished it was, dominated by a four-post bed turned so it faced the sliders that opened onto a patio that stretched the full length of the wall, with the rest of the furniture scattered around the perimeter—a pirate trunk of brass and aged wood, two walnut dressers, a writing desk bare except for a tiffany lamp.

There was also a white leather couch, a matching loveseat, and a natural, live edge coffee table that might have been redwood, judging by the reddish hue, all positioned in front a big-screen television that took up most of the wall, but even these did little to fill the space. The view was so unobstructed, so sweeping and spectacular, that they could have been on a cruise ship in the middle of the ocean.

Perhaps because of how still the other occupant was, it took Gage a moment to notice her driver—in the corner, next to her black hardshell suitcase. His skin was almost as dark as the suitcase, but not quite, more dark mahogany than black. He'd swapped his white turtleneck for a tan one, but otherwise he looked no different from when Gage saw him yesterday. A small, compact man, with rigid, angular features. He was small enough that he almost could have folded himself into her suitcase.

"Hello," Gage said.

The man bowed his head.

"Roko," Ellen said, "will you give us a few moments of privacy, please?"

With another slight bow, Roko stepped into the hall and closed the door behind him.

"He just sits in here with you?" Gage asked.

"He's quite loyal."

"I'd say. Is he just your driver?"

"It's nothing kinky, if that's what you're getting at. He's

more like a personal assistant and bodyguard. And he's tougher than he looks, I assure you. He has a black belt in karate, and he won many tournaments back in India as a young man. I just … I feel a little safer, having him close by." She held up her glass, then started for a dark cabinet around the corner. "Can I get you one? Or something else? This room has its own wet bar."

"It's a little early for me," Gage said. "Is there a specific reason you don't feel safe?"

She opened the cabinet and picked up a crystal decanter filled with bourbon, judging by the similar amber liquid inside, and refilled her tumbler, then poured a second one. She brought it to him. He took it, wondering if she hadn't heard or had merely ignored him.

"Should we toast?" she said, raising her glass. "Make it a toast to something good. I need to feel good right now."

"Why don't you feel safe, Ellen?"

"Hmm?"

"You said Roko helps you feel more safe."

"Oh, I don't know, just—well, with Stan gone, you know. I just feel a little more … well, exposed, I guess." She took a sip—more than a sip, gulping down half the glass in one go.

Gage put his own glass on the bar. "I am sorry for your loss," he said. "I want you to know that. I read your husband's obituary. He sounded like quite a man."

"Don't like bourbon?" she said.

"No, the opposite. I like it too much."

She scrunched up her eyebrows. She was swaying on her feet in a way that alarmed him. He started to reach for her elbow, afraid she was going to fall, but then she swung abruptly toward the window and took a few unsteady steps.

"Do you … do you like the view?" she asked. "I prefer warmer beaches, of course, but I … Well, it's quite—quite lovely."

"Maybe you should sit down," Gage said.

She gazed at the ocean, teetering like a woman on a ship at high sea. She took another stumbling step and saved herself from falling by clamping onto the leather couch. Her tumbler, however, bounced off the couch and rolled across the carpet, splashing what remained of the bourbon all over the floor.

Again, Gage started to go to her, but she shrugged him off. "When you knocked on the door," she said, then got so choked up all she could do was shake her head.

"I'd really feel more comfortable if you sat down," Gage said.

"When you knocked, I thought—thought you might be the police. I thought they might be here because … Well, because they found him. But not, you know …" She trailed off, but the word hung in the air anyway. *Alive.*

"Oh," Gage said.

"I've been dreading such a thing ever since I got here."

"We have no reason to think anything bad's happened to either of them."

"Shouldn't you be out there? Looking for him?"

"I *have* been looking for him," Gage said. "Both of them. But before I do so again, I need to know more information."

"What more is there to know? I'm afraid he's going to … going to … Well, we have to find him. That's all there is to it."

"You're afraid he's going to do what?"

"It's Lacy. She's upset him somehow. That's why he ran off."

Gage ignored this. "What are you afraid he's going to do?"

"He's not in a right state of mind, that's all. He's liable to do something … something foolish. We've got to find him before he … before he does."

"But what are you afraid he's going to do, Mrs. Carson?"
She didn't answer.

"Lacy thinks he … he might hurt himself. Is that what you think?"

"I wouldn't trust anything that woman says. She doesn't love him the way I love him."

"You didn't answer my question."

"We've … we've got to find him. He'll be all right. You'll see. He'll be all right."

Gage didn't want to talk about suicide. He didn't want to go there, especially now, with a stubbled face and grimy eyelids and a pounding in his skull so loud he couldn't even hear the ocean. But he sensed he was onto something here, that Ellen Carson had the same fear as Lacy but was much more reluctant to express it.

He sat in the loveseat, leaning his cane against the arm, thinking about how he wanted to do this. The leather was cold but firm, kind of like Ellen Carson. Kind of like him.

"Are you all right?" she asked.

"What's that?"

"Your knee," she said.

"Oh. That's an old injury. Just stiffens up sometimes, that's all. It's, uh, from my New York days."

Gage's throat tightened. What was he doing? It came out as if he were talking about where he grew up, what college he attended, or something equally trivial. Like it didn't matter that much. Like it was just another detail in his biography and not the most important, life-altering event that had ever happened to him.

He looked at her, his face warm, and he might have been able to skip right past this little bump in the road had she just let it go. But instead she nodded sadly.

"Yes," she said, "I heard about that from Chief Roland. From when—from when your wife died. I'm so sorry."

That was all it took. It wasn't just that Ellen Carson knew about the terrible thing—the mafia hit gone wrong, the Iranian strongman who'd turned his knee into a bag of broken glass and drowned his wife in the bathtub—or that she'd expressed sympathy. That would have been painful enough, but endurable. He'd endured it from so many others, after all.

No, there was something about Ellen hearing about it from Jo Roland that got to him in a much deeper way.

"Oh no," Ellen said.

"Hmm?" Gage said.

"I'm sorry," she said, "I seem to have upset you."

There was moisture on Gage's face. The sensation was so foreign that he assumed that the ceiling was dripping. Even when he touched his cheek and traced the moisture back to his eye, he found it hard to believe.

"Well," he said, "will you look at that?"

"I'm sorry," Ellen said. "I shouldn't have—"

"It's all right. Really."

"I've embarrassed you."

"No, it's all right. I think—I think it's just the exhaustion. It brings stuff to the surface, you know."

She made a sound akin to a laugh, but it was so pinched it sounded more like a strangled sob. "Yes. Yes, it does. I'm in so much pain. I can't bear it anymore. How do you manage? How have you possibly managed, all these years?"

Gage didn't have a good answer, but he thought he should gamely try anyway. "Life goes on, that's all. The pain is always there, but having other things to focus on … well, that helps. You just … get on with things."

"Get on with things," she said.

"It's not exactly Ann Landers level of advice, is it?"

"And if it's too much? What then? Oh my. I think I need another drink."

"How about you sit instead?"

"I'm afraid, if I sit, I'll never get back up again. I'm so tired, Mr. Gage. Can I call you Garrison?"

"Yes."

"And call me Ellen. I feel like we're getting to know each other, so it's good to use first names."

Gage patted the couch adjacent to him. "Please."

"I'd rather not," she said, but then she did. It was more like she was starting toward the wet bar but gave up after a few steps, collapsing onto the couch only because it was better than collapsing on the coffee table or the floor. She eyed her empty tumbler, still lying on its side on the thin tan carpet, but she made no move to reach for it.

"I've never been alone," she said.

"Oh."

"Not like this. I met Stan in high school. Then Wade came along. I've never had to be alone. Not really. Not without anybody. But I'm without anybody now. I'm really alone."

"We'll find him, Mrs. Carson."

"Ellen. Call me Ellen."

"All right. Ellen. I'm going to get right back out there. But I need some help. I feel like everybody's holding something back, and there's so much holding back that it's getting in my way, you see?"

"I—I suppose so. But I don't ... I don't know what I could possibly—"

"This might be hard to hear," Gage said, "but we've got to get things out in the open if we're going to find your son. I heard that Wade felt that Stan—his father, your husband—that he might have done things that he should have been ashamed of. Do you know what that might be?"

Ellen, so droopy and lifeless until now, sat bolt upright. "What? Where did you hear that? From Lacy?"

"It doesn't matter," Gage said. "Do you have any idea why Wade might feel—"

"Of course it was her," Ellen said, her eyes flaring wide, her pupils as dark as her nightgown. "She always hated him. She wants to ruin his reputation now that he's dead."

Gage had the reins now. The horse may have been running wild, but at least he had the reins. "Actually," he said, "Lacy said very nice things about your husband. She said she thought Stan was a very gentle soul, a very nice man. She said—"

"She hates him! She hates me! She wants Wade all to herself, so she's trying to … trying to drive a wedge between us."

"Tell me what Wade was talking about."

"It's a lie!"

There was a loud knock at the door. They both whirled in that direction.

"Mrs. Carson!" Roku called, from out in the hall. "Is everything all right? Do you need help? The door, it is locked."

"Ignore him," Gage said. "Wade said whatever Stan did would catch up with him eventually. What was he talking about? If you want to find him, you need to tell me."

"No, no, no. It has nothing—nothing to do with—"

"What does?"

She blinked. She'd curled herself into a ball on the couch, leaning so far back that the cushion curled around her, her legs tucked underneath her. "What?" she said.

"You said it has nothing to do with this," Gage said. "Or that was what you were about to say."

"No."

"Yes, you were. So there *is* something. There's something, something you don't want—"

"No, no, no."

"—to talk about. Did he embezzle? Did he hire prostitutes? What horrible thing did he do, Ellen? I can see it in your eyes. If you care about your son's life, you need to tell me."

"How dare you! How dare you say that to me!"

Again, Roko banged on the door. "Mrs. Carson! Mrs. Carson, please!"

"What are you hiding?" Gage pressed.

She made as if to go to the door, but Gage leaned into the gap between them. "Stay where you are."

"You can't keep me here!"

"If I have to beat the truth out of you, I will! Do you understand me? Lacy and Wade are not going to die because you can't face the truth. So I ask you again: What are you hiding?"

"No! There's nothing! There's nothing—"

"Tell me."

"—nothing—nothing—"

"Tell me!" Gage bellowed.

She screamed as if she'd been shot, grabbing her gut and curling even tighter. She screamed so loudly, and for so long, that he didn't hear the banging on the door until she was done.

"Mrs. Carson!" Roko cried. "Mrs. Carson, please! Let me in! I—I am going to kick the door down. I am going to kick it! Just say! Just say you need me!"

"Roko!" she cried to him.

"Mrs. Carson!"

"Roko! Roko! "

The door boomed and rattled, dust raining from the ceiling. She tried to get up again, but Gage stood first and threw her back against the couch.

"You're going to tell me what it is," he said. "You're going to tell me right now."

"No," she moaned.

"Tell me!"

"No, no, no, he didn't do that, he wouldn't do that, wouldn't touch him like that, it's not true, it's not it's not it's not it's not ..."

"Touch him? What do you mean?"

"No! No! Don't say it!

"Are you saying Stan—"

"No!"

"—molested his son?"

She covered her ears like a toddler and screamed so much that her face turned red.

Behind them, the door burst open.

21

There it was. *Touch him like that.* The truth, the terrible secret, the awful thing that Wade Carson had said his father should be ashamed of—it was right there all along. It might even have been obvious if Gage hadn't been so blinded by his own fear to see it. Fear of what? Suicide. It had so consumed Gage, his unease with the very idea of it, that it had blocked him from seeing what might have sent Wade down such a dark path in the first place.

Stan Carson had molested his son.

This revelation so shook Gage that it was a moment before he registered the approaching footsteps. From the corner of his eye, he saw an approaching blur—dark skin, bared teeth, and a hand rising. It was almost too late.

And it would have been, if Gage had been facing a tougher, more experienced adversary. But Roko was no experienced adversary, it turned out. When Gage felt the effeminate hand seize him on the shoulder, he swung his left elbow low and fast.

There was nothing to the man. Hitting Roko's stomach felt like plowing through thin cardboard.

With an explosion of exhaled breath, Roko folded in half like a paper straw, then fell backward. He crashed onto the coffee table, smashing the back legs. Ellen went on with her blood-curdling, inhuman scream, so long and so loud that it might have made Gage's nose bleed if Roko hadn't done something to finally snap Ellen out of her hysteria.

He pulled a knife.

He lay flat on the broken coffee table, gasping for breath, blood dribbling from a cut on his forehead. Ellen stopped screaming and gasped. The knife was childishly small, with an ivory handle inlaid with writing that might have been Hindi, something too delicate for combat, more fit for a museum display, maybe, but the blade itself still gleamed as if plenty sharp. Roko had yanked it out of a sheath strapped to his right ankle, a sheath exposed because his pant leg was hiked up to his calf.

"You going to stab me, Roko?" Gage said.

"You—you hurt Mrs. Carson," he said through wheezing breaths, "I kill you."

"I'm thinking you're not quite the black belt in karate you made yourself out to be, are you? Puff up your résumé a little, did you?"

"Roko," Ellen pleaded, "don't. Please don't. It'll just make things worse."

"He hurt you."

"I'm fine. I'm really quite fine. I'm sorry. I'm s-s-s-orry …"

And she had been fine, for a few seconds there, before she was back to bawling even worse. Burrowing into the corner of the couch, she rolled onto her knees and clutched her legs, hunching her back like a beetle in a protective crouch. Gage tried talking to her, but he could barely hear his own voice. He wanted to know more. As ugly as it was, he wanted the details, because those details might help him find Wade and Lacy, but it was no use.

The pathetic sight must have sapped Roko of what little fight he had in him because he dropped his knife and, crying himself, crawled to her as if Gage wasn't even there. There were shouts in the hall. Gage saw an astonished maid in the open doorway, her face as white as her uniform, before she vanished.

Time to go. Gage had made it down two flights when he heard police sirens. When he reached the lobby, a cruiser flashing its red and blues screeched to a stop outside the lobby doors. It was an impressive response time—too impressive, considering the traffic, which meant someone must have called 9-1-1 earlier, maybe Roko.

The cop Gage had talked to at Wade's truck, the kid with the buzz cut, came charging around the front of the Ford Explorer, his hand on his holster like he expected a gunfight. The sun, bright on the glass, meant the cop wouldn't be able to see inside. Gage stepped into the alcove they used for the complimentary breakfast, leaning on his cane and pretending to eye the one remaining apple turnover, while the cop rushed to the desk. There was a hurried conversation, then the cop punched the button for the elevator, grew impatient, and plunged into the stairwell Gage had just come out of.

After he was gone, Gage nonchalantly strolled through the lobby and outside, which was not easy to do when his heart was louder in his ears than the ocean. Nobody stopped him. Nobody stopped him on the way back to his van either, nor when he joined the steady throng of traffic on Highway 101.

———

Two AGONIZING miles and twenty frustrating minutes later, as Gage finally skidded to a stop in front of Books and Oddities, his phone rang. The caller ID read "BBPD Trunk," so it could technically have been anyone at the police station, but he had a pretty good idea who it was. As he steeled himself for the call, a cloud of gravel dust wafted over the boardwalk and the glowing green OPEN sign.

"What the *hell* did you do, Garrison?"

Wincing, Gage held the phone away from his ear. "Well, hello to you too, Jo," he said. "I think I might have permanent hearing damage from—"

"Will you shut the fuck up, you moron. I want to know what happened at the Inn, and I want to know right now. Otherwise I'm going to throw your sorry ass in jail, you hear me?"

He did. He definitely heard her. No perfectly timed wisecrack was going to get him out of this one. "Things might have gotten a little out of hand," he admitted.

"Out of hand? *Really?*"

"Well—"

"A fight in the penthouse suite at the Inn? That's your idea of out of hand? "

Gage swallowed. "I think I can make a case that it was self-defense."

"Oh, for attacking an old woman?"

"If she said I attacked her, she's lying. I didn't attack her —at least physically."

"What do you mean, physically?"

"I'm just saying, the conversation may have gotten heated. There may have been yelling. Mean words? Sure. But there were no physical blows until her little chauffeur tried to bum rush me."

"Mean words? What is this, kindergarten? What the hell did you say to her?"

"Are you going to arrest me?"

"I might if you don't tell me everything that happened right now! *Talk!*"

So he talked. With Alex ogling him from the Books and Oddities window, Gage told her what had gone down at the Inn in exacting detail. A gray-haired woman came out of Alex's store carrying a shopping bag full of paperbacks. When he was finished, Jo was silent. Across the parking lot, a steady line of cars and all their rumbling engines inched along Highway 101, but in his van it was so quiet he could hear Jo breathing.

"Mrs. Carson confirmed this?" Jo asked. "She actually said that her husband sexually abused Wade?"

"Well, she didn't use those specific words, but yeah. When I asked her, her reaction said it all, Jo."

"Don't call me Jo."

"But you just called me Garrison."

"I don't care. Don't call me Jo. And you think that's what drove Stan Carson to ... do what he did?"

The hitch in the middle of her last sentence was unmistakable. Knowing what he knew now about her father, Gage was not surprised that she, like Gage, had an aversion to the word *suicide*. "I think so, yeah. But the question is why now?"

The silence on the other end was long enough that Gage almost spoke again, and when she did speak, her voice sounded rougher, as if she was having to force out the words.

"Trying to ... understand somebody like that," she said, "somebody in that state of mind ... It's a ... Well, it can drive you crazy. It doesn't always make sense."

Gage hadn't been on the phone long, but the cell phone already felt warm against this ear. He knew he should ask her about her father, about Terminal Five, and about what was really going on between her and Tag Macklin, but he was afraid to go there. He was afraid of what he might learn. He knew he should ask her just what the hell she'd been doing with that gun, but he was afraid of what she might say. "Jo, about what happened yesterday at Secret Beach ..."

"I already told you, that's my personal business. It has nothing to do with the Carsons."

"I'm not talking about that. I'm talking about what happened between us."

"*Nothing* happened between us."

"But it did, Jo."

"I told you not to call me Jo."

The words may have been similar to what she'd said a moment ago, but her tone was softer, the pitch higher. He struggled with what to say next. There seemed no way forward.

"You know," she said.

"Yes?"

"You can—you can take back what you said. Emotions were running high. People—people can say things."

"I don't want to take it back."

"But you can."

"I meant it, Jo."

"But why?"

"I don't know. I just know I feel it."

"It's crazy."

"Maybe," he said. "But it's a good kind of crazy."

They sat in silence, her in her office at the police station, him in his Volkswagen outside the bookstore, alone in their separate worlds but somehow so close they could hear each other breathing. He could almost feel her breath against his cheek. The miracle of modern technology.

A woman carrying a toddler, a boy in overalls sucking his thumb, walked into the bookstore. Gage watched Alex greet them and point in the direction of the children's section, then all of them disappeared from view.

"Jo?" Gage said.

"I have to go," she said.

"You can trust me," he said. "I won't hurt you."

"Nobody can promise that, Garrison."

Then she clicked off.

———

WHEN GAGE WANDERED in a daze into Books and Oddities, Alex was still in the back helping the mother and her son. The row upon row of pine bookshelves under the buzzing fluorescent lights, rich with the scents of stained wood and old books, usually brought Gage some comfort, acting like a ship's ballast when Gage's life got most turbulent, but it didn't do so today. He felt lost. He felt alone. He felt desperate to find Lacy and Wade but more unsure than ever of how to go about it.

After Alex returned to the front, Gage caught him up on the new events, talking in a hushed tone because there were plenty of customers in the store. He noted, while he was talking, that Alex also hadn't shaved today; his heavy jowls, with his darker complexion, were pebbled with sprouts like grass on a newly planted lawn.

"Oh my," Alex said, settling onto the stool behind the counter. He took off his glasses and rubbed the bridge of his nose. "That's terrible. I guess that explains why he turned to drugs, huh?"

"Maybe, yeah."

"You look like crap, by the way. Have you slept at all?"

Gage shrugged. "A little. You don't look so hot either, my friend."

"Yeah, I didn't sleep much either. Gave up after a couple hours and got on my laptop to see if I could dig up anything else on Wade Carson that might be of use."

"Find anything?"

"Not really," Alex said, "though there was a short story he published in an online journal about a father and son who have a long drawn-out argument about burnt toast."

"Toast?"

Alex stroked his mustache, something he rarely did because he said he didn't want to look like a B-movie villain, but he must have been too tired to catch himself. "Yeah. I think it was supposed to be a metaphor for their relationship. After what you just told me, it puts it in a whole new light."

"Maybe the burnt toast didn't represent anything," Gage said. "Maybe it was just toast."

"Maybe, but I tell you something. The writing wasn't bad, Garrison. The kid does have some talent. But it's like … like he's hiding, you know. It's like he has a lot to say, but he's been afraid to say it. It kind of makes sense now, doesn't it?"

The woman with the toddler showed up at the front counter, forcing them to break off the conversation until Alex had rung up their sale—a couple books in the Lyle the Crocodile series. When they were gone, Alex asked him the question Gage had been asking himself ever since he walked out of the Inn at Sapphire Head.

"So what are you going to do now?"

"I have no idea," Gage said. "Some brilliant private investigator I am, huh?"

"Did somebody call you brilliant?"

"I'm open to suggestions is all I'm saying. I know that's shocking to you."

"Oh, you're always open to suggestions," Alex said. "You just never listen to them."

"Will you cut it out? I really need your help. If it's just a coincidence that Wade came to Barnacle Bluffs to kill himself, then why is Lacy missing? Did he grab her? Is he planning a murder suicide? I just don't buy it."

"Shh. Keep your voice down. There's kids in the store."

"Sorry. But you see my point? Coming all the way up here to do ...*that*, well, it would be a weird way to go about it."

"This whole thing is weird, Garrison. He's not in his right mind."

"But it's not weird in the right way. It doesn't feel random that he's here."

"You're talking about Tag and Jo."

"I guess so, yeah."

There was a stack of paperbacks on the counter. Alex picked one up, jotted a price in pencil on the first page, then set the book next to the stack. "Have you talked to her about any of this?"

"I can't."

"What do you mean, you can't?"

Gage had meant to simply say no, and now he felt defenseless against the questions his answer had raised. "I just mean, it's hard to go there right now."

"Because?"

"I'm not going to get into it, Alex."

"Because of what happened between you two at Secret Beach?"

"What did I just say?"

"So something *did* happen. I knew it."

"Alex—"

"Garrison, two people's lives might be at stake. If she's mixed up in something, or even if she knows something—"

"I know. I just ... can't. Not yet. And if she's *not* mixed up in this, and I push her too hard, then..."

"Then what?"

Gage didn't answer. Alex, giving him the kind of disapproving look he'd probably given his daughters when they were little, leaned forward on the stool and propped his elbows on his knees. The pens, pencils, and other paraphernalia bulging from his front pocket started to slide out the front, and he slapped his free hand over them.

"Good catch," Gage said. "That was a close call."

"Don't change the subject. You were about to tell me what's going on with you and our esteemed chief of police."

"I was going to do no such thing."

"Garrison, if you're not going to talk to Jo, then what else are you going to do? Just drive around aimlessly looking for them again?"

"That would be a waste of time, especially with this traffic. No, I need more information. Did I tell you that Tag Macklin keeps asking me if I want to work as a team? Why do you think that is?"

Alex chuckled. "Because he's more of a team player than you?"

"Maybe. Or maybe he's just trying to keep a close eye on me."

"Why?"

"I don't know, but he's the connecting piece, isn't he? He's the one that connects Wade, Stan Carson, Jo, and all that Seattle business. Yeah, I don't know that there really *is* a connection, but if there is, he's the hub of the wheel."

"Whether you believe his story or not," Alex said, "he'd be a lot tougher to rattle than Ellen Carson. A lot more dangerous too."

"That is also true."

"But that's not going to stop you?"

"Of course not."

"So what are you going to do, just ring him up and ask he if wants to go to coffee?"

"It's an idea," Gage said, then sat up so fast in the swivel chair that he banged his knees against the computer desk. "But maybe there's a better one. He told me he's staying at the Sea Witch. Maybe I just park myself outside and see what happens. Look, this guy is dirty. I can feel it in my bones, Alex. I don't know how it connects to Lacy and Wade, but if somebody's dirty, and there's dirty business happening around them, then it's a good bet they're involved."

Alex sighed. "I'm not sure that pearl of wisdom is something you'd find in a fortune cookie, but my own years in the FBI proved that's usually right. You know, your van is so distinctive that Tag will recognize it even if you ... oh, right. You'll be borrowing my Sienna again. Silly me."

"I accept your generous offer," Gage said.

<hr>

IT WAS a quarter to two in the afternoon when Gage left Books and Oddities in Alex's Toyota Sienna. It was a quarter to three when he finally made it to the Motel 6 across the street from the Sea Witch, his own sanity barely intact.

Anyone who had lived in Barnacle Bluffs for even a few years would have seen plenty of bad traffic, but this was something else altogether. Gage heard on the radio—99.3 FM, the BB Buzz, their local station—that this was the third day in a row Portland had crested 110 Fahrenheit, a record. The week before that, it hadn't dropped below 100. Here it was a gorgeous seventy-two degrees. That may have been considered room temperature in most of the world, but in Barnacle Bluffs, it seldom got hotter.

For once, even the fog favored the tourists. It was almost a given that all that heat in the valley would suck in the cool air off the ocean, and when the two collided, the air in Barnacle Bluffs would get so thick that even the cotton candy looked gray. Not today, though. Today the sun glared off all those bumpers and rear windows, so intense that even the sunglasses Gage borrowed from Alex's glove box couldn't keep him from squinting.

The Motel 6 parking lot was full, but Gage lucked out when a family of four, dressed in flip-flops and carrying beach blankets, piled into a Chevy Tahoe with Idaho plates and left to join the highway madness. Tag Macklin's black Mustang, parked directly across the highway in the Sea Witch's parking lot, was so distinctive that it took Gage only a second to spot it. Now all he had to do was wait.

The van faced the Motel 6 and all its garish orange doors, not the highway, so he had to use his rearview mirror to monitor the Sea Witch, but that was preferred anyway. Less a chance that Macklin would recognize him.

The Sea Witch was a rectangular, five-story structure with wood shake siding. All the doors were exposed to the elements except for the covered walkways that ran the whole length of the building, so it should be easy enough to spot Macklin if he came and went from any of the doors.

Gage's eyelids felt like they were coated with paint. His empty stomach, responding to the scent of deep-fried halibut from Freddy's Fish and Chips next door, grumbled loudly enough to be mistaken for an oncoming storm, and his nerves, already frayed from the monsoon of morons overwhelming their city, couldn't take one more honking horn on the highway, slamming door in the parking lot, or high-pitched screech of a kid piling into a minivan, so it took every ounce of will that Gage had left to sit there *another* half hour before his resolve began to wane.

In his line of work, Gage had been on plenty of stakeouts, but he'd never liked them. He didn't like being passive.

He preferred to force the issue. He was mulling whether this whole thing was a waste of time when the passenger door opened and Tag Macklin climbed in the van.

"If you're waiting to talk to me," he said, "I thought I'd just save you the trouble."

22

———————

Twitchy as Gage was in his sleep-deprived state of mind, it was probably good he hadn't had time to reach for the Beretta he currently had stowed under his seat. It wasn't just being surprised that might have prompted him to do something rash. It was also the condescending grin on Tag Macklin's face.

"Don't be too hard on yourself," Macklin said, his breath reeking of booze. "Even the best PIs can get sloppy now and then. And I'm a sneaky guy."

For once, he wasn't wearing his sunglasses, and Gage could see that Macklin's eyes were droopy and bloodshot. He wore his black tracksuit as usual, but the front was zipped down nearly to his naval, revealing a slick, muscular chest. When Gage didn't say anything, Macklin chuckled.

"No smart aleck remark this time?" he said.

"I'm just here to pick up a friend of Alex's from the Motel 6."

"Aw, come on, man, don't insult my intelligence. And after I went to all the trouble to climb off my balcony in the back just so you wouldn't spot me."

"So Ellen Carson's okay with you hitting the margaritas instead of looking for her son?"

Macklin laughed. "It was Coors beer, actually. But trust me, I've been hitting the phones hard, calling all over town, seeing if anybody's seen the kid." He gestured toward the endless line of slow-moving cars on the highway. "There's no reason to waste our time stuck in that madness, is there? So why don't you just be straight with me for once, and tell me what the hell you think you're going to accomplish staking out my hotel?"

"I'll give you a straight question, how's that? All those years you were working for Stan Carson, did you know what kind of man he was?"

Macklin shook his head. "You're still acting like a monkey on roller skates, man. You're making this *way* too hard. Are you asking did I know that Daddy Warbucks might have gotten a little too touchy feely with his son when Wade was growing up? That's what you're getting at, right?"

"How did you find out?"

Macklin shrugged. "Wade told me the first night I met him."

"He told you that he was molested?"

"Well, he didn't use that word. But he made it pretty clear that's what happened."

"Why?"

"What do you mean, *why?* You want me to get inside the mind of a sick fuck like Stan Carson?"

"That's a hell of a way to talk about your former employer," Gage said, "but I was actually asking why Wade would tell you that when you'd only just met."

"He told me lots of stuff," Macklin said. "And let's get one thing straight. I moved to Boise *because* of Wade, all right? I worked for Stan Carson *because* of Wade."

"I'm not following."

"What's not to follow? It pissed me off something fierce, that a guy would do that to a kid—to his own son, no less, and I went to Boise to see if I could fix the situation."

"How?"

"Turn Stan in, I guess. That's what I told myself, but I really wanted to show Stan Carson what it's like to be powerless against someone so much stronger than you. I was in a dark place myself, man. But Wade begged me not to do any of that." Macklin shrugged. "So I didn't. But I was there already, and, you know, I needed a fresh start."

"Why did Stan Carson hire you for so many other jobs?"

"Felt grateful. And I think he knew I knew. I let slip a couple comments. Couldn't help myself."

"So you were essentially blackmailing him?"

Macklin's easy-going-guy facade fell away, revealing the barely constrained animal underneath. "That's a pretty strong word. I wouldn't use that word."

"But that was it on the face, right?"

"Man, I know you're trying to push my buttons, but it was never about Stan Carson. It was about the kid, about Wade. I thought he was crazy, not turning his old man in for that shit, but I was worried it might break him if I did. Turns out I was right to worry. Look at Wade now."

"I still don't get why Wade told you," Gage said. "He wouldn't tell his own wife about any of that, but he'd tell a complete stranger?"

"You sure Lacy doesn't know?"

"I'm sure."

"If you say so. I think that girl might have secrets of her own, but whatever. Like I said, the night I found Wade, we bonded pretty quick 'cause we had things in common."

"Such as?"

"Such as we were both thinking of killing ourselves."

Gage didn't know what to say to this. Macklin stared at

Gage as if expecting a challenge, then looked to his left, past the parked cars at the traffic on the highway that had ground to a complete stop. Must have been another accident. It was inevitable, when traffic was this bad. There were just too many places along narrow and winding Highway 101 where it was tough to get a stopped vehicle off the road.

"Yeah, I said it," Macklin said. "I told you, I was in a dark place, man, and so was that kid. He couldn't get past what his father did. I was treated like a hero for what happened at Terminal Five, but I felt nothing but guilt. Dell Baldwin died and I lived. He was both a friend and a mentor, and I didn't know he was taking a cut of the action until it was too late to do anything about it. Call it survivor's guilt if you want, but it pretty much destroyed me."

"And that's why Wade opened up to you?"

Macklin looked at him again. "We both needed some-body to talk to. He just about OD'd, man. When I found him, he was naked on a dirty mattress in this shithole apart-ment in Renton. He was about to stick another needle in his arm. If he had, I think he'd be dead. And I was pretty close to OD'ing myself—in my own way."

"In your own way?"

"Yeah, I'm an addict too. Funny enough, my addiction never had anything to do with booze, drugs, or any of that shit. I didn't want to be numb. I wanted to *feel.* I wanted an outlet. I thought if I could channel all that anger, get it out of my system, it might help. It never did, though."

"Are you telling me that you *don't* wear that tracksuit to hide a bunch of needle marks?"

"Nope, but I do wear the tracksuit to cover the scars. They tend to make people nervous."

Macklin raised his right arm and used the point of his hook to pull back the sleeve. His arm was powerful and muscular, not like a body builder's arm, not shaped and sculpted as if were more fit for a photoshoot than a fistfight, but muscles lean and ropey, the veins laid on top like steel cables. Then there were the scars, so many scars, a tapestry of scars that left almost no skin untouched—scratches, gouges, and slices, a patchwork of white skin and pink skin, most of them faded and paled from distant healing.

"It's like this all over," Macklin said. "Worse on my arms and legs, course, because that's what's exposed the most. But I got scars like this everywhere."

"Is this some kind of self-harm thing? There's therapy for that, you know."

Macklin frowned. Taking his time, using his hook with an unnerving amount of precision, he reversed the procedure and rolled the sleeve back down. "My addiction is fighting, man. Not boxing. Not mixed martial arts or any of that shit that really doesn't hold up well in real-world situations. Nah. I went out into the world. I looked for people doing bad stuff, and I did bad stuff to them."

"Did you wear a cape and tights?"

"Look, man, I know you're trying to get under my skin, but I'm being honest with you, okay? I needed the fight the same way that Wade needed his meth. It was no different."

"What happened to the people you fought?"

"I never killed anyone, if that's what you're asking. This is what I was doing when Stan Carson hired me. This is the state of mind I was in when I found Wade in that shitty apartment. And I was getting more reckless because really I was trying to kill myself. Just like Wade. We just had different ways of going about it. When the fighting wasn't doing it for me anymore, I even tried to rejoin the force, in the hopes of getting on the bomb squad on account of my work with explosives in the army. What better way to go out than in a bang? But they wouldn't take me. I don't think it was just my hook either. I was just too far gone mentally at that point.

They didn't need a psych test to tell them that. They just had to look in my eyes."

"And this is what you told Wade?"

"More or less. After I got him back to my hotel room and got him cleaned up, I told him what I'd been doing to myself. I said it was seeing him in that shitty apartment that made me realize I was an addict too and that I was actually trying to kill myself. I just didn't know it until that moment. I actually thanked him. I think that's what got him to snap out of it enough for him to realize he had to make the exact same choice. But he had another reason to change."

"Lacy," Gage said.

"That's right. I may be suspicious of her, but it did give him extra motivation. See, we made a pact, the two of us. I swore I wouldn't go looking for fights, and he swore he wouldn't do drugs. So you see, I'm really here because of the kid. It tears me up, not being able to find him."

Gage gazed out the rearview mirror. The traffic had started inching along again, the sun beating down on the hood, the air hazy around their exhaust pipes. He wasn't sure how much of Macklin's story he believed, but it was just plausible enough to be true.

"Why don't you come in and have a drink with me?" Macklin asked.

Gage looked at him. "You're serious?"

"Sure, man. I think the Mariners are playing in a bit, my favorite team. We could kick back and watch the game until the traffic dies off, then both of us head out together to search for him."

"I'll pass, thanks."

"So you're just going to sit out here then?"

"Maybe. Maybe not. What really went down at Terminal Five?"

Macklin snorted. "This again. Did you talk to Jo about it

yet? No, I didn't think so. You know, since we're talking about addictions, Jo's kind of got one of her own."

"What are you talking about?"

"She puts up a hard front, but she's really kind of mushy deep down. When she's committed to somebody, she's all in, and I mean *all in,* and that's what scares her. Some people get so obsessed with the people they're with that they kind of lose themselves, you know? If you get my drift."

Gage didn't want to believe it, and when he spoke, he found his voice had gotten rough. "You're saying she was … helping Dell."

"I'm saying you have to ask her about it."

"Why didn't she end up in jail?"

"Maybe because I thought she'd suffered enough."

"Or she paid you off?"

"Man, you just won't let go of the idea that I'm dirty, will you? Ask her. Just ask her. It's her story to tell. But I'm saying this way she gets obsessed with people and kind of surrenders control of herself to them …Well, it's maybe why she's so scared of you too."

"I don't know what you're talking about."

"You know what I was obsessed with, before all the shit went down at Terminal Five? I was obsessed with my badge."

"Well, people can have weird fetishes," Gage said.

"I'm talking about the law. I used to believe there were good guys, bad guys, and the line between them was pretty clear. That's not how it is, and you know it too. All we got is our own personal code. Jo is like that too … except for people she loves. Then it all goes out the window."

"So you're saying she was mixed up with the cartel, just like her husband?"

"I'm saying you have to talk to Jo about it. You should go tonight, man."

"For somebody who claims he's being honest, you're still not saying an awful lot."

"I'm not holding back. It's just not my story. Look, all I'm saying is, Jo sees relationships with men the way I see fighting and the way Wade sees meth. It's an addiction that will ruin her life if she even lets herself try it one more time."

Gage had no answer to any of this. It might have been true. It might have been bullshit.

"So I take it you're not coming in?" Macklin said, finally.

"No."

"And you're just going to sit out here all night, twiddling your thumbs?"

"At least I have two thumbs to twiddle."

"You're a funny one, Gage."

"People tell me I should take my act on the road."

"Do they? I bet they do." Macklin slapped his knee with the side of his hook. "All right, man, but if you change your mind, the offer's there."

Macklin was reaching for the handle when it occurred to Gage there was one more coincidence about this whole situation that made him uncomfortable. "Do you know who Wade's dealer was in Seattle?" Gage asked. "Or how he was getting his meth?"

Macklin turned back to him. "You mean when I found him? No, I have no idea. Why?"

"It just seems interesting, Jo's husband involved in the meth trade, and Wade being hooked on meth. Both of them in Seattle at the same time. I know it's a bit of a stretch, since there are probably thousands of people hooked on meth in Seattle at any given time, but still."

"I don't think Dell would have known Wade from a hole in the wall, but maybe you should ask Jo."

"What about in San Diego?"

"How the hell would I know? I thought he was clean down there."

"Lacy told me she overheard him talking to someone on the phone last Monday. He was pretty upset."

There was the briefest pause, and the slightest twitch of eyelids, before Macklin responded. "Oh, that was probably me," he said.

"You?"

"Yeah. I figured with his dad committing suicide, you know, he'd go to a dark place, so I called him. I was trying to make sure he was okay."

"She said she heard arguing."

"I'm not sure I'd call it arguing. I was trying to calm him down."

"She said she heard him say 'I can't go through with this!' What was that about?"

"I don't remember him saying that."

"You're saying Lacy's lying?"

"I'm saying I don't remember him saying it. He said a lot of stuff. He was kind of ranting about how terrible his father was. Maybe he did. Yeah, maybe it was when we were talking about the funeral, he might have said something about how he didn't even want to go back. He couldn't go through with it."

Gage sat with this information a moment. "Why didn't you tell me this before?"

"Tell you what, that me and Wade talked on the phone? I told you, we talked all the time."

"Okay, but then why didn't Wade tell Lacy about you?

"Well, I guess that says more about their marriage than it says about me. Anything else, man? Or you want me to take a lie detector test?"

They stared at one another. Gage was absolutely certain that Macklin had made some kind of mistake, with this business of the phone call, but he couldn't say what the mistake was. After a tense moment, Macklin cracked another one of his trademark grins, then climbed out of the van.

"Hey, Tag," Gage said.

The big guy turned. In the sunlight, his hook gleamed like a sword.

"Have you heard that old Zen koan? What's the sound of one hand clapping? I was wondering if you could demonstrate for me."

With a snort, Macklin slammed the door and walked away.

23

Watching Tag Macklin cross Highway 101 at the streetlight down the road, Gage debated his next move.

He adjusted his rearview mirror to keep Macklin in view. The sun flickered off the hoods and windshields of the passing cars. The ocean breeze jetting through his cracked-open window was pleasantly cool, but it was not strong enough to keep the van from baking him like a crockpot. Sweat greased his neck and stuck his shirt to his back. His eyelids felt like they were coated in glue. It still smelled like beer in the car.

Macklin was lying. Gage didn't know for what purpose, but he could tell Macklin had been surprised when Gage brought up that phone call to Wade last Monday. But then why had he agreed that it was him on the phone in the first place? Maybe because he knew that the cell phone records might eventually prove it was him anyway?

But would Wade really not tell Lacy about this so-called special relationship? All addicts lied, of course. It was a truism as rock solid as the law of gravity. But why would

Wade not tell Lacy about Macklin? It was one thing not to mention Macklin's key role in Wade's long night of the soul, as a way to puff himself up in Lacy's eyes and make it look like he'd pulled himself from the edge of the abyss all on his own, the hero of his own story, but not telling her about repeated phone calls over the years?

I can't go through with this.

What if he was talking about something other than the funeral? If so, what would that be, and why would Macklin lie about it? Gage drummed his fingers on the steering wheel and watched Macklin, now on the exposed walkway outside the Sea Witch, approach his door. He turned and gave Gage an exaggerated wave, then fished a key card out of his pocket and slipped into the room.

Gage was reluctant to leave, but with his stakeout blown, he knew there was little point in it. The van's dashboard clock read 3:28 p.m. Maybe he should head back to Books and Oddities to talk things over with Alex and scan some of the side streets for his missing couple on the way? Or he could talk to Jo and try to get the real truth out of her? Rattle Ellen Carson some more?

There were a lot of options, and all of them were better than sitting here like a patsy in whatever game Macklin was playing. He started the van and made his way through the adjoining parking lights to the stoplight.

Yet as he passed the Sea Witch on his way south, inching along with the rest of the traffic, Macklin's curtains opened.

The big man stepped into view, his hook gleaming, a can of beer in his hand. He was smiling. The way the sun fell on the window, his teeth glowed as if phosphorescent. He even hoisted up his can in a parting wave.

The beer. The open curtains. Look, Macklin seemed to be saying, I have nothing to hide. I'm just going to be hanging out here watching baseball, just like I said.

And that was exactly why, at a stoplight three blocks later, Gage turned into the cluster of neighborhoods east of Highway 101.

Macklin was trying too hard.

Gage fancied himself a rational man, but he'd learned over the years to trust his intuition when his reason failed him. Where did this intuition come from? He could not say. He was not a religious man, but he did believe that there was a vast intelligence beyond his conscious grasp, connected to others and more in tune with the universe in ways that could not be explained, and that this intelligence could sometimes lead him to a deeper truth even if he could not articulate why. He just had to trust it.

Macklin might have surprised him earlier, but Gage could play that game too.

Now that he knew which room Macklin was in, Gage knew exactly where he could place himself without risking a repeat performance of what had just happened. A window seat at Dagen Dau's, the Chinese restaurant in a cramped stucco strip mall that also included a barber, an accountant, and a new age crystal shop, would afford him an excellent view of Macklin's room. It also had a second entrance from the gravel parking lot in the back, a fact that very few people knew.

Ten minutes later, after navigating through the neighborhoods so he stayed out of sight of the Sea Witch, Gage stepped through that very back door into a dimly lit room awash with red—red tablecloths, red vinyl seats, and red carpet. Paper lanterns hung from the drop ceiling. At this hour in the afternoon, only a handful of tables were occupied, so Gage had no problem convincing the perpetually smiling Mrs. Dau to give him a window booth.

Across the street, Macklin's curtains were still open. The black Mustang was still parked out front. Mrs. Dau brought him tea, steam smelling of jasmine rising out of the ceramic teapot. He ordered orange chicken and a side of egg rolls and watched Macklin's door and window while he ate. He saw Macklin pass by once, which at least reassured Gage that the guy hadn't slipped out his balcony again, but otherwise nothing interesting happened.

When Mrs. Dau collected his plate, he asked if it was all right if he waited here for a while since it wasn't too busy. Of course she agreed. He knew she would have agreed even if it *were* busy. Then she brought him an extra side of gyoza, no charge. Gage knew better than to insist on paying, but he made sure to leave a hefty tip when he paid his bill.

Then he waited. He waited some more. He received two calls—one, from Alex, just checking in, and two, from Ellen Carson, which he ignored. She left a message, demanding an apology for his behavior and further demanding that he call immediately if he discovered Wade's whereabouts. So much for the fragile flower. She sounded like her old cool self.

It was five o'clock by this time, with the dinner crowd trickling in, first a couple tables, then a couple more. It was not filled, Dau's almost never was, but it was busy enough that Gage felt uncomfortable taking one of their prime tables. The sun finally dipped into his view. The insane traffic on Highway 101 soon became slightly less insane, and by six o'clock it was still busy but not so bad that he wouldn't be able to get across town in a reasonable amount of time. That meant Macklin would be able to do the same, and if he was half the private investigator he boasted to be, he'd be out there looking for Wade in short order.

He didn't, though. Another half hour passed. When Gage felt he'd stretched the Dau's hospitality as far as he could, he exited through the same back door and walked to the corner of the building, near a stack of wooden pallets and a dumpster that smelled of sweet and sour sauce. Using the dumper as a shield, he was able to peer over the top at Macklin's room. The Mustang still hadn't gone anywhere.

The breeze that jetted between the building and the dumpster smelled more of car exhaust than the ocean. What now? Gage knew he was running the risk of drawing too much attention, but the longer Macklin remained in his room, the more Gage grew suspicious. The sun dropped still lower, a yellow ball just above the Sea Witch's roof, forcing Gage to raise his hand and squint into the glare.

Finally, his patience was rewarded.

Macklin, dressed in his usual Jersey Shore cosplay outfit, emerged from his room with a car fob in hand. He unlocked the Mustang from the landing, giving Gage just enough time to hustle to Alex's van and park it in virtually the same spot where he'd been standing a moment ago. The black Mustang was pulling out of its spot.

A minute later, Macklin was heading south with the mongrel hordes, and Gage wasn't far behind, trying to stay far enough back without running the risk of Macklin turning off without being seen. On the right, the sun threw daggers into his eyes.

As they made their way south, Macklin showed no sign he knew Gage was there. They passed the strip that contained Thackleforth Candies, the open sign still aglow on a busy Saturday night; the second floor was dark. He saw no sign of Wade or Lacy. They passed Arrow Outlet Mall, bustling with shoppers. When they closed in on the Starfish Motel, Gage expected to see the black Mustang turn right, but Macklin surprised him by continuing south on Highway 101.

Where now? To see Ellen Carson maybe? The answer came a mile later when Macklin turned west, into the hilly neighborhood north of the Inn at Sapphire Head. It felt like a ball of ice slid into Gage's stomach. Despite the risk, he made the same turn, taking his time up as he climbed the hill, slowing as he turned onto Alva. The black Mustang was parked in front of her garage. So was the white Malibu. Macklin was nowhere to be seen.

Gage puttered past, scanning the house. The windows on this side all had their shades drawn. He parked, five houses past, in front of a house with a FOR SALE sign. Only a few thread-like clouds hung in the sky, but the quality of light had already begun to change, growing duskier, grayer. Sunset may have been hours away, but the promise of it was already here.

Stay or go? Skulk around the house like a peeping Tom, or burst inside like a jealous husband, full of rage and righteousness? He wanted to go on believing that Jo Roland was the strong, beautiful, and incorruptible woman he'd fallen for, incomprehensible as that feeling still was to him, but he had to know the truth. He had to find Lacy and Wade, alive or dead, and all of his instincts told him he could only find out the truth by walking through Jo's door.

He took off his leather jacket long enough to slip on his side holster, checking his Beretta to make sure the magazine was fully loaded. It was. He hoped to God he didn't have to use it, but he didn't know what the hell he was going to find. Maybe Lacy and Wade were even locked in the house somewhere, crazy as that idea was.

He got out and headed for Jo's house, leaving his cane, barely feeling his bad knee with all the adrenaline pumping through his body. The little bit of wind Gage had felt earlier was gone, the ocean playing its usual symphony, and the neighborhood was as quiet as an enraptured audience. His heart wasn't playing a symphony. It was more like ragtime.

He tried the knob. Locked. He debated for a second, then knocked. He heard muffled voices, then footsteps. When the door opened, Tag Macklin stood there with his usual grin, sans sunglasses, but his tracksuit showing no sign that Gage had interrupted the occupants mid-tryst. He was almost ashamed to feel relief at that. There were bigger things to worry about here.

But he soon realized he'd caught them in the middle of *something*, whatever it was. When Jo peered around Macklin's broad shoulder—casually dressed in white blouse and blue jeans but no disheveling on her part either—she flushed bright red.

"Garrison!" she said.

"Can I come in?"

Rather than wait for an answer, he pushed his way past them into the house. Macklin did not seem concerned at all; he actually gestured flamboyantly with his hook, like a maître d' at a pirate-themed restaurant directing him to his table. The curtains were wide open, and the low sun gave everything a golden glow. He saw no Wade or Lacy on the couch or anywhere else. The sliding glass door was cracked open, but Gage could barely hear the ocean over his heart pounding in his ears.

"What are you doing here?" Jo said.

As he turned back to them, away from the sun, it took his eyes a moment to adjust. He could only see them in silhouette, but he saw Jo glance to her left.

There, in the middle of the dining room table, was the same steel box he'd seen at Secret Beach. The lid was open, but all the plastic bags appeared to be inside. She'd cleaned most of the sand off the box, but some remained, pebbling the rusty metal surface and the table around it.

"What's in the box, Jo?" he asked.

Before she had a chance to answer, Macklin chuckled. "You gonna shoot somebody, Gage?"

"What?

"You're packing. I can tell."

Jo raised her eyebrows. "Garrison? What do you think's happening here?"

"I don't know, Jo, why don't you tell me?"

"This has nothing to do with you."

"What about the Carsons?"

"It has nothing to do with them either. It's …" She shook her head. The way she was hugging her torso, she looked like a child, especially standing in front of Macklin. "Garrison, you're just making things worse—as usual. Just go."

"Not until I see what's in that box."

"You already saw what was in the box. You saw it on the beach."

"Did I?"

"Yes!"

Macklin raised his arms in what was probably meant to be a placating gesture, but once again that hook came off as vaguely threatening. The way the tip caught the sunlight, it was imbued with a vivid orange glow, as if it had just come out of a forge. "Look," he said, "I'll step out on the deck and give you some privacy. You obviously have stuff to work out."

"That's not necessary," Jo said.

"Oh, I disagree," Gage said. "I think it's absolutely necessary."

"Jo," Macklin said, "just show him what's in it. He won't stop until you do. And I'm not going anywhere, okay, man? I'll be right outside until you're satisfied this situation isn't what you think it is."

She shook her head. With an infuriating chuckle, Macklin slipped past them both. As the glass door slid open, the ocean's roar grew louder before Macklin closed it behind him. Jo, staring at the floor, said nothing.

Until now, Gage had been lost in his own jumbled emotions, his heart tumbling about like a child's kite in a hurricane, but then, for a fleeting moment, he was in the eye of the storm. It was calm. He was calm. He still didn't know what was going on, but he felt a sense of peace that had been eluding him for days, and that sense of peace gave him the clarity to make a decision he should have made days ago.

"No matter what's in that box," he said, "I'm not calling the cops, if that's what you're worried about. I want you to know that. I meant what I said before, Jo. You're right that nobody can promise they won't hurt somebody else. But I can promise you I'll never hurt you on purpose."

She looked at him, saying nothing. It may have only been a few seconds, but it was long enough for the quality of the light to change, some of the harshness of the late afternoon sun giving way to the promise of dusk—the hard edges, her jawline, the lid of the metal box, softening, everything turning more diffuse. It happened so fast that it must have just been a cloud darting in front of the sun, but it didn't feel like that to Gage. It felt like they were standing there while the Earth turned on its axis.

He hoped she might say something equally heartfelt, something about trust or love or the strange ways of the human heart, but instead she walked mutely to the box. She peered down into the plastic bags and sighed. When she looked at him again, her eyes, those magnificent gray eyes, which had always made him think of slate or steel, were more like the shifting vapors of smoke and steam—something, when you reached for it, that was ungraspable.

"Go ahead," she said.

He rifled through the bags in the box. He didn't know what he expected to find—wads of cash maybe, or keys to a safety deposit box—but he didn't see anything so obviously incriminating. What he saw instead were all the things she'd spread on the beach: the old cell phone in the green case, the John D. MacDonald paperback, the Swiss army knife, the Mariner's baseball cap, lots of other things. Almost everything was wrapped in individual plastic bags. Gage rifled through it. At the bottom was the foxed and faded photo in the silver frame, the one that pictured an army uniform.

"It's just the mementos?" he said.

"Just," she said.

"The photo is of your father, isn't it?"

"Yes. "

"I'm sorry, Jo. I'm really sorry that … you lost him like that."

She nodded, not looking at him, her eyes glossed with a wet sheen. When she spoke, her voice was rough. "The gun is Dad's too. I know, when you saw me on the beach, you must have thought I was going to … But I wasn't. I was just trying to … I don't know. Connect with him. Try to understand … what he did. I know it's strange."

"It's not so strange," Gage said.

"It was just Dad's stuff at first. I buried it in the woods above Secret Beach after his funeral. Then I came back and put Dell's things in there too. I … should have thrown all of Dell's things away, but I couldn't. I couldn't do it. What's wrong with me?"

"Nothing," Gage said.

"He didn't even love me."

"I'm sure that's not true."

"I *know* it's true. At least at the end. Otherwise …"

"Otherwise what?"

She didn't answer.

"Jo, just tell me. If it will help me understand what's going on here, just tell me."

She shrugged. "I found a letter, okay? I found a letter he was writing to some woman. It was hidden in his desk. He told her how much he loved her. He told her it wouldn't be long and they could run away together. He said … He said he never loved *me*. He said it right there, in black and white."

"Who was it?"

"I never found out. There was no name. It was typed and printed—a single sheet, with crease lines like it had been folded in quarters. No, I guess it was folded in *eighths*, like it had been in his wallet, you know? Otherwise why fold it so small? That's why I was following him that night, okay? It wasn't because I knew he was a dirty cop. I really didn't know about any of that. I was following him because I thought he was meeting her."

"And Tag?"

"I called him when I got to the wharf. I asked him if he knew who this other woman was. Tag didn't know either. He begged me to stay put, but I followed Dell on foot to Terminal Five. I was still so out of my mind that it didn't even occur to me that something else was going on. I confronted him. Then the cartel guys showed up, and everybody started shooting."

"And that's when Tag showed up?"

"Yeah. Thank God, otherwise I would have been toast. We managed to take out the cartel guys, but then Dell … Well, he was going to kill himself."

"He what?"

"He had his gun pointed under his chin. He was crying. He said his life was over. He said he'd be going to prison, so he might as well die. Tag begged him to stop. Me? I froze. I swore that I'd never stand by while somebody … while somebody did what my dad did, not if I could do something, and I froze. And that's when Tag made a play for Dell's gun."

"And that was how he lost his hand," Gage said.

"Yes. They were wrestling for control of it, and Dell shot him. I'm not even sure he meant to pull the trigger."

"And then …?"

"After Dell shot Tag, Dell kind of snapped. Tag was on the ground screaming, blood everywhere, pressing his mangled hand against his stomach. Dell looked at me and said this was all my fault. He pointed his gun at me, and that's when I shot him. I didn't want to. It was more reflex than anything else. I froze when my husband was going to kill himself, but I had no problem shooting him between the eyes. I don't think I'll ever get over that. Never."

"Why wasn't all this in the paper?"

"Come on, Garrison. How would all that look? The other woman? Tag trying to stop Dell from killing himself? It was too complicated. It raised too many questions. Tag was the one who said we should tell everyone that he was just trying to protect me instead of stopping Dell from committing suicide. He was amazing. He was in agony, as we waited for that ambulance, but he was thinking more clearly than me."

"I wish you would have told me this sooner."

"It wasn't any of your business."

"I know, but ..."

"And the crazy thing is, even after everything Dell had done, I still couldn't let him go. I still loved him. That's how ... broken I was. How broken I *am*."

"You're not broken, okay? You may be hurting, but you're not broken."

She swallowed. "When Tag showed up in town to look for Wade Carson, we talked. We were two cops who served together and went through something traumatic, you know? That's all it is. That's all it ever was."

"Okay."

"But it kind of shook me up, when I saw him on the bluff. It was like a ghost from my past."

"And that's why you took off so abruptly? When you, Lacy, and I were all on the beach near Wade's truck?"

"Yeah. After he swung by the office, Tag and I agreed to meet at my place. That night you saw us, I was telling him about the trunk, how crazy I was to keep all that crap. Tag convinced me that if I got rid of Dell's things, it might help me get closure, so I went down to get it. We were just about to go through it when you came in."

"But he came by last night. He told me."

"He did. I wasn't ready to let it go yet. I told him about you following me down there. I told him to come by in a day and we'd go through it together. So he did."

"And you felt like you had to run down there right away? With Wade Carson missing?"

"Tag thought it might help him get some closure too. I owe him that much. I owe him a lot more, actually. He lost his hand because of me."

"Well, it sounds more complicated than that."

"Not to me."

"But, Jo, Macklin hasn't been on the level. He's hiding something, and it has something to do with Wade."

She looked at the sliding glass door, where Tag was still standing on the deck, his back turned to them, before looking down at the open box. "I don't know what to tell you. Tag went through hell. I'm not one to judge him. I … I just want to try to put this behind me, Garrison. It's time. It's finally time. I knew it was time when you …"

"When I what?"

"Nothing."

"Jo, look at me."

"You really should go, Garrison. It would be better if you go. You've got Wade and Lacy to look for, and you shouldn't be wasting any more time with me."

"It's not a waste. Just tell me what you were going to say. You knew it was time to move on, when?"

"Well … when you asked me out."

"When I asked you out?"

"Yes."

"But you said no."

She finally looked up at him. There was something fragile there, something so exposed and vulnerable that whatever words were forming in his mind were forgotten. Whatever he could say, it would not suffice. It would not do. Somehow he'd moved so close that he could see all the tiny lines in her lips. She swallowed.

"Garrison," she said.

Before she got a chance to say more, Macklin shouted with such force that it rattled the sliding glass doors.

"Wade! Don't do it!"

24

I t may have been conventional wisdom that time slowed down in crisis situations, but that had never been Gage's experience. He used to think that because it had the appearance of being true, but then he realized it was only true in retrospect. Long after the emergency had passed, when the brain had time to interpret, decipher, and catalog every second in excruciating detail, as a way of processing, as a way of coping—only then did it *seem* like time slowed down.

In the actual moment, when there was only time for action and reaction, time felt like it was speeding up.

"Wade! Don't do it!"

At Macklin's shout, Gage whirled around to see what was happening, but Jo was even faster. One moment she was standing over the metal box, and the next she'd already sprinted halfway to the sliding glass door. How she'd gotten around him so fast, with both him and the table in her way, was impossible to know, but right away it put Gage at a serious disadvantage. He was trailing behind her, way behind her.

When she threw open the door, it cracked the glass.

Macklin, his hook-arm raised to block the sun, was pointing down at the beach with his right hand. Jo only paused there long enough to recognize whatever was down there before she was leaping over the wooden rail onto a patch of grass beneath her deck.

By the time Gage got to the deck—later, he would doubt whether even a second had passed—Jo was already darting through the gap in the blackberry bushes she shared with her neighbor along the mossy path that led to the wooden stair-case and finally down to the beach. It wasn't even like she was running. It was like she was being pulled by some gravitational force.

The ocean breeze. The salty air. The cry of seagulls in the distance. Gage took all this in as he squinted into the sunlight and saw what Macklin was pointing at down on the beach: Wade Carson stood at the edge of the surf with a gun pointed at his head.

Backlit, Wade was visible as a silhouette with a golden glow, but who else would be down there with a gun pointed at his head? Wade's identity was confirmed a few seconds later when Gage, following Jo but taking the steps off the deck to the left, made it far enough along the path through the blackberry bushes that he could see over the top. Both the angle and the light were different enough that he could make out more details.

The black pullover hat above a pale face. The hooded green sweatshirt with the yellow tie strings. The white tennis shoes caked with sand. The Smith & Wesson snub-nosed revolver pointed at his temple. It was Wade, all right.

By this point, Jo had already reached the last mossy step. Gage raced to keep up. He caught the briefest glimpse of her bare feet beneath her blue jeans—it was one of the details that would stick with him later—before she was darting across the sand. How amazingly fast she'd run without shoes,

Gage thought, and here he was, muscles aching, joints on fire, stumbling and gasping as he tried to keep up with her.

Briefly, as Gage plunged deeper into the blackberry bushes, both Jo and Wade disappeared from view. The wind funneled up the gap, thick with the smell of moss and mud and salty ocean air. His rubber soles clapped against the few stepping stones that remained; most of the rest had crumbled or been swallowed up by the grass.

Faster. He had to go faster.

He couldn't have been trailing her by more than a second or two, but when he emerged, Jo was way ahead of him, almost to Wade. He still had the gun pointed at his head. A long stretch of sand, yellow and sunbaked near Gage, flat and brown where the ocean had swept it smooth, lay between them. It was a continent of sand. It was way too much.

The tide was out. If it had been at high tide, things might have gone differently. At least that was what Gage told himself later, but that was probably just another lie that could only be believed with the benefit of hindsight. If Jo could have gotten there sooner, if Gage wouldn't have been so slow to react, if Wade hadn't had as much time to do what he was going to do … But no. Looking for what-ifs and rationalizations was a pointless parlor game more fit for random onlookers than actual participants.

And there *were* onlookers. It was only as Gage finally caught up to Jo and Wade that Gage became aware of them, a half dozen rubberneckers and looky-loos dressed in flip-flops, T-shirts, sweatshirts, and beanies, the typical wide range of attire depending on each tourist's familiarity with the Oregon coastal weather and also their tolerance for cooler beaches. A few had the presence of mind to reach for their phones; most merely gaped at the spectacle unfolding before them.

When Gage arrived, they formed a triangle, with Jo on the left, Gage on the right, and Wade, ankle deep in the surf, ten feet ahead of them. Gage was gasping for breath when Macklin finally joined them. Gage wondered why the big man, who was the first one to spot Wade, had been so far behind until he saw what Macklin was holding loosely at his side.

A revolver.

A .357 Magnum. A big gun for a big hand. Macklin must have gone back for it. Now it no longer felt like a triangle. Now it felt like a duel and that maybe this was the moment Macklin had been waiting for all along. Why, though? There were still no answers.

Wade looked nothing like his picture. With his hat pulled down over his eyebrows, the gaunt face beneath the black wool was pasty pale, the pallor of a corpse or someone who knew he might soon be one. Jo moved forward a step, and Wade moved back, breaking the perfect symmetry of their triangle. The surf splashed over Wade's tennis shoes, white and frothy, bubbling against Wade's jeans; they were soaked up to the knees, the blue denim so wet it looked black. Here, at the doorstep of the ocean, the wind was stronger, colder, the currents of air pushing the three still on the sand back as if it wanted to claim Wade for itself.

"Stay back," Wade said.

His finger was on the trigger. Where the compact barrel of the revolver pressed against his right temple, the flesh was dimpled inward and as white his tennis shoes. The nickel-plated finish gleamed in the sun.

"Don't do it," Jo said, her own voice choked with as much desperation as Wade's. "Please. Just—just put down the gun."

Wade started crying. "I have to do this. I—I don't have a choice."

"Hey, Wade," Macklin said. "Just put down the piece, okay? I know this isn't what you really want to—"

"Shut up!" Wade cried. "All of you, just shut up! I'm going to kill myself, all right? I'm going to kill myself, and there's nothing you can do to stop me!"

"Where's Lacy?" Gage asked. "Please, Wade. Just tell us where Lacy is. Can you do that?"

Gage wasn't asking just because he wanted to know. He was also asking because he wanted to break Wade's pattern, to get him to think of something other than his own pain, and what better way to do that than to bring up the woman Wade loved? Was it a mistake? It was just one of many decisions Gage would question in the hours and days to come.

Because Gage's question *did* trigger a reaction, a momentarily wilting of Wade's resolve apparent in his eyes. It was like he was looking past them.

Jo took another step forward, her bare feet submerging into the dark sand.

Wade, the gun trembling, edged backward, into the oncoming wave. The white-cresting water soaked his jeans up to his calves and threw him off balance. The barrel of the gun slipped off his temple—out of danger, if only for a second—as he staggered to regain control.

Jo took this as an opportunity to lunge for Wade's gun arm.

Fast. Everything was happening so fast. In hindsight, yes, there was time, there was time to do something, to stop it all, but in the moment, in the actual lived experience of moving bodies and saltwater spray and grit in Gage's eyes, Wade regained his poise and pointed the gun at his temple with renewed vigor. His trigger finger was moving.

"Dad, don't!" Jo cried.

By this point, there were two people on the beach recording what happened with their cell phones, but when the footage was reviewed later, the ocean was too loud, and Jo was too far away, to determine exactly what she'd said. Most people thought she'd merely stuttered the word *don't* twice in a row. But Gage had been there. He'd heard. It was the moment when he truly understood the invisible force propelling her forward.

For now, though, there was only Jo Roland lunging for Wade Carson's gun arm. Gage moved. He was sure he moved. It was just a step, maybe not even that, a little bit of a lean forward, but Macklin blocked him. It wasn't much of a block, just a little lean himself, but Gage sensed the movement.

Then, as the two blurry shapes became one, there was a gunshot.

The muzzle flare pierced the mist of splash water. The sharp *pop* rose above the ocean's roar. A mass of flailing arms and legs spun into the surf, splashing up a frothy veil. When the water came down, the arms and legs rolled away into two people. There were screams behind them.

Wade, on his knees, sobbed and covered his eyes, but he appeared to be unharmed. The gun lay beside him in an inch of water, foam clinging to the barrel. Jo was on her side and turned away from them, moaning and clutching her gut.

As the water splashed around her, it turned a dark and violent red.

25

Gage was no artist. He had never held a paintbrush in his life. The closest he'd come to even dabbling in something creative was the one photography class he'd taken at Montana State University as an eighteen-year-old fresh-man, and that was only because he'd thought being at least somewhat skilled with a camera might come in useful when he started his career in the FBI.

He also may have thought it would be a good way to meet girls.

The girl hunt was a bust, and his foray into photography was even briefer than his one in law enforcement, having barely touched a camera since. Even now, when misguided tourists asked him to take their pictures on the beach, he usually spotted them a few minutes later asking another passerby to take a similar shot. If that wasn't an indictment of his poor photography skills, Gage didn't know what was.

Yet in the heartbeat or two before either he or Macklin moved, in the precious few seconds until the cops showed up with guns drawn, and the agonizing full minute before the paramedics charged over the sand with their metal cot in tow, Gage saw the scene before him like an artist. He remembered a former girlfriend, a talented water colorist he'd briefly dated when he'd first moved to New York, talking about learning how to *see with your eye, not your mind.* He never really understood what she meant, no matter how many times she talked about contours, contrasts, and negative spaces while they were lazing about in her studio in Chelsea. Seeing was seeing, wasn't it?

But there on the beach in Barnacle Bluffs, just below Jo's house and barely a mile from his own, he finally understood. It was an odd time for the realization, to be sure, but learning happened in its own way and in its own time, not always when it was convenient for the person doing the learning. Sometimes it happened in a classroom with a gifted teacher, sometimes in the shower when you were thinking about something else, and sometimes it happened when the woman you'd fallen for was bleeding out on the beach.

It was not to say that the scene in front of him was art, not to Gage, and not to anyone with at least half a conscience still rattling around in their bodies, but he did *see* it like an artist. He saw it with his eyes and not his mind. He saw it as it was, meaning he saw it before his mind had a chance to interpret, label, and sort, as shapes and shadows and colors before the names of things were attached. Everything was connected and flowed into everything else. Foreground, background, none of that mattered, it was all just one thing. This, he finally understood, was the way an artist learned to see. This is what that girlfriend, whose name was lost to the mists of time like so much else, was trying to get him to understand.

If the artist could truly recreate what they saw, and not what they *thought* they saw, then true art would naturally follow because it would be a unique expression of how that person saw the world.

How did Gage see the world? He saw the sunlight lancing across the tops of the waves, yellow where the surf was frothy, emerald green where it was dark and smooth. He saw shimmering shades of crimson staining a white blouse pink. He saw bare feet pebbled with sand—such tiny toes, such delicate, tiny toes. He saw a sliver of flesh above the waistband of her jeans and below a yanked-up blouse, flesh so alabaster white it made the blood-drenched sand and saltwater look black in comparison.

It was not Jo. It was not really even a woman. It was just a form, lines and textures, light and shadow, contours and contrasts. It was just beams of light bouncing off the photo receptors at the back of his eyeballs.

It certainly wasn't a person he could love and lose.

What finally shocked Gage out of this timeless, artistic state of mind was Wade's pitiful sobs. They came in great, heaving gasps that rose over the roar of the ocean. This was no painter's canvas. This was Jo, bleeding to death on the sand, and somebody had to save her.

He splashed onto his knees next to her, both the pain shooting up his spine and the shock of cold water jolting him fully out of his reverie. When the surf retreated, he saw that she was pressing blood-soaked hands against her abdomen. Everything was so red it was hard to distinguish fingers, shredded cotton, and mangled flesh from each other; it was all one big gory mess.

Her eyes were closed. All the muscles in her face were screwed up tightly, as if drawn together by the kind of cord used to close up a hoodie.

"Jo, Jo," he said. "Jo, it's going to be all right. Just keep your hands there. Keep—keep them there."

Pointless words. Just something to say to try to get her to stay with him, but he didn't know if she even heard him. A wave splashed over them both, briefly submerging the bottom half of her face in the ice cold water.

As gently as he could manage, he scooped one arm under her neck, the other under her legs. He didn't want to move her, but he couldn't let her drown. She moaned. As he lifted her off the sand, the pain emanating from his right knee was so intense that the world briefly turned white, but then the adrenaline kicked in and he didn't feel anything at all—not unless he counted his heart banging around like a mad monkey trapped in his rib cage.

Macklin tried to step in and slip his hooked arm under Jo's legs.

"I've got her!" Gage said.

"I can help," Macklin said.

"I said I've got this!"

And he did, barely. When Macklin backed off with arms raised—holding Wade's gun in his good hand, the obvious source of his delay in reaching Jo—Gage staggered up the slope. He managed to carry her six feet before he collapsed. The pain was so great it managed to overwhelm the adren-aline, if only for a second, and he had to clench his jaw with all his might to keep from screaming.

He'd gotten her far enough from the water that there was no danger of getting wet, let alone drowning, which was the important thing. She whimpered a little, but that was it. He was not happy she was in pain, but he was glad to hear the whimper. She was alert and conscious enough to react, which was a good thing.

There was too much blood, way too much blood. He pressed his own hands over hers, trying to keep the life within her, slowly becoming aware of the wider world beyond just the two of them: sirens on the bluff, a growing audience on the sand, Wade moaning, "I'm sorry, I'm sorry," on a loop as endless as the waves, and the shadow of Macklin's hook darkening Jo's face. By now, cops with guns drawn were charging down the steps. Where were the damn paramedics?

"Get your hands up! Get your hands up where we can see them, all of you! Right now!"

But Gage wasn't raising his hands. He wasn't doing anything these cops wanted, not while Jo was dying in front of him, so he certainly wasn't raising his hands. He was keeping them right where they were, with hot blood burbling between his fingers despite his best efforts to keep the wound sealed. Jo mumbled something. He leaned in close, straining to hear her over the cacophony of crashing waves and angry shouting and, loudest of all, the booming of his heart in his ears.

"He—he didn't mean it," Jo said.

"Jo," Gage said.

"Not … not his fault …"

Then she stopped speaking. Then she stopped moving. Then she stopped breathing, just as the paramedics finally came racing over the sand.

———

For someone who despised hospitals, Gage had spent far too much time in them. It was bad enough when he was the one lying on an operating table or recuperating in a hospital bed, but far worse was the intolerable purgatory of passing endless hours on a hard plastic chair when someone he cared about was beyond the swinging doors and down a garishly lit hallway, in some cloistered, sterile room with masked strangers.

How long had he been waiting? There were no windows, but the clock on the pillar behind the reception desk—a white clock with black numerals that reminded him, oddly, of the clock in the cafeteria in his high school—showed the time to be 9:14 p.m., so he'd been here hours already. The two nurses at the reception desk were whispering to one another, heads bent low. Other than the two of them, Gage was the only person there.

This was not the main waiting room. If it had been, there was no way it would be this empty, not in August, not during a heatwave. It was simply a few green plastic chairs in the critical care wing, just down the hall from the operating rooms. One of the masked strangers had deposited him here. A jet of air whirred out of a vent above him, icy on his neck. He'd spent most of his time with his hands folded loosely in his lap, staring glumly at his shoes. White sneakers caked in sand. Neither his shoes nor his socks were still wet, which said something about how long he'd been there.

Finally the doors swung open, and a slight, narrow-faced doctor with glasses too large for his face stepped through. The lenses made his eyes, a shade of blue the same color as the mask pulled down under his chin, enormous.

"She's alive," the doctor said.

"Oh, thank God," Gage said.

"We've stabilized her enough to remove the bullet, that's the important thing." The doctor was a head shorter than Gage. In his surgical cap and gown, he gave Gage the impression of a child playing dress-up. His voice, however, carried all the authority that his physical stature didn't. "I've got to get back. They're prepping her for the next step. I'm just assisting, but I need to—"

"What next step?"

"As I said, we have to remove the bullet. Where it's lodged, so close to her spine, it's going to be very difficult."

"Will she be paralyzed?"

"Right now we're focused on saving her life."

"But that's a possibility?"

"Mr. Gage, I just wanted to give you that update. It was

good that you were trying to control the bleeding. That bought her some time. I'm telling you this as a courtesy even though you're not family. Now if you'll excuse me."

The doctor left before Gage could reply. Since he couldn't take out his anger on the doctor, Gage focused on the two men who walked up even as the swinging doors were still closing: Detective Bob Brisbane and Tag Macklin.

It was a study in opposites. Where Brisbane was a short potato of a man in a mustard-stained trench coat, Macklin was tall, sleek, and muscular, his black tracksuit like snakeskin about to be sloughed off. He'd at least had the decency to remove his sunglasses.

"Where's your partner?" Gage asked Brisbane. "Home shaving those stilt legs of his, as usual?"

"Detective Trenton is down on the beach," Brisbane said, his breath smelling of cigarettes. "Helping secure the area. What did the doc say?"

Gage didn't feel like answering this question just yet. "And the kid's in jail?"

"Where else would he be?"

"Did he say where Lacy is?"

Brisbane sighed and ran a hand across his sweaty scalp. There was so little hair up there these days that his moles were showing through. "No. He told us he has no idea, but that was before his mother showed up and made him clam up and wait for a lawyer. Now, are you going to tell me about my chief of police, or do I have to get the information from the nurses?"

"Jo said he didn't do it on purpose," Gage said.

"What?"

"On the beach. It was the last thing she said before she passed out. She said, 'Not his fault. He didn't mean it.'"

"Well, when she wakes up, she can testify to that. Until then, I'm treating this like at least a manslaughter charge.

Now, do you want to tell me what's up with Chief Roland, or do you want me to put you in jail next to Wade Carson?"

"She's in surgery," Gage said.

"How bad is it?"

"Didn't I just answer this question?"

"Hey, man," Macklin said, "there's no need to be that way. It was a terrible thing, what happened, and we're all praying she pulls through."

"Are we? I know I am, at least."

Macklin frowned. "What's that supposed to mean?"

"You tried to stop me."

"What?"

"On the beach. As Jo was making her move, you blocked my path."

"You're insane. Why the hell would I do such a thing?"

"I don't know, Tag, you tell me."

When the blood rushed to Macklin's face, the tiny scars around his eyes pulsed from white to vivid pink. "There was nothing we could do, man. I'm telling you. You're just feeling guilty, and you're lashing out. And if I stepped in your way without really thinking about it, maybe it's because I thought you were going to make it worse."

"That's enough out of you two," Brisbane said. "This is a hospital, for God's sake. Get a hold of yourselves."

Gage pointed at Macklin. "There's a metal box in her house. It's sitting on the dining room table. You need to get it before Captain Hook here does."

"Jesus," Macklin said. "Really, man? Now you're really grasping at straws. There's nothing in that box that has anything to do with this. You saw that for yourself. It's just Jo's stuff—from Dell and her old man. Mementos, that sort of thing."

"We'll see, won't we? "

"Gage, you should go home," Brisbane said. "Get some

rest. Her house isn't officially a crime scene, but nobody's going in or out tonight. I'll swing by and make sure everything's locked up, you understand?"

"I can't leave Jo."

Brisbane put his hand on Gage's shoulder. "I'm telling you, you look like yesterday's scrambled eggs. Go home. If you're worried about Jo, I'm going to station an officer outside her hospital door. I won't leave until that's done, so there's no reason for you to sit here."

Gage shrugged off the man's hand. "I'm not going anywhere until I know Jo's on the other side of this. And I'm telling you, this guy, he's at the root of this thing somehow. I just don't know how yet."

"Jesus," Macklin said. "You're fucking insane."

"Gage," Brisbane said, "you just said Jo told you the kid didn't mean to do it. So which is it? Was it attempted murder or just an accident?"

Gage simmered in silence.

"Yeah, that's what I thought," Brisbane said. "Well, until you *do* know, keep your mouth shut, okay? If there's somebody who always seems to be around when the shit begins to stink, it's you. The woman in there, she's a hell of a police chief, probably too good for our little town. If she dies today, I'm going to blame you."

26

———

Hours later, two doctors emerged through the swinging doors to give them the news.

They'd managed to remove the bullet, and she was alive, but she was in a medically induced coma. Nobody would be allowed to see her except immediate family. The worst of it was this: when she came out of it—*if* she came out of it— she might be completely paralyzed.

Her mother was on her way, but she was flying back from a Mediterranean cruise, and the soonest she could get to Barnacle Bluffs would be Tuesday. Twenty minutes later, the same young cop who'd helped search the streets around Wade's truck arrived to guard Jo's door, and Brisbane left shortly thereafter without even a grunt goodbye. Macklin slouched in the corner, far from where Gage sat in the plastic chairs, both of them avoiding eye contact. At 3:34 a.m., Macklin got a call on his cell. As he walked to the other end of the hall, Gage heard Macklin say "Yes, ma'am" before Macklin was out of earshot. He came back a few minutes later, slipping the phone into his front pocket.

"Well, I'm heading down to the station," Macklin said. "I

know you don't trust me, man, but I really do care about her. Will you let me know if she wakes up?"

"*When* she wakes up," Gage said.

"Right, that's what I meant."

"Was that Ellen Carson?"

"It was."

"She's talked to Wade?"

"She did."

"Did he tell her anything about Lacy?"

"He doesn't know where she is," Macklin said.

"He told Ellen this?"

"He said he hasn't had any contact with her since he left San Diego."

"I'd like to talk to him myself."

"Yeah, Ellen figured you might ask, and she told me to tell you no. He's refusing to talk to anyone but his lawyer or his mother. No other visitors."

Gage shook his head, then gazed at the swinging double doors, where he knew Jo lay in some nearby room, bandaged, tubes up her nose, enough drugs pumping through her veins to keep her slumbering. Thinking about how scared she was going to be, if she woke up and couldn't move, Gage found it hard to breathe. "Jo told me what really happened at Terminal Five," he said. "Right before Wade showed up on the beach, she told me. She told me how you *really* lost your hand. So you were lying after all, weren't you?"

He looked at Macklin again, gauging his reaction. He was hoping for indignation, or some telltale sign that Macklin was hiding something, but all he got was a tired shrug.

"If you want to call it that," he said.

"If I want to call it that?" Gage said. "A lie is a lie, man."

"Look, Jo and I did what we had to do to get ourselves out of that situation as cleanly as possible. Dell was gone.

What does it matter that we fudged the details a bit? It's been a long time. I lost my hand. She lost … well, I guess her heart, if you want to put it that way. You keep digging for something, but all you really did was cause her pain. Maybe if you hadn't …" He shook his head.

"Maybe if I hadn't what?"

"I'm saying, you just got Jo pretty rattled. Maybe, if she'd been thinking more clearly, if you hadn't gotten her so upset …" He trailed off.

"Oh, I see," Gage said, feeling his jaw tighten, "you're saying it's *my* fault that Jo got shot?"

"I'm saying that there's plenty of blame to go around, if blame is what you're looking for. But why bother? Now I gotta go before Mrs. Carson throws one of her tizzies." He took a step toward the exit, but Gage wasn't done.

"Who was Dell having an affair with?" he asked.

Macklin stopped. "What?"

"You were friends with Dell, " Gage said. "Who was he having an affair with?"

"I have no idea, and I told you, I really wasn't that close to him—to either of them."

"You were close enough that Jo thought to call you when the shit went down at Terminal Five."

"Yeah, that's because she knew I was a good cop. She knew she could trust me."

Gage studied his face. "You knew, though. You knew he was having an affair, didn't you?"

Macklin shook his head. "I didn't know who it was, okay? I didn't even know for sure. But yeah, I caught him reading a letter once in the locker room at the station, and he kind of hurriedly put it away when I walked in … So okay, yes, I had my suspicions. But that's all it was. Suspicions."

"But you didn't tell Jo?"

"Of course not. It wasn't my place."

"Didn't it ever occur to you that if you *had* told her, maybe things would have gone differently?"

"She found out anyway. I think she knew before I did."

"You think?"

"Look, whoever this mystery woman was, she disappeared into the wind after Dell died. I don't blame her. Now I'm leaving, man."

"I need to talk to Wade," Gage said.

"I already told you, that's not going to happen, but you go right ahead and try if it'll make you feel better. Listen, this is just a bad thing, man. Jo tried to help. It was like she couldn't stop herself, right? She wasn't about to stand there and let somebody off themselves when she might be able to stop them, right? Not after what happened with her father and her husband. No way. It's nobody's fault that she's just wired that way."

"I'm going to find Lacy," Gage said. "And when I do, I think the real truth will come out."

"You should," Macklin said. "After I talk to Mrs. Carson, I'm going to do the same—on my own dime. And I don't care if that broad likes it or not. Now are we good?"

Gage said nothing and Macklin walked away. What a loaded question. *Are we good?* Gage could not imagine a situation, either now or in the future, when he and Macklin would ever be *good*. Jo was in the hospital, Wade was in jail, and nothing added up. To the world at large, this may have seemed like nothing more than a suicide gone awry, but Gage was convinced there something else going on here. And that Macklin was involved somehow.

As soon as Macklin disappeared into the elevator, Gage headed for the stairs.

———

TRYING to stay as far back as he could, Gage pursued the black Mustang around Big Dipper Lake in the predawn gloom. There were few cars out at this hour, so Gage needed to be careful. While he drove, he called the BBPD on his cell and quickly found out that Macklin wasn't lying; Wade was indeed refusing all visitors except his lawyer and his mother. The Sienna's dashboard clock read 4:37 a.m. Was it Monday or Tuesday? Monday, Gage decided, though his eyelids were so heavy it felt like he'd been in the hospital for two days, not one.

Any hope that Macklin would lead him straight to Lacy Carson, or at least some other clue to her whereabouts, was dashed when Macklin turned into the police station. Had he done so just because he knew Gage was following? Either way, Gage didn't see a point in stopping there himself, at least not yet, not if Wade was refusing to see him. What he needed was more information, something to change the equation.

He could never prove it, of course, but he was certain Macklin had gone back into the house after Jo had spotted Wade on the beach, and for some other reason than to fetch his gun. Gage could not think of anything in that box that Macklin might want, but it was a place to start. If nothing obvious was missing, then maybe there would be something else in Jo's house that would help him understand what the hell was going on.

The moon, resurgent above the wraith-like clouds, splashed its milky-white glow on the deserted highway. The traffic that so infuriated him earlier was no obstacle now. Save for a handful of nondescript sedans and two noisy Harleys pulling out of Tsunami's empty parking lot, there was no traffic at all. When he reached Jo's place, he was glad that Brisbane had not designated her house a crime scene, because there was no police presence. Her Malibu sat alone in the driveway. He parked where he'd parked before, down the street between two houses. Except for porch lights, almost all the houses were dark.

Walking to Jo's house, the night air was so warm that he unzipped his leather jacket, but there was so little wind that it made no difference. His bad knee was so stiff from so much sitting that he brought his cane. The ocean was as loud as a lion's roar.

He tried the front door. Locked. He tried the side windows. No luck there either. He crept to the back, fearing there might be a crime scene set up on the beach bustling with cops who might spot him, but there was nothing down there but dark sand and an even darker ocean.

Why *would* the police be down there? After all, any crime scene would have been swept away long ago by the ceaseless ocean. The wood planks creaked. A neighbor dog yapped in response but probably nothing that would wake the sleeping beauties around him. He tried the screen door, expecting more disappointment, and was pleasantly surprised.

It was open.

Then Gage realized something. The door being unlocked was no accident. When Brisbane had said he was swinging by to make sure Jo's place was locked up, he was actually telling Gage he was going to do the opposite. He *wanted* Gage to be able to look inside. Brisbane may not have had any proof that the shooting was anything more than a suicide gone awry, but he wanted to know for sure, and he knew that Gage, unencumbered by police procedure, might be the one to do it.

The living room smelled faintly of lavender. Gage left the lights off, but the range light in the kitchen was more than bright enough to guide his way. The metal box still sat on the kitchen table, the lid open, all the plastic-wrapped contents still contained within.

Once more, Gage rifled through the bags. He didn't see anything missing. He didn't know if he would notice even if it were. The wallet, the framed picture, the phone in a green case—everything appeared to be as it was when he'd searched this box only hours ago. Maybe Macklin hadn't been lying after all. Maybe nothing in the box had the slightest thing to do with Wade Carson.

Gage paced the room, trying to imagine what he might be missing, his cane thumping dully on the carpet. Nothing came to him. He resisted the urge to hurl his cane against the glass. Looking at the window, and his own dark visage reflected back at him, this haggard-faced madman prowling around in Jo's empty house, it suddenly occurred to him that there was one big question that he had not asked.

Why did Wade choose to kill himself below Jo's house?

All along, he'd assumed that this had just been a coincidence, but now Gage silently chastised himself for making that assumption.

But why would he want to kill himself in front of Jo's house? It didn't make sense. Unless he *wasn't* going to kill himself? Unless it was all a ruse. Which meant what, exactly? That all along Wade had *wanted* to shoot Jo and he was just using the suicide as a sort of cover? But why? As far as Gage knew, Wade had never even met her. Assuming that was true, the only thing that linked Jo and Wade was Garrick "Tag" Macklin.

In the stillness of the house, Gage could hear his own breath catch in his throat.

What if Wade was just Macklin's tool? What if Macklin had made sure to be out on the deck at that moment quite deliberately so that he could point Wade out to Jo? Maybe, knowing Jo's psychology, Macklin knew she wouldn't be able to stop herself from trying to intervene. What if they'd actually planned to shoot Jo the previous night—after all, Gage had seen both Macklin and Jo at the window—but Gage and Lacy had inadvertently interrupted the plan? Or perhaps Macklin changed his mind anyway because he found out about something in Jo's box that might … what? Incriminate him somehow?

Why would Macklin want to kill Jo?

It didn't make sense. None of it made sense. Gage rifled through the box again. If there'd been something in here that incriminated Macklin, what on Earth could it be? The wallet was there, and seemed to contain everything that was in it before. Maybe there'd been a Swiss bank account written on a slip of paper?

Gage was grasping. Maybe there was nothing missing from the box. Maybe this whole thing really was just a suicide gone awry. But if that was so, where was Lacy Carson? Her absence was proof that something else was going on here, just as there might be a similar absence from this box that would suggest a different story than the suicide gone awry.

Story.

The book.

The John D. MacDonald paperback. What was the title? *The Dreadful Lemon Sky.* He could picture it in his mind, a yellow cover, a paperback with a cracked spine. Gage searched the box once more. The book wasn't there. Now there was something very strange indeed to be missing. Why? Gage had read that book long ago, and though the story was lost to him, he knew it featured MacDonald's most popular character, Travis McGee. He was a marine salvage expert by trade but a human salvage expert by nature, a sort of free-lance knight who helped people in need.

Gage took out his phone and looked up the book's description. A woman from McGee's past desperately needs him to keep a package of cash safe and sound, no questions asked, but then she dies under mysterious circumstances. McGee tracks down the truth. Was there a clue in there? Was there a code in the book, a treasure map that could lead Macklin to a metaphorical (or even real) buried treasure? It seemed insane. Why go to all the trouble? And why would Macklin need *this* book unless there was something unique about it, maybe some handwritten notes on a few of the pages?

Yet one indisputable fact remained: the book was missing. Confronting Macklin about it would get him nowhere. He knew that.

He also knew that Wade Carson was really the only other person who might shed some light on this, and the kid was refusing to see him. Wade may not have known where Lacy was, but he was the key to all of this somehow.

Gage returned to the sliding glass door. He was debating whether to leave the door unlocked when it occurred to him that there was another way to talk to Wade. If Brisbane had wanted Gage to look inside Jo's house, maybe Brisbane would also be willing to give Gage access to Wade in a rather unconventional manner. It was a risky move, maybe even outright crazy, but Gage didn't think he had time to play it safe.

He took out his phone and dialed 9-1-1.

"I'd like to report a burglary in process," he said.

27

"Hey, kid," Gage said, gripping the bars of his own jail cell, "how are you doing next door? You feel like talking? I'm here, when you do. About anything. You want restaurant recommendations?"

There was no answer—or at least no other answer than the obnoxious, nose-rattling snoring coming from the drunk in the cell to Gage's left. The cinderblock walls prevented Gage from seeing the occupant on either side. In the cell to Gage's right, where he'd gotten the briefest glimpse of Wade slouched on the metal bunk when Brisbane had shoved Gage roughly into his own jail cell, there was no sound at all. The kid could have been sleeping. He could have been meditating. He could have been dead, for all Gage knew.

Gage, standing inches from the bars, shifted his weight from left to right, his feet and knees still aching from all the walking he'd done. His back was also on fire, but he was pretty sure that was from carrying Jo. It had been fine at the hospital, but he'd had so much adrenaline pumping through his body that it was only now, hours later, that he was beginning to feel pain and fatigue catching up to him.

This was the fifth attempt he'd made to get Wade to engage with him in the past hour, each time to no avail. He'd tried the straightforward approach, explaining that Lacy had hired him to find Wade. Not even a grunt in response. He'd tried humor, joking about the stupidity of the average tourist, with the idea that building rapport might lay the foundation for a more meaningful conversation. Crickets. He'd tried appealing to Wade's vanity, saying that he'd heard Wade was a talented writer and that he wondered what someone with a writer's mindset made of kitschy Barnacle Bluffs. Nothing worked.

"Hey, you awake over there?" Gage said. "Make a sound if you are. You don't even have to talk. You can cough. Or burp. Hell, you can even fart. Just let one rip, Wade. I just want to know I'm talking to a living, breathing person."

There was the crinkle of clothing, but it wasn't from Wade; it was the drunk's duct-taped parka as the snoring maestro shifted in his bunk. Gage gripped the bars. He expected the metal to be cold, which it was, but he was surprised to find how smooth it felt. Worn smooth by all the hands that had gripped it over the years, most likely. He leaned out as far as he could, the bars pressing against his cheeks, and tried to get even the smallest glimpse of Wade, but all he could see were some of the bars and a bit of the cracked concrete floor.

It was not the first time Gage had been in the Barnacle Bluffs Police Department jail—either as a guest or as a prisoner. He couldn't say which side of the bars he liked better. The last time he was in here, less than a year ago, Zoe was the one sitting in this very jail cell. It had been one of the worst nights of Gage's life.

"I really want to help you," Gage said. "But I can't help you unless you talk to me."

Still nothing. Beyond the heavy metal door at the end of

the passageway, there came muted laughter from the cop stationed outside the evidence room, but otherwise it was just the drunk playing his nose trumpet and the hall lights emitting a high-pitched whine.

Gage remembered when those lights buzzed instead of whined. The difference between fluorescents and LEDs maybe? Whatever they were, the light was just as harsh, making all the metal and concrete that much grayer and colorless. He glanced over his shoulder. The high, barred window was still dark; dawn had not yet arrived. If the kid was going to talk, he had to do it soon. When Brisbane had locked the cell, he had whispered to Gage that Ellen Carson and her lawyer would be back at eight in the morning.

Since nothing else had worked so far, Gage decided to go with brutal honesty. "All right, kid," he said, "here's the deal. I think you shot Jo Roland on purpose. I just don't know why. I figure you're working with Tag Macklin, but I can't prove it. I can't prove any of it, but I'll promise you something right now: I'm not going to stop until I uncover the truth. I'll make it my life's mission ... especially if Lacy dies."

"She'll—she'll be fine," Wade said.

Finally. The kid had spoken in a croaked whisper, but it was something. "Do you know where she is?" Gage asked.

No answer.

"If you know where she is, you should tell me," Gage said. "The longer you go without telling me, the more at risk she is."

Still nothing. Gage breathed deep through his nose, his jaw tight, trying to stay calm, wondering if there was anything at all he could do to get this kid to open up before it was too late. He knew this situation probably required all the tact he could muster, but screw it, they didn't have time for tact.

"Why did you shoot Jo Roland?" he asked.

"It ... it was an accident," Wade said.

Okay, so anger was getting somewhere. Gage decided to go all in with it. "I don't believe you. I think you wanted to hurt her."

"I—I didn't want to hurt anyone but myself."

"She might still die, you know? Jo might still die. And even if she lives, she'll probably be paralyzed. Did you know that?"

"I'm—I'm really sorry."

"Why did you try to kill her?"

"I didn't. It was—"

"If she dies, you're a murderer. How does that sit with you, Wade?"

Gage heard sniffling, then a muffled sob. When Wade spoke again, it was difficult to make him out through all the crying and gasping for air.

"I want ... I want to die, okay?" he said. "I want ... I want to kill myself."

"I don't believe that either."

"I do! I hate myself. I hate what I did."

"Why did you do it, then?"

"She ... she tried to stop me. I ... I ... didn't make her do that. I was going to kill myself, and she—she—she just got in the way."

"Oh, so now it's her fault?"

"No. It's nobody's fault. It just happened."

"No, it's your fault, because you tried to kill her."

"I didn't—"

"There's something going on here, Wade. It's all some kind of ploy. I see that now. With the kind of lawyer your mommy is going to get you, you'll probably get off, or at worse, it's a manslaughter charge. Was that your plan all along?"

"There—there was no plan."

"Why did Tag Macklin take that John D. MacDonald book out of the metal box?"

There was a pause. "What?"

"Don't play dumb. He wanted that book for some reason. Why?"

"I … I don't know anything about—"

"Stop lying."

"I swear, I don't know anything about any book!"

"Why did you come to Barnacle Bluffs? Why here, of all places?"

"No … no reason. I just kept driving."

"Then why did you want to kill yourself in the first place?"

"I—I—I don't need to tell you anything. I'm—I'm waiting for my lawyer."

Gage was hitting Wade with a steady diet of hooks and crosses. Now it was time to go for the knockout. "I know about what your father did to you, Wade. I heard it from your mother. I heard it from Tag. You must have had a lot of mixed feelings when he died, but suicidal? I don't buy it."

Wade was silent. It had to be almost six in the morning. Ellen and the lawyer would be here soon. Time to try another approach. Maybe the key to getting Wade to open up to him was Gage opening up in return. Gage knew how too. He knew it, but it proved more difficult than he thought it would be. His face felt warm even before he started speaking.

"You know, I'm in love with her," Gage said.

Silence.

"Jo, I mean," Gage said. He cleared his throat. "I think she feels the same. I don't know for sure, but if she dies … I'll never know. Maybe you don't understand that. Maybe you don't feel that kind of love for Lacy."

"I do," Wade said. "I love her."

"I don't buy it. Your wife is probably going to die because of you."

"She's not. She's not."

"You got her killed, Wade."

"I didn't!"

"If you loved her, you wouldn't have done this to her."

"I did it for her! It's all because of her, okay! I had to! I had to do this or … or …"

There it was, finally, a crack in the facade. Wade may have dreamed of being a writer, but right now he was an actor playing the ultimate role, and Gage highly doubted it was Wade's choice to do so. Yet until this moment, all of this had merely been Gage's gut level instinct. This, and especially the word *or*, was the first real confirmation that his instinct was right.

"Or what?" Gage said.

"Nothing. It's nothing."

"Why did you *have* to do this?"

"I'm not—"

"You're talking about shooting Jo, right?"

"I didn't—"

"Let's skip the part where you keep pretending it was an accident. You said it was for Lacy. What did you mean? Are you saying *she* wanted to kill Jo?"

"No!"

"Yeah, I didn't think so. So, was it to protect Lacy somehow?

"I'm only talking to my lawyer."

"Does Tag Macklin have her held hostage somewhere? Is that what's going on? Maybe you were having second thoughts about shooting Jo, so Macklin took her and forced you to do the deed?"

Wade said nothing, but after a moment he started crying. It was all the confirmation that Gage needed.

"Where is she?" Gage asked.

"I can't talk to you."

"Wade, if Macklin promised he'd let her go if you did what you were supposed to do, he's lying. How can he let her go now? Don't you see?"

There was lots of sniffling. The bed creaked, clothes rustled, and the soles of shoes scratched against the concrete floor. Gage gripped the bars tighter, hoping the kid was finally coming to his senses.

"Wade," Gage said, "if you know where Lacy is, you've got to tell me. It's the only chance she has. If you want, it can stay between us, okay?"

The crying picked up. The shoes scratched a little more. A shadow flitted onto the concrete outside Wade's cell. A shadow? There were no overhead lights in the cells, so that could only mean one thing. Gage glanced behind him and saw the gray, hazy light of dawn brightening his cell window. They were almost out of time.

"Wade, please," Gage said, "I'm begging you. If you love Lacy, you've got to tell me where she is."

"I *told* you, I don't know."

"You're lying."

"I'm—I'm not. I was trying to kill myself. She—the police chief—she just got in the way—"

"More lies."

"I'm not lying!"

"Lacy's going to die unless you tell me the truth."

"I—I can't—"

"Where is she?"

"I don't—"

"Where is she, Wade? Tell me! Tell me right—"

"I told you, I don't fucking know!"

This came out as a roar, booming off all the metal and concrete, ringing in Gage's ears. He glanced at the access door at the end of the hall, waiting for a cop's face to appear in the thick glass window, but none did. Next door, the drunk went on snoring his nasally song. That was good too. The last thing Gage wanted was for the kid to think about the other prisoner as a potential witness.

"What *do* you know?" Gage said.

There was no answer, but Wade's breathing was right there, just inches from Gage's ear.

"Trust me," Gage said. "Wade, if you love your wife, please just trust me. Tell me something. Anything."

There was a long pause, and when Wade spoke, it was in a whisper. "Why should I?"

"Because Lacy's life depends on it."

"I'll go to … go to jail forever."

The kid was too smart to be placated by false assurances, so Gage figured the truth was better. "Look, I can't promise you anything, but I also know you're a victim in this too. A judge and jury would take all of that into consideration."

There were some shuffling footsteps backward. "If—if—if I tell you anything," he said, "she'll die."

"That's not going to happen," Gage said.

"You can't promise that."

"Why does Macklin want Jo dead? Start with that."

Silence.

"Wade?"

"He just … He just said he hates her. He said she ruined everything, and she has to … she has to pay for what she did. That's all he told me. And I told him … I told him about …" He choked off a sob.

"What your father did to you," Gage said.

"Yes."

Gage was starting to understand. "And so what, you made a kind of agreement? It's a little like that movie,

Strangers on the Train? He does something for you, you do something for him, and then you both have alibis."

"I—I didn't know what I was saying. I was high. I didn't mean it. I didn't mean any of it. It was a kind of joke. I didn't think Tag would go there. I didn't think he would."

It was all coming together for Gage now. "But he realized he could blackmail your father, didn't he? That's why he went to Boise. He threatened your father, told him he'd reveal to the world what he'd done to you, and that allowed him to keep squeezing him for more money. Isn't that what was happening?"

"I don't know. Yeah, I guess. I thought maybe Dad just gave him a job, but yeah, yeah I guess that makes more sense."

"And after Tag squeezed your father dry," Gage said, "he killed him. He made it look like a suicide, but he killed him."

Wade breathed out a strangled sob. "He called me. He said—he said I had to honor my side of the deal. I told him there was no deal. I told him I never promised him anything! I told him I wasn't in my right mind. He said—he said it didn't matter."

"Why did he take the John D. MacDonald book?"

"I don't know!"

"Stay calm. Please stay—"

"Oh God, she's going to die. I'm going to get her killed."

"When did you last talk to him? To Macklin?"

"Yesterday. He—he broke into this house just south of—of the police chief's. A mile down the beach maybe. Called me on the burner. Said it wasn't being rented, so I could use it. That's where I've been staying. He came by and told me Lacy was going to pay a terrible price if I did not go through with it. He said he had her now. He said if I ever wanted to see her alive, I needed to … to honor our original agreement …"

He could barely get out the words, he was crying so much. There was noise beyond the metal door. Muffled voices. A woman's voice. Maybe Ellen Carson's. They were out of time.

"Think, Wade," Gage said. "There's got to be something else. He wouldn't keep her at his hotel. Maybe another house? One close by?"

"I don't know. No, I don't think so. He drove away. He headed for the highway."

"Did he turn north or south?"

"I don't know."

"There has to be something else! Help me out here!"

"I'm trying!"

"But this was the plan? To fake your suicide so that you could get Jo to try to stop you?"

"Tag said she wouldn't be able to stop herself from trying to save me. He said it would look like an accident. He said my mom and her big-shot lawyers could get me off. He said all of these things. He promised me he would kill her, don't you understand? What was I supposed to do?"

"Why is he willing to kill Lacy but not Jo? It makes no sense!"

"I don't know. He just told me he wouldn't—he wouldn't—"

"What?"

"He wouldn't take the fall for it. For what he would do to Lacy. If I … If … I didn't go through with it. He said he'd pin the blame on someone else and he'd get away."

"Who?" Gage said. "Who could he pin it on? You're in prison, so it couldn't be you. It would have to be … to be …"

And then Gage had it. Who better to pin the blame on than someone who had been a pain in Macklin's side from the moment he'd gotten to town?

Gage himself.

If true, that still didn't tell him where Lacy was. Where would Macklin take her if he wanted to frame Gage? Not Gage's house—too obvious. Not his van. His yard maybe? No. It would have to be somewhere nobody would hear her, even if she was bound and gagged, and he couldn't think of any …

Gage pressed his face between the bars. "Hey!" he shouted. "Hey, I want to talk to Detective Brisbane! I want to talk to …"

He trailed off, because the main door swung open and there was Brisbane, rumpled and scowling as always, with Ellen Carson and her little Kung Fu master trailing right behind him.

Even then, the drunk next door went on snoring.

28

At six in the morning on a Sunday, Thackleforth Candies hadn't opened yet, nor had any of the other stores in the strip hugging Highway 101. Fog blanketed the blacktop, lapping onto the sidewalks. The way the fog moved and shifted, the neon Closed signs blinked on and off in an erratic fashion.

All the windows upstairs were dark. A few of the downstairs businesses, including Thackleforth Candies, were lit faintly from within, but it was mostly darkness all around. A lone jogger, bare legs glistening in the thick air, trotted north, but otherwise there was not a soul in sight. A few cars were parked here and there, but Gage saw no sign of Macklin's Mustang.

If his car was around, it wasn't close. Not that Gage expected it to be.

"Turn on 3rd and park next to the elementary school," Gage said.

"Have I told you this is a bad idea?" Alex said.

"Multiple times. Now park."

They were in the Toyota Sienna again. A gray sedan

floated past them in the other lane, but otherwise the highway was still. Alex parked next to the elementary school —a brick building surrounded by a chain-link fence—and killed the engine. A chihuahua in the window across the street barked at them, but otherwise all the little houses were quiet. Gage glanced in the side-view mirror, watching both the road behind them and the highway two blocks to the west.

"I should at least come with you," Alex said.

"We talked about this," Gage said. "If he's actually in that empty office with Lacy, I have no idea what he'll do. I need you out here as backup."

"That's not the real reason, and you know it. You don't think I'm up to it."

Gage looked at him. At the station, when Alex had picked him up, Gage had hopped in the van without really looking at his friend, but now he did. Alex wore a knitted gray hat along with a black hoodie and black sweatpants; everything was baggy—no surprise considering how much weight Alex had lost recently. That was the good news. The bad news was that he did look old, his mustache gray, the lines on his face deeply chiseled, his eyes more sunken than even a few years ago. It didn't help that he obviously hadn't shaved in a few days, though Gage wasn't one to talk.

"There's another possibility," Gage said. "Maybe I don't want you with me because you're dressed like a mugger?"

"Very funny."

"That gray wool hat really brings out the silver in your eyebrows."

Alex tore it off and tossed it in the back. The ring of hair around his bare scalp stuck straight up as if he were playing the part of a mad scientist. "I was cold, all right? I get cold sometimes. It doesn't mean I'm old and useless."

"You're *definitely* old, but you're not useless. Most of the time anyway."

"Gee, thanks. I was in the FBI, you know."

"Yes, you keep reminding me."

"I used to catch a lot of bad guys, once upon a time."

"Was *bad guys* the official term?"

"I was good at it too."

"That was during Prohibition, right?"

"The point is, you don't have to do this alone."

Gage shook his head. He unzipped his leather jacket and took out his Beretta, checking the cartridge before snapping it back into place. "I won't be alone," he said. "Besides, I really don't think he'll be there."

Alex sighed. "Tell me again why you didn't tell Brisbane? I'd feel a hell of a lot better if other people were in the know."

"I can't take the chance that word would get out," Gage said. "Surprise is our biggest asset right now."

"Garrison—"

"Alex, listen to me. I *need* you out here. If you don't get at least a text from me in the next … thirteen minutes, then call the police. Don't come charging into that office after me. Just call the police and tell them you think a murder is in progress. That's six in the morning, straight up. That's more than enough time for me to get inside and at least get the lay of the land. Now, are you going to give me that key or not?"

Alex groaned and fished the key, attached to a tiny plastic flamingo, out of his pocket. The key to the building—he and Eve had sometimes looked after the place, years ago, when the Thackleforths used to travel—was the other reason Gage needed Alex. Otherwise he may not have told him what he was up to at all.

Handing the flamingo to Gage, Alex nodded toward the dashboard clock.

"You've now got twelve minutes," he said.

———

It took three of those minutes for Gage to walk to the rear of the Thackleforth building. The light was gray, the neighborhoods just beginning to stir: a trash can lid clanked, a dog barked, a car door slammed. The thick air dampened his face. His knee ached. He'd left his cane behind, partly because he didn't want to be encumbered with it in situations like this one, but mostly because he knew that all the adrenaline pumping through his body would make the pain disappear in short order. Which it did.

The building, so wide and tall, muted the sound of the ocean. There was still no one parked in the three spots behind the building. The dumpster, bulging with boxes and black plastic bags, smelled of wet paper and moldy cardboard. As he approached, the sensor light over the rear entrance, a plain metal door that led to the back stairwell, illuminated. The top floor windows were still dark.

Slipping the key into the lock, Gage began to doubt himself. Maybe he'd grasped onto this crazy idea because he didn't want to accept that Lacy was probably dead. That he'd failed her? He thought about how he'd felt when he'd met her, how just the sight of her had made him want to protect her, to shield her from bad things. And yet he hadn't.

She was alive. She had to be, if only because he didn't know if he could take any more failures. There'd been too many people he'd failed already, and there was only so much guilt a man could carry.

With a quick glance over his shoulder, Gage took out his Beretta and turned off the safety.

Then he opened the door.

The stairwell was dimly lit by a caged light that cast a net of shadows over everything. There was a human-like shape by the entrance, but it was just a mop. The floor was bare concrete, the stairs beveled metal. There was a wheeled bucket, stacked boxes of cleaning supplies, and other junk, but no person.

Gage stepped inside and closed the door. He didn't realize he'd been holding his breath until now, and he exhaled slowly, his heart banging away in his ears. He started up the stairs, his Beretta nosing ahead of him. There was another door on the second-floor landing, and he eased it open and peered into the hall.

Nobody was there. It was the same hall he'd been in a few days earlier, with its plain white walls and thin blue carpet, with four unmarked doors. He listened for a long time, but all he could make out was the faint murmur of the ocean and the air whistling through the ceiling duct.

Then he heard something, the sound so brief that he couldn't make sense of it at first nor locate its source. Then he heard it again, and this time he was sure it was coming from inside the office he'd been considering renting: a high-pitched whine, not mechanical, more animal-like.

It was a kind of … *keening.*

Gage felt an iron glove clenching his chest. Lacy. Who else could it be? She was alive, and she was in that room. Not yet ready to abandon his caution, he crept to the door and stepped past it, staying flat against the wall with the Beretta in his right hand and the flamingo key in his left.

The keening noise came again, even briefer than the last time. Now Gage was close enough that he could make out the ocean. The window inside must have been open.

He tried the knob. Locked. It took some doing to unlock it from this angle, but he managed.

Then he swung open the door.

Fearing a trap, he waited a beat, then another. Nothing

happened. There was no keening, though the ocean was louder. A foul stench of piss and feces wafted out to him, mixed with the usual smell of dusty, exposed floorboards. Gage chanced a glimpse into the room.

It was only for only a split second, but it was enough. Lacy was there, tied up on the floor against the far wall and her mouth duct taped. There was something in the corner next to the old radiator. It took his mind a few seconds to make sense of what he'd seen—something small, black, with a tiny white head. It was a camera sitting atop a black backpack.

Cameras were small and cheap these days, and this one was tiny indeed, half the size of the typical cell phone. So Macklin was monitoring Lacy from afar? All right, but what was in the backpack?

Then Gage, thinking how the backpack had been placed right next to the radiator, figured it out. It all came back to one stupid comment that had Macklin made to him, a comment that Gage, only now, in hindsight, realized he should have given a lot more weight: *I even tried to rejoin the force, in the hopes of getting on the bomb squad on account of my work with explosives in the army.*

And now Macklin was going to put those skills to use by blowing up the radiator. Trying to make it look like some sort of accident maybe? It seemed a stretch, since the boiler was a long way from the room, but Macklin wasn't exactly in his right mind.

The camera may have been for watching Lacy, but the bomb in the bag was how he kept her from trying to escape. If Macklin was watching right now, he knew the door was open, and he'd probably seen Gage duck briefly into view. That meant every second that Gage stood here was another moment that Macklin might detonate his bomb.

Gage slipped his Beretta into his shoulder holster and

rushed into the room—one step, two steps, and he was already crouching in front of her, reaching for the duct tape wrapped tightly around her ankles.

He caught sight of a silver bedpan to her left, which explained the stench. She'd been forced to use the bedpan when she wanted to relieve herself. But how? She couldn't very well do it tied up as she was, which meant he had to show up from time to allow her to use the toilet. The humiliation of it all was just another reason to hate Macklin, and he was burning with this hatred when he saw Lacy's eyes widen.

She wasn't looking at him. She was looking over his shoulder. Gage had just enough time to realize that he'd made a crucial mistake: As he'd raced into the room, he'd failed to look into the doorless closet.

Stupid. So stupid.

And that was the word ringing in Gage's mind when something hard—most likely metal, most likely curved—thunked him on the back of the head.

29

————

W hen Gage opened his eyes, there was light and there was pain. The light was just a single exposed bulb overhead, the fixture missing, but looking at it still brought tears to Gage's eyes. He solved this by shifting his gaze to the floor, where he now sat with his back against the wall and legs splayed in front of him.

The throbbing in his skull didn't go away quite so easily. If anything, the slightest movement of his head intensified the pounding to the tenth degree—a throbbing concentrated in one bulbous spot above his left ear. Instinctively, he tried to reach for the spot, but his hands didn't cooperate.

That's because they *couldn't* cooperate; they were bound.

He tried to yell, but his lips wouldn't cooperate either. They were covered with duct tape. When his vision began to clear, he saw that his ankles and his wrists were bound in duct tape too.

"Welcome back to the land of living, pal," Macklin said.

Gage looked up, and there Macklin was, dressed in his usual tracksuit getup but sans sunglasses and wearing a blue surgical glove. There was also one other notable addition to his attire. In that gloved hand, he was holding a Ruger SR-22 affixed with a suppressor. It seemed this guy had all sorts of guns.

Judging by the Beretta-shaped bulge in Macklin's front pocket, Gage was no longer armed. Not that it mattered. He could barely stay conscious. Macklin said something else, but a wave of nausea washed over Gage, and the words turned into a garbled cacophony. He tasted blood in his mouth. His nose was stuffed up, each breath coming with rattling exertion.

"Did you hear what I said?" Macklin asked.

Gage shook his head, then, when the nausea intensified, regretted it.

"I said you really shouldn't have been on the beach when Jo got shot," Macklin said. "You really ruined everything, you know? I had a nice little plan, and you just had to meddle. But it's all right, man. It's all right. Like my daddy used to say, when the shit hits the fan, it may smell bad, but in the end it really doesn't change what has to be done. It just makes it stink more. And a little stink never hurt anyone. Right, Lacy? You sure made it stink in here, but it doesn't change what has to be done."

Lacy replied with a long, low moan, but Gage was still so disoriented that he couldn't tell which direction the sound was coming from. Taking in the world through a filmy, white veil, he glanced to his right and saw the window a dozen feet away, then glanced to his left and saw Lacy staring back at him. She was exactly where she'd been before, bound and gagged on the floor. Her jeans were dark around her crotch, and her UW sweatshirt was drenched around her collar.

As awful as his nausea was, Gage still felt a surge of sympathy for her. The only thing she was guilty of was loving her husband too much, and this was her reward?

"I didn't want to do this," Macklin said. "I want you both

to know that. I didn't want to do this to either of you. Wade and I had a perfectly good plan, and then the two of you couldn't leave well enough alone."

Lacy started to cry, big, pea-sized tears rolling down her face. Macklin walked over and nudged her chin up with the suppressor.

"Shut up," he said.

She inhaled sharply through her nose, glaring at him.

"There you go," Macklin said. "Hate me all you want, but just remember: You can still save Wade. He may go to prison, the dumb fuck, but he can still live. But I'm warning you, girl, you do anything, and I mean *anything* that pisses me off at this point, and I'll make sure he dies too. You got me?"

She blinked rapidly, the rage slipping away with each blink, then stared at her tennis shoes. There was still sand caked along the bottom of them.

"That's a good girl," Macklin said. "That goes for you too, Gage. You do anything at all, I shoot her first. You both made your decisions."

Lacy started crying again, but she did her best to muffle it. The throbbing made it hard for Gage to even think straight, but he knew his best chance was delay. He might be able to get on his knees, maybe launch himself at Macklin like a human cannon ball, but what were the odds that he'd come out on top? Not good.

No, his best bet was to wait for Alex to call the police. It couldn't be long. There might come a moment when Gage was required to do something desperate, to save Lacy if nothing else, but that moment hadn't arrived. Yet.

This was all going through his mind—along with wave after wave of gut-churning nausea—when he realized that Macklin was looking down at him with one of those big goofy grins.

"Thinking, thinking, thinking," Macklin said. "So much

thinking. I can see it in your eyes. You think all you have to do is just sit here and the calvary will arrive. Oh? What's that? Are you surprised that I know about everybody's favorite bookseller sitting outside in the van?"

Gage felt genuine surprise, but he did his best to look befuddled, as if he didn't have a clue what Macklin was talking about.

"Come on, man," Macklin said. "You think this is the only camera I have? I got them all over the place, all with feeds that I can see on my phone. You really think I'm just some dumb lug, don't you?"

Gage tried to speak, but it just came out *mmm-mmm.*

Macklin knelt in front of him. "I'm not talking that off, man, so you can forget about it. I already know what you're thinking anyway."

Gage lunged for Macklin. The tape duct bit into his wrists, hot pain flaring up his arm, but that was about all that Gage accomplished. Macklin chuckled and shoved him back against the wall with his hook. Then he pressed the suppressor against the middle of Gage's forehead. The metal felt ice cold against his sweaty skin.

"You want me to tell you what you're really thinking?" Macklin said. "You're thinking that Alex might be calling the police any second. But that ain't going to happen, you want to know why? Because your friend has something to prove. I could see that in him right away. When people have something to prove, they do all kinds of stupid shit. They do even more stupid shit when it's for somebody they really care about."

Something finally clicked for Gage. A missing piece fell into place.

"What the hell you smiling about?" Macklin asked.

Gage wasn't as practiced with a big goofy grin as Macklin, but he did his best with it. Macklin jabbed the Ruger under Gage's chin, tilting his head up.

"Stop that," he said.

Gage did the opposite. He smiled even wider. It was hard to do with the duct tape.

"I'm warning you," Macklin said.

Now Gage decided it was time to speak—or at least try to, enough that he could make Macklin crazy with curiosity.

"Mm mmm mmmm mmmm," Gage mumbled.

"What?"

"Mm mmm mmmm mmmm."

"Oh, for fuck's sake, I don't have time for this shit!"

It was almost a shout, which was good. It was good because it meant that Macklin was so focused on his irritation with Gage that he wasn't thinking about Alex's arrival, if only for a minute. With the precision of a surgeon, the hook slipped under the edge of the tape and ripped it free. The skin burned.

"What *is* it?" Macklin said. "Speak!"

"He was your lover," Gage said. "Jo's husband. Dell Baldwin. You were lovers."

"I don't know what you're talking about."

But he did. Gage wasn't the only one who had a hard time hiding his surprise. It was all in the eyes. In Macklin's case, those eyes were cobalt and surrounded by lots of scarred flesh, but the blue shrank to a thin blue line in the middle of two black pools.

"That love letter Jo found in Dell's desk," Gage said. "It wasn't to some woman. It was to *you.*"

"Bullshit."

"You and Dell probably exchanged letters in the books you were sharing. Is that how it worked? But maybe Dell, he played for both teams, you know. Maybe you both did, for all I know."

Macklin lifted his hook as if to strike Gage. Lacy sucked in her breath. For an instant, Gage thought Macklin was actually going to do it, but Macklin held the hook aloft, the metal vibrating, before finally jumping back to his feet and facing the door. Not good. Gage didn't want him facing the door. To give Alex any chance at all, he needed Macklin looking at Gage.

"Look," Gage said, "it doesn't matter to me who anybody loves. But why blame Jo? She didn't make Dell do what he did."

"She shot him," Macklin said.

"Because she had to."

Macklin still hadn't turned around. "She didn't, though. She really didn't. He wouldn't have shot her. He just wanted it to be over—the pain, the lying, all of it, and she gave him a way out."

Gage looked at Lacy, ten feet away. She glanced behind her. When he followed her gaze, he saw that she'd managed to loosen the duct tape considerably, to the point where she could certainly yank her hands free with one more big effort.

Why hadn't she? Her wrists were even more red and puffy than her eyes, so she'd obviously been working on it for a long time, but Gage thought he understood. The bomb next to the radiator. The camera. When Macklin wasn't around, she could never know if he was watching her, and if he was, he might light the whole thing up with a push of a button.

Even if he didn't, there was Wade to think about. She probably figured she was no match for Macklin physically, but with Gage in the room, the two of them would have a chance.

"It doesn't matter," Macklin said, turning around. "You don't really know anything, Gage. You never did."

"If you're going to kill me," Gage said, "then you might as well get it over with."

Macklin grinned. "You're trying to get me to do something stupid, aren't you? You're thinking if I shoot you, then Alex will hear it. It'll warn him."

"Jo is protected anyway," Gage said. "You can't get to her."

"Oh, I'll get to her. I waited this long."

"Why *did* you wait this long? You could have made a move before now. I don't get it. What was stopping you?"

"Nothing was stopping me. I just wasn't in a hurry."

"Bullshit. You were worried that she had proof of your relationship with Dell, didn't you? She had that letter. She hid it away, and you couldn't find it."

"No."

"You worried that even if she couldn't see that you were the one who wrote it, other people might. That's why you wanted to trade murders with Wade. If he did it, then no one would trace it back to you. And being hired to look for Wade also gave you a reason to get close to her and look for the letter."

Macklin shook his head. "You still don't get it. You think I'm such a simple person."

"Explain it to me then."

"I don't have to explain shit!"

"Tag—"

Macklin slapped Gage's temple with the suppressor, whipping Gage's head to the side and bringing tears to his eyes. "It wasn't about that stupid letter, you moron! I would have shot her myself if Dell hadn't … hadn't made me …" He whirled away from Gage and faced the opposite wall, shoulders hunched and breathing hard.

Gage pulled at his wrists, feeling the tape bite into his flesh, but there was just too much of it. If he had a day or two to work on it, he might be able to do what Lacy had done, but there wasn't much he was going to be able to do in a few minutes.

"If he hadn't made you *what?*" Gage asked.

Macklin didn't look at him. If Gage could get on his knees, he might be able to do something. Timing would be everything. He'd have to roll on his side first, and that would take time.

"It doesn't matter," Macklin said.

"He made you promise not to hurt her, didn't he?"

Macklin didn't answer, which was an answer all by itself.

"He actually loved her," Gage said. "Maybe not the way he loved you, but he cared about what happened to her."

"He … felt obligated to her. He felt he owed her. I told him he didn't. I told him the nicest thing he could do for her was to just walk away, but he … couldn't."

"Or … maybe he actually loved her."

"Dell was a complicated man. He just felt she'd been through a lot, and he didn't want to make her suffer any more than he had to. He just … He thought he could make everybody happy, and you just can't do that. Some people are going to be left out in the cold. It's just the way it is."

Then Gage finally figured it out. The insight came to him all at once, with the same kind of heart-pounding realization of seeing a train bearing down on him. Finally, it all fit. All the pieces. It actually came back to the way Jo had reacted when Gage first met her, when he'd told her he had a daughter. He could see the look of loss in her eyes. It was the way a person, and especially, in his experience, a woman, looked when they'd wanted children and hadn't been able to have them.

"The money was going to be for her," Gage said. "For fertility treatments, right? It's expensive. He thought he could give her a baby. He thought that might make it right somehow, all the pain they'd been through. He was never going to leave her, was he? Not really. He strung you along, Garrick. He strung you along like so many other people having affairs."

"That's a lie," Macklin said, but he had a hard time getting out the words. "That's—that's a total lie."

"And even worse, he made you promise not to hurt her. As angry as you are with him, you don't want to break that promise. You loved him that much."

Macklin spun around, the Ruger trembling in his hand. The look in his eyes was one of madness, of somebody about to plunge into the abyss. Seeing the way Macklin's trigger finger twitched, Gage remained silent.

"Nothing else to say, smart ass?" Macklin said. "Go ahead. You're a regular psychiatrist, aren't you?"

Gage said nothing, but then he thought he heard Alex's footsteps in the hall, and he realized that he had to keep talking just to cover the noise. "Why did you kill Stan Carson?"

"I didn't. He committed suicide."

"Come on, Tag."

"I *didn't*. He pulled the trigger on himself before I got a chance."

"Before you bled him completely dry, you mean."

"That child molester? You're defending *him?* I'm not sorry he's gone, if that's what you're asking."

"So you *did* bleed him dry?"

"Man, you just won't quit."

Now Gage was sure he heard something out in the hall, the distinctive creak of a footstep. "But killing him actually turned out to be a lot tougher than you thought it would be, didn't it?" he said. "You just couldn't bring yourself to go through with it, but then Stan Carson did it himself. That released you."

"It—it wasn't—"

"And it gave you the idea about Wade. You could use him to kill Jo, the whole suicide thing, and it wouldn't be *you* doing it. You wouldn't be breaking your promise to Dell." Then Gage decided to take a chance, one that could spectacularly backfire even if he was right, and undoubtedly so if he was wrong.

It was true that Gage didn't care who loved who or why. He'd never been attracted to the same gender, though he'd known plenty of good men who had. Good men who loved other good men. But Tag was not a good man, and his twisted, warped mind led Gage to believe there was a deeper trauma going on here, one that dated all the way back to childhood. "He touched you, didn't he?"

"What?"

"Your daddy. He touched you, when you were little. He did things to you."

Macklin raised the Ruger. "You fucker. You damn fucker. You don't know anything."

"You could keep your promise to Dell just like you kept your promise to daddy. He made you promise not to tell, didn't he? He made you promise, and little Garrick always keeps his promises."

"Shut up! Just shut the fuck up!"

"It's okay," Gage said. "I won't tell. I won't tell anybody, Garrick. Your secret is safe with me."

"Stop!"

"You're safe. I'll take care of you. Nobody can hurt you if you don't tell."

The Ruger shook violently in Macklin's hands, but so far the trigger finger hadn't moved. He was also crying—big, heaving sobs. This was what Gage had been hoping for, so much pent-up emotion coming to the fore, a maelstrom of shame and guilt and rage all swirling out of the darkest part of Macklin's heart that it would make it impossible for him to be aware of anything outside his own personal tornado.

It worked too. The door behind Macklin was opening. Gage glimpsed just enough to see Alex's revolver edging into the room—that old thing, the Smith & Wesson Model 13, something he'd bought before he'd even joined the FBI and probably hadn't fired in decades.

Macklin wasn't aware. Macklin was back with his daddy, in that horrible place, that place of betrayal and suffering. There was an opening here. It was the opening Gage had been hoping for, and all Alex had to do was take it.

"Drop the gun," Alex said.

And that was his first mistake.

30

I f only Alex had just pulled the trigger, things might have gone differently. What better opportunity could he ask for? Gage and Lacy were on the floor, out of the line of fire. Not only was Macklin standing, he was standing with his back to Alex, so frozen in place he might as well have been one of those two-dimensional targets they used to shoot at Quantico.

Alex had shot plenty of those targets when he'd been an instructor there, but that had been a long time ago, decades and decades, another life. The frumpy, bespeckled bookseller with the caterpillar mustache and the dark chasms under his eyes had about as much in common with that highly decorated former FBI agent as Gage had with Olympic gymnasts.

Still, when Gage looked back upon the fateful encounter later, with the benefit of perspective and hindsight, he would be fairly certain that rustiness wasn't the chief cause of Alex's hesitation. The explanation was far more straightforward.

Alex simply could not shoot a man in the back.

Gage possessed no such inhibition. He would prefer not to shoot *anybody*, of course, and would go to extreme lengths to avoid doing so, but if it had to be done, then there was no point quibbling about the doing of it. It made no difference to him whether it was in the back, between the eyes, or at point-blank range. If he decided that the situation required shooting somebody, then he would shoot them, and he would not indulge in such luxuries as to whether the act was honorable or not. That kind of thing would only get you killed.

This was not Alex's way, though, and at his command, Macklin flinched. He didn't, however, lower the gun. For a few tense seconds, he didn't do anything at all.

"I told you to—" Alex began, but he never got out the rest.

In one fluid motion, Macklin spun and sprang backward, squeezing off a shot even as he did so. Alex fired at almost the same time, the shots coming so close together that they sounded like one ear-ringing boom in the tiny office.

The drywall above Gage exploded. The doorframe behind Alex did the same. Both Alex and Macklin missed their first shots, the air pluming with white powder and wood debris. Gage's ears rang from Alex's unmuffled shot. Lacy screamed, so piercing that it penetrated his dulled hearing and the duct tape over her mouth.

Gage, on the floor, could see the disaster unfolding before him, but it was all happening so fast, with so little time to intervene. Both Alex and Macklin were recovering, bringing their handguns up for another shot, but Macklin was faster. He was going to shoot first. It was nearly point-blank range, and this time Alex didn't have the benefit of surprise.

In the chaos, Gage managed to clamber onto his knees, gritting through the pain, struggling to get one foot under him despite his ankles and hands still being duct-taped. The tape stretched and torqued but didn't rip, digging into Gage's skin.

This was where Gage was: mostly deaf, down on the

floor on his bad knee, weaponless, and with virtually no hope of saving Alex, let alone himself.

Alex was going to take it right between the eyes.

His best friend. His mentor. His confidant. This was the man who'd been there for him in all the ways that really mattered in life. One shot and he'd be gone. This was the real reason Gage couldn't allow Alex to truly put himself in harm's way, why he'd always done everything he could to avoid this possible scenario in the past, and yet here they were. Maybe this situation had been unavoidable all along. Maybe this was all that life ever had in store for Gage, just one loss after another, until he was good and truly alone. He brought death to everyone around him and only misery to himself.

No.

He wouldn't allow it.

Take my life, he thought. Take me instead. Give me the comforting darkness instead of making me live in the light with all that pain.

Something shifted inside Gage in that instant before Macklin pulled the trigger. He felt a tremor, like a crevice opening up in the deepest, darkest part of him, and hot rage gushed forth like flowing lava. It gave him strength he didn't know he had. It was strange that an act of total surrender would give him this strength, but he was not surrendering to defeatism. He was surrendering to the inevitability of death. It could happen now, tomorrow, or in fifty years, it didn't matter.

What mattered right now was *acting.*

So act he did. With his hearing still gone, he felt the duct tape rip more than heard it as he launched himself at Macklin's legs. Physics was still physics, and he ended up boring into Macklin's calves instead.

It was not a great target. Even Macklin's ankles might

have been better, more likely to break and bring the big man toppling down. But the impact with the calves only shoved Macklin sideways. He stumbled and staggered, but he didn't fall.

He also got off a shot.

But so did Alex.

Blood misted out of Macklin's extended gun hand. The Ruger went sailing through the air. Maklin stumbled to the right, blood dripping on Gage's face. What little hearing Gage had left was gone. What took its place was the sound of his own beating heart. Even before he rolled onto his side, he knew what he was going to see, and he saw it.

Alex lay on the floor near the door, blood already pooling around his gut.

He wasn't moving. Macklin was screaming, an inhuman sound, full of not just the pain of his wound but all the suffering he had endured, a cry of agony so piercing that it somehow reached Gage even through his deaf ears. Macklin writhed around, clutching his bloody hand against his chest, hardly more than another stump, the fingers mangled, the blood a deep, shiny red against the black tracksuit.

In his own personal agony, Gage reached for his friend's immovable form and was surprised when his hands were free. Somehow, inexplicably, he'd managed to rip them from the duct tape during his adrenaline-fueled tackle.

He had a chance.

He may have failed Alex, but he still had a chance to save Lacy.

Macklin, moaning and carrying on, had his back turned. Gage could only barely make him out from the corner of his eye. Gage curled himself into a fetal position, bringing his knees up so that he could reach the duct tape fastening his ankles. How long did he have before Macklin recovered enough to notice?

Not long. Seconds maybe.

He slipped off his right shoe and sock, then wet his fingers with his own saliva and slicked up his right foot and ankle as much as he could. Blinking away the sweat stinging his eyes, he slipped his fingers into the gap between his ankles and tugged with all his might. Macklin's moaning grew louder. Gage's hearing was coming back.

"You!" Macklin cried behind him. "Gage, this—this is your fault!"

With one herculean effort, Gage yanked his right leg free. The pain as his skin, rather than the tape, ripped free was so intense that his vision blackened around the edges. Footsteps. He both heard and felt them, a thundering over the floorboards.

There was a whistling in the air, and Gage rolled hard to his left. Macklin's hook struck the floor like the end of a spear. It missed Gage's face by less than a pinky width, the point so close that he felt the breath of wind.

Wood splinters speckled Gage's cheek. He saw his own eye reflected in the gleaming surface of the hook, the pupil distorted and huge, more like an inkblot than a human feature. He was still in a terrible spot, on his stomach with Macklin looming over him, and all it would take was one more swipe from that hook and Gage was probably done.

Then a miracle happened.

Macklin was frozen. It was like time had stopped, except that the blood from Macklin's hand dripped onto the floor. Gage rolled to the left, once, twice, and still Macklin didn't move.

"Damn it!" Macklin cried.

It was then that Gage realized what had happened. Macklin's hook was embedded in the floor. It wasn't so much a miracle as physics. The hook had gone in deep, and now he was struggling to yank it free.

It bought Gage the precious seconds he needed to climb to his feet.

With a howl, Macklin managed to rip his hook free. A fist-sized chunk of floorboard spun through the air and smacked against the ceiling. Gage dodged to the left. The hook sliced through his jacket as if it were made of paper.

Gage was no boxing expert, but he'd made sure to master the fundamentals, and he'd learned long ago that a decent hook, cross, and jab were all that he really needed when combined with his almost preternatural calm under pressure. He threw a hard undercut at Macklin's chin, but the big man swiveled at the last second, and Gage ended up punching Macklin's enormous shoulder instead.

It felt like hitting a brick wall. Worse, it left Gage exposed to another swing from that deadly hook. The point whizzed through the air, and Gage just barely managed to get his head out of the way, but his own shoulder took the brunt of it. The blade sliced through the jacket, the shirt, and much of the flesh underneath.

Pain radiated up his arm. He barely had time to feel it, and the hook was coming at him again. Gag ducked just in time, then plowed into Macklin with a right cross to the gut. He put everything into it, but again, he might as well have been punching ten inches of steel.

Macklin swung again, this time ripping Gage's polo shirt in half and slicing across Gage's stomach. The blade was so sharp that Gage barely felt the initial wound. What he felt instead was the blood pouring out of him.

Gage fought gamely. He got in a punch to the jaw, another to the ribs, and a third to Macklin's solar plexus, but nothing seemed to make a difference. Each one cost Gage another pound of flesh. Macklin was quite literally carving him up one slice at a time. There was blood everywhere. On his clothes. On the floor. On the walls. On

Macklin too, who was speckled with it like the strange embodiment of modern art made all the stranger by Macklin's ever-present leer.

He was toying with Gage. Despite his mangled hand, he was light on his feet, dancing left and right, easily avoiding most of Gage's punches. When the punches *did* land, it was almost like Macklin meant them to land, like he was trying to show Gage that no matter what he did, it would never make a difference.

The wounds all piled up: a minor tear on Gage's abdomen, a gusher along his shoulder, a nick off his left ear that could have removed his whole face. Finally Gage managed to land a jab to Macklin's nose, a real whopper, a punch that would have dropped just about anyone. But even as Macklin's head whipped backward, he was laughing.

Gasping for breath, Gage braced himself against his knees so he didn't topple over. Macklin probably could have taken Gage right there, but he only laughed harder.

"It's no fun unless I've *really* beaten you," Macklin said. "And now you're beaten, aren't you? You know there's no chance. Good, good. I want you in the darkest place imaginable, man. I want you …"

Macklin trailed off, tilting his head to the right. Gage was breathing so hard that it took him an extra second to make out the siren, and by then Macklin was already lunging for him. So much for being toyed with. Before Gage could even get his hands back up, Macklin had him in a choke hold in the crook of his ropey arm. Worse, with his other arm, the one with the hook, he pressed the sharp point so deeply into Gage's neck that it punctured the skin.

"There's still time," Macklin said, his breath hot on Gage's neck, his words gargled with the blood in his mouth. "I'll get out of this, you'll see. I'll blow up all the evidence. It'll all be on Lacy anyway. The crazy wife. The one who drove

Wade to suicide. She blamed you for failing Wade, and it all led to this. I've got it all figured out."

"Stop," Lacy said.

Macklin became very still. Her voice came from slightly behind them and to Gage's right.

"Stop, or I'll—I'll shoot," she said.

The gun. Macklin's Ruger. When Gage and Macklin were engaged in their crazy tête-à-tête, she must have gotten a hold of it. Gage couldn't move. One tiny move and that hook would cut his throat.

The approaching siren rose into the silence. A second passed, maybe two. Nobody moved.

"Let him go," Lacy said. "Let him go or—"

With a sharp, bark-like laugh, Macklin spun them around so they were both facing Lacy.

"—shoot," she finished.

It happened that fast, in the gap between two words, but it probably wouldn't have mattered if she'd had an hour. The truth was in her eyes. Through her veil of disheveled blonde hair, Gage saw it.

It was not weakness. It was not cowardice. It was what Gage had realized the first time he'd met her. There was just something about her. You felt for her. You wanted to protect her, to shield her from bad things. Back then, when this thought had first occurred to Gage, he hadn't known why he felt this impulse for somebody he'd just met, but now he did. It wasn't just goodness. It was the goodness that refused to be corrupted by the world. It was a rare thing, when it was seen, because it was that part of the human spirit that everyone wished they had but few really did.

Gage didn't want to see her lose it. If she shot Macklin, she'd never be the same. If she shot Macklin *and* killed Gage in the process, that part of her that was wholly good would shrivel up and disappear. But that was the choice, wasn't it?

She could let that pure goodness go, and live, or let it be consumed by the evil that had always been flitting around the edges of her life.

Gage could not protect her. He could not shield her from bad things. Looking at her now, he saw that it was true. It was true not only for her but for Zoe, for Jo, for Alex, for anyone that he cared about. He could not shield them from the evil in the world.

Something else happened in the long pause after Macklin spun around. He heard something else over the sirens.

He heard Alex moan.

Alex. His friend. His best friend. He was alive. He was still alive, so there might be hope yet.

No, Gage couldn't protect them. He could, however, give his life for theirs. That was something worth doing. Some part of the goodness in them would remain. It may have been lost to him, but some small kernel of it would live on in others. To do it, she would have to do something terrible, and he would have to give her permission.

With Macklin's arm clinching down on his windpipe, it was hard to breathe, much less speak, but Gage pulled at Macklin's arm with both hands enough to gasp out a few words.

"Shoot—shoot him, Lacy," he said.

"I'll hit you."

"Doesn't matter. Shoot! Then you get to live."

She started crying.

"Just pull the trigger and keep pulling it. He won't live. You can do this. It's all right. I want you to do this. I want—"

Macklin squeezed Gage's neck even harder, choking off the rest of what Gage wanted to say. "Here's what's going to happen, Lacy my girl. I'm going out that door with Garrison here."

"Don't," Lacy said.

Macklin laughed and took a sidestep toward the door, dragging Gage along with him. When he did, he relaxed his grip on Gage's windpipe just a little, and Gage was able to cough out a few hoarse words.

"If he leaves," Gage said, "he'll blow this place up. Shoot him. Don't let—"

"Shut up!" Macklin cried.

He squeezed Gage's throat so hard that his vision tunneled, black on all sides, unconsciousness threatening to remove him from the game. He blinked hard and fought to stay awake. His vision narrowed until all he saw was Lacy, her face contorted with anguish, her eyes bloodshot, her nose a pink and puffy mess.

The Ruger dropped again, even farther than before, though it wasn't pointing all the way to the ground.

"Don't," she begged. "Please don't. Please don't leave."

Whether it was her pleading tone, the hopelessness in her body language, or that the Ruger was no longer really pointing at him, Macklin stopped. The sirens were so loud they must have just been down the street. The police would be in the building in seconds.

It was Macklin's best chance to escape, but he stopped. Why? Because he was enjoying himself? Because he took perverse pleasure in the utter desperation in Lacy's eyes? Whatever the reason, Macklin once again released his grip on Gage's windpipe. The hook still dug far enough into Gage's flesh that blood trickled down his neck, but there was enough room for Gage to make a move.

He could roll to the right, toward the blade.

He might cut his own throat in the process—he was quite sure he would—but it would get him out of the way. It would give Lacy a clear shot. She still might not be able to pull the trigger, but Gage couldn't be the reason she and Alex died in this room. So he gritted his teeth and rolled hard toward the hook, feeling metal cutting in deeper, the blood flowing even faster.

Even this might not have been enough to free him from Macklin's grasp if it hadn't been for Alex.

For Macklin's fixation on escaping into the hall had made him forget where Alex was on the floor. *Right there next to Macklin's feet.* And just as Gage was beginning his move, Alex reached out and grabbed Macklin's ankle.

Gage, as he spun, saw it happen. He saw Alex's blood-drenched hand clamping through Macklin's tracksuit to take a fierce hold of the ankle beneath. The hook still ripped across Gage's neck, but he didn't black out. Gage fell to the floor next to his friend, grasping at the blood gushing from his neck.

When he hit, he was looking at Lacy. He was looking at his own Beretta. It was firm. It was aimed in the right place. More importantly, those green eyes, so soft and diffuse the first time he'd met her, looked like blocks of limestone.

She fired.

The first bullet hit Macklin in the chest. He barely moved. Then she fired again, one shot quickly after another, four in all, each hitting him center mass.

The second bullet made him stagger back a step, grunting and grasping at his bloody chest. The third bullet sent him careening against the far wall, banging into it with all of his weight. The third must have hit him directly in the heart, because when Gage finally turned to look at him, he saw Macklin sliding down the wall, dead-eyed and slack jawed, his poor, miserable life finally and swiftly coming to an end.

The world wavered, black clouds encroaching on Gage's vision from all sides. Lacy dropped the Ruger with a clatter and fell to her knees, covering her face with her hands.

Fighting the pain, fighting the nearly irresistible pull of the darkness, Gage crawled across the floor to his friend.

The sirens grew louder. Through the open window, he heard tires screeching. There was so much blood on Alex's face that his mustache was stained red. He was holding his side, where he'd been shot. Gage pressed his hands over Alex's, covering the wound, the blood soon overwhelming both their fingers. He couldn't tell whose hands were whose.

"You're an idiot," Gage said.

"Tell Eve, okay? Tell Eve I love her."

"Will you shut up? You're not going to die."

"It hurts. Jesus."

"Hey. Hey now. Look at me."

"I'm sorry. I know—I know I messed it up."

"Alex, stay with me."

"You've been a good friend," he said, then closed his eyes.

31

———

There were moments in life, terrible moments, that could break a person in half. Everybody faced them sooner or later. Everybody knew they were coming too, even if they denied it to themselves—an inescapable crisis, a tragedy so overwhelming it blotted out everything else, a mistake so big and so painful that it swept aside all the comforting lies people spun to themselves about what things meant and why.

Gage had faced more than a few such moments in his life, certainly far more than should have been allotted to any one person. Nobody should have to suffer this much. Nobody should have to bear this kind of burden. And yet, he did, and he had. He would also go on bearing these burdens because there was no other way for him to be. It was who he was, and he'd long since accepted that maybe some people got to float through life on feathery wings, but he would always be down in the muck.

He could get shot, punched, yelled at, fired, slapped silly, and all other manner of indignities that could be piled on a person. Lose a wife? He'd checked that box. Alienate a daughter? Sure, sign him up. Watch his best friend die in front of him? Yep, Gage had no doubt that he deserved to have that particular spitball of meanness.

Fortunately, even if Gage deserved it, the universe wasn't *quite* that mean. Not yet anyway.

"I know we're not in heaven," Alex said, "because Eve's in here with us, and she's got to be still alive. Unless I'm dreaming?"

Once again, Gage was at the Barnacle Bluffs Hospital, but this time he was not in a waiting area but an actual room. Gage sat in one of the two chairs near the door. Eve had been sitting next to him in the other one, pretending to read her Kindle, but she sprang out of it as soon as Alex spoke.

The blinds over the window were closed, but the midday sun was so fierce and so bright that it filled the room with a golden glow even though the overhead light was off. Other than a tiny bandage on his forehead where, ironically, Alex had gotten scraped with his own fingernail as he'd fallen to the floor, there was hardly any immediate sign that he'd been shot. If they pulled back the sheets, however, his whole abdomen was a mess of bandages, bruises, and enough stitches to knit a pair of gloves.

There was no heart monitor, no IV, and no other equipment to make a sound. Gage could hear the nurses talking just down the hall, some soft laughter. Shoes squeaked on the tiles. He should have been annoyed at the laughter—didn't they know his friend was on the mend in here?—but he was too relieved to be irritated by minor things.

Gage smiled. "You're definitely not dreaming, but what makes you think either of us would deserve to get into heaven?"

"Good point," Alex said. "And that's how I know I'm

really not dead, because there's no way Eve would be in the other place."

He laughed, but the laugh quickly morphed into a wince. Eve, blinking back tears, grabbed her husband's hand. She was still dressed in the charcoal-gray pantsuit she'd been wearing during a city council meeting when she got the call that both Alex and Gage were on their way to the hospital. Despite not having slept, despite having cried much of the time Alex had been in surgery, and despite having paced the soles right off her shiny black pumps while he slept in this room, she somehow still managed to look resplendent. It was some kind of voodoo magic. It had to be.

"You two," she said. "You just never quit. You need rest, dear. Rest."

"I'll be all right," he said. "Dear God, it hurts like a son of a gun, though."

"They told me it's a miracle the bullet missed your heart," Gage said. "I told them it wasn't a miracle if somebody didn't have a heart in the first place."

"Don't make him laugh," Eve said. "And shouldn't you be getting back to your room?"

"Are you going to call the nurses on me, Mrs. Cortez?" Gage replied.

"Nurses? I'll have you arrested. I'm the mayor, you know."

"Wow, a power play from the Greek goddess."

She looked at her husband and squeezed his hand again. "Our daughters are on their way."

"Good, good," Alex said.

He smiled big enough that even the bandage on his forehead raised a few inches, but his eyes also turned watery. They were all silent. The tone had been light up until now, but it shifted, a heavy weight pressing down on them like one of those lead-lined blankets they draped over patients during an X-ray. There was something he needed to say to Alex, something difficult.

First, though, the easy part. "I'm sorry about what happened," Gage said.

"Ah," Alex said, with a shrug. "I just wish I had gotten there sooner."

"No, you were amazing. I wouldn't be alive if it weren't for you. Or Lacy. We owe you everything."

"You saved me too, you know," Alex said.

"Well, I did that for Eve. Otherwise she'd never forgive me."

"Damn straight," Eve said.

"Eve!" Gage said. "I'm shocked, shocked at your profanity."

Alex, his eyes distant, continued as if he hadn't heard this exchange. "I just wish I'd been a little quicker, you know. Just too rusty, I guess."

Gage swallowed. Here was the hard part. "Well, there's nothing wrong with being rusty, you know. Getting old. It happens to all of us. There comes a time when we've got to face the music. I know that's a cliché, but it's got a ring of truth to it, as all clichés do, and, well …"

Alex laughed. "Garrison, if you're trying to tell me something, just spit it out."

"I was just thinking, you know, you're a very good bookseller. A *damn* fine bookseller, to use Eve's new favorite word."

"Oh, stop," Eve said.

"And maybe," Gage said, warming up to it now, "maybe it's just time to be a bookseller and, well, leave all the Dick Tracy stuff out of the equation."

"Dick Tracy stuff?"

"You know what I mean."

"Uh huh. You're saying I'm too old to be shooting it out with psychopaths, is that it?"

"Well, it's not so much about being too old ..."

"Too fat and out of shape?"

"Hey, I didn't—"

"Too rusty, washed-up, out of practice, out of touch, and out of time to be worth a damn out in the field with a young whippersnapper like you?"

"Alex, come on, I—"

"Well, you're right," Alex said.

It caught Gage by surprise. "I am?"

"Yes. It's obvious, isn't it? It's obvious I had no business being in that office with a gun in my hand. It's obvious I had no business going out on a late-night stakeout with you. It's obvious that whatever skills I once had are long gone, and this wrinkled and saggy old man is barely a shadow of his former self."

Gage felt his face warm. "I never said all that. I just—I just don't want you to get hurt, that's all. Neither does Eve. Neither do your daughters."

Alex raised his hand. "Don't get all riled up. I actually agree with you, okay? You're telling it to me straight, and I appreciate it. I'm a long way from my FBI days, and the smartest thing to do is to own up to the truth of who I am now."

They were all silent for a time. Gage, his emotional bruises now equal to his physical ones, found it difficult to speak. It came to Eve—of course it came to Eve, stalwart and steadfast even in her distress—to take up the conversational baton.

"So you'll leave all the private investigative stuff to Garrison?" she asked.

Alex's face was unreadable. Nobody moved. The only change was the sun. Bright and golden on the blinds until that moment, some clouds must have floated across the sky, and the light in their room turned dusky. It was so like the coast. The weather never stayed the same for long, and the sun, always welcome when it showed its face, would depart with little warning, like an ungrateful houseguest.

"Absolutely not," Alex said.

"Oh God," Gage said.

"Actually," Alex said, chuckling, "there's a new judo dojo that just opened up in the outlet mall. I was thinking of trying them out."

"Honey," Eve said, "I know this is hard, but you don't have anything to prove."

While looking at his wife, Alex jerked his thumb toward Gage. "You think I'm going to let him have all the fun? Besides, I think I have *plenty* to prove. That's the point."

"You're going to get yourself killed," Gage said.

"Okay, so what?"

"So what? What do you mean, *so what?*"

"I'm not saying I'm going to *try* to get killed. I'm not an idiot."

"I beg to differ," Gage said.

"Will you let me finish? I've got something to say here, and you need to hear it."

"*I* need to hear it? You're the one who won't listen to reason."

"No, I think I finally caught a clue, that's all. I'm not saying I'm going to try to become some kind of Chuck Norris wannabe—"

"You're dating yourself, dear," Eve said.

"—but what I *am* saying, if the two of you will stop babying me for one second, is that I want to do better. I want to get in shape. And I'm not going to let my fears get the best of me. What's so wrong with that? I'm not denying that I love my books, but is that all I have to be? Is there some rule that I have to sit at home rereading James Michener, listening to Miles Davis on vinyl, and drinking twenty-year-old scotch?

Or am I allowed to do something else? To *be* something else?"

His tone was stern but still somewhat playful; there was an obvious glimmer of amusement in his eyes. When Gage had no reply, Alex leveled a finger at his wife.

"And you," he said, "you're not one to talk, are you ... *Mayor Cortez?*"

Eve said nothing, but it was obvious she was trying to hold back a smile.

"Right," Alex said. "You faced something difficult, a big health scare, and it made you think about your life in a new way. That's all I'm doing, okay? And I have every right to do whatever the hell I want, so you both need to shut up."

"I guess I did the same thing, didn't I?" Gage said, feeling appropriately chastised. "After Janet died, I came to Barnacle Bluffs to wallow in misery, but a young dead woman on the beach helped me get back into the game."

Alex shook his head. "Not really."

"What?"

"I mean, yeah, you did *kind of* get back into the game—in your usual half-assed way."

"I'm confused. Alex, I'm just trying to apologize."

"Is that what this is?"

Gage shook his head. "You're hopeless."

"Is that why you *still*, after all these years, don't have an office?"

"I don't need an office to be a private investigator."

"No, but you don't even have a business card."

"Oh, is that what I need to make it official? A tiny piece of paper. Jesus. When did *I* become the focus here?"

"There's more," Alex said. "Don't worry, it gets worse."

"Oh goodie."

"Because here's the thing. Ever since you came to Barnacle Bluffs, you've always had one foot in, and one foot out. And I'm not just talking about being a private investigator. I'm talking about *life.*"

"You're crazy," Gage said.

"Oh yeah? Is that why, with all the women who've come through your life since you got here, that you've always found your way to being alone again?"

"*Me?* I didn't do that. They all left on their own."

"Because they always knew you had one foot out the door."

"I'm really getting tired of you saying that."

"Already? If you don't start committing to something, *anything,* you can look forward to hearing me saying it a lot more in the days ahead. Because here's the thing, Garrison. Here's the thing." His voice sounded pinched. Their conversation, despite the rising tension, had remained more friendly banter than serious argument up to this point, but now there was no doubt that Alex wasn't kidding around. "Yes, I'm old. Yes, I almost died. Yes, I can probably never be who … who I once was."

"Honey," Eve said, touching him gently on the shoulder.

"No, I'm not done. I have one last thing, and my best friend here, he's the one who really needs to hear it. It's like this, Garrison. Just because you can never be what you once were doesn't mean you can't be something else."

32

There was another patient in the Barnacle Bluffs Hospital who wasn't nearly so feisty as the aspiring judo master down the hall. If Alex Cortez had gotten incredibly lucky in how a handgun had torn through his insides, then Josephine Roland was the opposite.

The fates had not been kind. When Gage looked in on her from the doorway, she was exactly as she had been when he snuck down last night, barely managing to get to the door before the nurses apprehended him. Eyes closed, a mess of tubes everywhere, and her face waxy and yellow, she was hardly recognizable. She looked small, like a child even, which was partly because someone had brushed her blonde hair in a neat part down the middle.

It was not a style he'd ever seen her wear before. She looked so tiny and helpless. That was when he realized that the young cop who'd been stationed outside Jo's door, the one who'd been here last night, was gone. He clenched his jaw and turned to go get his phone so he could call Brisbane and demand an answer for such incompetence.

"Hello," a woman said.

Gage flinched. He'd been holding onto the door frame for support, and it was good he was, because otherwise he would have fallen for sure. That would have not only been painful but embarrassing, because his hospital gown wouldn't provide him with much cover once he was down there.

It was Jo's mother, perched like a watchful owl in one of the chairs. Gage recognized her from the picture in Jo's office —same build, same high cheekbones, same severely straight hair, though silver instead of blonde. She wore a powder-blue cashmere sweater over a white V-neck blouse, charcoal gray slacks, and blue pumps that matched the color of her eyes. In person, her eyes weren't gray, as they'd seemed in the photo, but some of the saddest, bluest eyes he'd ever seen.

"Oh," Gage said, "I didn't know anyone was … I'm Garrison. Garrison Gage. I'm … I'm a friend of Jo's."

"I know who you are," she said.

"You do?"

She nodded, taking her time answering. "She said you were the most difficult man she'd ever met."

"Ah."

There was another long pause as she gazed upon him with her owl eyes. He would soon learn that this was the norm for her; she was never in a rush with anything. "Among other things," she said. "I'm Vivian Robles. I'm her mother, as I'm sure you already guessed."

She smiled faintly. That was when Gage realized he'd been wrong about her eyes. They weren't sad so much as … soulful. Possessing extraordinary depth. That was not to say she wasn't sad. The puffy pinkness around her eyes was a clear sign she'd been crying. It was just to say her sadness did not define her. There was something else there, a sense of presence, of peace even amid tragedy, that radiated from her the way heat radiated from the sand after a day under a relentless sun.

She beckoned for him to sit in the second chair. When she did, her diamond ring flashed in the sunlight slanting into the room from the cracked-open blinds. A wedding ring, if she was following the usual custom. Two suede jackets hung on the rack, one much bulkier.

Vivian followed his gaze. "Robert has gone to get coffee," she said. "He won't mind giving up his seat anyway. Too much sitting is not good for his arthritis, especially here, where it's so much colder than in Miami. Please. Sit."

She patted the empty seat. Gage resisted. It wasn't because he didn't want to sit. It was because he didn't feel he belonged. Yet he found himself sitting anyway, such was the magnetic pull of Vivian Robles. When he'd seen her in the photo, he'd formed an impression of her as a lonely old widow, but she'd obviously forged a new life for herself— remarried, moved to Florida. He wondered now why he'd assumed she wouldn't. He wondered what it said about him.

The cushion was still warm, so her husband couldn't have been gone long. His gown was so thin that it felt like he was wrapped in cellophane. He tugged at it self-consciously.

"No change?" he said to her.

"I'm afraid not. And yes, I'm completely up to date on her condition. I know she might not wake up. And even— even if she does ..."

Vivian might have been a woman of rare poise, but her voice still cracked. It was the sort of thing that would usually elicit a comforting response, how everything would be okay, but Gage was not in the business of giving people false hope or even reassuring lies, however much he might want to, and he certainly wasn't going to do it with Vivian Robles. But he had to say *something*, so he said the same three words most people would say, as hollow as they were.

"I'm so sorry," he said.

"Yes. It's a terrible thing, seeing your child this way."

"I know. I just wish I could ... I don't know, *do* something for her."

"You're here. That's something."

"It's not enough," Gage said. "If it wasn't for me ..."

"Oh, don't blame yourself, dear. That kind of thing will eat your soul. It's what made life so hard for Jo all these years. She just wouldn't stop blaming herself. As Alan Watts wrote, 'No work or love will flourish out of guilt, fear, or hollowness of heart, just as no valid plans for the future can be made by those who have no capacity for living now.'"

Gage swallowed away the lump in his throat. "How much do you know about what happened?"

"I talked to Detective Brisbane on the phone when we were driving here from Portland. He gave me his version of events."

"His version?"

"Well, there are always many versions of such things, aren't there? It was like my Chaucer classes. No two students ever interpreted *The Canterbury Tales* quite the same way."

"That doesn't mean the actual story is any different, though, right?"

"Doesn't it?"

She offered up another one of her fleeting Mona Lisa smiles. Gage didn't want to argue the point.

"Speaking of Brisbane," he said, "where's the officer that's supposed to be stationed here?"

"Dismissed. Now that the danger is past."

"Uh huh. Well, I'll have to have a little chat with Detective Brisbane about that. Seems a little premature, don't you think?"

She didn't say anything to this. He didn't blame her. There wasn't really anything to say, and he was being petty anyway. It wasn't a time for being petty. This was just more avoidance on his part about facing up to the hard thing. But what *was* the hard thing? His inability to accept that he and Jo just weren't meant to be together, no matter how he felt about her?

"What's going to happen to that poor boy that shot her?" Vivian asked. "I'm having a hard time getting a straight answer from anyone, but it doesn't sound like they think it's an accident anymore."

Gage nodded. "It's complicated, but … yeah. Yesterday, when Brisbane came by to take my statement, I learned that Wade actually confessed to shooting Jo intentionally—over protests from both his mother and his lawyer, I might add."

"Oh. Well, good for him."

Gage shot her a skeptical look. "Good for *him?*"

"Yes. In the sense that it's almost always a good thing to take ownership of our mistakes."

"Aren't you angry at him?"

"Of course," she said, but she didn't sound angry. She didn't sound like she *ever* got angry. "That doesn't mean I want him to see the electric chair. Oregon still has capital punishment on the books, correct?"

"Technically, yes. But the last one was decades ago."

"Still. He's just a boy, really. And it sounds like he was very much coerced into this terrible business."

"He's twenty-seven, hardly a boy. And no one forced him to pull that trigger. That's on him."

She nodded. "Which is why I'm glad to hear that he's trying to take responsibility for his part in this … I see you shaking your head. You think I'm being hopelessly naive?"

"I guess a more positive way to put it is that I'm in awe of your grace."

"You have a hard time forgiving, don't you?"

"I would never forgive somebody for shooting my daughter, no. It's more likely that I would take them apart piece by piece and enjoy every moment of it."

It wasn't Gage's intention to get a rise out of her, but if it had been, he would have been disappointed. Her gaze softened, and her voice, while still cool, carried an undercurrent of warmth. "Forgiving other people is actually the easy part," she said. "Not that any of it is truly easy. But forgiving yourself? That's hard. It's also what will actually change your life."

Gage clamped down on the arms of the chair, trying to hold back the tidal wave of emotion threatening to overwhelm him. This was hardly the time, the place, or the person to unburden himself with all his rage and guilt, but it was like the dams he'd built up around his heart were crumbling. It was like there was nothing he could do.

Then Vivian Robles did something quite unexpected. She reached over and patted his hand. For a woman who came across so coolly detached, her fingers were surprisingly warm and soft. Just like that, it was better. He no longer felt like screaming. He just felt hollow.

"I don't know if I can do that," he said. "Forgive myself, I mean. I don't know if I'm capable of it."

"It's worth the effort, you know."

"Hmm."

"My daughter keeps trying. Maybe one of these days she'll get there. Maybe you can even help each other."

She gave his hand another pat, then let it go. Despite the skimpy hospital gown, Gage felt warm. Sweat trickled down his back. He also felt naked next to her, and it wasn't just the lack of clothes; he felt vulnerable in a way that was intolerable.

"I should go," he said.

"Are you sure? My husband should be back any minute. I'd like you to meet him."

Gage stood, having to use the chair for support, now

feeling all the aches and bruises in a way he hadn't before. "Maybe another time," he said.

"I wish you'd stay, at least for a little while."

"I don't think that's a good idea."

Vivian looked at Jo. "She'd want you to."

"Would she, though?"

"Sometimes Jo says the opposite of what she means. More often than not, I think."

Gage, with no answer to this, could only nod. He should have left right then. That was certainly what he intended to do, what he believed he *should* do, but instead he found himself shuffling in his bare feet to Jo's bedside. Either the vinyl floor was ice cold or he was burning hot. He no longer cared that the flimsy gown exposed his backside to Vivian. He'd already felt naked in front of her. It had taken her only a minute to see right through him.

Woozy, he grabbed onto the bed's metal frame for support. Why was he here? He looked down at Jo, tubed up and helpless, and didn't have an answer. He would only hurt her. He would just go on hurting her because that was what he did.

"Please wake up," he said.

She didn't, of course. There were voices in the hall, two men. When they entered, and saw Gage, they both stopped in the doorway. The one on the left was a stranger, a short man with a slight build and hair so dark and thick it was probably a toupee, given the age evident in his deeply lined face.

The man on the left was Detective Bob Brisbane, looking as frumpled as ever in his baggy gray trench coat.

"What are *you* doing here?" Brisbane said.

The emphasis was on the word *you,* as in *you don't belong.* Gage looked back at Jo.

"I don't know," he said.

33

———————

Gage couldn't smell the coffee. If there was anything left of his sense of smell after spending two days communing with bleach and paint primer, it was hard to say. The coffee was still hot, at least, hot enough that it was hard to hold onto the paper cup for long even with so much white paint on his hands that he was practically wearing gloves.

The weather had turned cool the last few days, and the morning breeze was a welcome relief on his sweat-stained overalls. Both windows were open, and a box fan whirred in the corner. He set the cup down on the stool and stepped back to appraise the window frame. Since there was no carpet, they hadn't bothered to put down drop cloths, and there was white paint all over the floorboards too. It was white everywhere.

All it needed was some padded walls and they could bring in some crazies in straight jackets. If Gage had to smell this primer any longer, he might be one of them.

"I think you need another coat," Zoe said, behind him.

He turned and gave her his best smug smile, but it was hard to look smug when his face still hurt. She was on her

325

hands and knees inside the doorless closet, painting the baseboards.

"You're not even looking at it," Gage said. "How the heck can you tell?"

She dabbed one last time in the corner, then leaned back and looked over her shoulder at him, arching one eyebrow. She wore a PSU baseball cap with her brown hair pulled out the back in a short ponytail, and most of the logo was hidden behind white paint. Her denim overalls were more white than blue now too. Her hair hadn't been long enough to wear in a ponytail the last time she'd been in Barnacle Bluffs —at least he didn't think so.

"I was looking at it plenty while you worked," Zoe said. She dropped the paintbrush in the blue plastic cup in her other hand and set it on the floor next to her. "And if you didn't take so many coffee breaks, you'd get done sooner."

"I was just in the hospital, you know," he said. "Some allowances for my condition must be made. And you're the one who brought me the coffee. What did you think I was going to do, not drink it?"

"And you're the idiot who thought it was a good idea to clean this place up when you should be home recuperating. I still can't believe the police let you. Isn't it still a crime scene?"

"They got everything they needed," Gage said. "It's not really that complicated when the deceased is a murderous psychopath and the three people who killed him did so in self-defense."

Zoe nodded. "And so Brisbane officially gave you the okay, huh?"

"Well ... official might be too strong a word."

"I knew it. I saw that police tape in the dumpster. "

"Hey, what Mr. Grumpy Pants doesn't know can't hurt

him. And you didn't have to do this, you know. If you're worried—"

"Why do you keep saying that?" Zoe said. "Of course I didn't *have* to do this. And I'm still pissed that you didn't call for a damn week, Dad. Sometimes you have your head so far up your ass, I'm surprised you don't die of a methane overdose."

She glared at him. He was worried he'd really wounded her, then she laughed, and he *knew* he'd wounded her. She did call him *Dad*, though. No matter how many times he heard it, he still got a kick out of it.

He swallowed. "I really am glad you're here, though. Truly."

"Funny way of showing it."

"Hey, work with me here."

"Okay, okay," she said, waving him off with her paint brush as she turned back to the closet. "Now let's get back to work. My boss was nice to give me a few days off, but I *am* going to have to go back to Portland on Thursday. I can only help out your lazy ass for so long."

He laughed. His instinct was to let the conversation go at that, but then he remembered his conversation with Eve. About how he and Zoe needed to turn *toward* each other rather than *away*. There were other things that needed to be said. Important things.

"Hey," he said.

She looked at him, and all at once the world collapsed to the ten feet between them in that tiny white room in the backwater coastal town there at the ends of the earth. It felt like somebody was squeezing his windpipe. It felt like someone had dropped an anvil on his chest.

As usual, it was Zoe who made the first tentative move. Her brown eyes were wide and unblinking, her face was almost as white as the paint on the end of the brush, and the rest of her body was frozen with mannequin-like stillness, but somehow, even then, she found a way to speak. She was so much stronger than him. Always was.

"It's ... it's okay, Dad," she said. "Really. I'm—I'm okay. With everything that happened last year. I'm okay."

It was the wrong thing to say, because it was a lie. It was also the right thing to say, because both of them *knew* it was a lie. It was the comforting lie the two of them had held between them like a baby in a bassinet, a precious thing, or so they'd thought, both of them unwilling to set the lie down long enough to see that it wasn't comforting at all, and it certainly wasn't precious.

"Are you really?" he said.

Her throat moved as she swallowed, but otherwise there was no movement. She didn't nod. She didn't shake her head. She just stared at him. The breeze picked up, cool and smelling of the ocean as it stirred through the empty room, a reminder of the world outside and all that came with it. They weren't alone. Not out there. Not even in here. She blinked a few times.

"No," she said, wiping her eyes.

"Well, I'm not either. I'm so fucking messed up, Zoe, I barely know who I am."

This was enough of a surprise to startle her out of her tears. "Really?"

"Yeah. I—I thought I was going to lose you. I was so scared. I didn't—I didn't feel like myself."

When she put her brush into the blue plastic cup, her hand was shaking. "You always seemed so strong."

"I thought the same thing about you. She's so strong, how can I be so weak?"

"Oh, Dad. So many times—"

"I know."

"—I wanted to talk to you."

"Me too."

She got shakily to her feet, this young woman with paint on the end of her nose, this fierce and fiery soul who'd once been a troubled teenager who'd not only lost her parents but her grandmother too, and for the first time in months he really saw her. She was all of that, but she was also vulnerable in the best possible way, because she was real. And they needed each other.

They hugged. Neither of them were great huggers, but it was a good one.

"Maybe we can start now?" she said. "Talking about it? Otherwise, I'm pretty sure I'll—"

"Chicken out?"

She nodded. He laughed.

"Me too," he said.

So THEY TALKED. They talked for an hour, then another hour after that, the two of them sitting on the floor in that white room. The pleasant breeze became a cold and brittle wind, the cobalt sky turned gray and overcast, and the paint dried on both their brushes, but that was all fine. It didn't even matter what was said. It only mattered that they were saying it.

Around noon, Gage heard voices in the stairwell. The two of them hastily cleaned themselves up, wiping their noses with paper towels, trying to make their faces look less puffy, and each of them grabbing brushes and turning back to their respective walls as heels clicked onto the hardwood floor behind them.

"Oh my," Ellen Carson said. "Do you two have any brain cells left?"

"Well," Gage said, "you'd have to know how many we had to begin with, wouldn't you?"

He turned and was surprised to see that it wasn't Ellen Carson's diminutive personal assistant standing behind her but Lacy Carson instead. He hadn't talked to Lacy since she'd visited him in the hospital, so he wasn't sure what to expect. He'd been so drugged up with painkillers that he hardly remembered the conversation anyway, only that the stony-faced woman who'd stood at the foot of his hospital bed hardly looked like the same person who'd tentatively approached him to find her missing husband.

The difference was even more stark now. Lacy was different. It was mostly in the eyes, a hardness there, but it wasn't just that. It was in her posture: a stooping of the shoulders, a tightening of her hands into loose fists, and a slight crouching at the waist, like someone waiting for a blow to come from any angle. It was even in her clothes. The UW sweatshirt was gone, replaced by a gray hoodie and matching gray sweatpants. He wondered if she'd ever wear husband's sweatshirt again. He wondered what that meant.

Next to Ellen Carson, she looked like a small-time crook about to rob a convenience store. In a sleek and form-fitting blue pantsuit, Ellen looked like she was dressed for court. Which, in a way, she probably was.

"Now these are two people I didn't expect to see in the same room together," he said.

He expected nervous laughter or at least an exchange of awkward glances, but though they looked at each other awkwardly, it was not the kind of awkwardness he expected. They acted like teenagers who'd just shared their first chaste kiss.

"Tragedy makes strange bedfellows," Ellen said.

"I thought that was politics?"

"That too."

"This is my daughter, by the way. Zoe."

Introductions were made all around. There was a moment, when Zoe and Lacy were nodding toward one another, when Gage felt like he was looking at one of those preschool inkblot projects, the ones where kids put paint on one side of the paper, fold it, and then create a mirror image on the opposite side of the page.

What a strange thing. When he'd met Lacy Carson for the first time, he never would have imagined that she'd go through something that would make her more like Zoe, but there it was.

There was a little idle chit chat, the usual stuff about the weather and the tourists, which seemed strange after everything they'd been through, then some updating on Wade's situation, mostly from Ellen. Their lawyer was trying to plead down the attempted murder charge, despite Wade's confession. It was apparently a tough sell. The hope was that since Macklin was dead, and since a lot of what had gone down could be pinned on him, they had a good chance of a greatly reduced sentence.

A lot depended on whether Jo Roland recovered. Gage nodded mutely to this. Lacy spent most of the time staring at her pearly-white tennis shoes. There wasn't one grain of sand on them. They'd been scrubbed raw.

When Gage looked up from her shoes, she was staring at him, and for the briefest of moments he saw beyond the concrete barriers she'd recently erected around herself to something vulnerable and terrified underneath. She looked away.

"I need to go," she said.

"Okay," Gage said.

"I'm sorry. It's—it's just hard to breathe in here, that's all."

"I understand. But hey, how are you doing?"

"I'm doing okay," she said.

She wasn't, though. That was obvious, but what did it mean to be okay? Lacy was here. She was still standing, still getting on in the world. He may not have been able to protect her, but she was alive. The rest was up to her. Maybe it always had to be that way.

"I just wanted to thank you," she said. "For helping me. You didn't have to do that and … I want you to know how much I appreciate it. Wade and I … we'll get through this. Somehow."

"If you need anything, Lacy," Gage said, "anything at all, you just let me know."

She nodded, murmured to Ellen that she'd be waiting outside in the car, and started toward the door. Gage searched for anything else he could say to her, anything that might make a difference, and he came up empty. Then he realized that maybe it wasn't words she needed.

"Hey," he said. "While you're waiting, why don't you go take one last look at the ocean?"

She shrugged. "Why?"

He could have said the obvious about paint fumes and fresh air, but he could see that she suspected he meant more than that, and he did. "Just do it. It helps. I don't know why, but it does."

She nodded and left. Zoe, who'd gone back to painting the baseboards in the closet, put her brush down in the paint and wiped her hands on a paper towel.

"I want to go check on Alex," she said. "Do you want me to grab us some lunch on the way back?"

"Sounds good. I'll take care of your brush."

Zoe left the room in enough of a hurry that Gage figured she had an ulterior motive for leaving just then: she wanted to talk to Lacy. Good. One hard woman deserved another. After they were gone, it was just Gage and Ellen in the room, and the two of them stared at each other with the wariness of people who weren't enemies but weren't exactly friends either.

"Lacy's going to have a tough road ahead of her," Gage said.

"I'll be there for her," Ellen said.

"*You'll* be there for her?"

"Surprised, are you?"

"Mmm. It's not a bad surprise. Where's Roko?"

"I let him go. With a nice severance, I might add. And a plane ticket to India. He wants to visit his mother."

"Ah."

She took a few steps toward him, heels clicking on the floor, navigating around the splotches of white paint the way she'd navigated around all the other obstacles in her life—deftly and somehow instinctively, with barely a glance at them, as if it wasn't so much her avoiding the obstacles as the obstacles scurrying out of her way.

"I want to thank you too," she said.

"Thank me? I figured you'd want to kill me."

"No, I owe you an apology for how I treated you. I owe an apology to a lot of people. That's part of why I'm going to look after Lacy. I have a lot of making up to do."

"You're not angry? About everything that's happened?"

"Of course I'm angry," she said. "I'm angry at everyone. But you know what I'm *not?* Drunk. For the first time in as long as I can remember, I've gone more than a day without a drink. I haven't had a drop of alcohol since ..." Her preternatural poise briefly faltered, and she glanced away. "Since, um, the last time we saw each other. Anyway, being angry is not a bad thing. I'm just trying to channel that anger in better ways. "

"I see. Well, I pity our legal system, having to bear the brunt of all your fury."

She swallowed. "Yes, well, the best thing to come out of this is that nobody's lying anymore. Truth is the best disinfectant, as they say. So what are you doing here, exactly?" She gestured to the surrounding room.

"What do you mean? I know the owner of the building. Cleaning this place up is the least I can do for her."

"Is that all it is?"

Gage hesitated. She smiled.

"I thought so," she said.

"I haven't officially decided."

"I think you have. And I'm glad."

"Glad?"

"Yes. Because if you rent this place, then I know you'll be able to help more people, and that's exactly what I want. You won't be hiding anymore."

"I haven't been hiding."

She stared at him with the eyes of a woman who wasn't going to tolerate any bullshit.

"Maybe a little," he admitted.

"A little?

"Okay, a lot."

She smiled. "See? No more lies—from anyone. Now I have to go, but I have something to give you first."

She pulled a white envelope out of her purse, which she handed to him. The paint on Gage's fingers was sufficiently dry that he could risk opening the envelope, which had been closed but not sealed, but not so dry that he was willing to take out what was inside once he realized it was a check made out to him.

That didn't surprise him so much, considering the size and lightness of the envelope. What surprised him was the amount.

"Is this a joke?" he said.

"Of course not."

"A check for a million dollars? Really?"

"Yes. It's yours."

"No."

"Yes, Garrison. It's real, I assure you. I transferred the money to my account yesterday, and I've already alerted my bank, so you will have no trouble depositing it. They may want to contact my bank first, of course, but—"

"This is insane."

"I won't accept no for an answer."

He tried to hand the envelope back to her. She took a step back.

"I can't accept this," he insisted.

"You *will* accept this, Garrison, or you'll never stop hearing from me."

He looked at the check again. "It's way too much."

"It's not nearly enough."

"Mrs. Carson—"

"Ellen. *Ellen.*"

"Ellen, your son might go to prison for life because of me. Are you out of your mind?"

She smiled again. He was getting very tired of seeing her smile. "I see what you're doing, you know. You're trying to make me angry at you so I change my mind. It won't work."

"Damn it, Ellen, I don't need this!"

"Will you shut up and listen, you stubborn fool? I'm old. I'm rich. And as I told you, I have a lot of amends to make. This is one way I can do it. I just ask that you use it for your business, to make sure you're spending your time helping as many people as possible. Get yourself a secretary. You can charge the people you want to charge, but you won't have to, not all the time anyway."

Gage shook his head again and stared dumbly at the envelope. The top flap was still open. The whole check wasn't revealed, but the important part was. *One million dollars*

... Until now, he didn't even know a check could be written for that much money. "This goes against every instinct I have," he said.

"Good. I think a few of your instincts deserve to be challenged, just as mine have been. You don't have to thank me. I know that's a bridge too far for you right now, but you *will* take it. Even if I have to deliver bags of cash to your doorstep, you *will*."

"Ellen ..."

"Goodbye, Garrison."

He started to speak, but she reached out and placed her hand over his own, the one holding the envelope. Her fingers were bony and cold. He tried to think of something else to say to change her mind, but the way the skin around her eyes quivered and her mouth tightened into a firm line stopped him.

She was right that he couldn't thank her, though he was pretty sure he would find some way to do so eventually. What he could do was nod. She gave his hand a little shake, then turned and headed for the door. She stopped at the doorway.

"I hate for this to go to your head," she said, "but I want to say it anyway. You're a rare breed, Garrison, far rarer than you know. You're like some kind of knight for a lost world. Keep doing what you do. It matters. It matters so very much."

34

———————

Later that evening, before the sun had fully set but the sky was already dusky and pink, Gage stopped at the Barnacle Bluffs Hospital.

Just down the hall from Jo's room, he ran into a neighbor who lived down the hill from his house, a retired high school science teacher named Don Lipton who was there because his wife was having kidney surgery. "Lipton like the tea," Don had announced the first time they'd met, when Gage was out for one of his nightly walks. Standing there in the middle of the hall, with rubber squeaking on the tiles and the smell of antiseptic in the air, Don said his wife was out of surgery and she was fine. The man looked like he wanted to cry.

They chatted for a few minutes, about the road construction on Highway 101, about the annoyingly high number of short-term vacation houses around them, and of course about the unseasonably warm weather. Usually it was Don who would talk Gage's ear off, with Gage trying to pry himself away, but this time it was the opposite. Eventually Don abruptly told Gage that he had to use the little boy's room, so he'd be seeing him, leaving Gage alone in the hall to face the inevitable.

When he went inside Jo's room, he had this image in his mind that Jo would be sitting up in bed, her eyes wide open, and she'd smile upon seeing him. The reality was that she was still lying down, her eyes closed, and she didn't react at all to his arrival.

He *was* greeted by a smile—two of them, in fact. Vivian was there, as was her husband, Robert.

"Oh my," Vivian said. "Doing a little painting, are we?

"Yeah, sorry about that. I just thought I should stop by on my way home or … or I'd …"

He caught himself before he said the rest. *Or I'd chicken out and not do it.* The silence—if it could be called silence, filled as it was with the infernal beeping and whirring of the machines—lasted for a long moment before Vivian stood. She retrieved their coats from the rack.

"I was about to get some dinner," she said, "and Robert was going to stay, because we don't like leaving her alone. But maybe, now that you're here …?"

She raised her eyebrows at him, handing her husband his black London Fog trench coat. It caught Gage off guard since stopping had been an impulse and his plan was to scurry out of there as fast as he could if Jo was still in a coma, but what could he say now?

"Sure, I can stay a while," he said.

"Oh good! It won't be long."

Robert thanked him, telling Gage they'd be back within the hour if they could. Vivan turned at the door.

"Talk to her," she said. "I think she'd like that. Maybe it will help."

"Oh." His face felt warm, and the knot in his stomach, the one that had been there ever since Jo had gotten shot, grew tighter. "Vivian, I'm not sure … well, I'm … I'm not …"

"Maybe try the Sleeping Beauty thing," she added.

"Excuse me?"

"You know, see if a kiss wakes up the princess."

"You want me to kiss your daughter? While she's in a coma?"

"It's worth a try at this point, right?"

"I don't know. If … if she found out later."

"Humor me, Garrison. I'll tell her I gave you permission."

She left. He stood for a long time looking at Jo. The light on the blinds was hot neon pink, and some of that light brushed across her face and gave her bangs a reddish glow. He scooted one of the chairs to her bedside. For a long time, he just sat there, but then, almost as if it happened of its own accord, he started to speak.

He felt ridiculous at first, but it got easier. He told her that he was sorry for what had happened. He told her about Janet, how he could never forgive himself for how she'd died, and if Jo didn't wake up, how he'd never forgive himself for that either.

He begged her to wake up. He promised he'd never let anything bad happen to her again. He promised that he would love her forever, even if she didn't love him back. He promised her that he would stay with her forever, if she did. If only she would open her eyes. God, if only she would open her eyes.

"Please wake up," he said.

She didn't, of course. It was foolish to even think so. This was no place for a priestly confession. He needed to go right now before he started crying again, and what would that get him? What would that possibly do for *her?*

He stood. He turned to go, but then he remembered

Vivian's last suggestion. It was not the sort of thing that any modern, self-respecting man should do, kissing a woman when she couldn't say no, but what the hell. He wasn't a modern, self-respecting man. He was barely a man at all.

He leaned close enough that his breath moved her hair, stayed that way for a time gazing at her face, then kissed her. It was not a chaste kiss, but it was not a long one either. It was the way you might kiss somebody goodbye.

Or hello.

Because when Gage leaned back, Jo's eyes were wide open. Not only that, but she was also cupping the back of his neck with fingers that were surprisingly warm.

"It's a miracle," she said, grinning.

That was when Gage knew he'd been had. "How long have you been awake?"

"Since this morning."

"And you can move …?"

"Everything. Even my toes."

With her other hand, she reached up and touched his face. It was too much.

"What's this?" she said, wiping her thumb across his cheek. "Crying for little old me?"

"Will you shut up? You're going to ruin our storybook ending."

"Yeah, well, I'm going to hold you to all that, you know. Everything you said, I'm going to hold you to it."

Gage feigned a surprised expression. "What did I say?"

"Don't get cute with me, Gage."

"You're hallucinating," Gage said. "All those drugs have got you imagining things."

The fingers on the back of Gage's neck turned into claws as they clamped down on his skin, and it was the best feeling in the world. "Oh no you don't," she said. "You're not weaseling your way out of this. I've got a lot of lawyer friends who will work cheap for me, you know. I've got a lot of dirt on them, so they have—"

Gage kissed her. It was a good way to shut her up, maybe the only way, and he knew, even then, that it would be a method he'd use a lot in the days ahead.

Weeks.

Months.

Years.

ABOUT THE AUTHOR

SCOTT WILLIAM CARTER's first novel was hailed by *Publishers Weekly* as a "touching and impressive debut" and won an Oregon Book Award. Since then, he has published dozens of books, including the popular Garrison Gage mystery series set on the Oregon coast. His book for younger readers, *Wooden Bones*, chronicles the untold story of Pinocchio and was singled out for praise by the Junior Library Guild. In past lives, he has been an academic technologist, a writing instructor, bookstore owner, the manager of a computer training company, and a ski instructor, though the most important job—and best—he's ever had is being the father of his two children. He lives with his family in Oregon.

Visit him online at
www.ScottWilliamCarter.com

ALSO BY SCOTT WILLIAM CARTER

Garrison Gage Mysteries

The Gray and Guilty Sea

A Desperate Place for Dying

The Lovely Wicked Rain

A Shroud of Tattered Sails

A Lighthouse for the Lonely Heart

Bury the Dead in Driftwood

A Deep and Deadly Undertow

A Cold and Shallow Shore

A Kiss of Sand and Sorrow

Myron Vale Investigations

Ghost Detective

The Ghost Who Said Goodbye

The Ghost, the Girl, and the Gold

Karen Pantelli Novels

Throwaway Jane

Lethal Beauty

Dead-Eyed Drifter

Other Books for Adults

The Dinosaur Diaries

A Web of Black Widows

The Man Who Made No Mistakes

Ask Hagan

Looking for Little Red

Young Adult Novels

The Last Great Getaway of the Water Balloon Boys

President Jock, Vice President Geek

The Care and Feeding of Rubber Chickens

Books for All Ages

Drawing a Dark Way

A Tale of Two Giants

Wooden Bones

The Castle on the Hill at the Edge of the World

The Dragon Lottery